GLORY: HUMANITY'S LAST HOPE

GLORY SERIES
BOOK 1

IRA HEINICHEN

CRAIG MARTELLE

CONNECT WITH THE AUTHORS

Craig Martelle Social

Website & Newsletter:
https://craigmartelle.com

Facebook:
https://www.facebook.com/AuthorCraigMartelle/

Ira Heinichen Social

Website & Newsletter:
https://iraheinichen.com

Facebook:
https://www.facebook.com/iraheinichen/

Twitter:
https://twitter.com/iraheinichen

Instagram:
https://www.instagram.com/iraheinichen/

Copyright © 2021 Ira Heinichen and Craig Martelle

Published by Craig Martelle, Inc

PO Box 10235, Fairbanks, AK 99710

First US edition, November 2021

ACKNOWLEDGMENTS

Thanks to our Beta Readers

Micky Cocker, James Caplan, Kelly O'Donnell, and John Ashmore

If I've missed anyone, please let me know!

Editor Lynne Stiegler
 Cover designed by Chris Kallias

We can't write without those who support us
 On the home front, we thank you for being there for us

We wouldn't be able to do this for a living if it weren't for our readers
 We thank you for reading our books

CORVUS SEPTIMUS

Unclaimed Space

CHAPTER ONE

EVERY SHIP HAS A SWAN SONG, the cry it makes when it meets its end. The Navid word for it is "*ingletu*." Humans have no word for it, but the Navid do. The *ingletu* is an honor to witness.

The *Ulysses* was singing its *ingletu*. Shrieking it, in fact, as its bulkheads ripped apart. A swell of living voices accompanied it like a chorus, rising with each direct hit as its crew was ejected into space, where the vacuum would snuff out their screams.

The Paragon were out there, waging a holy war, cleansing the cosmos of the unfit. Coming for *her*.

Through the portal window of her tiny secret quarters, Idri the Second Born caught glimpses of their glittering ships lighting up the darkness with weapons fire and explosions. The *Ulysses* was in orbit over a gas giant, the name of which she could not remember. The Paragon made clear outlines as they passed over its swirling oranges and reds. Only small craft surrounded the *Ulysses* now, carving her up, removing her defenses, knocking out power, destroying her hangar bays. Idri saw no return fire in the swarm. The *Ulysses* had never had a chance to launch a response. Her squadrons had been trapped or destroyed in the first barrages of the surprise attack. Truly, a surprise it had been; *Ulysses* had never even raised an alarm. Idri and her chaperone had been caught unaware.

It was a concept utterly foreign to the Navid, but human ships—and indeed all the other races of the galaxy—traveled the stars through a network of gateways, massive hulking arcs with crews in the thousands that ripped holes in the fabric of space. They were nothing like the precise, minute majesty of a Navigator's jumps. More like wrecking balls. They worked, albeit clumsily, but they had a downside: between such gateways, ships were forced to crawl at sub-light speeds for long stretches, slow, tedious. And vulnerable.

Such was the *Ulysses* when the Paragon attacked.

Soon, the Paragon single-pilot fighters would retreat, having disabled the unclean vessel, and that would signal the end. Their carrier ship, presumably out in the stars where Idri could not see, would unleash its big guns and destroy the *Ulysses*. Or, perhaps, the ship would simply be left derelict to fall into the crushing gravity well of the gas giant, lost forever. Either way, space would be purified. Idri's threat to them would be snuffed out.

And she *was* a threat. One would never guess from her diminutive stature, soft-spoken manner, and oversized eyes and ears that made her look younger than she was. It wasn't her appearance that made her so dangerous; it was what she could do. Because of that, the *Ulysses* and all aboard her were dying.

The ingletu was not something to fight, stop, or bemoan; it was something to accept. *The end comes to us all.* So said the Tome, the ancient book Idri clutched to her chest as she watched. The Tome was the scripture for the Navigators, those who could fold space, a set of commandments to be followed to the letter. *Go down with the ship* is what those words meant. Their weight made Idri burn with shame.

At her feet was a crumpled EV suit, and it made her think of Warren. Warren, her human warden, escorting her to Earth. Warren, a behemoth of a man, forever clad in armor. Warren, the skeptic. Sidelong glances and rolled eyes whenever Idri tried to practice. It made her uncomfortable. On edge. As on edge as *he* was, constantly pacing about the small cabin, clunking in his heavy plastiform and metal armor. Not for a second did Idri see him out of that armor, and with every step, it creaked and groaned. It made it impossible to concentrate.

"Hey, kid," he'd called to her early in their voyage. "Listen up."

She had been in the middle of a recitation, eyes on the Tome. She didn't look up until she finished.

Warren had been holding something in his arms, motionless for once, and he'd had a sour expression. "Do you ever stop reading that book?" he'd asked.

Idri had blinked at him. "I must practice my recitations."

"All the time like that?"

"The Tome requires constant practice."

Warren had flexed his jaw. "You don't think maybe you could bend the rules, close quarters and all? Be flexible? 'Constant' seems a tad excessive."

Idri had bitten back a retort involving his noisy pacing and drawn herself up ramrod-straight. She'd turned back to the book. "Perhaps it does to you."

There had been a moment of silence before Warren

said, "You don't like me, do you?"

Idri had reddened. She hadn't replied; she knew it wasn't necessary. She *didn't* like him. She suspected the feeling was mutual.

Warren had thrown what was in his hands to her, and a shiny mess of fabric with a hard dome had clunked at her feet. "Put that on," he'd said.

"What is it?"

"An EV suit. I want you in it at all times. For safety."

"Safe?" Idri had begun, wondering what this hulking human thought she needed to be kept safe from, but Warren had dismissively cut her off.

"It doesn't matter," he had said. "Just put it on."

Idri had regarded the suit, then the robes she wore, inscribed on the seams with passages from the Tome. The robes of a Navigator were never to be covered and never to be removed. To hide them from the stars was blasphemy. Idri had told Warren as much. "I cannot wear this."

Warren's face had reddened. When he spoke, his voice had been tight and sharp. "Then you have a conundrum, don't you, kid?" he said. He had jabbed a giant gloved finger at Idri and the Tome. "You can do what that book says, or you can do what I say. You'd better figure it out before we get to Earth because when we get there, you'll be a soldier just like me. Soldiers follow orders, and I'm giving you an order. Wear the suit."

He had resumed his pacing and said little else for the rest of their voyage. Idri had been left to wonder if she'd made a grave mistake. Were all humans like this one?

She thought of Warren's order now and stared down at the EV suit. He was gone. Stepped outside for a reason she couldn't remember. She wondered if he was coming back. But the suit was there. Waiting.

The deck plating trembled as *Ulysses* struggled toward her demise. From the pattern of the noises she'd heard before, she knew the growing sounds were the Paragon coming back for another strike. It was only a matter of time before the destruction reached her. To her chest, she clutched the Tome, the only path she'd ever known. *Accept the ingletu*, it said. *The end comes to us all.*

It came as quite a surprise and with an immeasurable amount of shame when Idri realized she was not ready to die. She was ready to live. Warren with all his noise and his pacing and his doubts be damned, she wanted to be here. She wanted what had been promised to her on Earth and denied her at home.

She wanted to become a Navigator.

The first in a hundred years.

She grabbed the EV suit and prayed to the stars for forgiveness. She was struggling with the blasphemous garment—she had no idea how to put it on—when, as expected, the Paragon fighters returned. This time, whether by luck or design, their weapons found her. The bombardments slammed into the ship around her. Their might roared in her ears, and the portal window went white with light. It felt like punishment for her transgression.

Idri only had time for a fleeting thought about Warren. Where was he? Why wasn't he here? Then everything exploded.

THE MISSION WAS FUCKED. Of all the fucked missions Warren had ever been assigned to—and there had been so very many—this one took fuckery to new levels.

Warren stood deep in a press of dozens of panicked

bodies, unable to move. The air stank of sweat and smoke and reverberated with the cries of the desperate and the lamentations of the forlorn. The deck and bulkheads around them screamed and groaned with the sounds of the battle raging just outside. He blocked it all out with a hiss as he sealed the helmet to his suit armor.

The Paragon had come. They weren't supposed to, which was fuckery level one. This mission had been of the secret-est of secrets, unknown even to the commander and crew of this (woefully inadequate) ship. Nonetheless, Warren had known they could come—would come; deep down, it was always "would"—and he'd allowed this to happen anyway, which was fuckery level two. He'd dropped his guard. He'd become separated from his charge at the moment he most needed to be with her, all for banality. All for a good, lonely shit in the crew head down the corridor. A moment of poo-scented peace.

Goddammit.

The enlisted crew of the *Ulysses*, those not high enough on the social ladder of rank and privilege to be stationed near the escape pods, now filled the tight corridor. They were desperately trying to flee, but there was nowhere to go. The *Ulysses* was a pinnacle of the new Fleet, a perfect example of everything that was wrong in the modern age with its abundance of style and criminal lack of substance. For all its ample, shining corridors—lit beautifully, mind you, as they filled with smoke and panic —there was no escape plan. There had not been an alarm to warn them of the incoming attack, nor was there any sound of return fire. Put into combat, a real test of military might, the ship crumbled. Her crew, falsely confident that such battles were a thing of the distant past—peace was at hand, after all—had crumbled as well. They were going to die. Warren was going to die with them if he didn't find a way to move.

He stood a full head above the mass of panicked bodies. Their faces, smooth and shiny with fear, were two decades younger than his. It wasn't their fault. They'd been told the lie that this would never happen to them. They were going to die anyway, and that was a universal kind of fuckery.

The hatch to their quarters, those he and the Navid girl shared, was mere meters away. So close to the head. To step out had seemed innocuous, just a moment away from her and her incessant recitation and prayer. It was enough to make Warren wonder if he was losing his edge. "Out of my way," he bellowed as loud as he could, letting the projection speakers on his suit amplify his voice. It was no use. Gridlock.

He wasn't going to reach her.

A panicked face, that of an impossibly young man—he couldn't be a minute past eighteen—clawed into view and pressed against Warren's faceplate. His pale white skin was slick with sweat, and he had a nasty gash on his forehead. "I don't know where to go," he said. His voice cracked, and his eyes were wide and glassy. Warren couldn't help him. He couldn't help anyone, but he was spared saying the words because a moment later, the deck on which they all stood erupted into and through them.

With a great shriek of tearing metal and a thunderclap of expanding air, the corridor's bulkhead ripped open. Those who were not immediately dumped into space were sucked out after a split-second delay as the ship's atmosphere emptied into the void.

Warren was part of the latter, and he spun end over end as shrapnel pummeled his suit. He idly thought as he spun about the sound of the weapon that had breached the hull:

none at all. No booming explosion. No sizzling plasma fire. Only the groan of the ship being ripped apart. The bastards were using gravity weapons, which had been outlawed except in the darkest corners of the galaxy—like this one.

Warren would have spun off into the darkness forever had it not been for a cluster of shrapnel. He slammed into it hard, bouncing between chunks of debris from the explosion. As he slowed and his suit was finally able to compensate for the wild movement and allow him to get his bearings. He realized he wasn't bouncing off pieces of the ship and plastiform. Bodies had slowed him, men and women spewed out of the ship. They were writhing in the vacuum, suffocating to death and slowly freezing.

Behind them, streaking toward the *Ulysses*, Warren caught sight of a small craft bathed in brilliant white light— a Paragon fighter. Dozens of them, actually, in formation, returning to make another strafing run, this time with missiles and plasma cannons to burrow into the holes the gravitic bombs had ripped open. Their fire lit the faces of the dying, casting moving shadows that crept over the noses and brows. It was ghoulish and grotesque. A fucking waste.

He maneuvered his suit to angle him back toward the ship, which was backlit by the gas giant Corvus Septimus. Corvus lay almost perfectly equidistant from the Argeron Gateway, which they'd exited two days before, and the Beta 27C Gateway that was nearly two days out—the longest stretch at sub-light in their journey to Earth. The planet glared an angry red and cast the *Ulysses* into shadow except for the plumes of plasma fire erupting across its hull. The flames were concentrated in the lower part of the ship, right where their quarters had been, and where, only a few bulk-heads deeper, the ship's batteries lay. That area was belching flame, a surgical strike. It could have been miti-

gated with the proper evasive maneuvers, but as unprepared as the enlisted of the *Ulysses* were to die, their officers
were even less prepared to give them a fighting chance to
live.

There had been a time in Fleet history—a time before
Warren's   enlistment,   unfortunately—when   a   ship's
commander, stuck at the farthest point between gateways as
they were, would have his ship and crew at the ready
around the clock as a matter of course. Particularly in the
shadow of a large planet such as Corvus that could hide an
entire fleet of attackers. The attack was so obvious. But this
was not that time in Fleet history. Warren didn't have to be
on the command deck to know they'd frozen when the
attack came. No alarm had been raised. The Paragon only
gave their enemies a split-second chance to respond. It had
been squandered in deadly ineptitude.

The batteries would explode any minute. The explosion would be massive enough to split the ship in two, and it
would incinerate everything in its path. That included
Warren and everything—everyone—around him. It was a
lost cause. He had to move.

The hangar bay, farther astern, was close enough to get
to and far enough that it would likely remain intact once the
ship blew. Seeing the hangar relatively undamaged sent a
surge of adrenaline through Warren's dour nerves. There
was a shuttle down there, tucked into a crash box. Standard
procedure for any op, a way out in an emergency. Warren
could probably make it in time, hightail it to Beta 27C, and
hope the Paragon didn't see them leave. They probably
wouldn't in all the chaos. It could work. There was escape
with some luck, and he had to head for it now.

But the girl was nowhere to be seen.

The girl.

Warren supposed she was the last level of fuckery. The final fuckery. What was he even doing out here? Babysitting a child wasn't the purview of black ops, no matter how special she was. Warren had said as much to his briefing officer, not that he'd listened. Nor was there any indication the kid *was* special. She'd done nothing to indicate she was —quite the opposite, with her pious whispering and defiant attitude. Warren didn't like kids. He didn't have any and wasn't ever going to, thank you very much, which he'd also told the up-and-ups.

Warren had been told she was a Navigator and that she would change everything. He'd had no idea what that meant. He'd heard of the Navid, sure. Stories. Religious fanatics, much like the Paragon. They'd been a fixture on Earth ships a very long time ago, but that had ended for a reason. They were weird. Not to be trusted. He hadn't said that to his briefing officer, but he hadn't needed to. "Keep her safe," the officer had said. "You have your orders."

Fuck.

Chances were, she was already dead.

He laid a course for the hangar bay into his suit. It would be easy to just report she'd died in the attack. It was probably even true.

Probably.

His finger hovered over the execute icon. All he had to do was click it. Bug out. Leave all the fuckery behind. Goddammit, it was right there.

To his ever-loving, mother-flubbing, never-ending frustration, he found himself pulling up the comm channel controls instead. "Idri," he called once he had the channel open. He'd pre-programmed the Navid's suit with it. If she was in it, she would hear him. "Idri, can you hear me?"

A burst of static in his helmet made him jump. A signal.

His suit locked onto it, triangulated, and a small highlighted form flickered onto his faceplate display. He zoomed in on it. She writhed in space, clawing at her open suit—she had the damned thing on—dying.

Dying. Not dead yet.

He ground his teeth as he rerouted his suit's flight plan and fired its thrusters on an intercept course with the girl. She was still twitching, albeit weakly, when he reached her. His suit thrusters slowed him at just the right time for him to wrap her in an embrace. She was tiny under all those robes. They collapsed around her like a balloon.

Her helmet wasn't fastened. She'd done the rest—inconceivably, she had listened—but not fast enough and not well enough. There was no seal to contain an atmosphere. Warren clicked the helmet into place with practiced ease, and the faceplate fogged over. A good sign. Maybe. "Idri," he called through the radio. She didn't answer. "Idri," he repeated. He had been too late, after all. Wouldn't that just be the most perfect shit?

A ragged breath came through.

Warren again grabbed her body with both arms and rubbed her vigorously to stimulate circulation through the fabric of the suit and the robe stuffed within. "Hey, can you hear me?" he said.

"I see nothing," she croaked in a weak panic.

Warren grabbed her suit's wrist controls and tapped in the sequence that would equalize the faceplate temperature with the air. The fog evaporated instantly, and he was left staring into her oversized eyes. They were bloodshot but very alive. She wasn't dead.

"Warren," she said when she recognized him, surprise in her voice.

He clenched his jaw and wanted to look away, but he held her gaze. "Yep."

He didn't miss it when her eyes focused beyond him and her expression turned to one of abject terror. In the shininess of her faceplate, he saw a reflection of what was coming from behind.

Flames. Towers of them.

The batteries had exploded.

He glanced over his shoulder to see a massive shock-wave led by white-hot plasma rushing toward them, vapor-izing everything it touched. It would do the same to them. On the inside, Warren laughed. It was all he could do. This was it. He'd saved her just to die anyway. This was the bull-shit that was finally going to get him.

But instead of dying, Idri grabbed him with surprising strength, wrapping him up as he had wrapped her. Warren gasped as he felt his body stretch. The air he'd sucked into his lungs expanded too, along with his chest, arms and legs, and head. His mind, his thoughts, every part of him reached out toward the stars in every direction with one great inhale, and for a moment, Warren felt a peace he'd never known, never been able to conceive of—a connection to every molecule in the cosmos all at once. There was no longer a Warren, only everything and everywhere. That everywhere became a point, and he was drawn into it until he became the point, and then, with as giant an exhale as the inhale had been, Warren was back in his body, back in his mind, normal-sized, thinking normally.

"Holy shit!" he exclaimed, panting. His head spun, as did space around him, and he tried to marshal his senses. It had been glorious. Achingly beautiful. He felt the loss of that place, and all he wanted to do was go back.

Idri was limp in his arms.

That yanked him back to the present.

"Idri!" he shouted as he took stock of where they were —...or rather, where they weren't. The fireball from the *Ulysses'* explosion was no longer milliseconds away, ready to consume them. It was nowhere to be seen, in fact. No, check that. A small glimmer of red, orange, and white caught his eye several hundred, perhaps thousands of kilometers away. It belched from the ship, which was a mere speck in the distance. They'd traveled that distance in the blink of an eye, the span of a breath. Idri roused in his arms. "Holy shit," he repeated breathlessly. "Idri, are you okay?" He shook her lightly.

Her eyes fluttered open, and she saw Warren. She nodded weakly. "I am okay."

"Did you do that?" he asked her.

She nodded again.

"You did that? Just you. You folded space?"

"I will recover soon," she answered.

"Fuck me," Warren said, and with the expletive came a flood of realization and purpose.

She *was* worth it. Goddammit. She was worth *all* of this. He couldn't believe it, but he did. He had to. It was real. The Navid were real. A goddammed Navigator. The first in a hundred years.

Holy shit.

The swarming Paragon pushed aside the revelation, and Warren eyed the *Ulysses*. The ship had split in half from the final and fatal explosion and started its slow descent into the angry red gravity well of the gas giant. Fighters peppered her, making sure the destruction would be complete, drawing forth *Ulysses'* ingletu.

What caught Warren's eye, however, was her stern, which was still intact. The hangar bay.

He turned back to Idri, who, as promised, was becoming more alert with every second. The two of them locked eyes, and Warren inhaled.

"Can you do it again?" he asked.

CHAPTER TWO

THE HANGAR DECK was on fire.

Warren and Idri threaded their way through burning husks of fighters, personnel transports, and other support craft that had never been launched. Still, not even the general quarters alert had been sounded, such had been the swiftness of the Paragon attack. The deadliness. Warren spurred Idri onward, taking her arm to keep her from stumbling.

They'd managed to get back to the ship on their suits' thrusters and slip into the hangar through an exterior airlock. Their entry to the ship caught the Paragon's attention because new weapons fire spat through the open hangar bay doors as soon as they came into view. It sizzled through the flickering white atmospheric barrier and slammed into the decking around them. A squadron of enemy fighters swarmed in space beyond.

Warren cursed. If there had been any doubt this attack was about Idri—and there really hadn't been—it was beyond the shadow now. They knew. Warren didn't know how, but the Paragon knew she was there, knew she was coming to

Earth. It was a deeply unsettling, deeply problematic thought.

By the time a second barrage rained down upon them, Warren had activated the weapons on his suit. Without turning around, he charged a pair of .6-caliber ECP tactical plasma shoulder cannons, aimed with infrared sights that fed into the corner of his display, and blasted the control panel next to the hangar bay entrance. It exploded in a shower of sparks, and with a great rumble, the giant metal doors on either side of the hangar opening began to close. The tactic went against every rational notion Warren had, cutting off their only escape route, but these were not rational times. When someone could fold space using their mind, standard tactics need not apply. Idri could blink them anywhere using what lay ahead of them.

Once the blast doors were closed, the Paragon's weapons fire ceased, leaving the two with only the flames and smoke of the dying ship. A moment later, ducking past the billowing hulk of yet another destroyed un-deployed fighter, a large black box came into view. Relief washed over Warren. It was intact.

The crash box was a miracle of the modern age, one of the few that actually worked. Made from a material humans had yet to analyze and understand, the indestructible boxes were generously traded by the alien race that made them. An object placed inside could be dropped from orbit and collected intact after it crashed on the surface—no parachute, nothing—without a ding or a scratch. Incredibly useful in a pinch. Warren keyed in the unlock code from his suit's wrist control pad, and with a thud that roused Idri, the walls of the box fell away.

A shuttle lay inside, untouched. It was their way out.

"We're escaping in that thing?" Idri wondered, and Warren pulled them forward.

It was old, the shuttle. Not much to look at. "Just wait till you see what's inside," he promised.

As they approached the hatch, an alarm warbled low and distorted in the hangar bay. "Intruder alert," it moaned. An automatic recording, playing back at slow speed. It was the first alarm Warren had heard in all this. Paragon troops had entered the ship, a thought which was swiftly followed by a plasma bolt that sizzled millimeters from his head.

"Down!" Warren barked as he dove to the deck, pulling her with him.

Weapons fire peppered the area. He estimated the firing points from the impacts and the line of fire and determined that their current face-down prone positions were safe. For the moment they were, thank the stars. Paragon, for all their arrogance and bombast, were deadly good shots. One did not tangle with their shock troops and survive.

Warren low-crawled a half-meter to see past a smoldering troop carrier and found two squads of Paragon troops streaming into the hangar bay through an access hatch on the far wall. Their gleaming white-gold armor was covered with cold, angry blue dots, concentrated mainly on their faceplates. Visual sensors. They had the effect of making the troopers look insect-like, which they might be. No one Warren was aware of had seen a Paragon outside of a suit of some kind. They didn't show their faces to lower life forms. The way in which they moved made their tactics obvious: a pincer attack. Warren and Idri would be surrounded.

The shuttle was several paces away, but if they made it inside, they'd be safe from the troopers' weapons. They just had to get there.

Warren keyed another unlocking sequence from his

suit's wrist pad—this one for the shuttle door—before he slid back to Idri. "When I say go," he murmured to her, "you get up and run, okay?"

She nodded.

The shuttle door remained stubbornly closed.

Warren keyed the sequence again. This time, with the grinding of old metal on even older metal, the door cracked open. It was the kind that swung down and made stairs once it touched the ground, but it didn't touch the deck. It creaked to a halt two-thirds of the way there. Paragon weapons fire instantly focused on the movement. Warren swore. It would have to be enough.

"Go!" he shouted to the girl.

Dutifully, she got up and ran. Warren was behind her, shadowing her halting steps. In the surprise of their flight, the Paragon fire sought to catch up. When they reached the half-open hatchway, their luck ran out. The back of Warren's suit screamed as blasts pelted it. He stood with his legs braced, shielding the girl with his body.

The force of the energy bolts pitched him forward, nearly crushing Idri against the hatch. He planted his feet and grabbed her and, riding his forward momentum, he tossed her over the door and into the shuttle as he fell in behind her. They crashed to the deck, and Warren reached up to slam the controls to shut the door. In that split second, a plasma bolt sniped his wrist. Warren recoiled with a shout.

With a shrieking groan, the shuttle door rumbled closed. The weapons fire couldn't reach them but continued to rain on the outside of the shuttle.

"You're hurt," Idri said as Warren cradled his left hand.

"Don't worry about it," he said, lifting it to take a look. His suit was smoking, and the pain from the injury coursed through his body. He looked away lest he drive off the adrenaline he needed to keep going until they were safe. "Long as we stay in here, we'll be fine." He tried to flex his wrist, but no dice. He'd have to wait for the shock to wear off to get a sense of what was still there and what wasn't.

As for the shuttle, now that it was occupied, lights flickered on at a dubious pace and in a suspect number. Ironically, that put him at ease. He knew these things. Relics they might be and rough around the edges, but they were from a time when the important stuff worked, the stuff you counted on to get you out of a mess. He used them as often as he could. Warren stood and got the rest of the lights to flicker on with a few well-placed bangs. He and Idri took off their helmets.

Idri took a grateful, deep breath and wrinkled her nose.

Warren was inclined to agree. Musty. Not the best smell in these things, but that wasn't what mattered. "It should be around here somewhere," he said, thinking about what *did* matter. He bumped into the walls of the small craft as he turned this way and that in his oversized suit, looking for what they'd come all this way for. "Here," he called from the aft end after he found it.

With a flourish, he grabbed a thick canvas-like shroud and pulled it aside. A puff of dust followed it, which caused him and Idri to wave at the air, but what it revealed stopped Idri dead in her tracks. At the center of a series of portal windows that ringed the shuttle's rear bulkheads from ceiling to floor stood a pedestal. It was about waist-high, bolted to the deck and topped with an orb of absolute darkness like a hole had been cut out of reality. It reflected no light and did not appear to have a surface or a shape other than its round nothingness.

Idri gasped and fell to her knees.

"It's beautiful," she whispered, transfixed.

Warren had seen one of these before—several, in fact—in old shuttles such as this one; he'd never paid them any mind. Never had any use for them. But a distant memory from his training days of manuals and diagrams, he knew—hoped—Idri had a use for one. A fulcrum, a folding device from the lost age of Navigators. "Do you know how to use it?"

To his relief, she nodded and finally broke her gaze to stand and shed her suit. Her robes billowed out, and something heavy clunked to the floor—the book. The old one she was always reading. How'd she manage to stow that away? She picked it up and leafed intently through its pages, tracing passages with her fingers and muttering along with them.

Warren had to throw out a steadying hand when the shuttle suddenly rocked. Heavy weapons fire. Idri looked at him, frightened. He strode to the cockpit, the Navigator in tow, and peered out at the hangar deck. More flashes of golden-white light streaked among the still-burning wreckage. Thick plasma bolts led his gaze to the tripod weapons that had fired them. Heavy weapons, which would make quick work of the stationary shuttle. "We're surrounded," he said through gritted teeth before turning back to Idri. "Whatever you need to do to get us out of here," he said, "now is the time."

"Wait, what?" Idri asked, eyes going wider than normal.

"Fold us out of here."

Idri blinked. "I can't."

Warren took a step toward her and pointed at the fulcrum. "I thought you said you know how to use that thing?"

"I do."

"Then, let's go!"

"I can't, without the stars."

It was Warren's turn to blink, and his chest felt hollow. "What?"

Another direct hit to the shuttle rocked the floor beneath them. "To fold space, I must see the stars," Idri said.

"What are you talking about?"

"It is the only way."

"This isn't some Navid, Tome bullshit like that not-wearing-a-suit-over-your-robes, is it?"

Idri shook her head.

"Because that would be really inconvenient, kid, seeing as we're stuck in this hangar bay."

Idri's voice trembled as she repeated, "It is the only way."

Warren tilted his head back to curse or scream, but all he could do was close his eyes and shake his head. Of course. He turned to stare through the cockpit windows again, through the smoke and flames, at the dull gray of the blast doors. Closed. By a cannon shot. His shot. Why hadn't she told him?! He wanted to shout the question at her, but he knew it wouldn't do any good. She hadn't known. He hadn't told her about the fulcrum. He hadn't asked her before closing the blast doors. He'd almost left her out in the cold.

Goddammit.

This was his penance, wasn't it?

Goddammit.

"What are we going to do?" Idri asked.

Warren turned back to the shuttle's controls, connected the wrist interface on his undamaged hand to a data port, and began to punch in commands with his bulky gloved fingers. Dutifully, the console lit up, and with a cough, then a shudder, the shuttle began to hum. "We're going to get you out of here," he growled.

He was interrupted by a clank as something solid hit the shuttle. A horrible whooshing sound followed, and the shuttle shuddered from nothing its engines or power cells could cause. Warren froze and gripped the console as his heart skipped a beat, then breathed a sigh of relief when the shaking and whooshing went away. Bastards were using gravity weapons, almost useless in an artificial gravity field but deadly at point-blank range. He squeezed the solid metal controls gratefully; this old bird still had gravitic plating on her, which had just saved their lives. And she'd do it again, at least for one of them.

In retaliation for the G-bomb, Warren used the shuttle's onboard plasma turrets to lay down a wild spread of return fire. Satisfactorily, it sent the Paragon troops scattering. Warren saw the data transfer from his suit complete, set the turrets to continue firing in a random pattern, and punched in a series of flight commands.

The shuttle was spinning up to lift off, and he was halfway back to the hatch when Idri grabbed him by the arm.

"What are you doing?" she asked, shaking.

"I told you," he said. He slipped loose and clicked his helmet back into place with a hiss. "Getting you out of here."

Her voice rose in alarm. "What about you?"

"I have to get the door open."

"You can't do that from here?"

He shook his head.

"The Paragon are out there!" Her eyes were so wide Warren nearly fell into them.

But he didn't. "I'll be fine," he lied.

"They'll kill you."

"They're after you, and you're safe in here. They'll ignore me."

"I don't know how to fly the shuttle."

"It's set to automatic, Idri."

"I won't leave you!"

"Idri!" he said, and he grabbed her shoulder and stared her in the eyes. Hers showed a resolve he wasn't expecting, a clarity, and it forced him to look down for what he said next. "It'll stop for me." She started to protest once more, so he lifted his eyes back up to continue. "I've programmed it to stop for me. I just have to get the doors open." She searched his face to see if he was telling the truth, so he held fast as long as he could. "It's the only way," he said when he no longer could.

He opened the airlock before she could protest any further. A blast of hot, smoky air greeted him, as did a pair of near-misses from Paragon troop fire. A well-timed volley from the shuttle's cannons covered him. "Be ready to fold!" he shouted. She was pressed into the corner of the cockpit, looking like she wanted to disappear, but she nodded. Then he was out. He hit the deck running.

The shuttle roared behind him, lifting off. Weapons roared, too, and he ducked into a roll, cradling his injured wrist. It worked, and his momentum lifted him back to his feet. He took off in a dead sprint toward the hangar bay doors, then his suit's servos kicked on and his speed increased twofold. At first he was deluged with plasma fire, which shattered deck plating and rained down debris as he flew through the fiery, smoking hulks strewn across the hangar. Within moments, the weapons fire lessened, then died. He'd been right: the Paragon weren't after him. They continued firing at the shuttle, hoping to slow it down with a lucky shot or through sheer, unrelenting effort. Warren needed to move quickly.

He skidded to a halt at the charred wall of controls. The controls were worthless, blown to hell. Not a surprise. He ripped off the interfaces, exposing the circuitry behind them. They sparked, which was a good sign. There was still power here, so there was a chance. He switched his helmet's holodisplay to heat signatures, searching for the live wires. The warmest of them was the one he was looking for.

The blast doors on every ship worked on a very simple mechanism: an electromagnet held them apart and open. Cut power to that magnet, as Warren had when he'd shot up the panel, and the doors closed. Restore power to that magnet...

He found a severed and sparking wire that was thicker than the rest and pulled it toward him. The shuttle was almost to the blast doors. He hoped his suit could handle the current, but he didn't hesitate. He slammed the ends into each other.

Energy surged through his suit, and bolts of electricity arced up and down his skin. The hangar doors creaked and shook. Warren pressed the cables together harder, his teeth chattering and every muscle in his body taut.

The doors opened.

Plasma fire from the Paragon fighters outside blasted through the hangar bay, missing the shuttle by a meter. It glided through the doors, and Warren whooped through clenched teeth.

"Warren?!" came Idri's voice through the comm, desperate. "The shuttle didn't stop!"

Warren watched the back of the shuttle clear the edge of the hangar through the atom field; it was now free and clear in space outside. A gas giant loomed beyond it, with swirling red clouds a seeming hair's breadth away. The *Ulysses* had been listing during their time inside the hangar. The planet's gravity well was pulling them in. A cry of twisted steel reinforced the ingletu.

This is the way it needed to be. The only way it could work. Warren had known, and he'd lied to Idri; he'd never intended for the shuttle to stop. The plasma fire that had briefly obscured the shuttle stopped. She was visible now. She needed to jump.

"Warren!" Idri repeated over the comm.

He let go of the power cables. The blast doors began to screech closed. "You have to go," he urged desperately. "Right now."

"You can fly to me. I'm not leaving you."

Warren shook his head and ran ahead of the closing doors to see her as long as he could. "There's no time, kid," he said. "This is the only way."

"You told me the shuttle would stop!" She was crying. He could hear her heaving breaths through the comm.

"You have to go," he repeated. "That's an order." The doors caught on shrapnel that had spilled into the track and stayed open. A blessing. He'd get to see her go. But she was hesitating, the shuttle sitting in open space. "I'll be fine," he pressed. "Remember, you don't even like me."

Idri sobbed.

Beyond the shuttle, the Paragon fighters were repositioning, readying to fire again. Armor plating or no, it would not withstand the coming blasts.

"Now, Idri!"

The Paragon craft fired. It seemed like their energy bolts hung in space for a moment, crawling in slow motion toward the shuttle. With a brilliant flare of multicolored light, the shuttle disappeared. The space behind it pinched, then expanded, warbled back and forth as the plasma bolts ripped past, and then it was gone. All sign of her—the shuttle, everything. It was glorious.

Warren cheered. She'd done it. She was on her way to Earth. He nearly crumpled to the hangar deck, so great was his exhale of relief. Instead, he looked at the wristpad on his suit and ran a gloved hand over it. The shuttle carried a recording of what had happened here, downloaded into the flight console. They'd have that. They'd know what the Paragon had done. Best of all, Earth had Idri now. The girl who could fold space. The first in multiple generations. The victory filled him up to his eyes and spilled over onto his cheeks.

Far beyond the point in space where her shuttle had disappeared, something rounded the horizon of the gas giant. He instinctively stepped forward to gain a better look and nearly passed into the atom field at the edge of the hangar opening. But Warren didn't need a better look, not for the size of the approaching behemoth.

It had been odd to see the Paragon fighters alone, so quick, so covert without their carrier nearby, standing over the proceedings like an imperious general. That was their way. Proud. Blatant. They could be called over-confident if they weren't so indomitable.

What came toward them now was indomitable, certainly, but it was no carrier. It was a craft unlike any Warren had ever seen. There were no windows, no hangar bays, no launch tubes— nothing except a single giant opening on one end and a massive, pulsing, moon-sized power station behind it. A unique weapon. One that looked like it could crack the core of a planet.

A fleet of ships in the more conventional style of carriers and battle groups rose from the horizon to surround it and escort it during its lumbering flight forward. There were dozens of them. Hundreds. An invasion fleet.

"Damn," he whispered.

Idri had escaped a minute too late, it seemed.

He hoped Earth already knew.

He hoped Idri was part of a plan to stop what was coming. Because if there was no plan...

Weapons fire splattered against the back of Warren's suit, forcing him to tear his gaze from the invasion fleet. Tendrils of red gas were oozing into the hangar bay. The *Ulysses* was making her final descent into the planet. The gas made halos around the quickly advancing Paragon troops, now solely intent on him with no shuttle left to draw their aim. He had seen their great secret. They did not intend to let him survive the knowledge.

Warren scanned the deck and spotted something he could use, a plasma cannon from a wrecked fighter. It took all of his suit's assisted strength, and he had to grit his teeth at the pain in his charred wrist, but he managed to hoist it onto his shoulder and reconnect its batteries.

The cannon hummed hungrily. Warren looked at the Paragon. "Come and get me, fuckers," he shouted and fired.

EARTH

Terran Federation Space

CHAPTER THREE

THE DRONE APPEARED in the sky at noon.

Drake noticed when the auto-posthole digger broke. The power-aided metal jaws hit a rock, the servo motor whined and began to smoke. Drake tried to reach down to shut it off before it ruined itself, but all he got for his troubles was a snap from a breaking metal cable. It gave him a nice little slice in his palm, and he cursed. He looked at the sky in pain, and that was when he saw it.

The drone was a pale, blinking dot of light in the midday sun. Drake squinted at it for a long moment, then cursed again. With a shake of his hand, he took a handkerchief from his back pocket and tied it off over his injury.

The drone was still there when he arrived in town to get legumes, hard sours, and a new posthole digger from the feed store. It was almost impossible to find a traditional one without the motor and AI-assist. The store help had scratched their heads, and called for help before Drake just went digging through the shelves on his own. He finally found one, two wooden handles with a hinge and metal scoop-shaped blades on the bottom. Nothing fancy. It would work till the metal rusted.

"You sure you don't want one of the normal ones, Cap?" LeBranch said at the checkout counter. He was a young one, early twenties, slight, with a sun-reddened face and dirty fingernails. He barely filled out the weathered flannel hanging off his shoulders. He was half-watching the holo-screen in the corner.

"I'm sure."

LeBranch shook his head. "Hard to believe, huh?"

"This one won't break."

LeBranch tore his eyes from the holoscreen to look at Drake with a sheepish smile. "Oh, no," he said, "I mean this peace-summit shit." He gestured at the screen, enraptured. "Can you believe it?"

The reporter on the screen spoke of soon joining one of the Fleet ships out at the Jupiter Gateway. The Paragon peace delegation was due in a couple days' time. History was at hand.

Drake didn't say anything, but he thought about the drone in the sky.

"Hey, you were in the military, right, Cap?" LeBranch looked at him earnestly, eyebrows raised. "That's why they all call you that, yeah?" Drake again chose to stay silent and still. LeBranch leaned forward. "What do you think about all this? Paragon treaty and whatnot. Sounds like they've finally come around. Peace in our time. You believe it?"

Drake chewed the inside of his cheek. "How much for all this?"

The boy leaned forward. "Come on, Cap. You think those shiny bastards are serious?"

LeBranch wasn't going to let it drop. "Doesn't matter

what I think," Drake said, and he pulled out his credit chip. "Not anymore."

LeBranch whistled, then laughed. "You're a cool one, Cap." He winked. "I like that about you." He took Drake's credit chip and scanned it. Then, with a gesture at the holoscreen, he said, "Personally, I think they're full of it. All this trade deal nonsense, trading tech. Smells like shit to me." He handed Drake his chip back, then pointed at the feed bag and posthole digger. "You need help with those?"

Drake shook his head and pocketed his chip. He held out the palm-sized canister of hard sours and cracked it open with his thumb and forefinger. LeBranch grabbed a candy and popped it in his mouth.

"I can handle them myself," Drake said, and he pulled the bag and the digger off the counter and hauled them to his waiting vehicle.

THE DRONE HUNG stationary in the sky that night, and Ellen caught him staring at it, standing out on the porch with his night brew in hand. He leaned against the peeling white rail as he heard her footsteps creak the floorboards behind him.

"Someone's coming?" she asked.

Drake nodded. "Yeah."

The air was filled with the sounds of crickets and the tat-tat-tat of the sprinklers in the closest field. It was old-school and less efficient than robotic misters, but the sound couldn't be beat.

"You get that fence fixed?" She had a gravel in her voice that drove him crazy, all business and sass. Her salt-and-pepper hair flowed onto her shoulders, unpretentious and beautiful, as was everything about her.

Drake shook his head. "No."

"Can't put the yearlings in there 'til it's fixed."

"Nope."

They continued on like that until the ground car made its way down their long driveway. Its turbines kicked up dust as it went, collecting it so that when the car finally reached the house and stopped, the cloud coated everything in fine grit. Drake tasted it in his mouth, and with a grimace, put down his cup of hot brew. Ellen tensed and backed toward the front door, where they kept the shotgun.

A figure stepped out of the car, backlit by the starry sky. A man. Tall.

"Who goes there?" Drake called. "What do you want?"

The tall man walked forward slowly, almost sauntering. His hands were out at his sides, and he was smiling broadly. "You went full country, huh, Cap?" His voice was familiar. Mocking. He stopped when he reached the edge of the porch light. "What's the matter, you don't even recognize your old XO anymore?"

Drake's breath caught in his throat as Commander Alexander Oh stepped into the light. His face had wrinkled since they'd last set eyes on each other, but he was unmistakable. The tall, burly man still sported the high and tight haircut, was as clean-shaven as the day he was born, and his snug uniform accentuated his wide silhouette.

"Commander," Drake said, pausing in a moment of shock.

The officer filled the silence with large strides up the porch steps. Drake stuck his hand out, but the larger man laughed and shook his head, his arms wide. He wrapped his former captain in a giant bear hug that threatened to squeeze the life out of him, then stepped back to look him up and down.

"You can still call me 'XO,' Cap," he said, still grinning. His bass voice rumbled the same way it always had, and it snapped Drake back to old times. Happier times. "And you got old, old man."

"So did you," Drake rumbled back in his own deep voice. "You're still in the Fleet," he said, again noting the uniform. It gleamed in the porch light. "I didn't know that."

XO nodded, and his smile faded. "Indeed I am, sir," he said with a crisp salute. He then turned to look at Ellen, who was by the door, casually cradling a shotgun and scowling. "Captain Einhard," he said, saluting again. The gesture couldn't quite hide his surprise. "I didn't know *you* were here."

Ellen grunted. "This is *my* farm, soldier. Your intel missed that."

"Well, it's a pleasure to see you." The XO turned back to Drake, and gave him a look and a nod toward Ellen. His eyes were shining. "You two." He shook his head.

"You disapprove?" Drake asked.

"The opposite, Cap," XO said. "Precisely the opposite." He squeezed Drake's shoulders, looking him up and down at arms' length. "It's *good* to see you."

And it was. The warmth in the gesture filled Drake up. It had been so long. Too long. How had that happened? "You should come inside for a drink," Drake said. XO smiled again.

"Why are you here?" Ellen pressed. She was guarding their house like a sentry. She looked at the car, which was military-issue. XO was in uniform. Always had a nose for bullshit, Ellen did. Drake loved that about her.

This wasn't a social visit.

XO straightened. "I'm an envoy. With an offer for you."

Drake's eyes narrowed. "An envoy," he repeated slowly, letting the words roll off his tongue.

Behind them, the door of the car clicked open again, and another figure stepped out. Drake squinted into the darkness, and he set his cup down on the porch railing. The shadowy figure walked toward the pool of porch light. Drake ambled down the steps to meet him, the warmth leaving him and a cold certainty filling in its absence. A cold rage.

XO followed, calling, "You should hear what he has to say, Cap."

"Who goes there?" Drake said as the figure approached the light. He cocked his head to the side and balled his fists.

The figure stepped into the light, and he saw the face of Admiral Jack Sturgess. Of course he did.

Drake felt sick to his stomach. He practically frothed at the mouth when he said, "You son of a bitch."

"Nice to see you again, Augustus," Jack said. The admiral was hawkish and had severe features that had become exaggerated with age: a sharp nose to match his sharp eyes, which were always shifting back and forth. Jack was the type of man who knew where the exits were at all times, in addition to the deepest, darkest secrets of everyone around him. He was the head of intelligence for the United Earth Space Fleet, and he was a bastard.

Drake closed the distance between them with two large strides, raised his fist, and clocked him in his smug face.

Jack fell hard. Drake followed him to the ground, set his knee on the admiral's chest, and raised his fist to hit him again even harder. He didn't get to land the blow because Oh was in his ears and had wrapped his burly arms around Drake's chest and shoulders.

"Stop!" he yelled.

Drake didn't listen. He lunged toward Jack, but XO's grip was firm. The admiral scrambled backward along the ground, crab-walking to keep Drake in sight until he could get back to his feet. Blood streamed from both nostrils as he panted through his mouth.

Drake wanted nothing more than to beat the man into the ground. "Let me go!" he bellowed. Oh held on, tightening his grip to keep his friend from causing more damage. "Let me at him, you son of a bitch!"

More figures emerged from the car and leapt into action. Guards, except they hardly registered for Drake. He didn't care. Years of pent-up rage erupted like a volcano. He saw nothing but the red of his fury.

Jack would pay for what he'd done to him, and he'd pay with his smug fucking face.

A gunshot ripped through the night air, and everyone stopped.

It was still booming off the barn and the fields when XO turned Drake back to the porch. Ellen was in a wide stance, the shotgun's barrel in the air, stock resting on her hip, a telltale wisp of smoke rising from one of the two barrels. Her face was hard. "Y'all will stop right now," she said, and she leveled the gun at XO. "Let him go."

XO let Drake go, but not before putting himself between Drake and the admiral, who had regained his feet and was dusting himself off. The guards bracketed the admiral, protecting him while he teetered satisfyingly. Drake had landed a good punch. Or, they'd gotten old. Drake's hand throbbed.

"Now, get on out of here," Ellen commanded.

"Captain," XO said, angling himself to cover the admiral from both Drake and Ellen—...or was it to cover them from the admiral? He spoke insistently, desperately. "You need to listen to what the admiral has to say."

"You need to do what she says and leave," Drake said. He backed toward the steps and stopped next to Ellen. "Now."

"You should listen to him," Jack said.

"You shut your mouth," Drake snapped, the fire rising in him again.

"Cap, please." XO pleaded.

"I'm not a captain anymore."

"Just—"

"Leave!"

"They're giving you back the *Glory*!" XO shouted to get his attention and distract him from the rage that bubbled from every pore like sweat on a hot day.

Everything went silent and still as his last word rang across the night.

Glory.

XO closed on Drake. He was shaking. "He's here to make amends."

Drake found words had left him, and he couldn't move. His mind was reeling, and he was having a hard time believing he'd heard what XO had just said.

XO continued. "They need you," he said, then looked at Jack. "*We* need you."

Drake cleared his throat. "For what?"

———

"I THOUGHT the *Glory* was sitting on a scrap heap."

The atmosphere in the living room was tense. Drake held out a steaming cup of brew like it was the hardest thing he'd ever done in his life. The statement/question was for the admiral, but he'd said it as though he were addressing the room.

Jack took the mug.

With his other hand, Drake held out an ice pack.

Jack took that, too.

"*Glory is* sitting on a scrap heap," Jack said slowly, sipping from the mug and dabbing gingerly at his cheek and nose. Drake had gotten him square. Good. Bastard deserved it. A young soldier dressed in black, the uniform color of the Intelligence division, watched Drake's every move. A sharp-looking young man with piercing blue eyes. Jack had always recruited the best. He'd recruited Drake way back when. The thought disgusted Drake, and he retreated to the other side of the room to stand next to Ellen. She squeezed his arm reassuringly. She was right behind him, ready to act if need be.

"They're bringing her out of retirement," XO said of the *Glory*, his eyes lighting up. His excitement was genuine. "Her and the rest of us. CAG with the flyboys. She stayed in the service, like me. Already agreed to the assignment, like me. DLC on the flight deck. Recommissioning. Once we get ahold of Doc, it will be all of us." XO stopped himself. "That is, if you agree to come along, Cap."

"Come along?" Drake said, rolling the phrase around in his head. He leveled a look at the admiral. "Where?"

"Can't tell you that," Jack responded with a snap.

Drake smirked and shook his head. "Classified?"

"Yes."

"Of course it is."

Jack coughed. Hard. At first, Drake thought the old man had choked on his brew. His young attendant provided him with a handkerchief, however, and when he was finished with the fit and dabbing his mouth, it came away smudged with black blood. Drake frowned. Jack pocketed it and shook his head. Drake wasn't to ask.

"We are in need of an experienced crew," Jack said. His tone was casual, like he was asking for more sweetener in his brew or bringing up the weather, but Drake knew how practiced and fake it was.

"Surely," Drake said, baiting him, "you have a whole fleet of experienced crews."

XO snorted.

"I'm speaking of very specific experience."

That caught Drake's attention. "You mean the Paragon."

"Of course I'm talking about the Paragon."

Drake thought of the coming peace talks and what he'd seen on the holovids earlier. "What are they doing? Are they planning something? Something with the peace talks?"

Jack shook his head. "I cannot talk about it with a civilian."

That boiled Drake's blood. "Fuck you," he said, and he meant it.

From somewhere on his person, Jack brought out a palm-sized flat box covered in deep blue velvet with a hinge at the back. He leaned forward in his chair and held it out. Drake didn't move, so Jack leaned forward farther and wiggled it at him. Finally, the admiral sat back and passed it to his attendant, and the young man walked it over to Drake and thrust it into his hands.

Drake felt the lush velvet and the shape of the box. It was familiar, intimately familiar. His stomach turned over. "You really are a son of a bitch," he said, and he cracked the box open.

Inside was a gleaming gold bar the length of a middle finger and about as wide, with four solid stripes cut out of its center. It was a badge of office, captain's rank. There were tiny signs of wear around the edges, rounding from use, knicks and tarnish from combat and flame. It had been *worn*, but it still gleamed with pride.

"It's yours," Jack said.

"I know it's mine," Drake said, and he touched it. His hand was shaking.

"I mean, I'm giving it back to you."

Drake flared. "I don't want it."

Jack flared back. "Bullshit."

"You don't know a fucking thing about what I want."

Jack threw his head back and looked at the living room ceiling. "You want your commission back." He leveled a finger at Drake. "I know you do. You have since the court-martial. You want to reclaim your rightful place on the command deck of your starship."

Drake shook his head with barely contained fury. "You took all that away from me."

"And now I'm offering it back to you." The admiral produced another object from a uniform pocket. It was a small cylinder, matte silver, pneumatically sealed. "Your orders are inside, effective the second you accept recommissioning."

Drake closed the velvet box. His hands were no longer shaking. "Why?" There was no answer from Jack, so he accused the admiral, "I petitioned for reinstatement for almost a decade, and you blocked me every time. I saw your name on the letters, Jack. You *personally* made sure I never made it back into the Fleet. So, you tell me why now?"

Jack chewed on the side of his mouth the way he did when he was obfuscating. It made Drake bristle. He knew whatever answer was coming would be bullshit. "I need you," the admiral said, finally. Vague. The worst kind of bullshit.

"For *what*?"

Jack tapped the sealed metal cylinder. "It's all in your orders."

"It's the *Glory*," XO said, stepping into the conversation for the first time as it was starting to go irreversibly south. "Come on, Cap, trust us."

"Absolutely not." Drake shook his head at the admiral.

"Then trust *me*," XO pressed.

"No," Drake said. "No more games." He pointed up toward the ceiling and the night sky beyond it. "No more hiding or drones hovering in the sky, watching me. You tell me what the hell is going on out there. Right. Now."

Jack stood at that. "It's classified," he said coolly with a final shake of his head. "And for good reason." He looked at XO. "Even Commander Oh here doesn't know his orders beyond reporting to the *Glory* for refitting and deployment as soon as she's spaceworthy. And I can assure you such secrecy might save this farm of yours and all the other farms in this godforsaken dust bowl and all the farmers on them. Because that is the work the Fleet does, Augustus. We do what needs to be done." Jack took a purposeful step forward, and Drake got a good look at the man's face. The lines there had deepened. "You used to do what needs to be done. Do it again."

Time had ravaged the admiral as much as his secrets had, and of all the things he hid, the spymaster could not hide his age. Nor could he hide his fear, Drake realized. It was there, flashing in his sunken eyes. Drake had only seen that fear once before, right before Jack had stabbed him in the back and run him out of the Fleet for knowing too much. Seeing it again made Drake seethe.

"No," he said, and he tossed the velvet box on the floor.

"No?" Jack blinked.

"Cap?" Oh asked in disbelief, face contorting at his friend's defiance.

Drake looked firmly at them both. "My answer is no." He stepped over to Ellen, who wrapped an iron-strong arm around him in support.

Jack's face reddened in anger. "I'm not going to ask you again."

"Then don't."

"You're a fool!" Jack spat, which caused him to cough again violently. Blood speckled his lips. He wiped it away, eyes wild and disbelieving. "A fool."

"The ship," XO pleaded, trying a softer approach and coming close with a lowered voice. "Come on, Cap. She needs you." It was too late for that, though. Far, far too late.

Drake shook his head and pulled his former XO into a hug. "It's good to see you, XO," he said, then released him. "But all of you, get the fuck out of my house."

"*My* house," Ellen said from behind him. She was still holding the shotgun, bless her.

"Ellen's house."

Jack coughed again, even worse, which made his face purple. He raised a hand like he was going to shout at Drake again, some cutting or furious remark, but the fit would not allow him. Instead, he hacked some more before giving Drake one last poisonous glare and turning on his shining black boot heel to exit through the front screen door. It clanged after him, causing his attendant and XO to snap to and follow him.

Drake felt immediate relief as he watched the vile old man go. His anger subsided like the tide, and in its wake, he felt tired. Very, very tired. Ellen set down the shotgun and wrapped him in a hug.

The embrace was interrupted by another clack of the screen door. It was XO.

"Cap," he said, throwing his giant hands up in response to the glares he got from Drake and Ellen. His demeanor was gentle, and it belied his massive, sloping frame. "We're spending the night in town before shuttle pickup in the morning. Fleet boarding house. Idea was to give you time to pack up and settle things here..." XO cleared his throat awkwardly. "Anyway, we'll be there till 0600. If, uh, you change your mind."

"It *was* nice to see you, XO," Drake said with a small, sad smile.

"You too, Cap."

"Call me Augustus."

XO wrinkled his nose. "No, thanks."

The large man lingered. "You really getting the old officers back together?" Drake asked him.

Oh nodded. "All except you. And Doc. Can't find him."

That got a small smile from Drake, and a nod. Good. "Good luck on the *Glory*," he told his old friend.

XO stayed for one last moment, then nodded and turned to leave. Another thought made him pause. "One more thing," he said, frowning. "You mentioned a drone to the admiral?" Drake nodded. XO shook his head. "He didn't send any drones. He wanted us showing up to be a surprise. For obvious reasons."

Drake frowned too but didn't say anything further. There was nothing left to say.

"See you," XO finally agreed, getting the hint. He gave a small wave, then he was gone.

Drake didn't see the velvet case on the floor until the

ground car was nothing but a dim cloud of dust in the darkness. He stared at it until Ellen stooped to pick it up.

She handed it to him and locked his eyes with a meaningful gaze. "It's yours now."

Drake realized with surprise as he held his former badge of office in his hands—the thing that had been stripped from him so many years before—that he believed Jack had meant what he'd said.

The offer had been real after all.

CHAPTER FOUR

"WHAT IS IT?"

Jack punched the comm button on the door's armrest. It connected him to the front of the ancient-feeling vehicle, where his attendant and the driver were taking them toward the tiny town closest to the Drake farm and seemingly hitting every bump or dip in the road along the way. His face still smarted, and it was no less the source of his irritability than the constant jostling or that he'd failed in his mission, the reason he was out in this godforsaken place. He didn't have time for failure. And he didn't have time for comm requests. Behind the irritability, he was burdened by the freezing cold of desperation. Jack decided he didn't have time for that either, but he couldn't make these go away by force of will.

They'd signaled him. Next to him in the back seat, Oh raised an eyebrow. Something was up.

"Incoming transmission, sir," his attendant said.

The admiral frowned. "Put it through."

The partition that separated him and his companion flickered, then disappeared, replaced by a holographic screen that displayed a written message. It was gibberish. Jack's heart rate quickened. Encrypted. He swiped it off the partition projection, and it winked into his palm. The microscopic holoprojectors embedded there tingled as they activated. Jack ground his teeth and reminded himself to yell at his attendant later. Such transmissions were not for mixed company.

He keyed in an access code in mid-air, and the projection unscrambled. He inhaled sharply as he read the contents of the message. It was from Aegis Station.

Damn.

He'd thought he'd have more time.

He didn't.

"Trouble, Admiral?" Oh was looking at him, concerned. The big dolt. Loyal to a fault, competent with his men, certainly not someone you'd ever want to challenge physically, but not an ounce of insight or radical thinking. No, all that, they'd just left behind. If their fate rested on *his* shoulders. Jack shuddered to think. Then again, Jack had been wrong before. Not often, and nothing he'd ever admit, of course. But it had happened. He cringed to think that such honesty was being wasted at this moment and might have been better applied back at that farmhouse.

"Change of plans," he said to the XO. "You're leaving tonight for the shipyards."

"Yes, sir," Oh replied briskly. Such a good order-following officer. At least Jack knew he could depend on *him*.

"Get her flight-ready. She needs to ship out in forty-eight hours."

Oh's eyes widened, and there was a tremor in his voice, but all the man said was, "We'll get it done, Admiral."

Jack nodded. He knew what he was asking. The *Glory*

was in mothballs. Probably literally, given the pest problems retired ships notoriously had. She hadn't been spaceworthy in twenty years. She was a dinosaur. They didn't make ships like her anymore, but that was precisely why Jack needed her for what was coming. Why he needed all of them, especially *him*...

"And you, Admiral?" Oh asked as the ground car bounced over a particularly rough patch of road.

Jack sighed and looked out at the landscape, featureless in the darkness except for the twinkle of running lights from the watering drones. "I'm going to wait in town and hope that our old colleague back there changes his mind."

ELLEN HATED it when Drake lay awake, so he got up and stood at the bedroom window. She hated that too, but it was better than him being in bed. She said she could feel his open eyes staring. It creeped her out. Drake didn't keep track of how often it happened, but if he had, he was sure it would be a depressing number. Best not to count such things.

His hand hurt. It was likely broken. He'd shown it to Ellen, who'd moved his fingers back and forth a few times, one by one. The middle and index fingers hurt right down to the knuckles with which he'd hit Jack square in the jaw. Ellen said they'd go to town in the morning to the vet station, see if they could get a service member to look at it.

But it wasn't his hand that kept him awake.

"You're thinking about your ship," said Ellen. She found herself behind him, wrapping her arms around his torso and pressing her chest against his back. The flannel of her nightgown was soft, as was her cheek against his shoulder.

Drake nodded.

The stars outside the window shone glittering in the clear night sky, unobstructed by the saturation of city lights. It was one of the very few places left on the planet that could claim that view of the stars. It was one of the reasons he'd picked this place to settle. That and Ellen.

"You ever think about yours?" he asked. She was a retired captain as well.

"Aug," she said, a pet name only she could call him, "I *left* the Fleet when I retired."

The insinuation was that he never had. And she was right. Ellen was always right. Guilt stabbed through him as he realized what he wanted but had been too afraid to admit. He'd chosen this place a long time ago, made promises, commitments—to himself most of all. His former life had burned him, so he'd turned his back on it. For his own good.

But had he?

He'd tried. He really had. He didn't miss it. Not in the daylight, anyway. But at night...at night it was quiet enough to hear the ghosts of unfinished business. He knew that was why Ellen hated it when he lay awake in bed or stood by the window. But tonight, she held him tightly.

"You never left," she said. "I've always known that, and that if the chance were ever to come again, you'd want to go."

"I don't want to go," Drake said, anger briefly boiling up inside him. But he couldn't be angry at Ellen. Not for the truth.

The Fleet had meant nothing but pain and headache for so long. Why would any sane person want to go back? He'd risked life and limb for his crew, for the admirals, for people who deserved it and many more who didn't, and in return, he'd been humiliated, cast aside, and labeled a menace. Now they wanted him back? He'd be insane to go.

"But you do," Ellen said. It wasn't a question.

"But I do." He hated himself for it. He hated Jack most of all. He clenched his fist again, which made the pain flare.

Ellen unwrapped her arms from around him and pulled his shoulders around to get him to face her. Drake resisted. He couldn't look her in the face, not after the promises he'd made for their life together. What a failure he was. What a hypocrite and a liar. She persisted, and he let his body rotate. He didn't know if he could take the berating he knew was coming or the pep talk about what he'd committed himself to do away from the Fleet, the life he'd chosen for himself that they could never touch or ruin, but had ruined anyway.

"It's okay," she said, and she raised his bowed head to meet her gaze. It was filled with love and understanding. "You're a good farmer, Augustus. And you're a wonderful lover. You make me very happy. But your place is on the command deck of that starship. It always has been."

"I can't go back." Drake shook his head. As much as he wanted to, as much as he thought about his former life, his ship, his crew, he couldn't allow himself to go back. He had promised.

They had burned him. *Jack* had burned him, and to be fooled for a second time, as the phrase went, shame on him. "I'm not going back," he said, and he wanted it to be final.

Ellen sighed and put her head on his chest. "Yes, you will."

Drake was about to protest, but the whirring of a rotor caught his ear. It was coming from outside the window. He turned to look. Something was in the darkness, hovering, mechanical. For a second, Drake thought it was one of the neighboring farms' mister drones gone astray. It had happened before. But there was no water pouring from this one, nor did it have the customary running lights so as to always know where they were from a distance.

"Aug," Ellen said, leaning back in alarm and putting a hand on his chest.

A tiny white dot no bigger than a pinhead was visible. It was a miracle she'd seen it. They weren't meant to be seen.

"Get down!" he shouted, and he shoved her away from the window.

The drone opened fire before they hit the floor. *Pop-pop-pop*. Three bursts of wicked orange-yellow light belched from the front of the remote-controlled craft. The energy projectiles crashed through the window where Ellen and Drake had been standing a moment before. The glass shattered and rained down on them. The plasma bolts slammed into the far wall of the bedroom, blasting wood and plaster in a cloud of debris that filled the bedroom.

Drake covered Ellen with his body, his hand screaming in agony from where he had hit the floor hard.

"Aug!" Ellen called from beneath him, not knowing if he was alive or dead.

Drake scrambled back, pushing with his feet toward the outside wall, moving them below and beside the window and out of sight. "I'm okay," he growled through gritted teeth, rolling onto his back to cradle his aching hand. "I'm okay," he repeated more softly, as much for himself as her.

His mind raced, the mind of a captain in battle. What did he know? What *didn't* he know, and how could he find out? How could he survive the next few seconds, then stretch it to a minute and more? Space battles were fierce and short. Survive to fight again. Hit and run.

To stay put would mean death and an easy one, exposed

as they were. How out of practice was he? How much of his training, his edge had he lost after all this time? Just how old, slow, and worthless had he become?

"The shotgun," Ellen hissed as she crawled toward the bed.

The room exploded as the drone fired again, targeting her voice. Plasma fire tore into the bedcovers, shredding the pillows and starting a fire. Ellen was a blur of motion as she scurried around it and bolted for the bathroom, which was the closest door.

"No!" Drake shouted. There was no way out of the bathroom. She'd be cornered in there.

The drone stopped firing in the split second after he'd shouted. That made Drake freeze. There was only the whir of the machine's blades to fill the silence, then a new sound. A *pop-hiss*, and an object flew through the shattered window and clanked on the bedroom's floorboards. Drake squinted to see what it was, fighting through floating embers and light spots in his vision. A chill gripped him when he saw what the drone had deposited inside.

A tiny sphere no larger than a marble or a ball bearing, impossibly black. So black, it was as if it weren't there. But it was—a little black dot.

Drake roared a curse as he launched into action. He bolted as if the devil himself chased him.

The next few moments played out in slow motion, a unique feature of the black dot weapon. The ceiling, the floor, and the walls constricted and began to cave in. Air was sucked in, as well as the still-floating embers. They traced orange-red lines as they collapsed toward the black dot. Drake lunged through the doorway to the living room, his body stretching. If he hadn't made it past the event horizon, he was dead. He'd fall into that black dot for eternity, and so would Ellen if she wasn't safe in the bathroom. The fabric of space-time bent inward, ripping at the edges. Drake froze in mid-air on the edge of a great funnel or drain. Then, with a flash of light and a thunderclap, things returned to normal, and Drake fell to the floor hard.

Behind him, what had once been their bedroom was now a perfect sphere of nothing. Destroyed electrical wires sparked and flickered, and ripped pipes geysered.

"What was that?" Ellen yelled from across the void. She'd made it to the refuge of the bathroom.

Drake rolled over. Now, not only was his broken hand stabbing with pain, so was his shoulder. He gritted his teeth. His body couldn't take a fall like it used to. "Stay put!" he shouted. "I think it's only after me."

On cue, as if to back up his assumption, the drone once again opened fire, pelting the living room through the kitchen wall. The crisscross of plasma fire and the flames and debris it kicked up made it impossible to see where the shotgun rested, and the shots were getting progressively more directed as they went. Homing on him.

It was tearing down the house around him. Damn.

Drake growled at his soft edge before running toward the front door. He doubted he had much more of a chance out in the open, but there was a ground car next to the barn. Maybe with some speed and some luck, he could lead the damned thing away from the house, away from Ellen, and somehow turn the tables.

Bolts of red-orange peppered his footsteps. He stole a glance at the kitchen and saw the drone tracking him through the twin kitchen windows as he ran, making Swiss cheese of the wall. There was another *thunk-swoosh*, and a second black dot plunked onto the floor. Drake dove for the front door, smashing into it with the shoulder he'd fallen on.

It stabbed with pain, but the force was enough to splinter the old wood.

He spilled onto the front porch and rolled down the stairs in a heap just in time to see the kitchen and part of the living room crumple and collapse into nothingness. The flash and thunderclap from the weapon stung his eyes and took his breath away. The house groaned with the suddenly missing support of its walls, ceiling, and floors. With a pop, a gas line caught fire in where the kitchen used to be. Embers, splinters, paper, and other shredded detritus floated in the air, remnants of the latest attack.

The house was ruined.

He staggered to his feet, pain burning in his hand and shoulder. "Ellen!" he shouted, desperately hoping she was okay.

The only answer he got was the rotor droning behind him. He turned and found himself face to face with the enemy. It had lights now, no longer a darkened shadow in the night but even less visible. They blinded him, and he instinctively raised a hand to block them. He tried to make out the shape of the thing, what make or model, where it came from, *who was trying to fucking kill him*, but he couldn't see. Not that he needed to, he realized. There was only one foe that used those cursed little black dots.

Drake felt a tickle as a new, tighter beam of light scanned his face.

"It's me!" he shouted at the machine and whoever might be controlling it. "Do it!"

The drone hung in the air, indecisive. Or perhaps just toying with him, playing out his end as long as it could to watch him squirm or beg or both. Drake wouldn't give it the satisfaction. He found a chunk of wood—the arm from his favorite armchair, as it turned out—and flung it at the drone with as much strength as he could muster. It wasn't much. His left shoulder, his injured shoulder with the broken hand, was his throwing arm. Drake gritted through the pain and threw anyway.

For all the effort it took to fling the wood, it bounced off the drone harmlessly.

Weapons whined within, and the gleam of the tiny white dot on his chest, the one that had tipped the drone's presence when he'd been standing at the window, told him the end had come.

He wanted to have his eyes wide open when it finally happened, to face his death with the grace and bravery befitting a warrior. The kind he imagined himself to be, at least one last time in his life. But the involuntary nervous system didn't work that way. There was a loud boom of a weapon firing at close range, and his eyelids constricted of their own accord. He flinched as well. One last humiliation. He'd blinked in the face of his death. Damn it all.

When he opened his eyes—Drake found it miraculous that he could do so—it was dark in front of him, save for the sparking flames of the drone at his feet. It writhed, glitched, and burbled in its death throes, and Drake could see why. A rather large hole had been blasted through its body and two of its four circular rotors.

Drake turned to see a bloody, disheveled Ellen standing above him on what was left of their porch. The house was on fire behind her, and in her hands, she held the still-smoking shotgun. Her hair was streaked with soot and grime, but it dangled on either side of her face, sexier than Drake had ever seen. He flushed, and a surge of emotion broke his voice when he said, "Thank you."

She nodded like it was nothing and lowered the

smoking gun. She regarded the still-sizzling drone writhing on the ground. "You get a good look at it?"

That snapped Drake back to the here and now, and he stepped to the thing with one purpose. He stomped on it, crushing it beneath the heel of his boot. The machine fell silent. He hooked the toe of his boot under the drone's body and flipped it over. His mouth twisted into a snarl.

"Whose is it?" Ellen asked when he'd been silent for too long.

Drake looked at the sky. "One of ours," he said. The drone had the distinct Earth-and-star logo of the Fleet. "Outfitted with Paragon tech."

"How is that possible?"

Drake shook his head in disgust. "I don't know." He gazed at Ellen, taking stock of how she looked. In the distance, sirens wailed. Fire control was on its way, and probably medics, too. "You okay?" he asked her.

Ellen shrugged. "Bumps and bruises."

Drake set his jaw and nodded. He tightened and untightened his good fist. He turned his back on the smoldering drone and stalked into the night, heading for the barn and the flatbed.

"Where you going?"

"Town," he said, building up a head of steam. "I'm gonna ask Jack why he blew up our fucking house."

"Don't ask nicely," Ellen called after him.

"I won't."

CHAPTER FIVE

THE VETERANS' Building was one Drake knew well. There was one in every town on Earth, the result of centuries of warfare. Not warfare amongst each other, though that still happened sometimes, but out in space. Space was a dangerous place. It teemed with life, the kind that had become reachable once humanity had figured out gateways and slip drives and whatnot.

With all that life came conflict. Imperialistic zeal was not a trait exclusive to humans. No, in fact, it seemed endemic to life, full stop. Territories were fought over, alliances and enemies made, and wars were waged on a near-constant basis. Earth had been drawn into several of them.

Thus, the majority of the world's population served in the Fleet, at least for a time. It wasn't mandatory—not now, although it had been at times in the past—but it was such a massive part of the human economy, most still did. Veterans' Buildings were ubiquitous everywhere you went, even in the sleepier corners of the world, those few that still existed. Like Plainsville, Iowa.

The Plainsville Veterans' Building lived up to its name; it was plain. It was a gray block slightly wider than it was deep or tall, featureless, unimaginative, and functional. It did its job. Medical services, recruitment, bunks, a rec and fitness center, a buffet-style cafe that served its employees, anyone staying there, and the public at large should anyone have a hankering for cafeteria-style chow, which some did. Many a retiree came in from the farm or the hills for a cheap meal that reminded them of their service days.

That kind of thing wasn't for Drake. He'd turned his back on military life, and that included its shitty food. He stayed the hell away from this place as much as he could, which was damn near all the time. He regarded the gray building with contempt through his truck window. The admiral's ground car was nowhere to be seen, but one of the corner top-floor windows was lit up—a visiting officer's suite. Only someone of the admiral's distinction would be given that room. Jack was there.

Drake parked askew in the front lot, not bothering to fit into a single spot, then heaved himself out of the truck, slamming its creaking, rusted door behind him. He was in the lobby a few long strides later and stalked past the crewman on duty, who couldn't have been more than a day past eighteen. He punched, literally, the lift controls before the kid could even speak.

"Here to see the admiral," he growled in response to the meek question from the front desk. The lift dinged, and its doors parted, revealing a dingey but functional interior. "He's expecting me," Drake said as he stepped inside.

With another ding, the lift doors closed, and it lurched upward before settling into a smooth rhythm. One of the incandescent light tubes overhead was on its last leg, illuminating the lift in a sickly green glow instead of a steady, pleasant military white. Drake found it suited his mood, and he readied his fist and clenched his jaw. A final ding announced that he'd arrived on the top floor, and Drake was out the doors before they had fully rumbled aside.

His boots clomped as he stalked over the aging white flooring. It was spotless, of course, nary a speck of dust to be seen, but somehow, that highlighted its age and disrepair. Leave it to the military to polish a turd. The building was probably fifty years old, and the flooring, walls, lights, lift, etc., were the same. None had been replaced in all that time, just cleaned over and over. It was so *government* it made his skin crawl, which gave him a small thrill of satisfaction at the thought of Jack staying here, far from his slick offices and fancy housing. It must be making his skin crawl too.

Drake pounded as hard as he could on the doors of the quarters whose lights he'd seen on.

"Jack!" he shouted, making no effort to lower his voice. He pounded again before anyone would even have had time to answer. "Get your ass over here and open this door!" He pounded again and didn't stop. "I know you're in there! Open up!"

The door flew open so fast that Drake nearly punched the hawkish-looking man in the face. That would have suited Drake fine, but Jack was already stepping to the side to let him in. *Mistake*, Drake thought.

"Augustus," the admiral greeted him. "Please come insi—"

His words were cut off by Drake taking his throat in his bare hand. Drake pushed Jack farther into the room, grabbing his shoulder with his bad hand to shove him up the wall and then using his foot to slam the door behind them.

"You *fuck*," Drake seethed as Jack's eyes popped wide

open. "You piece of absolute fucking shit. How dare you?" Drake squeezed on the man's throat tighter, causing his face to redden. He started to gurgle and writhe under the assault. Drake dimly thought he should have checked the room to see if one of the admiral's guards was there, but the thought was squashed by the realization that he didn't care. Not one bit. Having his hands around the throat of the snake who'd ruined his life was sufficient in this particular moment.

"You blew up our house!" he hissed. When Jack made no effort to respond, Drake used his weight and strength to pull the admiral's head forward, then slam it into the wall. *"You blew up our fucking house, Jack!"*

Jack gurgled as though he were trying to say something, and he shook his head violently.

"What are you trying to say?" Drake yelled, but he didn't take his hands off of the man's throat. No, he squeezed even tighter. What could Jack say except more lies? Drake didn't want to hear it. Anger surged through him like a tidal wave, building and building. His vibrating body felt white-hot. And as it built and exploded, he squeezed harder.

The admiral was purple now, his eyes bloodshot. His hands clawed futilely at Drake's, but he couldn't tear them away. Not the hands of a man possessed. Again, Jack tried to speak, shaking his head. Drake bellowed at him, past words, past thoughts. There was only sound and action now and what this man had done to him. The bellow became a scream, and when it was over, Drake blinked, physically blinded by rage, lightheaded, and shaking.

Jack was on the floor, coughing on his hands and knees. He must have let him go.

Drake watched the admiral, pathetic, old—so old now.

He looked frail, and his coughs were turning into retching, getting louder and more forceful. Behind him, Drake heard the door of the room fly open and slam against the wall. The admiral's guards came rushing in, disheveled and bleary-eyed. One grabbed Drake while the other rushed to Jack, but with a sickening realization, Drake wondered if they were too late. He looked down at his hands, which moments earlier had been wrapped around the old man's throat. Now, Jack was gasping desperately for air between bone-shattering coughs.

The coughs came sharper and faster, and with a great heave, Jack coughed up a dark-red, almost black slick of blood that splattered on the floor. It was thick, and it seemed to shimmer and undulate in the dim light of the room. Drake narrowed his eyes and stopped fighting the guard holding him by his arms. Everyone in the room stopped moving. No, the blood slick didn't *seem* to shimmer or move. It *did* move. Sharply. Like a worm stretching out after having been curled.

For the second time that night, Drake felt cold certainty and horror settle into his chest. Drake recognized the creature, and it *was* a creature. He'd seen one before, and it was not of this world. It started to glow, burning away the blood slick that covered it, and two golden eyes the size of pinheads glared open. The guard who'd been attending the admiral gasped sharply and jumped back. Behind him, the guard holding Drake did the same, and Drake, acting on instinct, lunged forward. He crossed the distance between him and Jack before anyone could move, including the glowing, bloody creature. On the last stride, he brought his work boot high into the air and slammed it down on the thing with a crunch and a splat.

It sparked and gurgled, followed by the hiss of smoke

and steam leaking out from around the sides of Drake's boot. He lifted it off the floor to make sure the damned thing was dead.

It was, smoldering in the midst of Jack's innards. Now still and dark, it was easier to see it for what it was: a grotesque cross between a silverfish and a centipede, about half a palm-length, with beady eyes, a corrugated, sectioned body, and sharp-looking legs and antennae. The shapes were all off, the proportions wrong. Even without its glow, it was alien. Paragon.

Beside him, Jack wheezed and moved into a sitting position, leaning against the wall and away from Drake and the Paragon bug. He gave a grim smile. There was still blood dripping from his lips and chin.

"I was trying to tell you," he rasped. He coughed again and shook his head. "It wasn't me who blew up your house, Augustus." He pointed a shaking finger at the dead bug. "It was them."

JACK SAT at the cheap kitchen table in his quarters in the Vet Building. It was laminated with a plastic dyed to look like wood, but the illusion, which had never been convincing, was ruined by the worn patches that exposed the white synthetic material underneath. The corners were split too, with sharp edges poking out that would scratch someone who wasn't paying attention. Drake fingered the one closest to him, trying to wrap his head around what Jack was telling him.

"H-how?"

"Could be anyone." Jack waved the question away like it was hopeless. He leaned toward Drake for extra emphasis. "*Anyone*," he repeated. "This thing goes up to the highest levels of the Fleet, Aug. Hell, it could be one of my attachés." With that, he fell into a coughing spell. More blood, but specks of it now. The big bug was out, or one of them. There would be more.

"How long?" Drake asked, thinking about the monstrosities growing inside of his old boss.

Jack shrugged weakly and wiped his mouth. "I don't know. Days? Weeks? You know how it goes."

Drake did know. He'd seen a person succumb to this particular nasty and effective weapon before. They were called something extremely technical by the Paragon, autonomous, self-replicating, high-growth factor biosynthetic programmable somethings. The Fleet called them "bugs." Ostensibly, they were medical devices. Nanotech. They could repair cell walls, but they could also be programmed to tear them down. They replicated and multiplied, growing by a factor of billions in size, and they were customizable down to a person's DNA. They were activated in the right host's body, which made them easy to deliver since they did nothing to the wrong host. And they were always fatal. Always.

There were millions of them inside Jack, tearing his body apart from the inside. It was a gruesome death, one Drake would not have wished on his worst enemy. Well, one or two of his worst, and maybe that was Jack, but he didn't feel the hatred now that he had earlier. There were nights when he could have reveled in what he saw across from him at that cheap table, the great spy of the Fleet hacking out his lungs, but the fantasy did not match the reality.

"It doesn't matter," Jack said about his impending doom,

his weary eyes sharpening with purpose. "There's no more time left anyway."

"No time left for what?" Drake asked. He focused on the admiral's eyes to the exclusion of all else. Jack was going to tell him what the fuck was going on. They were alone now, secrets be damned.

Jack nodded. "They're coming," he said simply.

"The Paragon?"

Jack nodded again.

"For Earth?"

"For everything."

"When? Does it have anything to do with this peace conference?"

"I don't know exactly when, but there is no peace conference, Augustus. It's a ruse. There will be no peace. You and I both know that. There will never be peace with them."

"War, then?"

Jack's eyes filled with horror. "Or worse." He reached into his uniform pocket and pulled out the small metal tube with Drake's orders inside. The admiral's hand was shaking, so much so that the tube slipped out of his fingers and clattered onto the table. Drake recognized it as a top-secret orders capsule, the kind that could be programmed to open for a specific person or persons, at a given time, or in a predetermined location. "Damn," the admiral muttered as he put a palm down to stop the capsule from rolling and steady himself. When he looked at Drake again, the bravado, the pride, the contemptible air of knowing and controlling everything that made Drake want to pop his head like a water balloon was gone. Even the weary sickness was gone. In its place were horror and haunting. "I fear for the spirit of the Fleet, Augustus. I don't know if we have it in us to fight what's coming, to defeat the Paragon."

Drake bristled. "If anyone in the Fleet is giving up, Admiral, it's you on them. Not the other way."

"Which is why I need you," he said, and Drake considered that he actually meant it. He put his hands together. "Desperately."

"For what? What do you need me to do?"

Jack shook his head. He still wasn't going to say.

Drake slammed a fist on the flimsy table. It bounced so hard it felt like it might shatter. "Dammit, Jack," he said, nostrils flaring.

"I can't tell you," the admiral wheezed. "I can't risk it. I can't." He tapped the metal cylinder on the table. "I couldn't even risk typing it, Augustus. I had to write this all out. I've suspected for a long time that they're logging my keystrokes and recording all my verbal interactions. And thank the stars I did, because if the attack on you tonight means anything, it's that they *are*. And even more than that, they're anticipating."

Drake's anger cooled when he saw the paranoia in the admiral. It had always been there, but this was different.

"No one was supposed to know I was coming to you tonight," Jack continued, not pausing to catch his breath. "Not anyone at HQ, in the intelligence division, my subordinates... Hell, my attachés didn't know who we were going to see. Oh suspected, but I didn't even tell him. But *they* knew. They knew out in the Corvus system, too." Drake didn't understand that reference, but Jack plowed on. "They're one step ahead now, or so they think." He finally stopped to inhale. He'd worked himself up, and he closed his eyes and gripped the metal tube tightly.

"What's in there?" Drake asked.

"A fighting chance," Jack said, opening his eyes. A coughing fit proceeded, one that was violent enough to leave him wheezing again, and he leaned back against the wall, trying desperately to catch his breath. He let go of the metal tube in the action, and it rolled across the table toward Drake. "A *weapon*."

Drake picked it up and shook his head. "Jesus. What have you gotten yourself into?"

"Us," Jack coughed back. "They're trying to kill you too now."

Drake nodded grimly.

"That was unfortunate," Jack said in the silence that followed.

Drake sighed, thinking about his smoldering house and feeling weary. "We survived. And the house...well, it can be rebuilt," he said. "Ellen will make sure of that."

"Not your house," Jack said gently, a tone Drake had never heard him use before. "Though, that's also unfortunate."

"Oh," Drake said, tensing. He knew where Jack was now, but he was not sure where he was going. From the Admiral's demeanor, he suspected he was thinking further back. Much further. He waited for Jack to speak. It was some time before he did.

"I was going to reinstate you, you know. If you'd just waited. A year at most. I was going to make sure you got your rank back."

Drake flexed his jaw muscles. "It wouldn't have been enough."

"I know."

"You sold me out when we were supposed to protect each other."

Drake's words echoed across the chasm that had grown

between the two men, and they both let them reverberate for a good long time. Then Jack said, "That was a mistake."

It still wasn't enough.

No words would ever be enough. Nor was it an apology, a real apology, the kind a man should make when he regretted his actions and owned up to what he'd done, the mistakes he'd made. But it was close. It was as close as Drake was going to get. At least, it was as close as Drake had ever heard from Jack.

"Fucking hell, Jack," Drake said, leaning back in his chair. He rubbed his face and tapped the metal cylinder on the table.

Jack sensed the opening. "I need you," he told him earnestly and without pretense.

"*Fuck*," Drake repeated, avoiding meeting the gaze of the other man by looking at the ceiling.

Jack gestured at the tube. "I've worked out a chance in there. I don't know if it will be enough, but it's a fighting chance." His body came alive, and he repositioned himself in his chair so he was leaning toward Drake. His voice was freshly invigorated. "Shuttle departs in the morning, bound for Jupiter Station."

"I can't just leave Ellen."

"There's time for goodbye."

Drake was silent for a long time, then sighed heavily. When he spoke again, it was with firm conviction.

"You said you couldn't find Doc," he said. He leveled his gaze on Jack. "I can."

CHAPTER SIX

EVERYTHING about the Thames Delta was salty. The wind, the splash at the bow of the hover skiff, the smell, all of it was saturated in brine. Drake steadied a hand on the gunwale as they bounced over the whitecaps. His knuckles matched their color. There was no sense in getting tossed into the frigid, super-saline water. He wasn't a cucumber. Nor was he a sailor. The misty, early morning air made him want to draw his far-too-thin coat in closer around his neck and torso, but he didn't dare take that hand off the boat edge.

Doc would call him a landlubber. Drake wouldn't correct him. This was not his element. It was Doc's. That was, Doctor Lazare Broussard, surgeon, and former Chief Medical Officer of the TDF cruiser *Glory*. And an old salt.

Behind bouncing skiff, stretching for several kilometers, was the London seawall, holding all the ocean brine back from pouring into the old river basin and flooding the metropolis towering in the distance. Ahead of them lay a forest of wind turbines, slowly spinning on the horizon as the frothy sea slapped at their white stalks. It was the largest offshore wind farm in the world, which was saying something given such farms were on nearly every coast. Their rotors spun in great, lazy arcs that belied the fierce, cold wind, as far as the eye could see. That was not Drake's destination, however, nor the bouncing skiff's.

The small boat's pilot, a broad man with a white beard as salty as the sea around them, made a shout over the wind and the slapping waves, and pointed ahead. Drake followed his outstretched arm and squinted against the gray sunrise. A structure of a different kind loomed. Several structures, in fact. Boxes on stilts, like some kind of fantasy story where a house up and walked out to sea.

The Maunsell Forts were military, originally, built for a war that had ended two hundred years ago; they were constructed on barges, floated out into the Thames Delta back when it was several meters shallower, and then sunk so only the boxy structures and the concrete columns on which they stood remained above water. The sea level rise meant the lower floors of those boxes weren't usable anymore, but more floors had been built over the many decades, and their metal structures reinforced. In fact, several of the forts had been re-floated to be moved to this one, last remaining location outside the metropolis and its seawall.

"Sealand" had been in existence since very nearly the beginning of these forts, a forever-unrecognized, independent principality with a checkered and entertaining history. The forts were, and remained, just remote enough, just unstrategic enough, and just worthless enough to remain unbothered. Once abandoned by the military, they'd become an attraction for all kinds of offbeat folks, from radio pirates to data miners to just plain folks who wanted to stay really, really away from it all. Even back then, it had been one of the last, true places to find solitude and independence; something that was exponentially harder to find in Drake's time. The skiff ride out was still a two-hour trip. It took a very rare, very special person to live beyond the edge of the world. Doc was just that rare, and just that special.

The skiff finally, blessedly reached a mooring spot. Not a dock. Not in these wind-tossed conditions. A line was tossed down from above to keep them from drifting, and the pilot attached it to a ring on the gunwale. Then came down a loading hook. The ride out to Sealand had not been to deliver Drake; he was a barnacle, allowed to attach himself for a price to an otherwise occupied vessel. That vessel's mission was to bring supplies, which is what the hook was for. It was also the only way up onto the forts.

Drake helped the pilot secure the various crates and packages and watched them hauled up into the structure above. Once they were all gone, it was his turn, and instead of a hook, down came a swing. It looked very much the way they looked as a child: a small, narrow bar for the bottom, a rope rising from each side, left and right, and both spanned above by another narrow bar that was attached to the loading hook.

Drake looked over at the pilot, oozing skepticism. The white-bearded man just smiled at him and laughed. "Only way up, boyo," he said, reveling. Welsh bastard. Drake had only been out this way once, decades before, and he'd come with Doc by air. This would be his first time on the swing.

It was just as terrifying as Drake had imagined. The second he was lifted off the tossing boat, he swung back and nearly lost his grip, which would have plunged him down into the freezing water. But he didn't, bad shoulder be damned, and he gritted his teeth to bite back the terror and not let it show. There were no smirks or laughter when he reached topside, which told him he was successful. A woman waited there to haul him in, regarding him silently with narrow eyes.

Drake touched down on the ancient metal grating and thanked her. He could have kissed the rust beneath his feet, but he bit that back, too. He vowed this was the last time he'd sail. It was the land or the stars for him, thank you.

"And who're you?" the woman asked him, voice thick, guttural and rising at the question in the distinct inflection of a Scottish accent. They had quite the varied collection of backgrounds out here, didn't they? Doc would be another kind, added to the mix.

"Here to see Doc," Drake answered, understanding she'd know him by the familiar term rather than his actual name. When the woman continued to stare at him through skeptical, slitted eyes, he added, "I'm a friend."

"He know you're coming?"

"Yes," Drake lied.

"You know where to find 'im?"

Drake looked ahead, finally taking in the rest of the fort complex. There was a dozen or so of them, all connected by cabled suspension bridges, each with a wild collection of scrap metal and plastiform panels adorned in all manner of graffiti, rough handmade sculptures, or amateur artwork as well as practical considerations like clotheslines and radio towers. In the approximate center was one square structure that caught his eyes (and ears) in particular. At the end of its bridge was a hand-scrawled sign that read "Pub."

"Yes, I do," Drake finally answered the Scottish woman. He looked at the offloaded crates and packages sitting on the bulwark near the crane and recalled that it was good manners on Sealand to pitch in at every opportunity. "You need any help?" he asked.

The woman looked around and located a torso-sized plastiform crate, lifted it, and handed it over to Drake. It tinkled with glass inside as she did. Bottles. "If you're heading that way," she said.

He was. He gripped it tight, and headed out onto the suspension bridge, which swayed in the wind. Between rusting metal slats, Drake could see the sea churning and frothing below. The wind was picking up. Maybe there was going to be a storm. The cold cut right through his civilian coat.

He made it across as quick as he could, then kicked at the door on the other side to get someone to open it for him. It took him a couple tries before a giant of a man with dark skin and a beer-soaked apron yanked it open. Written in permanent black ink on the bib of the apron was the name "Tre."

Tre scowled at him and wiped his hands with a bar mop. Inside it smelled musty and sour, a comforting aroma for Drake that was different from the salty outside air. It smelled like a bar. Drake lifted the plastiform crate for Tre to see and give a jiggle so the bottles inside tinkled. Tre grunted and stood aside.

The "Pub" was dim, and fashioned almost entirely from old, pockmarked steel covered in a shellacking of ancient military-grade paint. The bar itself was riveted to the metal floor, and the rest of the decor was fashioned out of more metal scrap. Drake wasn't sure where they took their electricity from, but it was enough to power string lights, which hung around the edges of the room and across the bar. Sitting there, lit from below, Drake immediately recognized Doc.

He was slumped over, his hand on a pint, with skin darker than Tre's, a mess of wild, curly hair on top with a graying beard to match. Though he'd clearly long-abandoned military etiquette for hairstyle and facial hair, he had a Fleet jacket draped around his shoulders.

"Here," Tre said to Drake, pointing to a spot beside the bar. It took Drake a moment to realize the giant bartender meant the crate he was holding. Drake bought it to where he'd indicated, set it down, and gave Tre a nod as he straightened. He felt his eyes follow him as he walked around to the customer side of the bar, and approached Doc. Everyone's eyes in the bar followed him, in fact. There were, perhaps, a dozen other people inside; some drank quietly and alone, others drank loudly in groups. But, everyone took a pause to watch the outsider. Drake made himself as large as he could and walked with confidence and purpose. He suspected if he were to show anything less, this group would turn him right out and send him swimming with the fishes. Sealand wasn't inhospitable to visitors, per se, but they weren't exactly friendly either. It depended on whether you were bothering someone who didn't want to be. Protective. Drake liked it. Doc needed protection sometimes.

"Hiya, Doc," Drake said and slid onto a stool next to his friend. He ignored the eyes on him.

Doc ignored him too. His wild-haired head didn't budge, forehead pressed to the polished wood of the bar. His fingers danced beside it, tapping and drumming to music only he could hear. All the while, Doc's drink sweated into a pool of water, which was starting to run toward him.

Drake grabbed a nearby rag and reached for the drink. Doc's nearest hand snapped out to grab him by the wrist. The grip was iron-strong, unwavering.

Doc was upright now, staring into Drake. "Mingled

cream an' amber," he said in a gruff voice like that of a smoker long past his prime. He slurred the words even though his grip stayed steady. His eyes were glassy and distant. It was a quote; one Drake couldn't place. "I will drain that glass again."

He dropped Drake's wrist, and his head began to sink back down to the bar.

Drake caught him by the temples and held steady, trying to reclaim his gaze. "Doc," he said again, but he got nothing but a flat stare.

This was not the work of alcohol. No, not this far gone. He worked his fingers around to the back of the man's neck and found a derm patch there on a clear area of skin: sugar-soft; a potent depressant usually laced with hallucinogens. Drake looked again at Doc's eyes. Definitely hallucinogens.

"It's me, Doc," he tried. "It's Augustus."

The man stirred at the name. His eyes focused. Widened.

He jerked back, barely staying on his stool. "The spirits of the dead may walk again," he quoted again, voice hushed and wild. His Estuary-London accent was thick and raw. He pointed at Drake. "You are not here."

"It's me," he repeated and tried to pull him back toward the bar.

Doc shook his head violently and waved him away. His face was pale and panicked. High as the clouds.

Drake reached into his pants pocket and pulled out the time-locked cylinder Jack had given him. He set it on the bar with a smack to make sure Doc would fix on it. The emblazoned Fleet logo sparkled in the dim light of the bar.

Doc stared at it. He drifted in and out of focus, then a huge smile came up from deep within. He laughed. The bellow nearly knocked him off his barstool again, and then he laughed more. It turned maniacal. Hysterical.

Not the reaction Drake had been hoping for. A giant hand clamped on his shoulder from behind. Drake looked up into Tre's mirthless mug. "Time to leave." He yanked Drake up.

Drake spun and shoved the man back as hard as he could. Tre didn't flinch. Drake stumbled back instead. Every chair and stool in the bar scraped across the floor in unison, and a tense silence followed.

Drake set his jaw. "I'm here to talk to my friend," he repeated.

"He doesn't want to talk to you," Tre replied.

Doc continued to howl. The orders were in his hands, dancing back and forth.

This wasn't working. Drake reached into his pocket and fingered his last resort. He should have known it was going to come to this, but goddamn if Doc hadn't backed him into a corner this time, all these men staring him in the face. It had to be quick.

So Drake was quick.

In a blur, he pulled a needle from his pocket, bit the plastic tip off, spat it aside, and lunged for Doc. He caught him at the base of the neck. Not ideal, but his shoulders were covered by the tattered blue uniform coat. He plunged the anti-narcotic serum into his old friend. Doc shrieked and fell off his stool. Hands seized Drake from behind.

They grabbed him, too many to be only one man, and pinned both arms to his back. Then Tre was there to deliver the heaviest punch Drake had ever suffered. The wind exploded from him, and he sagged and gulped for air. Tre's face split into a lopsided grin. The two behind Drake kept him from dropping to the floor and started dragging him toward the exit.

Before Drake could recover his breath, free himself, and fight back, a shout silenced the bar. Drake was thrown free, and he crashed across a table and slid to the floor. Drinks showered him. A single pair of hands hauled him to his feet, supporting but not restraining him.

"Stay back!" the voice bellowed from too close to his head. Drake wiped off the alcohol stinging his eyes and got a blurry look at who belonged to that voice. Doc.

His eyes were already clearer. He swung a fist back and forth at the tense mob that surrounded them. A grin formed on his lips, and he looked at Drake. "We can take 'em like old times," he said. "Eh, Cap?"

Doc coughed once lightly and puked on Drake.

He sagged. Drake caught him on the way down.

There was a prolonged silence in the bar. Drake fixed on Tre while fighting the urge to join Doc in spewing ingloriously. The stench attacked him like a three-day-dead body.

"You gonna help me with him or what?" Drake asked.

"Here."

Drake accepted the wet, brown bar mop Tre offered and continued to dab at the front of his vomit-drenched shirt. It was probably a lost cause, but there wasn't much else to do as he sat on an overturned bucket outside the back of the pub, waiting for Doc to sober up. It was an activity Drake knew well. As brilliant a surgeon as Doc had always been, so too had he been brilliantly and fiercely an addict. Drink. Medication. Drugs. Anything he could use to alter and escape his reality when the opportunity afforded itself. Rarely an issue on deployment. A persistent issue land-side. Or sea-side as it were. Drake had expected this.

They'd removed the derm patch. It was clear from the sheen of sweat that now drenched him and his dark blue coat that the anti-narco was working its magic, but Doc had yet to come to.

"You want food?" Tre asked, but Drake waved him off. He was not hungry given the smells around him, vomit aside. The brine, fish, grease, and curdling alcohol cocktail didn't get him salivating, nor did the cold. On the horizon, behind the white windmills, the rising sun peeked through the gray cloud cover. Below the railed platform they sat on, the ocean waves splashed against the concrete stilts.

"How long is this going to take?" asked the giant man, eyeing Doc, who was propped up against the tin of the shack, mouth slack and eyes closed.

Drake shrugged. It varied.

Tre grunted and lumbered back into the pub's kitchen. He returned a moment later, holding a sweating glass of cold water.

Drake held his hand up. "No, I'm not thirst—"

Splash. The large man threw it in Doc's face.

Doc woke with a start and fixed his eyes on Drake, panicked and disoriented. Drake thought he'd scream again, that maybe the sugarsoft hadn't yet oozed its way out of his pores, but then the man's dark eyes cleared. Softened.

Tre grunted again in satisfaction. "That's how we sober him here," he said to Drake, then he turned to Doc. "*You* hungry?"

"Starving," Doc said, blinking.

Drake waved off the request. "No food," he said. "He'll

just throw it up anyway." Drake stared at Doc. "You can sober up en route."

Doc laughed wearily. "En route, Cap?" His Oxford-educated received pronunciation was back, clipped and polished. "Am I going somewhere?"

"Jupiter Station," Drake said.

Doc stopped laughing.

"Doc," Tre said, eyes on Drake, looking for any excuse to pummel him once and for all. "You needin' me?"

Drake braced himself.

Doc leaned against the wall. He shook his head. "No, thank you, Tre," he said. "You can let me talk to the ghost here."

Tre left.

"'The ghost?'" Drake repeated.

Doc leaned forward again and shivered. The medals on his old uniform shivered with him, tinkling. Up close, Drake could see how threadbare and faded the coat had become over the years, just like Doc. His face was lined and weary. Wisps of white and gray peppered his cheeks and chin. The hair on top was the same and wild. And Lord, did he stink.

"Dead is what we call someone who disappears and never comes back," Doc said.

Drake winced. "I'm here now."

Doc stared at him, impenetrable, till Drake looked away.

His hand and shoulder ached, roughed up in the fight. He flexed the former, and gingerly put his other hand on the latter, slowly rotating it and trying to stretch it out. Hand. Shoulder. Drake was falling apart.

"Boys inside give you trouble?" Doc asked.

Drake shook his head. They had, but not really. "This isn't from them."

"Who then?"

Drake allowed himself a small smile. "Admiral Jack, actually."

Doc's eyebrows raised. "You don't say."

"Got him good."

"Finally." Doc, too, smiled despite himself. A real one. Finally, he looked down at the vomit on Drake's shirt. "Is that mine?"

Drake nodded.

"Apologies for that."

Drake shrugged. "Apologies for *that*," he said, and he pointed toward Doc's neck where he'd stuck him with the needle.

Another beat passed.

"So. What's with this nonsense about Jupiter Station?"

"Not nonsense." He pulled out the cylinder, which he'd recovered from the bar floor after the scrum. He showed it to Doc again. "At least, I hope not."

"What is that supposed to be?"

"Orders from Jack."

Doc raised an eyebrow at him. "You can't order someone who isn't in the Fleet."

Drake reached into his pocket and produced his badge of office. Drake had started to polish it on the flight over. Half of it was still tarnished, but the other half gleamed in the rising dawn. Drake could see on Doc's coat where his used to rest, the spot bare and faded now. He handed the small piece of metal to his friend, who took it and gripped it tight as if to see if it were real.

"It's *Glory*," Drake said.

Doc said nothing.

"I need you with me."

"You left," Doc said after another long silence. "Left all of us." Pain shone in his eyes, uncovered.

It was true. Drake hadn't talked to anyone after he'd quit the Fleet. Everything had been crazy then, but that was just the excuse he told himself for not even talking to his own men. His best friend.

"I'm quite angry about that."

"I'm sorry."

Doc sighed. "I'm weak, Cap. Too old. It's a young man's game."

Drake pointed at Doc's hands, which were white-knuckled as they held onto the badge of office. "You look strong to me."

Doc looked at him, not daring to believe, and Drake met his eyes. Below, the ocean swelled and crashed against the supports. It sent a salty mist showering down over them.

"So, how about it?"

CHAPTER SEVEN

THE HEART of Earth's military lay in DC.

When the world's governments had coalesced into a single body—the United Earth, or "UE" as it was commonly called; a miracle in its own right—those chambers and halls and offices were drawn to Paris, across the ocean. The politicians had uprooted for a nicer view, more grandeur, food, the things the French still held over other parts of the world and seemingly always would. But the soldiers had stayed behind, at least those in what had once been called "the Pentagon." It wasn't called that anymore.

All branches of that ancient tree had become "the Fleet," and Fleet HQ had remained in DC, even when the off-world colonies, both in-system and out, had multiplied and grown beyond just the UE into the Terran Federation. The rest of Earth's soldiers, and those from the colonies, had come there too and taken root in the flat, humid, simpler land. Not that DC was simple, or that it didn't have as much of incessant hand-shaking, back-slapping, and politicking as the other side of the pond. But it had been different once, DC from Paris. A long time ago.

Jack was old enough that he could remember.

The admiral strode through the early-morning throng of HQ's grand entrance, lungs on fire. Banners hung from the eaves of the hall, proclaiming victory for the peace talks that were just days away. Peace with the Paragon. A treaty that would end hostilities once and for all, negotiated by the politicians, of course. A century of war gone just like that.

It was a triumph of the modern age, one in which conflict was considered a thing of the past, a relic of an undesirable history that should never be repeated, a time that was encapsulated by fanatics like Jack. That was why he was being pushed aside, relegated to less responsibility, fewer personnel and resources. They were bleeding his authority dry drop by drop.

Jack was a microcosm of the reach Paris had into DC, hollowing out the military, and it was impossible to stop. Perhaps it could have been stopped once. Jack had even seen it, but he hadn't acted when he'd had the chance. That ate at him, even though he knew why: he had wanted to believe them. He had wanted to believe peace had a chance, that none of what he'd done was necessary, that none of what he feared would come to pass.

A message buzzed on his commlink, and he flipped his wrist over to view it. He slowed in the throng and his two escorts slowed with him, making sure the crowd parted on either side of them.

Encrypted.

"We're making a detour to my office," he said, suppressing a cough. It would make him late for the all-hands meeting he was due to attend, but that would allow him to make a blustery grand entrance; one of the few he had left in him at this rate. Anything disruptive had to be considered a plus these days.

In stark contrast to the bustling entrance, the Admiralty's offices were quiet. Jack and his guards—"aides" as far as anyone else was concerned, but Jack knew what they really were—strode across the polished stone floors, heels clicking and echoing. It was still early morning at HQ, and everyone already here was headed to the meeting. "You two stay put." Jack motioned as he reached his door. The guards raised their eyebrows in response to the command. "I'll just be a moment."

Jack left them behind with a swift opening and closing of his office door. The encrypted message was not for them to see or know about, as it had been with the itinerary to go and see Drake with Commander Oh. Jack was on his own now. He had to be. The eyes and ears he was trying to avoid were everywhere. His secrecy had very nearly not been enough. Iowa had proved that.

The message was waiting on his desk terminal, flashing insistently. It required bio identification to unscramble, and Jack let it prick the tip of his left index finger and ingest the tiny drop of blood like a cold, polished-plastiform version of a vampire. A pleasant chime sounded, and the coded message changed from gibberish to words. An intel dispatch. Jack sucked his index finger and sat.

Drake was on his way to Jupiter Station. Good. With Broussard in tow. Excellent. The message indicated the latter had increased the chances of the mission being successful by a small but not insignificant amount. That was all fine and good, but it was the second part of the encrypted message that caught Jack's attention.

Probable that Glory *crew infiltrated with Paragon operative. Sleeper [high confidence]. New tech. Unscannable.*

Drake leaned back in his chair. After each assertion in the dispatch was a string of values that indicated the degree to which the intel was predicted to be accurate. All of those values were extremely high.

Damn.

The Paragon were always a step ahead these days.

The desire for peace had certainly blinded the politicians across the pond in Paris, but it had also blinded much of those in this very building. But not Jack. He could still see the Paragon for who they were: a deadly combination of religious fervor and xenophobia. Even the name "Paragon" was a testament to their obsession with supremacy.

The Paragon believed their place in the cosmos, and theirs alone, was ordained. All other species, cultures, and races were unclean. Their presence polluted the heavens, and it was the decree of the Paragon religion that such pollution be eliminated. Stamped out. Exterminated. They'd been trying to accomplish that ever since humans had first encountered them more than a century before, and Jack knew they would never stop. Zealots, true believers, never stopped. They had to *be* stopped.

Drake needed to know about this message.

"Marquette?" He called for one of the guards by name and coughed again, violently. Nothing. "Stevens?" Still nothing.

He froze when the door to his office opened. Through it stepped neither of his guards. A man appeared, tall, broad, suit precisely tailored, sandy blond hair expertly coifed as only a politician could wear it. Jack recognized him. His name was Jurgen. Assemblyman Jurgen. A perennial bayonet in Jack's asshole.

"What an unexpected pleasure," Jack said, standing and locking out his desk console in one fluid motion.

"Unexpected," Jurgen repeated humorlessly as he stared at the console. He looked up to meet Jack's eyes before sweeping the rest of the office, then clucked his tongue. "I have to say, *I* expected something...I don't know, less normal for the office of the Fleet's head of intelligence. Monitors everywhere, perhaps, for all your surveillance, stacks of intel reports, a board with pictures and lines of red felt between them. You know, spy-chief stuff."

"Spy chief," Jack repeated with a forced chuckle. "Nonsense."

Jurgen raised an eyebrow. "Is it not the spy chief who would receive an intelligence communique about operation threat levels from a masked probability AI, as you have just received?"

Jack's blood ran cold. He blinked. "I don't know what you're talking about."

Jurgen sighed. "You really have become a problem for us, Admiral." He looked Jack up and down. "How are you feeling? I heard about your near-death experience in Iowa."

"Fine." There was a weapon in his desk drawer. He inched his fingers toward the handle.

"Believe me when I say it's a miracle you survived. Now, tell me, please, what was in the dispatch?"

"Dispatch?"

"The one you just received."

"I just told you, I don't know what you're talking about." His fingers found the handle. They closed around it.

"Like I said, you really have become quite the problem." Jurgen turned slightly toward the office door without taking his eyes off Jack. "Could you come in, please?" he called.

One of Jack's guards, Stevens, stepped into the room. He was holding a gun, but it wasn't pointed at Jurgen. It was pointed at Jack. "Stevens," Jack breathed. As the young man stepped past Jurgen into his view, Jack saw something was off. His eyes were vacant. And his face—...his face was crawling. Vibrating under the skin, rippling. He was sweating profusely. Breathing hard.

"The admiral is not cooperating," Jurgen said to the young man.

Stevens slowly pulled the trigger and shot Jack in the chest.

Jack bellowed in pain. The projectile shot ripped through his left shoulder, a non-fatal but excruciating shot. The force of it sent him flying into his chair, then he toppled onto the floor. Jurgen was around the desk in an instant, Stevens close behind.

"Get him up."

Jack grunted and groaned as the guard hauled him up and into his chair. He got a close-up look at the young man's strained face, and what he saw there was horror. Something was inside him, writhing. A light-gray liquid oozed from the pores on his forehead, cheekbones, and around his eyes. His breath was ragged, feverish. In his gaze, there was nothing. Stevens was not in there.

"The dispatch, please," Jurgen said once Jack was back in his chair.

Jack tried to respond, but the bodily trauma had rattled loose the damage already done to his lungs, resulting in a violent coughing fit.

Jurgen shook his head with mock sympathy. "Terrible thing, those Paragon bugs. They sure take their time, don't they?"

"Fuck off," Jack gurgled.

Jurgen sat on the edge of the admiral's desk and leaned closer. "We thought they would move faster."

Jack spat in the man's face and laughed, which caused him to break into another coughing fit. "They're contagious," he managed to wheeze as he watched blood drip down the assemblyman's face.

Jurgen stumbled back. He wiped his face hurriedly with his hands, and when that was woefully insufficient, he dug into his suit pockets until he produced a handkerchief and a small metal pouch. With the blood cleaned off his face and hands, he fumbled open the small metal case and pulled out a tiny syringe no larger than a thumb, the kind that was one and done, a single dose. He stabbed that into his neck and sighed in relief. It was still hanging in the side of his neck when he addressed Jack.

"You know what that is?" the assemblyman asked, a dark edge to his voice. He pointed at the metal case. Jack could see there was another syringe inside, perhaps several. "A cure to your malady." That caught Jack's attention, and Jurgen noticed. He smiled cruelly. Coldly. "I could give it to you, you know? If you were to cooperate. Show me what's in that dispatch."

It was a lie. Jack knew that as clearly as he knew the sun rose in the east. Jurgen was never going to give him one of those syringes. They were only there to taunt him, to give him hope and then snatch it away. He even doubted the seriousness with which Jurgen needed to see the intelligence information.

Jurgen was here to kill him.

So Jack didn't cooperate.

Jurgen ordered Stevens to force his finger into the verification slot on his desk computer. Jack fought it, of course, as hard as he could. Snap. He received a dislocated pinky for his trouble. Stevens, for his part, seemed to be breaking down. His body shook as he stepped aside to let Jurgen look at the computer readout. Jack could smell his cologne and his sweat. The assemblyman was not as cool and collected as he pretended to be.

"Let's see what we have here," Jurgen said as he scanned the brief message. "*Glory...Glory, Glory, Glory,* what is that?" He punched up another monitor on Jack's desk, and the readout of a ship appeared. Jurgen frowned at first, looking at its details, complement, armament, and commission date. Jurgen laughed and turned to Jack.

"That is your plan?" he asked, pointing. "That is what this has all been about? All your secret, quiet little personnel reassignments?" He was incredulous. Gleeful. "*That* is your plan? A junkyard ship." He roared with laughter. Stevens, behind him, was slick with sweat, his face streaked with gray ooze. "It won't make a difference," Jurgen said, still howling and clutching his stomach. "Not an ounce. Oh, my word. Not when they come, Admiral. One ship!" He shook his head, tears in the corners of his eyes. He wiped them away with another incredulous headshake. "One ship. We thought you were up to so much more."

"We?" Jack repeated.

Jurgen's laughter subsided. "We," he confirmed, the coldness back in his voice.

"What have you done?"

Jurgen placed his hands on Jack's desk and leaned forward intently, ferociously. "Ended the war."

"There will never be peace with the Paragon." Could the man be that stupid? Misguided?

Jurgen shook his head. "No peace, but it will be over all the same. A fresh start." He said it as if it were laundry day. Jack's stomach turned. Jurgen stood. "And, Admiral," he said, "I'm afraid you won't be around to see it." Jurgen gestured at the desk monitor that still displayed the intelligence report. "Shame *Glory* won't get this. For them, I mean. 'Sleeper.'" He said the word with air quotes. "That sounds ominous. Someone who doesn't even know they're working for the other side. Someone being controlled, and they don't know it." Jurgen gestured at Stevens, who was shaking uncontrollably. "Like your guard here."

Jack felt sorry for the young man.

"Mr. Stevens," Jurgen said to him, "kill the admiral, please."

Jack turned to face him. The young man trembled so badly he could hardly raise the gun.

"The control isn't perfect," Jurgen droned on. "As you can see. But it is still effective in quick, short bursts. We're pushing the limit here, but I think Mr. Stevens is holding on."

Stevens had the gun up now, shaking but trained on Jack's head. The man's eyes were wild, his expression distorted and his skin crawling. Something was under there, working furiously. Jack could see Stevens desperately fighting it, and he tried to lock eyes with him. Maybe he was still in there.

"Fire," Jurgen called. "Let's get this over with."

Stevens screamed. Something broke through one of the pores on his forehead—a tentacle, gray and slick.

"Fire!" Jurgen ordered again.

Stevens fired, but not at Jack. And not, unfortunately, at Jurgen.

He fell to the floor, a smoking hole in his own head.

Jurgen clucked his tongue. "That was supposed to come next," he said, and he strode around Jack to crouch by the dead soldier.

Something began to pool in Stevens' vacant eyes. It was viscous, slimy even, and it undulated and slithered. Jurgen reached for it, and a tentacle stretched from the pooling blob and snagged the assemblyman's hand. It pulled at Steven's head as it went, tentacles rising from every pore in his face. It was huge, the creature. It covered Jurgen's hand, and with a thud from Stevens' head hitting the floor as it sucked free, it slithered into Jurgen's suit coat and disappeared.

"Nasty creature," Jurgen said as he took the gun from Stevens' limp hand. "But effective." He turned to Jack and smiled ruefully. "Kind of like you."

Jack swallowed.

"Admiral Jack Sturgess killed," Jurgen said almost wistfully. "Murder-suicide with one of his own guards." He raised the gun.

Jack eyed the metal case on the desk, still where Jurgen placed it and still open, syringes waiting. "You're a madman."

Jurgen shook his head, dead serious. "I'm a politician. I make deals. And this," his finger started to squeeze the trigger, "is the deal." He aimed between Jack's eyes.

Jack kept his eyes on those syringes and wished the poser would get it over with.

"Goodbye, Admiral."

Jurgen fired.

JUPITER SHIPYARDS

Terran Federation Space

CHAPTER EIGHT

It was a long time coming, but Lieutenant Commander Eunice Carrol finally felt like royalty. Outside the shuttle window, Jupiter was her king, ready to anoint her.

Carrol let the monarch-planet fill her eyes with swirling oranges, yellows, and reds as the shuttle picked its way, arcing and slow, toward the shipyard facility. In the Fleet, rarely was it what you did or what you knew. It was *who* you knew, who *you* were, and where you came from. Carrol had done great things, filled out quite the resume, and she knew much—everything, in fact, about what she wanted—but she came from nowhere. She was no one until she made the right connection. Until now. Finally.

Command. Second Officer on a ship.

Oh, did she hope it was *Olympia*.

It had to be *Olympia*. Admiral Lyle had nearly said as much when he'd put in his recommendation.

Nearly.

Carrol ran her fingers over the insignia clasped to the thick fabric of her uniform. The metal was fresh, still shiny.

Large. Larger than lieutenant, that was for sure. She reveled in its weight and size, and when she was done, she grabbed her jacket cuff with her fingers and wiped away her fingerprints to make it spotless again. Nothing was going to dull her shine today. Nothing.

The sound of retching came from the rear of the shuttle.

Carrol wasn't alone in her sojourn on the craft. She'd been joined at the central hub docks by two older officers. 'Salts.' If Carrol were ever in the mood to be unkind, which she never was, let alone now, she might be inclined to say the two were so salty they were practically fossils. But she wouldn't say that. Not out loud.

The one making the retching sounds looked like he was at death's door, face slick with sweat, his uniform jacket threadbare and draped around his shoulders. She couldn't tell if it was just the sick man who stank or if it was both of them, but Carrol couldn't press herself far enough forward in the shuttle cabin to escape the stench. It was the lone discordant note in her triumph.

"Excuse me," the sick man slurred to no one in particular, and he rose to stumble back into the rear chamber of the shuttle, which had a small head. The head wasn't large enough for a man to kneel over the toilet *and* close the door, however, so when he began to puke for real, the sound was audible. Puke in space was inevitable. The weightlessness. The assault on the human body. More so when they let their bodies go. How people responded after puking would show their mettle. Carrol avoided it all by not eating before shuttle rides. It was like these two had forgotten what they'd learned.

Carrol wrinkled her nose involuntarily. She could see the other salt, a bigger man, quiet and poised, clock it. She dropped the expression and turned back to Jupiter, but the moment of disgust had been shared.

"You traveling to a posting?" she asked to fill the uncomfortable silence.

She had to look back to see him nod. He was rugged, with dirt under his fingernails and a sun-leather effect to his skin. Such an odd thing to see on a salt. She wondered if he'd somehow been planetside for an extended time. Maybe at Command? She'd never seen him there. Or the Academy? Nonetheless, he held himself with an authority she recognized despite his rank insignia being hidden by his open coat. This man was a captain. It was hard to believe he still was at his age, but Carrol did her best not to let that thought show. What the Fleet did with its older lifers was none of her business. Not today, anyway.

"What's your ship?" she asked.

"*Glory.*"

Carrol frowned. "I haven't heard of it. It's a new ship?"

The man shook his head with a small smile but offered nothing further.

"Well, congratulations anyway." She waited for the man to ask her where she was going. He didn't. "I'm going to a posting, too," she finally volunteered. Saying it made her chest swell, filled her so much she felt like she might burst. "My first."

The man raised his eyebrows slightly and nodded. "Congratulations," he replied emotionlessly once Carrol had smiled and nodded back long enough.

"Thank you. I hope it's the *Olympia*. You know the *Olympia*?"

He shook his head.

"Really?"

"Really."

This guy must have been stuck in the darkest ass-end of the service. "She's the best and the brightest," Carrol said, taking it upon herself to show him the light. "And she launches in twenty-four hours. Just in time for the peace delegation to arrive." She looked at the man again. "You do know the Paragon peace delegation is coming?"

"I do know that," he said.

Carrol nodded before turning away to look out through the forward shuttle window. "I've been command-rated for six years, but no dice. Had to ride a desk and kiss ass, just waiting for a post to open up. I've been watching *Olympia*'s development since the project started—she's a new class, you know—and never dared to think maybe my posting might line up with her launch window, but..." Her voice trailed off into a huge smile, and she shook her head. "They didn't tell me. Lyle, one of the admirals—you know Lyle?" The captain shook his head. "I worked in his office. He kind of took me under his wing, put in a good word. I think he wanted it to be a surprise."

As Carrol spoke, she could picture the posting officer who'd delivered her orders and the slight snicker he'd given. It had been unnerving—and a complete surprise since she'd expected Lyle to deliver the news, if only informally—but now, in the shuttle heading toward *Olympia*, she realized it must have been jealousy from the posting officer. That gave her a certain amount of satisfaction. She'd seen jealousy in every step of her journey in the Fleet, and it usually gave her impetus to do more, work harder. Her efforts had finally paid off.

In the captain on this shuttle with her, however, she saw none of that. He didn't know what she was talking about. "You really haven't heard of the *Olympia*?" she asked.

"I haven't." He gazed past her into space, his mind less than engaged with the conversation.

There was a chime from the shuttle's front panel, and Carrol again turned her attention forward. Their course was automated, no pilot. Ferrying people around the complex didn't require one, with its prescribed routes and strictly organized schedules. The chime had been a ping from a proximity beacon. They were approaching the shipyards. Carrol rose to get a full view and called to her companion, "Well, come get a view, sir." She pointed ahead of them.

Olympia rose into view like a colossus. She dwarfed the docking complex that held her. Her sleek lines, all curves and arcs that looked as though they could cut the stars, screamed that she was meant to fly, to be let loose, not confined and still as she was. Carrol imagined being the one to let her loose, to give the command to fire up those engines, to unfurl those sails. It made her gasp, which she realized she had done aloud, and she reddened as the salt captain lumbered up next to her.

"She displaces four million metric tons," Carrol rattled off from memory, unable to stop smiling despite the embarrassment. "And with the new air-light spaceframe, her conventional mass is less than half that. Crew complement is 3,513 with a carrying capacity of thirty thousand troops, a top velo of ninety percent light speed—that's Earth to Jupiter Gateway in eighty-seven minutes, ungated—unlimited range, an FRC-42 seventh-generation defense system with an intuitive AI core, 147 RIM6k plasma cannons, the new maxLoad missile spaceframe—gift from our new Paragon allies, there—and a top of the line countermeasure array to go with triple-plated diamond shielding, and my stars, how she shines."

And she did. She glistened, just as she did in Carrol's dreams. "I've read every report they've ever made about her," Carrol breathed, hardly able to take it all in. "She's the best there is."

There was a snort from behind her, and Carrol turned into the stench of the other older officer, who was standing next to the captain and swaying despite bracing himself to the ceiling with a grimy arm. "She'll win a beauty contest," he said with an unsteady smirk. His breath was overwhelming in the confined space, acidic and rank with vomit. "I'll grant you that, my dear." With another snort, he teetered to the back of the cabin again.

The captain stayed where he was, taking in the *Olympia*. His expression was neutral, and he offered no apology or excuse for his sick friend.

Sick.

Carrol wasn't born yesterday; the man was hungover, and from more than just alcohol by the look of those sweats. She wondered how a person in such a state would be allowed in the Fleet, wearing that officer's rank he had pinned to his threadbare uniform jacket, but she bit it back. These two were not her concern, after all. "Charming friend of yours," was all she said to the captain. "Sir."

"I'm sure she's a fine ship," the captain replied before leaving Carrol alone at the front of the shuttle.

It was all the same to Carrol. She would bask in the glory of this moment on her own as she had so often. Too often. She wished Lyle could be here, the damn old codger. They'd finally got her through. Past the bullshit. Lyle was very much an outsider, just like she was, risen through the ranks through merit and pure dogged determination, as he liked to tell her at every chance he could get. He had no connections to powerful families, no long lineage of warriors to carry his reputation, only himself, just like Carrol. And he'd become an admiral. Carrol would too someday. This was a huge step forward. Second in command on the Fleet's flagship. A front-row seat to the peace talks starting in one day. It was a triumph for both of them. *Olympia* was right there, looming ever closer. Close enough to touch.

Until...

Until the shuttle passed the logical point of delivery to *Olympia*'s hangar bay and arced away from the shining ship.

Carrol frowned.

First, she double-checked their vector to make sure her eyes weren't playing tricks on her. No. They were definitely angling away. Second, she checked the shuttle console to see if it was malfunctioning.

"Shuttlepod zero-beta-niner, don't mess with your automated flight controls," came the terse radio response seconds later.

"Just checking we're still on course," Carrol explained, trying to avoid letting the panic that rose within creep into her voice.

"Course confirmed," the voice squawked.

Then silence. Silence as the shuttle swooped past the *Olympia* and the gleaming ship slid out of view. Silence as the shuttle cruised out to a section of the shipyards Carrol didn't recognize, holding derelict vessels in various states of disrepair or assembly. Many of their shapes and configurations she didn't recognize, then she did for a few. That was half of a CVN-65 attack carrier, and that was a Black Star cruiser from the second Elyree war. There was another of them. Dozens, in fact.

Mothballed.

They were flying through the mothballed ship graveyard.

Carrol lost time after that. Her thoughts swirled and she became lightheaded, unable to comprehend what was happening. She couldn't reconcile the events within her mind. All she could see was the *Olympia*, right there, so close she could have touched it. She saw Lyle's face too, replaying their last conversation in her mind, searching for something she'd missed. She hadn't. She'd known him for years now. His excitement for her had been earnest. Real. The only thing she could hold onto was that smirk on the posting officer's face when he'd handed her orders over. She shivered. Tried to shake it from her mind. But it stuck.

Thunk.

The shuttle jerked, and Carrol nearly lost her balance.

They were docking.

It snapped her back to the present. Flustered, she blinked and looked around. The shuttle's docking hatch was at the rear, so the view out the front window faced away from their destination. Still, from an overhang peaking above and around them, Carrol could tell they'd docked with a dry dock facility, the kind you'd use to refit or repair a large craft. Or, as in the case of the mothball shipyards, junk one. Cut it up for parts.

With another clank and a loud hiss, the hatch at the rear of the shuttle opened, and the musty smell of old plastics and corroding metal wafted in. The sick man rose and stretched. The old captain did the same, and together, they strode off the shuttle. That left Carrol alone, and she stayed long enough to confirm that this was, in fact, their last *and terminal* destination. That earned her another terse talking-to from System Flight Control.

She fled the shuttle. The hatch clanked shut behind her

with finality. She'd been delivered to the right place. Except she hadn't. None of this was right. The corridor she found herself in featured a long, grimy window to the interior of the shipyard facility, which was to say, a view of the ship the facility held.

It was long and wide. Boxy. Adorned with a dark metal cladding Carrol recognized as a type of mattered armor that hadn't been used for decades. Weapons bristled from her sides. There were very few windows. Her lines were utilitarian, optimized for the space they gave the crew inside or for access, like the fighter launch tubes and the yawning cargo bays. She had nothing like the *Olympia*'s curves, which hid all that behind an elegant design. She was also riddled with pockmarks, charred armor, and flat-out missing sections of her hull. She'd been in battle many times. She bore the scars to prove it.

She looked like she belonged in the mothball yard, and if one wasn't paying attention, it would be easy to assume she was here to be dismantled. But no. The cranes, suited workers, and engineering drones that surrounded her were adding to her bulk, not taking away. She was being patched up. Like putting lipstick on a pig.

"You coming?"

Carrol looked up. The old captain was standing with his friend down the corridor, at the entrance to a long gangway that led into the ship.

"That's *Glory*?" she asked, pointing.

The old captain nodded. "We're expected."

Carrol felt nauseated. The deck swam, and she had to steady herself against the grimy window—mistake—but she managed somehow to follow the two older officers down the gangplank. Every step made her feel more ill, more out of touch with reality.

"Captain on deck!"

The booming voice refocused her. It came from a man even larger than the old captain, with an experienced-lined round face. A commander. He was saluting. Behind him, a line of disheveled men and women snapped to attention. One brought out a boatswain's whistle and blew the ritualistic three tones, down-uuuup-down. The chimes snapped Carrol rigid as well.

The old captain returned the salute of the round-faced man, and with all the seriousness of a Fleet officer, recited, "Commander Oh, I relieve you as commander of the TDF *Glory*."

"Captain," said Oh, just as serious. "I am relieved." Their arms snapped down in unison. And then, breaking protocol but only in the view of his superiors, Oh cracked a giant smile. He turned to Carrol, the smile growing even wider. "You must be Carrol," he said with a quick salute. Carrol returned it, then Oh addressed his captain again. "The commander here is our new second officer."

The old captain smiled ruefully. "We've become acquainted. Somewhat."

Carrol felt her cheeks burn, which she hated. "Sir, I..." she began, then lowered and shook her head, unable to meet his eyes. She desperately wanted to put on the face she'd worn so often and mask what she was feeling, hide the sickening disappointment, and say the bare minimum, just speak the tiniest of pleasant lies. She found she couldn't. She couldn't say anything.

There was some grace in the old salt when he said, "No need, Commander." His arm slid up in a practiced salute. "Captain Drake," he said. "Honored to have you."

The ritual took over, and she saluted back. "Captain."

Drake gestured at his friend. "And this is Lieutenant Commander Broussard, the ship's surgeon."

Carrol saluted him too.

"Welcome aboard the *Glory*," Oh proclaimed to all of them, and he stepped aside to allow them to enter the ship.

Beyond him, engulfing the ragtag formation of crew still at attention, the ship was in chaos. Bulkheads were open or missing, with conduits, wires, and pipes spilling onto the decking, along with containers and crates, some empty and piled, others heavy and full, waiting to be taken inside where they were supposed to go. It was the kind of pressing clutter that made it hard to breathe. The crew looked sweaty and disheveled. They'd been interrupted mid-task and were caught between curiosity about their new commander and wanting to get back to work.

Above the first officer, and Carrol didn't know how she'd missed it before, a long, rectangular metal plate had been fixed to the bulkhead that covered the gangplank entrance. In hand-scrawled letters, torched into the metal, it read 'Where Angels Fear to Tread, Drake's Demons Give 'Em Hell.'

Drake's Demons.

The old captain stopped to look at it as well, his expression becoming stoic. Oh stepped up to him, beaming, with his hands clasped behind him. "It's so good to have you back, sir," he said softly.

Drake looked down at his crew. "Company dismissed," he said. Once they'd dispersed or gone back to whatever it was they were doing, Drake gestured at the sign. "The old sign is still up," he said.

Oh nodded, and looked at it, then back at the captain. "Should I remove it, sir?"

Drake considered, then shook his head. "No," he said, eventually. "Leave it. It's history."

Oh smiled. "Yes, sir." He approved. His smile then fell as he remembered something. Out of his pocket, he fished a palm-sized data pad. He held it out to the Captain. "This . . . came in Earth-side, sir, while you were in transit."

Drake took the pad, read it, and frowned. He showed it to the doctor, and Carrol took the opportunity to look over his shoulder.

It was a news report.

Fleet Admiral Presumed Dead and Assemblyman Missing.

Someone named Jack. His blood had been found all over his office. And someone else named Jurgen had been seen entering there, but never coming out. Carrol had no idea what it meant.

The captain didn't look too surprised, but the doctor did. Drake gave him a look that said he'd explain later, and handed the data pad back to Oh. The two shared a grim, but expected expression. "Thank you," he said, and he sniffed the air to refocus on the ship before them. "Shall we?" he gestured to the Commander.

Just then, a telltale whirring-down sound came from the corridor ahead. The lights inside died, and all the chaos within was engulfed in darkness. Sounds of frustration and disgust from the crew deeper in the ship rose like a chorus. A moment later, some—but not all—of the lights flickered back on, and there were a couple of scattered rounds of sarcastic applause. Carrol realized this must not be the first time it had happened.

"We're working on the power core," Oh said with a grimace.

Drake nodded and began to stride off with purpose.

"Department heads meeting in twenty," he called behind him.

"Aye, sir," Oh acknowledged. "And where are *you* going?"

"To get some flashlights."

Carrol regarded the hand-made sign one more time and then followed the men inside.

CHAPTER NINE

"FLASHLIGHTS, FLASHLIGHTS, FLASHLIGHTS..."

The enlisted crewman helping Drake crawled exuberantly through stacks upon stacks of equipment containers large and small. "I'll find them, sir," he said, and his voice cracked as he leapt from one pile to another. "We've had so many shipments these past couple days. I know it's around here somewhere in an r-9 container. Whole mess of them. I scanned it in myself."

He was small and spry, this helpful crewman, and young—very young—and he sported an ancient apparatus that rested on his face from his ears and the bridge of his nose. Its frame encircled each of his eyes, and the transparent material within made them bulge from the magnification. Drake believed they had once been called "glasses."

"Aha!" he called from the bottom of yet another pile. When he emerged, he was hauling a light yellow-striped plastiform cube that was nearly as big as he was. An r-9 multipurpose container, just like he'd said. "Told you, sir." He beamed. With a thunk, he set it at Drake's feet.

The two of them opened the top hatch, and inside, as

promised, were dozens of palm-sized flashlights. Drake fished one out, clicked it on, and waved its beam of light around the piles of containers.

"Apologies for the mess, sir," the crewman said, still catching his breath. "Personally, I'd opt for a little more organization myself, but the deck officer says all this stuff is going elsewhere on the ship anyway, so don't waste the time."

Drake clicked off the flashlight. "How would you organize?" he asked the young man.

The crewman scratched the back of his head and looked around the cargo bay as if the question surprised him. "Me?"

"Yes, you."

"Well, sir, I mean, I know what's vital and what's not, you know? It's gonna be engineering and power core parts first. Put those in front, life support up there too, like our air scrubbers. Rack stuff's gonna be last, you know? Just kind of go from top to bottom. Put the most important stuff closest to the door since that'll be used first, I guess. Work my way back and group by department?" He leaned ruefully on a stack of wobbly containers and pointed at it. "Big stuff on the bottom, smaller stuff as you go up."

Drake surveyed the room and nodded. "Make it happen," he said. "I'll let your officer know the plan."

The crewman grinned. "Yes, sir!"

"What's your name, Crewman?"

"Snyder, sir. This here's my first posting, and I couldn't be more happy. I know a lot of the guys around here think this old ship is a piece of junk, but I don't think so, sir. Old doesn't mean junk, just like these things." Snyder pointed at the glasses on his face. "My eyesight's bad. Normally no problem, right? But my eyes are super sensitive, sir, and the normal implants would dry them out too much, so these old things it is for me, and I can see great."

He tapped them, then chuckled to himself, leaned toward Drake, and spoke in a hushed tone. "You know what they used to call these things back in the day when they'd give them to you at boot camp?" Drake waited for him to continue. "Birth control glasses." Snyder busted up laughing. "Cuz you're not finding nobody to—you know what—with these things hanging off your face." He giggled gleefully.

Drake couldn't help but smile back. "You have someone at home?"

Snyder shook his head. "Oh, no, sir. Not yet. But I'm looking. Ever hopeful, and I figure I have time."

"How old are you, Mr. Snyder?"

"Eighteen, sir."

Drake had figured as much. "Well, thank you for your help. It was a pleasure meeting you."

"You too, sir," he replied earnestly. "You too."

"To your task, Crewman," Drake said in his command voice and straightened to leave. While Snyder had been talking, Drake had fished out the interior liner of the storage crate, a strong mesh-like fabric, onto which he dumped a couple of dozen of the flashlights. He twisted the top to close it like a sack, then handed one of the flashlights from inside the crate to Snyder. "And keep one of these on you so you can always see. Power and overhead lighting may not be a given in the near term." He threw the sack of flashlights over his shoulder and strode out of the cargo bay.

"Thank you, sir!" Snyder called after him.

THERE WAS a small conference room right off the command deck on the *Glory*, complete with table and chairs, but it was as Drake had left it years ago: charred and full of damaged consoles and equipment. They'd been hauled off the bridge and dumped there in the midst of battle. Paper printouts littered the floor, many of them half-burned as well. Nothing had been touched in nearly two decades. It still smelled of smoke.

Drake closed the hatch and shut out the memories before they could rise. Memories of fire, screaming, and thunder...

They'd have the meeting on the command deck.

There weren't enough chairs, but that would be fine. He retrieved those that weren't bolted down from around the command deck and placed them around the tactical multipurpose console in the center of the bridge, which often doubled as a table. He plopped down his sack of flashlights in the center of it.

People began to filter in a few minutes later.

The first was a face he didn't recognize. The young woman introduced herself as Sudan, an engineer. She couldn't have been a day older than Snyder down in the loading bay. Behind her, Doc arrived with a fresh uniform and a quick shave of both his face and head. He ran a hand over top his head and down his chin with a sheepish smile at Drake. The Doc cleaned up very nicely; he looked every bit the officer again.

Oh blustered in next, and Carrol a moment later, the latter still looking rather shell-shocked and hauling a massive stack of printed papers. Behind them were two more new faces, both plopped on top of bodies built like brick houses. Leading the two was a woman who introduced herself as Efremova, their master at arms. Her pure-white hair was shaved askew and pushing regulations, she had tattoos shining from her sweat-slicked and very non-regulation bare arms—she'd lost the sleeves to her uniform, apparently—and perhaps most notable, she was covered in blood.

"Rats," she said, then made a horrifying gesture with her hands to indicate their size. "Big ones."

Behind her, getting his introduction from Efremova, was a mountain of a man. Nothing about him was non-regulation, at least not in appearance. His hair had been cut to a high and tight, angled to perfection, his uniform was crisp and without a crease, and he stood rigidly alert, waiting for the meeting to begin. Smith was what Efremova said his name was, and he nodded the affirmative in response.

Drake had needed no introduction. Not really. He could tell instantly from the man's demeanor, size, and look that he was as much a relic as the ship they were standing on. More so, even.

Smith was the surname given to all enhanced Marines. It had been a program in the first Paragon war to boost Earth's fighting force. The program had been outlawed and shut down shortly thereafter. Drake had assumed all such soldiers had been destroyed or died by now, but there he was, large as life and terrifying. He was over a hundred years old, yet to the eye, he wasn't more than late twenties. A killing machine. There'd been a good reason the program had been outlawed.

Those who recognized him for what he was inched away. It was subtle, but Drake knew if he saw it, the Marine did too. He therefore greeted him the same way he'd greeted everyone else who'd arrived. The Marine returned a sharp salute, then gripped Drake's hand in a bone-crushingly firm handshake. He repeated his name, Smith, in a low rumble, and that was that. He went rigid again, awaiting orders. Drake was eager to oblige him.

A moment later, the loudest of the department heads arrived in the form of Lieutenant Martha Kluger, their flight group commander. That position was still called a CAG, Commander Air Group, for the sake of a millennium-old terrestrial tradition, and it was by that moniker that Kluger preferred to be called. With her was Flight Deck Officer De La Cruz, who went by the initials DLC for "De La Cruz." Drake was happy to see them.

"It's been years, Cap!" CAG said as she hobbled in, one leg swinging more than walking and the hugest smile on her face Drake thought he'd ever seen. CAG had a drawl she rolled out when she was excited, and it was as thick as molasses right then and there. She reached the table, and with a giant thunk, she threw her swing-leg up onto the table. "Check that out," she said as she hiked her uniform pant leg up to expose a pale right knee gashed down the side with a glaring pink scar. She slapped it eagerly. "Just had that done to fix up the bum knee." She then slapped her thigh the same way. "Hip too, but not showing you perverts that part." She belly-laughed at that and hauled her leg off the table with a spry hop. "I feel like I'm forty-seven again!" She laughed some more.

At her side, DLC, a slight, tall man who spoke more quietly than his pilot counterpart, stepped forward to shake Drake's hand. "So good to be here," he said, bobbing his head up and down to go with the greeting. "So, so good, Cap. So good to see you."

Drake nodded in response, and DLC proceeded to rattle off information about the state of the fighter squadron and the modifications they were going to make for their new pilots.

DLC had been a young man the last time Drake had seen him. Now there was more silver in his hair than black, and he had lines under his eyes and on his forehead. They all looked older, in fact. It was a sharp contrast to the fresh faces who were watching the old crew with a mixture of uncertainty and interest.

"Couches are coming on the next transport in," DLC was saying eagerly, "but the neural modules are here, along with the transition kits, so I'm already halfway through the P7s."

CAG snorted at that. "Bunch of hooey," she said with a wave of her hand. "That couch nonsense." She was referring to the fact that these days, fighter pilots flew their craft remotely rather than strapped into the cockpit. Drake was inclined to agree with his officer, but then, the loss of a spacecraft without the loss of life did have its merits. "It's vulnerable!" she continued. "Anything that requires ship-to-ship comms is."

Drake waved her off the subject. It was time to start the meeting, not debate advances the Fleet had made in their lengthy absence. He looked at the chronograph built into the display cluster hanging over the tactical console. It wasn't working.

"McCourt is on the next cargo transport." XO spoke preemptively of their Command Master Chief, reading Drake's mind. "Same shipment as those flight couches," he added, pointing at CAG, who rolled her eyes.

"Right, then," Drake said with an inhale. "Just waiting for Chief Engineer..." He paused, searching for the name. McCourt was an old hand. An original Glory crew member. This new engineer was not.

"Fredrickson," XO supplied.

Drake nodded. "Then we can get started."

Sudan, the fresh-faced engineer who'd been first to arrive, cleared her throat. "Oh, uh, Fredrickson can't make it, sir." Drake turned to her with raised eyebrows and she wilted. "He sent me in his place."

Next to her, Drake watched as XO's face reddened. "This is a department heads meeting," XO snapped, voice tight.

"Yes, sir." She swallowed. "He said he was busy working on restarting the power core."

"Busy working—" XO bit out, then he turned to storm out, no doubt to grab Fredrickson and haul his ass up to the command deck.

Drake intercepted him with a hand to his elbow, which surprised XO. "Hold on that," he said evenly. "I'll go and speak with Mr. Fredrickson myself once our meeting is over."

XO hesitated, still red-faced, then relented to stew in his own juices. Drake turned his attention back to the tactical table and the faces around it, old and new. He could feel their attention re-center as well, drawing in on him, waiting for him to speak, and most importantly, to lead them to a better place.

He turned to Carrol. After a moment's hesitation, she took the non-verbal cue and plopped her massive stack of papers on the tactical table, then slid them around to everyone in the meeting. Everyone, new and old, began leafing through the printed material, using their flashlights.

"This is our operational plan," Drake said of the print-outs, then leafed through his copy, which he hadn't seen yet. Densely worded checklists and procedures filled the hundreds of pages, an intimidating document that contained everything that needed to happen for *Glory* to once again be spaceworthy. He turned to Oh, who'd put the document together based on the one he'd been working on in space dock for the last week-plus. "If you would fill us all in, XO?"

Oh straightened. "Yes, sir. She is airtight, sir, on all decks, and both life support and gravity are nominal." That was good. The bare minimum, certainly, but good. "Deliveries, however, have been slow 'til recently. Only yesterday did power core parts start arriving after we'd requested them right at the start, so we're behind schedule, that's for sure." He pointed at the operations plan. "That's up to date as of this second. This is what's left to do to have *Glory* fully operational."

Inside, Drake grimaced. A cursory look at the document —its size alone—told him they were way behind. Impossibly behind, given the information he was about to share.

He reached into his uniform pocket and took out the cylinder Jack had passed him back on Earth. Its location-delayed lock had released the instant he'd boarded *Glory*. Drake had opened it and read the paper inside before coming to the meeting. It was frustratingly sparse, a total of two short phrases, and there was *another* set of location-sealed orders inside, locked in another small canister. Of course. Jack and his infuriating obsession with secrets. But the orders Drake had been able to read were clear.

And intimidating on their own.

Drake laid out the small script for his department heads to see. It looked like a finger scroll, print tiny and sparse, spelling out their fortunes.

"Our orders from Admiral Jack Carrol of Fleet Intelligence are to be underway for the Neptune Armory in twenty-four hours."

There were audible gasps from several of the new crew and gapes from the old. Only XO didn't seem fazed at their timeline. He'd spent time with Jack these last couple of days. Weeks, it would seem. It made Drake wonder what else the admiral had told him that he hadn't even shared with the captain.

That had been the first line of the orders: *Deploy to Neptune Armory 0700 Standard*

"Neptune?" Oh repeated with a frown. It was their destination that had him puzzled. Then again, perhaps Jack hadn't shared shit with him. That was more likely. XO looked at Drake with a frown. "What would he possibly have waiting for us out at the Armory?"

Drake shook his head, then tapped the still-sealed second canister. "Your guess is as good as mine," he said, hiding his own frustration and concern.

"Forget Neptune," Carrol said, still leafing through her copy of the operational plan and adding a green hue to her look of shock. "There's a month's worth of maintenance, repairs, rebuilds, checks, and re-checks to do in here. We cannot possibly get this done in twenty-four hours."

CAG chuckled and tossed her printout on the table so she could cock one hip to the side and put her arms akimbo. "Hooey," she said. "We've turned her around in less before, Cap, back after that skirmish with the Drakson Hoard."

"With a full complement," Broussard pointed out, speaking up for the first time. He was still looking sickly, but he was steadier. He could stand up straight, at the very least, and he was picking his way slowly through the voluminous checklist.

CAG waved off his sentiment. "Everything we need is already on board."

"CAG is right," Drake said. She'd hit upon exactly the point. "We have everything we need, save for the fighter sims—"

CAG gave a *pshaw*. "My point exactly, Cap," she said with a grin. "Don't *need* those!"

Drake pursed his lips to hide a smile that would say he agreed with his lieutenant and held up a hand to keep her from interrupting further. "Save for our Command Master Chief and the aforementioned equipment for our onboard squadron, we are loaded, and our orders are to be flight-worthy." He stressed that last term.

XO picked up what his commanding officer was putting down. "We'll get our systems to a minimum, and the rest we can work on en route."

Drake nodded in confirmation.

"Guess that means we don't have time for a fresh coat of paint," DLC said from beside CAG. His tone was grudging, but the small smile on his face said otherwise.

XO gave the tone right back. "That's number 111 on our top hundred most important list," he said. "Even food is number ninety-seven, so get used to protein bars and water."

"I'd like to talk to you about that," Drake quietly said to his XO without interrupting the flow of the banter. "After we conclude." His first officer nodded.

"I suppose this means we'll all be pulling day-on, stay-on," Broussard piped up with a groan.

"Racks have to be number 3,043 on the top one hundred if I know the Fleet," CAG agreed, then she grinned wide and leaned forward to grip the tactical table. "It'll be just like those two weeks in the Quasar."

The old crew was excited. Drake could see it in their body language. He could feel it, too. The rush of the challenge. They could do it. The ship could. They all knew she could. And so could they. They'd been there before.

The new crew was a different story.

"Begging your pardon, sir," the quiet-voiced Sudan piped up, "but there may still be a problem even with minimum power. I know Lieutenant Fredrickson is operating under a weeks-long timeline, currently, to retrofit and test each of the core's systems."

XO flared. "Well, Fredrickson would know there was a change in plans if he was here, wouldn't he?"

Again, Drake stayed his first officer's wrath, this time with a look. Oh set his jaw and deferred to his captain. Drake regarded the young woman. "I will talk with the chief, crewman. Thank you for bringing that to my attention."

Sudan gave him a meek nod and put her head back down.

Carrol picked up where she'd left off, however. "I have to concur with her, Captain," she said, her nose still deep in the printout. "These systems, and in particular structural reports, are alarming at best. Our beams and rider plates are still showing damage from whatever the ship went through when last underway in several areas. Decks eleven, thirteen, seven, six, five, in sections up and down the ship. Bulkheads have been compromised all along the starboard exterior, even if we do have them airtight. And to what Crewman Sudan was saying about Engineering, sir, that power core hasn't been hot for two decades."

"Not to mention the ship is full of shit," Efremova said with her arms folded across her chest. "Rat shit." Beside her, Smith nodded with a grimace.

The distinction between the gray hairs and the shiny new faces could not have been more stark. He could see the new officers thought this was madness. Admittedly, it was. Possibly much more than even he knew. But then again, mad didn't mean impossible.

XO tapped the printout. "I've been over this, sir, person-ally. We'll be rough around the edges, but we can launch in twenty-four." Oh glanced at the command deck chronome-ter, saw it wasn't working, and pulled out a pocket time-piece. "Twenty-three," he amended, then put it away and addressed the rest of the officers in addition to the captain. "As ordered. The rest we can keep working on while we're underway."

Drake drew himself up tall and inhaled to back up his first officer, signaling that the debate was over and the meeting had come to an end. It hadn't been a conversation but a demonstration of what it took to realize a command vision. "Quite right. It'll be all hands on deck, catch rest as catch can for the next twenty-three hours. Commander," he said to Oh, "you've been handling the retrofit to this point; you'll continue as the lead. Mister Carrol, you'll handle the commander's supply chain and our last incoming shipment. Let's get the equipment sitting in our bays and holds where it needs to go. Doc." Upon hearing his name, Broussard drew himself up as well. "Sickbay is high on the list of the hundred most essentials. Get func-tional down there." Doc nodded. "DLC, you're on your flight deck, and CAG, get to know your pilots. I want flight drills as soon as those couches are in. Efremova..." Drake paused to look her up and down again, noting the large gun she was toting and the blood splatters on her grimy uniform. "You're doing just fine down below, clearing out our rodent problem. Please continue. Crewman Sudan—"

Perfectly on cue for the second time in as many hours, the power on the command deck went out and cut Drake off mid-sentence. There were rueful chuckles from several of the officers in the darkness, but when flashlights clicked on and re-illuminated the space, the expressions were all business.

Good. They had a lot of work ahead of them.

"Sudan," Drake continued once everyone had their lights on, "I will head down to Engineering to speak with Mr. Fredrickson."

She nodded.

Drake looked each member of his crew in the eyes. "Dismissed."

They dispersed with haste, all except Oh, who hung back. Drake let him stand there for a moment as he once again scanned the personnel list in his printout.

"Quite the motley crew," Oh said, reading his mind.

Drake didn't outwardly agree with the judgment in any way, though it was a fair observation. Jack had certainly given them an interesting bunch, ranging from the incredibly inexperienced to, in some cases, the outright insubordinate. The name Drake had landed on was his next challenge, the one and only Mr. Fredrickson. An archivist. He'd worked on restoration assignments all over the mothballed fleet as an expert on obsolete technologies—the Fleet's words, not Drake's; just reading them made his teeth grind—but Fredrickson had only ever worked alone, and only on non-operational ships. He was a historian, not a chief engineer. Then again, outside of *Glory*'s former chief, who was no longer among the living and for whom Drake suddenly felt the pang of loss, Fredrickson was probably the only person who knew how *Glory*'s engines worked.

They were stuck with each other. All of them. Drake understood that. He'd have to figure out a way to make sure everyone else did too.

"They'll do just fine," he finally said to his XO, and he set the roster down. "With the right support and guidance."

"A kick in the ass?" XO stood tall and nodded. "They'll do fine because they have to. Whatever Jack had in mind for us, he expended a great deal of energy and capital on this. It's important." XO shifted his weight. "Was that *really* all the admiral's orders said?"

Drake fished the small container out of his pocket and handed it to his first officer.

Oh opened the cannister and pulled out the small piece of handwritten paper, and the second location-sealed tube. He frowned as he read. "'Use the girl,'" he said, repeating the second phrase in Jack's orders. Oh looked up. "What does that mean?"

Drake shook his head, equally mystified. And he didn't have time to contemplate it. Not now. His mind was already moving a million miles an hour. Oh returned the contents back to the cannister and returned it to Drake. The captain expected him to excuse himself, but the commander remained. Drake realized he was waiting patiently for something else.

"You said you wanted to speak to me about the food, sir?" Oh reminded him.

"Ah. Yes. Bless you, XO. That I do. Who's the shipyard quartermaster?"

"Young fellow by the name of Harris, sir."

"Harris, as in Damon Harris?"

"Junior, sir."

"*Junior.*" Drake took a moment to feel very, very old; then, "Tell Mister Harris I'd like to speak with him about his father, and perhaps a favor."

CHAPTER TEN

DRAKE, in addition to passing out another dozen flashlights from his bag and meeting each of the crewmen he gave them to, was able to skim through the second most important document XO had prepared for him above and beyond the operational plan: the personnel reports on his new officers.

He scanned as he walked, pausing here and there to get a closer look when something caught his eye—and a lot caught his eye. Nearly everyone on the list had infractions of some kind, some of them serious. Efremova, for example, had been in several fistfights. Smith had done the same and sent a young man to the infirmary, though that had been almost a decade ago. Even the meek Sudan had several reprimands for tardiness and insubordination. Nearly all of them had either been shipped out or requested a transfer from every posting they'd ever been given.

Jack had handed him a stack of numbered cards of four different suits, with a couple of jokers thrown in for good measure.

Only Carrol stood out from the group in a positive way.

She'd graduated from officer training near the top of her class, she was a skilled pilot, or during training she had been, she'd been riding a desk since then, and she had glowing recommendations from her previous superiors. And yet, she'd been assigned to *Glory*. That seemed to be the only thing she had in common with her rough-around-the-edges fellows.

Drake was under no false illusions, and this list of personnel only strengthened his preconceived notions. *Glory* was a shit posting for anyone not in the original crew. Drake wondered what she'd done to piss somebody off since her assignment smacked of retribution. Of bullshit Fleet politics. And it was clear as day that it had blindsided her. He'd seen the shock settle in. It was still there. Beyond, perhaps, his old crew, *nobody* on this ship wanted to be here.

Drake aimed to change that.

As he reached the engineering section, he lingered over one last name. Fredrickson. He was a microcosm of the others. The list of reprimands, reports, and infractions was long. Impressively long. And it told a very consistent tale: nobody liked him. Insubordinate. Arrogant. He was impossible to get along with. Didn't listen. Coworkers avoided him. Superiors loathed him. Once, during an emergency core shutdown, he'd told an executive officer to "eat shit" and locked him in the head for twenty minutes. From the XO's report, it would have been a lot longer, save for the junior chief's intervention.

An amusing story, but the kind that gets someone a big chicken dinner: a bad-conduct discharge. And that was where Drake saw a glimmer of hope, a crack he could leverage and break through to this asshole. It also explained why he hadn't been kicked out of the Fleet after such insubordination; he'd been right. What that angry official report was missing was that the XO had probably asked Fredrickson to do something that would have melted down the ship's core, at best leaving them stranded, at worst killing them all. But Fredrickson had known it, and he'd refused. He'd refused because he knew something the XO didn't. He'd been right. To Drake, that was worth a great deal more than blind obedience to orders.

Fredrickson was an expert engineer. On old systems, specifically. He'd managed to repair and keep running half a dozen older ships before being transferred into the archivists' task force at this very shipyard with some direct, hands-on work with *Glory*. It was a posting he miraculously hadn't been forced out of or requested a transfer from, and Drake noted with chagrin why he'd stuck as an archivist to this point: he'd worked alone.

Maybe brilliant. Definitely not a team player.

Drake sent up a silent curse and a thank you to Jack. Drake had always wanted the best on his crew, no matter their foibles. Being right was the trump card he had used to make his career. Still, he was going to have his hands full.

He tucked the personnel report inside his uniform jacket as he reached the hatchway to Engineering and took a deep breath. Already, he could hear shouting from inside; even though the door was closed, the sound carried through. With a purposely loud *thunk*, he unlatched the door and swung it open.

Fredrickson was a small man, no more than five and a half feet tall, with a light build and a young face. His personnel file said he was mid-thirties, but he looked a decade younger. His scowl lines matched his sharp features, high cheekbones, and glittering, dark eyes, which raked Drake as he entered. The engineer was mid-rant.

"Captain on deck!" some poor soul called from deeper within the long, cavernous room, and things got very quiet as everyone stopped what they were doing to stand at attention.

"Thank you," Fredrickson called to the voice sarcastically. "Little late."

"Lieutenant," Drake said by way of greeting, but Fredrickson brushed right past such formalities and strode over to his new captain.

"Yes, yes, I know all about you," he said and brandished the mess of papers he held in his hands. "You want to tell me what absolute fucking idiot came up with these?"

Drake surmised what the engineer was referring to were the operational plan checklists, and as Fredrickson waved them in his face, he could see he was correct. His mind flashed to XO, feeling very grateful the large, excitable man wasn't here. Otherwise, Fredrickson might quickly have another reprimand on his personnel file. Or a broken nose. "You have a problem with the restart procedures?" he asked in a flat, practiced diplomatic tone, and he stood his ground.

"You bet I do," Fredrickson up close was red-faced and spun up. Volatile. "I'm glad you're here, Captain. Sudan, get over here." Sudan cautiously walked toward them, and once she was within reach, Fredrickson pulled her in by the arm and re-addressed Drake. "You send her down here with this shit, this imbecilic shit about restarting this power core to get underway." He repeated the last word with another furious shake of both the printouts and Sudan. "*Underway,* and then all these idiots are going to start touching shit and doing things, you understand?" For the last point, he gestured to all the crew members who were standing around the main engineering room. Some looked shell-shocked. Others looked tired and fed up. One was wiping down a control surface and caught Fredrickson's eye. "Stop touching that," he shouted at the young man. "Yes, you. Stop. Everyone, stop!"

"We have orders to be underway within twenty-four hours," Drake said, keeping his voice calm and measured, hoping the engineer would match. He didn't.

"And I'm telling you those orders are lunacy. Nobody is listening to me."

"I'd be happy to discuss any modifications to the procedures that you'd like."

"You're still not listening to me! There aren't any procedures." The engineer waved frenetically at the power core, which stood in the front of the main engineering room and stretched back along the central axis of the ship for a hundred feet before it disappeared into a thick bulkhead that separated them from the main propulsion assembly. "This core shouldn't be re-started. It, and this ship, have been cold for almost twenty years. It should be preserved, not messed with. Certainly not re-commissioned. None of these people should be in here messing with it. You shouldn't be here; there shouldn't be any mission. It's *all* lunacy, Captain. This ship should be goddamn left alone, not dug up from her grave for her old captain's joyride!"

The accusation hung in a collective inhale from the room, and Drake took another deep breath, then let it out slowly. The toxicity in the air was palpable. "Lieutenant," he said, carefully, "why don't we step outside to better discuss how you're going to use your genius to get this museum into the sky?"

At that, Fredrickson stiffened, and his eyes went wide, then narrowed. "Absolutely not," he said. "No fucking way. I've told you my concerns. There's nothing to discuss."

Drake set his jaw, wanting very much to grind his teeth.

Wanting very much to do more than that, not because of the verbal jousting, but because it was wasting time they did not have. He stayed still until his anxiety passed. Then he turned to the rest of the crew. "Crewmen," he said loud enough that it would echo down the long chamber, "give us the room."

They couldn't scramble out of there fast enough. With a great clattering of tools, crates, and equipment, two dozen or so crewmen and junior officers streamed past Drake and Fredrickson. Sudan stayed for a moment longer than the rest, but Drake glanced her way, then the room was empty. The captain turned away from Fredrickson to close the door behind them, then sauntered to him.

The engineer, so upright and in Drake's face before, shrank, his eyes sharp and cagey. "Are you going to hit me?" Fredrickson said, his voice quieter now, though no less tight and volatile.

Drake shook his head and spoke in a slow and measured tone. "No, Lieutenant. We don't have time for that stupid crap."

Fredrickson, consciously or unconsciously, took a shuffle step back from Drake's imposing size and clenched and unclenched his fists. Drake let him retreat. His statement had been taken as a threat.

"I'm going to talk to you," he said, and he splayed his hands at his sides, palms facing Fredrickson. He had no desire to intimidate this man.

Fredrickson blinked, then shifted his weight uncertainly. "There is nothing to talk about," he said, and he looked at the closed hatch. "I didn't just say all that stuff for show. I know who you are, Captain. I know this is your old ship, and I mean it when I say we shouldn't take her out. She's not meant to be resurrected. Not for kicks."

Drake considered that. "*Kicks.* Why do you think that, Lieutenant?"

"That you're here for some unfathomably selfish egomaniacal reason?"

Drake almost smiled at the brazen lip of this man—it was so over the top as to be borderline comical—but he just shook his head. "No. I mean that the ship shouldn't be resurrected."

At that, Fredrickson drew his frame straight, all five and a half feet of him. "I am an archivist," he said with no small amount of pride. "I preserve ships like *Glory*, Captain, so that their knowledge or place in history is not lost. I keep them as they were, safe, still, and not bothered."

"So, your objection to our orders is a moral one, not technical?"

Fredrickson reddened and shook the papers in his hand. "My objection is absolutely technical," he said. "These procedures will ruin that core. Probably even destroy the whole damn ship."

"Why?"

Fredrickson dug into his stack of papers with relish and again approached Drake, this time to show him what he was pointing to. "Right there," he said, circling his finger around a hastily printed checklist next to an elaborate schematic of the power core. "These are the steps for a simultaneous startup." Fredrickson said the term like it was insanity.

"That's standard procedure, is it not?" Drake asked, recognizing the steps from his distant past; they looked as familiar as if he'd gone over them yesterday. He went through the steps on the printout, and yes, they were.

Fredrickson shook his head, incredulous and frustrated. "You're not listening again," he growled and rubbed the bridge of his nose before slapping the checklist. "There is no 'standard procedure' for restarting this core. It's been cold for twenty years. Those chambers and their seals, not to mention the length of the propulsion lines and the battery systems, almost certainly cannot handle the stress of a full startup. That's why we don't do this! We don't restart twenty-year-old cores. So, this checklist, Captain, is drivel."

To punctuate his last point, he threw the printouts on the deck.

Drake, for his part, pursed his lips, nodded, and folded his arms. "So," he said in a calm and measured tone. "How would you do it?"

Fredrickson blinked again. "What?"

"I'm listening, Lieutenant. The procedures are outdated. Don't apply. Agreed. Well-spotted, in fact. So, I'm asking you: how would you do it?"

"I wouldn't do it."

"Not from a moral standpoint, but a technical one. The orders are confirmed. We need to start this core."

"I'd complain to whoever issued those orders."

Drake tapped his own stack of printouts with the personnel files. "I believe you already have."

"They didn't fucking listen, the bastards."

"I'm listening."

Fredrickson swallowed and closed his eyes, the moment overwhelming him. He was about to scream, cry, or attack this man who was the embodiment of all his frustrations, but Drake appreciated that he did none of those things. He put his hands on his hips instead and turned to face the old, cold, silent power core. His back was to him, so Drake couldn't see what he was doing or thinking, but when he spoke again, it was clear he'd relented, if only a crack.

"I'd do a staged restart," he said, jaw flexing between his words. "Start with the chambers and injectors that look like they've held up the best. And monitor the propulsion and power grids with the fractional power, see how they handle it. And those that can't, we can skip and then come back to replace." He turned back to Drake, defiance creeping into his expression. "It'll take longer than twenty-four fucking hours, Captain. I can tell you that much."

Drake nodded. "Can we have partial propulsion in that time span?"

Fredrickson shrugged. "Maybe."

"That's our goal, then. Our orders are to be underway for Neptune in twenty—twenty-three hours."

Fredrickson let out a giant sigh and shook his head. "I can't promise anything." There was a long pause. "But it's doable."

Drake again had to hide a smile; displaying satisfaction would destroy this small, impossible victory. Fredrickson was just the kind of man to rip everything up in response. So, he kept it to himself and gave the engineer a simple, curt nod. "That's all I'm asking. Get us going, and that requires a hot core."

"Captain," Fredrickson said to him before Drake could turn around to leave. The captain raised his eyebrows, listening. "I request to be reassigned from your command. I'll deliver a letter to you today to make it official."

Ah, yes. There it was. One last stab of defiance.

Drake nodded. "Get us to Neptune and I'll accept it, Lieutenant."

Fredrickson remained stoic while Drake picked up his bag of flashlights, turned away from him, and strode to the hatchway. He could feel the archivist's eyes on his back as he opened the hatch and poked his head outside. Packed to the gills in the otherwise spacious corridor were the dozens of excused crewmen and junior officers, all straining to listen to the fireworks they'd been sure were going off on the other side. They all snapped rigid when Drake appeared. The woman closest to him hit her head on one of the bulkhead support struts, and she grimaced more from embarrassment than physical pain.

"Back inside," Drake said to the group. "Step quickly, now. There's a lot of work to do. Do as the lieutenant tells you. He has my full support, and by all that's holy, we will be underway in twenty-three hours."

The group mobilized as if a fire had been lit under their butts, and as they passed Drake, he emptied his bag of flashlights into their nervous, waiting hands.

Progress.

CHAPTER ELEVEN

The HR officer smelled like shit. Human feces.

"It's all backed up on deck five," he explained in a manner that indicated to Carrol that he was tired of the shit and tired of explaining. "Old fucking pipes, you know? Who knows what's in them? And my God, Commander, there is *everything* in them. You know we have a rat problem, right?"

"Please," Carrol pleaded, trying unsuccessfully to stay far enough from the man to keep her nostrils from singeing. "I just want to know where my quarters are."

"Racks haven't been assigned yet," he said with a scratch of his head. The movement released more stench and Carrol closed her eyes, feeling as though she would burst into flames or tears. Either would be preferable. Anything other than this smell.

"I know racks haven't been assigned, Mr...?" she trailed off, searching her brain for his name, and of course, drawing a blank.

"Liu," he said with an appropriate expression of disdain and offense.

"Yes, Liu, of course. My apologies. I know racks aren't assigned, but surely there are designated officers' quarters." He looked at her with disgust, but Carrol pushed through it, not caring at that moment. "I just need to know where to put my stuff."

With deliberate slowness, Liu reached into his uniform pocket and pulled out a crumpled and worryingly brown-stained piece of paper that Carrol could see was printed with a list of names, dozens upon dozens of them, accompanied by a grid diagram of the ship.

"Second Officer's quarters are 327," he said after moving his finger slowly over the diagram.

"Thank you!" she called back to him, already hauling ass.

"That's Deck Three," he shouted to her half-heartedly.

"I know!" she yelled back.

It was more than the stench. It was more than wanting to put her trash somewhere. Carrol knew she'd just insulted a junior officer too, but it was far more than all of that. She felt as though she was going to suffocate. Like the walls of this damn, smelly, rickety, dark—always dark everywhere, never a light you could count on!—loud, old-ass ship were going to come crashing down on her.

She ducked past working crewmen too fast for any of them to ask her any questions or otherwise stop her, and by the grace of the stars, she didn't run into any fellow officers. The operational plan weighed impossibly heavy in her hands, and when she finally reached Deck Three, found the officers' quarters section—quiet and empty in the corridors, thank God—and located the hatch inscribed with 327, she dropped the plan on the floor as soon as she had the hatch open and closed again.

It was quiet inside.

Carrol took a quivering breath and let it out as slowly as she could. Her hands were shaking. Her entire body was, in fact, and her fingertips lips felt numb.

I'm hyperventilating, she realized.

She grabbed a small metal chair that had been tucked under the tiny little table in the corner of the small room, and its surface crumbled at her touch. Corrosion. It would get rust all over her uniform if she were to sit down in it, but she didn't care. She sat and tried to control her breath.

What am I doing on this ship?

The panic that had driven her to ask that question was reality setting in. She was not on *Olympia.* Not where she was supposed to be. She was here. This was her post. This rusting chair and the tiny room it belonged to. The shit-covered HR officer. And the absolute mountain of work in that operational plan lying scattered on the floor.

"What the fuck is going on?" she whispered to herself as her breath caught in her throat.

There were a million things waiting for her to do out there. The sheer volume of work was overwhelming, as was the microscopic amount of time they'd been given to do it, but Carrol found she couldn't move, not now that she'd found a private moment of silence.

Her breathing slowed eventually. Her heart pounded less thunderously in her ears. She decided she wanted to learn what in the hell was going on.

Her small quarters—and they *were* small with about a body's length of room in any direction—did have a computer console. She clicked it on, and with no small measure of relief, the Fleet logo appeared on a 2-D monitor with the resolution of a screen type she hadn't seen since she was a child. The text was blocky, nothing like the usual crisp, holographically augmented screens she knew were installed at every station on new ships like *Olympia*, but she could nonetheless read it.

She tried the communications portal to see if it was operational, and she was in luck. It was.

Carrol logged into the system with her credentials, keyed in a face-to-face message request with Admiral Lyle's office, and waited.

There was no response. The terminal informed her that an alert of her call had been logged with the admiral's profile and asked her if she wished to leave a further message. She said no and tried the live call again. Still no response.

She tried one more time, got the same, and slapped off the console.

She sat in silence for a long time. It was the only thing she could do to keep from falling apart. Rising from that rusted chair felt as though it would cause her to disintegrate. *What had happened?* What the *fuck* had gone wrong?! All she wanted to do was to yell that question over and over into Lyle's old, wrinkled, kind, lying fucking face. Had he known this was coming? Was he trying to humiliate her? What had she done wrong? What had she done, how had she failed him to deserve this?

Carrol was unaware of how long she'd been spiraling, searching through every conversation the two of them had ever had, every interaction where she'd not gotten it perfect or forgotten something, missed a detail when her console beeped.

She stood so fast the chair spilled over.

Someone was requesting a face-to-face with her.

Hands shaking again—or was it still?—she accepted the call.

A familiar smiling paternal face appeared on the screen.

"Admiral!" Carrol gushed, leaning forward and nearly head-butting the comm screen. Relief surged through her, raw and uncontrollable. "Admiral," she repeated, blinking away her emotions. "It's so good to see you."

"Eunice," Lyle said, still smiling. "It's good to see you, too. How is the posting going?"

Carrol hesitated.

"Is it everything you were hoping for, Commander?"

What? "Admiral?"

"I do hope you're settling in nicely. Big step!"

"Yes, sir. Um, I'm just surprised, is all."

"Surprised?"

Did he not know? By the stars, is it possible this *was* a mistake? "Sir," she said, picking up intensity, "I'm not on *Olympia*. I think something's gone wrong because I'm on another ship, sir. It's some old, mothballed ship, sir, named *Glory*."

"*Glory*," Lyle repeated, the smile still plastered to his face.

"Yes, sir."

"Yes, that's right."

Panic started to rise again, but she pushed it down. "No, sir, it's not right. Remember? You put me in for *Olympia*? We talked about *Olympia*."

Lyle just kept smiling. "I trust that everything is going well? You're settling in? Big step!"

That was when Carrol noticed something wasn't right. The admiral wasn't right. His eyes weren't focused on her. They were focused on something else. Past her. On the other end of the transmission. Someone else, perhaps? Fuck, it was impossible to tell.

"Admiral," she said carefully, quietly. "Are you okay?"

"You're settling in?" Lyle repeated, ignoring her question, and that damned smile on his face was getting more unnerving. Infuriating. Confounding.

Something was wrong. Terribly wrong. And it was impossible to know what.

Their transmission glitched with some kind of interference.

"It's so...see..." Lyle said, his words halting and the image choppy. It froze on Lyle's discordant face.

"Admiral?" Carrol said and leaned forward to try to make out what he was saying.

The transmission glitched some more, with flickers of static and other interference that were brilliant enough to make Carrol's head hurt. She blinked and turned away in pain.

"It's so good to see you," she could hear him say, and she looked back at the console to see his smiling face one last time before the transmission ended, and she was left alone again in her quarters.

She leaned against the desk, too unnerved to pick up the chair until her hamstring cramped from the unnatural position. She didn't know how long she'd been leaning there, and she didn't care. She finally lifted the chair and sat in stunned silence, unable to put together a coherent thought about the inexplicable conversation she'd just had, why she was here, and worried for the admiral. Had someone gotten to him? Forced him to reassign her? Someone who had it out for her? Or was it him? Could it have been lies all the time?

Something was wrong. Very, very wrong. She could feel it working through her stomach like a worm, twisting and writhing—the certainty that there were forces in play she couldn't see, just beyond her grasp, and that they were dark and sadistic and evil. It was something she'd always dealt with in this damn Fleet, something she just couldn't figure out: decisions made behind closed doors, whispers around the corner, glances of disdain in the periphery. Nothing she had ever been able to confront directly, but it had all made it known that she didn't belong.

What she didn't know. It scurried out of sight every time she turned to look at it. It spoke a language she still didn't understand, an insider code she'd never been able to break. And they'd won. She was here now. Stashed away in oblivion. So close, and yet so far. And they'd used that, hadn't they? To twist the knife. It hurt with physical pain as if she'd been stabbed, and it had left a horrible wound.

The deck rumbled and then lurched violently, accompanied by the sound of a thunderclap. Carrol was thrown from her chair and hit the plating hard.

An alarm started to wail a moment later.

Carrol scrambled to her feet, disoriented. She had the sense of lost time, and though she hadn't moved, things didn't feel right. Or look right. The comm screen was static, a snowstorm of black and white that indicated a long-severed connection. Beside her, on the table, her printouts were neatly stacked. Her shoulder was sore, presumably from her fall, but so were her hands, which were clenched tight and white-knuckled. How long had she been staring into nothing? Jesus.

The alarm wail reset and repeated, which snapped her into motion. There was an emergency somewhere.

"Fuck."

She was up, then, and rushed out of the hatchway to her quarters, then tore down the corridors until she found another rushing crewman. He had soot on his uniform jacket, and he reeked of smoke.

"What's going on?" she asked, grabbing him.

"Fire," he said, pointing back. "In the docking..." He

wiped his face, desperately searching for something in his head he couldn't find. "I don't know which number it is," he finally confessed.

Carrol let him go and took off, running as fast as she could.

She wracked her brain for the layout of the ship, struggling as mightily as the shell-shocked crewman. Dammit. *Dammit!* Okay, she knew she was starboard, and she knew the docking bays were stacked on top of each other in the mid-sections. They went in a row down the length of the ship, so she headed in that direction. The chaos should be easy to spot when she got close.

It was. Smoke filled the corridors, making it hard to see. Carrol's foot caught on something as she rounded a corner, and she crashed to the deck for the second time in as many minutes, this time banging her knee hard on the grating. She looked back to see a pile of crates against the side bulkhead. Ahead of her, similar crates clogged the accessway; she saw several crewmen fleeing and falling over the clutter in their haste.

Carrol picked herself up and headed toward the door they were spilling out of.

A docking bay control room awaited her, and through the quickly blackening windows, she could see that a cargo vessel was askew inside the ship, on fire, and from the pops and jets of sparks coming from its rear, its propulsion system was about to explode. Flailing beside it like an entity possessed was a docking arm. It slammed into the cargo ship over and over, sending a shower of sparks every time it did. The controls in front of her and all around the control room blinked one simple message over and over.

Malfunction.

"We need to vent the bay!" she shouted to what she

hoped was someone still left in the control room. A fire needed oxygen to thrive, and the vacuum of open space was excellent at depriving anything of oxygen.

"Commander!" a voice shouted back, and Carrol was relieved to see one other person inside. A crewman who'd remained at his post. But rather than respond to the command she'd given, he was pointing out the windows. Carrol followed his gesture.

On the docking bay deck, motionless and lying at a sickening angle, Carrol recognized CAG. If they were to vent the docking bay, she would suffocate if she wasn't dead already. And if they didn't vent, that ship was going to explode, and they would *all* die.

The crewman looked at Carrol, panicked. "What do we do?!"

CHAPTER TWELVE

"Vent the fucking bay!"

Carrol gave the command and ran out of the control room, searching desperately for the ladder down to the deck below and the entrance to the bay. She found it half-covered by more cargo containers, which she tossed away with expletives, then slid down the ladder to the deck below. Her knee twinged in pain as she landed, but in front of her was the entrance to the docking bay.

It was locked.

Good. It meant the crewman above had followed her instructions. The door had sealed to preserve pressure on this side, and from the distinct lack of slamming and screeching sounds or vibrations on the other side, Carrol found it likely the crewman had secured *all* power to the bay to shut down that loading arm as well.

Bad. It also meant that CAG was suffocating on the other side, and the door was locked. If she was even alive.

Carrol desperately looked for the door controls. She found them behind a bench leaning up against the wall. They weren't in a configuration she recognized, nor was the door anything she'd seen before—heavy, solid metal. The controls were no more helpful. There was no manual override that she could see. She continued to search frantically for the right button to push, panic rising inside her. Precious seconds were ticking away.

"Manual lever!" came a shout from behind her.

It was XO, and the captain was huffing right behind him. XO was pointing at something below the control panel.

"CAG's inside," Carrol called over her shoulder breathlessly as the two men arrived.

"I know," XO said. He muscled his way between her and the control panel. Below the screen and buttons was a small metal hatch, and he pounded it open. Carrol saw Drake do the same on the other side. Two hand-levers popped out, and the men went to work jacking them up and down.

With a grinding of metal and the pop-hiss of air escaping, the door cracked open.

"It's not going to hold!" Drake shouted to her as she moved toward the slit.

Carrol wasn't listening. As soon as the doors were open enough for her to turn sideways and get through, she did, plunging into zero-pressure.

It sucked the wind out of her, which she realized was her first stupid mistake—holding in her breath. Her next stupid mistake was dropping to the floor and putting her hands on the deck plating. While the fire had been extinguished in the vacuum and the smoke had blessedly been sucked out along with it, the heat remained. Her fingertips singed, and she yanked them back in pain. Shaking it off, it took her only a split second to find CAG, and she jumped to her feet and sprinted over to get her. She hooked her arms underneath CAG's limp shoulders and began to haul.

Anyone who has ever tried to carry an adult human, particularly a limp one, knows it's nearly impossible. Humans are as easy to carry as a three-fourths-filled sandbag, and CAG was not petite. Carrol was doing that with limited air from the trickle coming in via the partially opened door. Her head started to swim, but she held what breath she had left and redoubled her efforts. She thought, *You might just rather lay down and die,* but she pushed the thought away and focused on one action: move. One step after the other, she dragged the woman toward the bay door.

It was shut again when they got there.

Carrol pounded on it with her elbow, frantically, which didn't make much of a sound. But if she let go even with one hand from underneath the woman's shoulder, she didn't know if she'd be able to hoist her up again. There was no movement from the door. Carrol pounded again, and this time lost her grip. CAG slumped to the deck. Carrol's lungs burned worse than her hands, and her vision started to tunnel. She pounded one last time, then collapsed. The fiery-hot plating began to singe her uniform and started to work on her flesh.

She fell backward.

She thought it was the inevitable collapse into oblivion, but above her in the pinprick of sight that was still available to her, she saw a face leaning over her. A face she recognized. And then hands were upon her, dragging her into the interior of the ship.

With a great clank, the door shut inches from her booted toes, and air rushed into her chest. She coughed. Violently. More hands helped lift her into a seated position, and she held herself there with her burned hands against the raw, rough corrugation of the deck plating. Standing in front of her was Smith, the giant e-Marine. Next to him was Efremova, who bent down to her level.

"You okay?" she asked in her thick accent.

Carrol nodded. She asked for a hand to help her stand and Efremova obliged, hauling her up like she was a feather. Carrol nearly toppled over, but another set of hands caught her, the same hands that had hauled her through the door while Smith kept it open. She turned to see Drake standing there.

"What happened?" he asked, his face cavitating between anger and concern.

Carrol shook her head. "I don't know, sir. The fire was already in progress when I arrived."

"Who was the officer on watch?"

Carrol shook her head, trying to access information she was dimly aware she should know but drawing an utter blank. "I will find out, sir," was all she could say.

Drake nodded, accepting it. "See that you do," he said, then he turned to CAG, who was still lying limp on the floor with XO kneeling over her.

She had burns up and down her exposed flesh, along with a nasty gash on her forehead. Her uniform was charred, portending more bodily harm underneath, and it was hard to see under all that if she was breathing. If she was alive.

XO looked up at the group and nodded. "I have a pulse. She's alive."

Carrol was in too much shock to feel any relief. Everything was a flood of information.

"Let's go. Sickbay," Drake said, reaching for CAG's legs.

XO angled to grab the officer by the shoulders, but without a word, the giant e-Marine stepped forward and grabbed the woman by the waist, lifted her like a rag doll, and slung her over his shoulder. Drake and XO looked at him in surprise as he lumbered toward Sickbay. Carrol hesitated.

"Commander," Drake said to her, stopping. He pointed at her hands, which she realized were red with burns. "You're going to Sickbay too."

Carrol looked at the hangar bay doors and thought about the flailing docking arm. "I should..." She pointed back, unable to find words.

But Drake was following. "Efremova."

The master at arms snapped a sharp "Yes, sir."

"Would you be so kind as to make a preliminary investigation as to just what happened down here? I'm taking the commander with me to Sickbay."

There was another "Yes, sir" from the Russian woman, and the captain ushered Carrol away.

As they were leaving, a sweaty group of young men carrying fire suppression gear clambered into the corridor behind them, banging noisily off the bulkheads and panting. They skidded to a halt in front of Efremova, who remained in front of the hangar bay door.

The damage control team had arrived.

"It's about time, you motherfuckers!" she shouted, moving close to loom over them.

CHAPTER THIRTEEN

"SHE'S GOING TO MAKE IT."

Doc was bloody as he stepped around the makeshift surgical curtain he'd thrown up to give poor CAG privacy as he cut her out of her uniform and tended her wounds. Given the blood, Drake didn't dare think about how much of her skin had come off with the uniform, but the doctor's expression was one of relief. That gave the captain solace. He trusted the old man.

"The lieutenant has third-degree burns," he explained. "But nothing that a dermal spray and some regenerative implants can't take care of for the most part, which we have around here somewhere if my damned manifest is to be believed." He kicked a cargo container with no small amount of frustration.

"That's our top priority, then," Drake said, thinking quickly. "I can have one of the offloading crews assigned to—"

Doc cut him off with a tired wave of his hand. "Please don't. More bodies in here will only complicate things. I'm sure it's here. I and my staff can handle it."

Drake stopped and nodded, physically trying to slow his brain. He had to trust his people. Sometimes helping when it wasn't needed was a hindrance and a waste of time, neither of which he could afford.

CAG was okay. Doc was going to take care of her. It was hard to listen through the insanity that surrounded them, and Sickbay was in chaos, with new crates of supplies mixed in with old ones that needed to be removed, spare parts, and what looked like conduits that had been dumped here during decommissioning. It was a madhouse, but he was trying. Doc seemed to be handling it well. That was all that mattered.

"I'm going to keep her sedated until the implants can work their magic," Doc continued. He sighed heavily, with one hand over his heart and the other over his head, "She should make a full recovery, Cap."

"How long?" XO asked, which Drake realized was a logical question.

Doc shrugged. "A day or two."

Drake and XO shared a look at that, and he could see his officer's mind starting to swirl. They'd have no commander for their fighter group until she was back on her feet. Those logistics needed to be thought of, dealt with.

"And you," Doc said, taking a couple of careful steps through the detritus on the floor to address Carrol, who sat on the only other examination table they'd managed to clear. "How are your hands feeling?"

Carrol turned them over a couple of times and flexed. They were still deep red, particularly the fingertips, but they were now coated with a thin regenerative film. It would slowly absorb into her skin and push out the dead cells, which would peel away until the accelerated healing process had finished. "Like I'm wearing gloves," she answered the doc's question.

"Any pain?" he asked.

She shook her head. "Not anymore, no, sir."

"You can call me 'Doc,'" he told her with a genuine smile and a sly wink. Carrol smiled in return, something Drake hadn't seen from her yet.

A call from the Sickbay entrance interrupted the moment. Efremova was standing there with a smoking piece of circuitry in her hands. "I've found it, Captain," she said, waving it at him and picking her way through the maze to join them before plopping it on the bed next to Carrol. "That's the docking arm control board. It's fried to shit. Arm went bananas, knocked the cargo shuttle into the hangar wall during its entry burn, which caused the fire."

"Any idea why the control board fried?" Drake asked with a frown.

Efremova shook her head. "More digging needed," she said and shrugged. "It—probably just old, sir."

That possibility hung in the air for a moment.

"Did the fire crew have an explanation for why they were so late?" Carrol asked, entering the conversation.

"I ripped them new and big one, if that is what you mean," Efremova told her with a scowl.

"I'll double the number of drills," XO said with a scowl of his own.

"If I may, sir," Carrol said, looking at Drake, "part of the problem is almost certainly all of the cargo that we still have in the hallways. It slowed me down getting to the cargo bay, and I wasn't hauling any of the gear they have to wear."

Drake nodded. It was an excellent point, and he told her so. "What's the state of the shuttle's cargo?" he asked, turning back to Efremova.

She got even soberer at that. "Some salvageable, sir, and most unfortunately, every fighter sim unit look melted to shit, but..." She took a moment to decide how she was going to say what was coming next, presumably with a measure of diplomacy, before ultimately just coming out with it. "Sir, Master Chief McCourt was on that shuttle. He is dead, sir."

Drake heard XO inhale next to him, and he stiffened. "You're sure about that?"

"Yes, sir."

There was a moment of stunned silence from everyone in the room before Drake spoke again. His voice creaked, dry. "Let's get a crew down there to recover the, uh...recover..."

"Let me handle that." Doc stepped in. "I'll take care of recovering the chief."

Drake nodded.

Damn.

Everything stopped for a moment as the group collectively considered that a man had died. *McCourt* had died. Drake saw McCourt's face in his mind's eye. He tried to think of the last time they'd seen each other. It must have been twenty years ago near the very spot he was standing right now. Drake realized the image he had of the chief's face was also twenty years old. Outdated. Out of touch. And now, he'd never get to fix that.

XO cleared his throat. "Captain," he said, "we're going to need to appoint a new Command Master Chief and a new CAG, sir."

"Yes, of course." Drake pushed the spiraling thoughts away and forced himself to refocus on the present. "Of course." His mind went to the crew and officers' manifest and the reports therein. "Efremova," he said, "you'll continue in your current duties until we're underway, but once we are, you'll act as the new CMC."

She snapped to rigid attention. "Yes, sir." Her acknowledgment was grave and serious. Without dropping that, she continued, "Sir, that means you'll need new master at arms, yes?"

Drake nodded. "I suppose that's true, though you're welcome to perform both duties."

"If I may, sir, I have someone in mind for job."

"At your discretion, for the time being."

Efremova nodded in satisfaction but didn't share who she was thinking of. Not yet.

"Commander Carrol," he said, turning to her next. "You're the new fighter group commander."

Carrol looked at him in surprise. "Sir?"

Drake frowned, going back over her personnel report in his mind. "You are fully rated, are you not?"

"Yes, sir."

"Is there a problem?"

Carrol hesitated for the briefest of moments, then shook her head. "No problem, sir. Just surprised it's a priority, sir, with the couches out of commission."

Damn. That was a good point. There was something else to the hesitation, but Drake didn't have time to dig into it. She'd have to figure it out herself, whatever it was, and in the meantime, she brought up a damn good point. Drake turned to XO. "Talk to DLC," he said. "See if it's feasible to return the fighters to manual controls."

XO nodded. "Done."

Back to Carrol. "While we work on getting your squadron up and running, you can assist Efremova with the clearing out of the lower decks. The clutter in the corridors is indeed a problem, well-spotted. Use your pilots to assist."

Despite the gravity of their circumstances, Drake saw a smile creep onto Efremova's face at that. Pilots. Hauling garbage and cargo. That was going to be a sight to see.

"They can help with rats, too. Sharpen their shooting eye," Efremova offered, smiling wider.

Carrol's look grew more dread-filled, but to her credit, she offered no protest.

"Dismissed," Drake told the two of them, and they ambled off together.

Once they were gone, Drake let out a giant sigh and leaned wearily against the bed while staring at the deck. The weight on his hand caused him to jerk it back up and flex it. It still smarted from its run-in with Jack's face.

Doc put a hand on his shoulder. "You alright, Cap?" he asked, and pointed to the hand. "Should I take a look at that for you?"

Drake shook his head and looked at XO. "No more load-ins," he said. "It's too dangerous."

XO nodded. "It was one of our very last, anyway."

"I want all the arms inspected, and I want you to seal off that hangar bay until we can do a thorough inspection of exactly what went wrong."

XO nodded again.

"Dammit," Drake growled, and he closed his eyes.

A question hung silently between the men before Doc put it into words. "Is she going to hold together for us?"

Drake looked at the disheveled Sickbay. At the old bulkheads, which were dulled with age and in desperate need of a fresh coat of paint. She was an old ship. So very old now. Damn. Was she too old?

"I hope so," he said.

Dammit, she needed to.

The Ready Room could not be missed, even for those such as Carrol who were unacquainted with the ship's layout. Roars emanated from it, and something crashed into the furniture. Carrol steeled herself for what she'd find inside. She'd never enjoyed fighter training. It wasn't standard. She'd put in for it at the Academy but quickly decided it wasn't for her, even if she showed some level of skill and promise. It was too nerve-wracking, predicated as it was on a degree of showmanship and hubris she'd never felt comfortable with. That brought her to the second thing she'd never enjoyed about flying: fighter pilots. Cocky. Brash. Competitive. A small part of the much larger machine that was the Fleet, yet to a man or woman, they acted like their shit didn't stink.

Beside Carrol, Efremova must have noticed her stiffening. "I am going to relish giving these jockeys hauling detail," she said out of the side of her mouth. She was carrying a hefty-looking rifle in her arms, which she insisted was for the rodents.

Carrol shook her head. She wasn't going to relish anything. They'd likely riot. She knew that without having met a single one of them. The only thing that made her feel slightly better was that Smith was there, lumbering behind Efremova and carrying a large gray bag. She supposed nothing could get too out of hand with him around unless he was the one getting out of hand. She'd heard stories. E-Marines gone berserk. Lots of people dead. She thought they'd been outlawed, stripped from the Fleet.

Looking at him, she realized how fucked up such a thing would be, though no less fucked up than a massive killing machine like him going on a rampage. But here he was, following Efremova around like a puppy, as quiet and compliant as could be. It made her head spin if she thought about it for too long, just like *everything* on this ship did. So Carrol didn't think. She just sucked it up and threw open the hatch to the Ready Room with an intentional slam, hoping to startle those inside and perhaps make an authoritative entrance.

It made no difference. The room inside was an assault on every sense. A haze hung in the air. Smoke. Cigars? And it reeked of sour sweat and the telltale smell of booze. Music was blaring from the overhead sound system the briefing projector plugged into. There was a large flat wall with a screen the projector was pointed toward, a podium off to the side of it, and an arrangement of stadium seating that took up most of the rest of the room. Those chairs looked like they'd been to hell and back, tattered, askew, and bursting with a yellow-white filling from a myriad of holes in the once-intact padding. Two dozen or so young men and women were at the center of it all, howling and laughing and carrying on, oblivious that they had visitors.

Someone was in the middle of the scrum, twisting and flipping a Ka-Bar between his hands and egging on the crowd. Money changed hands, along with—yes, it was cigars —and a metal flask the size of a pectoral muscle. The man in the center called for silence, cocked the standard-issue Navy dagger, took aim at one of the disheveled stadium chairs, and threw the knife. It plunged into the headrest of its target, sending a poof of old stuffing flying, and the crowd of pilots roared. The man at the center of it all roared too, took a celebratory toke from a cigar someone handed him, called for new bets to be made, and pulled in the next person to step up and give a throw.

That was when Carrol recognized him—the one in the

center, the ringleader. He was tall, muscular, and sharp-eyed, and the same went for the angles of his face. He looked like the goddamn captain of the football team.

"Zed," she called. He didn't hear her, so she shouted a second time. "Zed!"

Still nothing.

Next to her, just inside the threshold, Efremova cocked her rifle, pointed it at the ceiling, and let fly a thunderclap of plasma. The bolt sent a spray of fireworks onto the crowd of pilots, who shrieked and ducked, looking frantically for the source of the attack. Some of them ran for the door, thinking the room was about to collapse on them. Efremova stood with her gun cradled and grinned at one fresh-faced pilot with a cigar drooping from his stunned face. She stepped up to him, swiped it from his lips, and stuck it in her own. Chewing on its end from the side of her mouth, she bellowed, "Flight Commander on deck!"

Involuntarily, since it was muscle memory, the entire group snapped to attention. In the sudden quiet, the music blaring from the speakers above was excruciatingly out of place. Only one pilot hadn't snapped to attention—Zed. He calmly walked over to the podium, picked up a personal media device that had been hot-wired into the system, and shut it off, leaving the room in silence.

Someone coughed awkwardly, and Zed turned to look at Carrol. "Carrol!" he said with wide-eyed recognition and then a frown. "I thought CAG was...that older woman."

Carrol stepped forward to be flush with Efremova, and she heard Smith lumber in behind her. "Lieutenant Kluger has been in an accident," she said, putting as much bass as she could in her voice.

"She okay?" Zed asked neutrally.

"She's stable but unconscious." The room didn't react to

the news. They stayed silent and rigid. "The captain has named me the acting commander air group. I'll be your CAG until the lieutenant is back on her feet, hopefully in no more than three days."

Zed reacted to *that* news. He let out a snort, then covered it quickly. A moment of awkward silence followed in which he impressively managed to maintain a straight face.

"You find funny? Is it problem?" Efremova growled at him.

"Absolutely not," Zed said, raising his hands in feigned surrender while not taking his gaze off Carrol. "Just surprised is all. I thought you hated flying."

"Pilots," Carrol corrected him with a forced smirk. "I hate pilots."

Zed smiled, disarmingly. "Well, lucky us."

"Mind telling me what the hell is going on in here?" she asked the room as much as she asked him.

It was Zed, nonetheless, who answered her. "Just killing time, sir," he said.

"By destroying Fleet property?" Carrol gestured at the torn stadium chairs.

He shrugged "Kluger said they were being replaced. She told us we could do whatever we wanted to pass the time, so we did."

Carrol ground her teeth. Not something she could confirm with the unconscious officer, and Zed knew it.

"Not much we can do until our sims get here," someone from the crowd said.

Carrol straightened. "I'm afraid I have bad news in that regard. All of the fighter sims were destroyed in the same accident that befell CAG."

That finally caught Zed off-guard, as it did the rest of

the group. His mouth worked a couple of times before words came out. "Well, then what the hell are we going to do?"

"De La Cruz is working as we speak on retrofitting the fighters for manual flight."

"Manual? As in, in person? Inside the actual fighter?"

Carrol nodded. Zed's shock gave her satisfaction. Manual flight was, of course, part of every pilot's training in the Fleet. That was how fighters had been flown for hundreds of years, and there was no telling when such skills might come into play, but nobody flew in person anymore. Not on deployment, and certainly not in combat. Of course, it wasn't like combat was in danger of taking place inside the Solar System, but still. Carrol knew that what she was telling Zed and this group of pilots was making them shit their pants. It was the upper hand she'd been looking for.

"Fully manual," she assured him. "In addition," she continued and finally found her command voice, "the captain has ordered us to work on Petty Officer Efremova's detail while those retrofits are being completed."

"What kind of detail?" Zed asked, eyeing the new CMC's rifle and her blood-splattered uniform.

"So glad you asked," Efremova said, enunciating each word, finally taking out her stolen cigar so she could give a nice big smile. "Lower decks full of waste and old cargo. You," she pointed a rough finger at them, from one side of the group to the other, "are helping clean it out." There were cries of disbelief from the group, which made Efremova laugh. "I have not even told you fly-fucks best part." She turned to Smith and gave him a nod. He stepped forward, hauled out the bag he'd been carrying, and began to hand out handguns to each of the pilots. "Lower decks full of fang rats. Good hunting."

The chorus of groans that followed made Carrol smile. Maybe Efremova had been right. Maybe she would relish this after all.

CHAPTER FOURTEEN

"Watch out!"

The warning came a split second before a white bolt of plasma sizzled past her ear. Carrol whirled to see Zed standing behind her, legs braced into a shooting stance, his pistol raised. She was about to scream "What the fuck?" at him when he pointed past her. She turned to see a torso-sized furry black mass topple from the crate stack ahead of her and land on the deck, smoking.

He'd nailed the thing between the eyes while missing Carroll's head by mere inches.

Fang rats were the stuff of legend. She'd never seen one until this moment, but she had heard stories. They bred insanely quickly, had tiny babies that could stow away on any ship, and they grew up to be huge. Looking at one in the flesh, they *were* gross and larger than she'd thought. And their two front fangs, again larger than Carrol had imagined, were poison-tipped because they came from the galaxy's version of Australia, where everything had evolved to kill you. Not that a fang rat could kill you, Carrol didn't think. That felt like the bullshit part of the legend. But then again, looking at the damn thing, she wasn't so sure.

"You almost shot me," was all Carrol could say to Zed, who finally lowered his pistol.

"You're welcome," he told her.

Efremova, with Smith in tow, rounded the corner and sauntered up. "We got another one!" she said with glee, and she bent down to scoop up the creature. She gave it a shake to be sure it was dead, and bloody brain-like stuff oozed from the hole in its head. "Nice shot." She nodded at Zed.

The pilot grimaced, apparently feeling as queasy as Carrol from how she'd handled the beast. No wonder the CMC had blood all over her uniform.

"Back to work!" Efremova said, gesturing with her rifle.

Zed managed a nod to the new CMC, then looked at Carrol, who shared his glance for a moment. Efremova took off down the corridor and Carrol followed her, leaving him behind.

Efremova snorted when Carrol caught up with her. "You have history with that guy?" Her Russian accent was as thick as ever.

"No."

Trailing them, Smith snorted. It was the first sound Carrol had ever heard that colossus of a man make. She glanced over her shoulder at him. His eyes were trained dead ahead, his rifle at the ready, but a smile twitched behind the stoicism. It made Carrol's cheeks burn.

They did have history, she and Zed. Ancient history... but they'd dated in her flight school days. Not the only crash and burn from the time period.

"He got a name other than Smith?" she asked Efremova to change the subject.

"Ask him yourself," she said, stopping at a waste chute.

She slung her rifle onto her shoulder, and while holding the dead rat with one arm, opened the chute hatch with her other hand. A thousand smells wafted from it, so foul that even Efremova had to turn her face away from it, then she dropped the rat inside and let it slam shut. She pointed at Smith before wiping her bloody hands on her uniform. "He can hear, you know?"

Carrol's cheeks reddened again, but she tried to hide it with the same question. "So," she asked, "do you?"

"Just Smith, sir," he rumbled in response. His voice was exactly what Carrol would have expected: low, rough, and quiet.

Carrol nodded and searched for something else to say. "Not, uh, many like you out there anymore, are there?" was what she finally settled on.

"There's nobody like me anymore," he said matter-of-factly. "All the others have been killed in action or terminated."

Carrol swallowed, feeling a fool. Of course they had. What a stupid thing to bring up.

Efremova laughed and shook her head as she took point to lead them down a new section of corridor. "You have gift for making people uncomfortable," she said as they strode into the darkness and switched on the light at the end of her rifle. Carrol did the same with her flashlight.

"I didn't mean to—"

"Oh, *nyet*," she said, waving off the awkward, inadequate apology that was coming. "Smith is used to it. It is same everywhere we go, is it not?"

The question was for him. He just grunted in response and continued walking behind them.

"He can hear," Efremova said with a grin, "but he is not liking much to talk." She called back to him, "You know you are going to have to fix that, right, if you are going to be new master at arms?"

Master at Arms. Right. With Efremova taking over as Command Master Chief, it would leave a hole in the command chain. Smith must be the person she intended to recommend to the captain. "Congrats," she said to him.

He grunted once more. "I can talk when I need to," he replied to Efremova.

Carrol noticed he wasn't using his flashlight. She thought perhaps he was letting the two women in the lead light their progress down the corridor, but he deftly side-stepped a pile of conduits Carrol hadn't seen at the side of the walkway, and she realized he didn't need a light to see. His eyes glowed faintly with a barely perceptible red. Night-vision implants? Holographic overlays? She knew the enhanced Marine program had tried it all, and she wondered what they'd put inside of him, but she didn't dare ask.

"How about here?" Efremova said of the first cargo hold door they came to.

If the rest of the ship was a madhouse, these lower decks were the creepy-ass moldy basement. From the near-complete lack of working lights to the piles upon piles of trash, rotting biomatter, and hastily dumped electronics, machinery, and spare parts. Carrol gagged at the thought that no one but the rats had been in these levels since the day the ship was mothballed. There was an astounding amount of cleaning to be done, nothing that she, Efremova and Smith, or her crew and Carrol's two dozen pilots could hope to handle in a few hours, but orders were orders. They'd get as much done as they could while they waited for the fighters to be retrofitted.

The thought of flying once again, particularly in space

as opposed to the holographic interface of a simulation couch, was enough to make her queasy, but decidedly less queasy than the stench of the cargo bay made her as they entered.

"Try the lights," Efremova asked Smith, who dutifully searched next to the open door. He found something and gave it a click, but nothing happened.

Carrol swept her light over a pile of crates in the corner, which were askew and half-open. Their contents might once have been food, but now it was a slimy black slick that oozed out of them onto the floor, and it stank to high heaven.

Even Efremova pinched her nose in disgust. "Fucker," she mouthed. "Reminds of street after New Year's celebration in Moscow."

There was a flicker of movement behind the pile of crates, and Carrol snapped her light toward it. Efremova and Smith jerked their rifles up, ready to fire. "I saw something!" Carrol said, her heart pounding in her ears. She brought up her pistol, which felt tiny in comparison to her comrades' weapons, and she held it close to her light, sweeping back and forth as steadily as she could, watching for new movements. The trio moved farther into the room, slow and tense.

"What did you see?" Efremova asked, doing the same with her rifle.

"Just a blur. I don't know."

They fanned out, and Carrol saw that Efremova took some satisfaction from how she matched their moves without being told to do so. She had tactical training. She knew how to sweep a room, even if she hadn't done it in years, despite feeling like she might pass out.

A clatter rang out not two yards away from where she was standing.

"There!" she shouted and fired in the direction of the sound. The shot boomed and reverberated in the small hold. "It's behind there."

Carrol couldn't see what it was, hiding behind the pile of crates, but she knew it was there. The group converged next to her. Something rustled around where she pointed.

"You think it's another rat?" Carrol whispered, hardly wanting to breathe since it seemed much bigger than the earlier creature.

Efremova didn't answer. She just kept her eyes trained on the spot, searching, trigger finger at the ready.

What happened next was so fast, it nearly spun Carrol's head off her shoulders. There was a howl from behind the crates, then a massive shadowy figure exploded through them and slammed into the trio, catching Efremova full-on and clipping Carrol and Smith and knocking them to the side. Carrol spun away and barely managed to keep her balance. The creature took a scrambling bound off the Russian woman's chest and smacked into the wall to the side of the still-open cargo bay door.

"I got it!" Carrol shouted, and she raised her pistol to take a shot. The creature skittered back to its feet, clearly dazed. Against the wall, she could see the silhouette of something giant, furry, and four-legged.

"No!" She heard a deep shout, but she was already pulling the trigger.

A giant arm smacked her gun up toward the ceiling just as it fired, and there was an animal's yelp of pain before the shadowy figure leapt through the doorway and into the darkness beyond.

Carrol turned to Smith, who was towering next to her,

watching it leave. "What the hell?" she asked, panting. "I had the rat right in my sights."

He didn't answer her. Instead, he strode to the doorway and looked down the corridor in the direction the creature had run. "Not a rat," he said, and he bent down to the floor to wipe something up with his hand. He returned to Carrol and Efremova, who was back on her feet, now, and rubbed blood between his fingers for the two of them to see with their flashlights. There was hair mixed in, brown hair, and white, unlike the jet-black Carrol had seen on the fang rats. "That was a dog," he said, his voice hushed, almost reverent.

"A dog?" Efremova repeated, incredulous.

Smith nodded. "Enhanced," he said. "Like me." He turned to Carrol and looked at her with his eyes glowing their dull red. "And now he's injured."

CHAPTER FIFTEEN

CLEARING A HOLD WAS BACKBREAKING WORK, and there were dozens of them on the lower decks. It worked up an appetite, both for food and gossip.

"I didn't know it was a fucking dog!"

Carrol sat on a crate. Most of the stench from the space was gone, and she picked through her ration pack, trying in vain to find something palatable to eat.

It was folly to try to defend herself. Joining them for a meal break were most of the pilots and several of Efremova's security team. The team had howled as Efremova related the story of how their second officer had nearly lost it in the face of a canine.

"And Smith says it's an enhanced," Carrol said, still picking through her disgusting pack, which was little more than a protein bar. "Isn't it?"

Smith sat beside her, methodically munching on his food, and nodded.

"No shit," Zed said. He'd particularly enjoyed the story, which annoyed Carrol no end. "Those things are dangerous, I thought."

"That's what I'm saying. More dangerous than a fang rat. And I'd have got it, too, if Smith hadn't knocked my shot off." She turned to him. "Why the hell you'd do that, anyway?"

"He was scared," Smith rumbled. "Not dangerous."

"It attacked us."

"He was cornered and didn't know us."

Carrol shrugged. "Well, I think if anyone else sees it, they should take it down."

At that, Smith smiled. "No one else will see him." Carrol looked at him questioningly. "He has been trained to disappear when necessary. Your attack on him will make him impossible to find. For most."

"For most," Zed repeated, pointing his uneaten protein bar at the Marine. "But not for you, I bet?"

Smith's smile remained. "Not for me."

Zed looked up and called to the rest of the group, who were listening. "All right, who wants to take bets? The Marine finds the dog first, or the rest of us?"

Several calls came in to take that wager, but before Carrol or Efremova could shout them all down, an announcement chime came over one of the loudspeakers in the corridor outside. It was just loud enough to reach the hold.

"Chow in the mess," it said in a squawking hum. "Chow in the mess. Come and get it."

Zed looked at Carrol, eyebrows raised. "You think they mean real food?"

"I wouldn't wait around to find out," she said. "Let's move!"

The mad dash was worth it. The mess hall was still a disaster, nowhere close to up and running, which made Carrol think about that list of a hundred things to do the XO had mentioned in the staff meeting and how far down the list real food had been. But, it made the vats of hot food —*real, steaming, delicious-smelling food*—all the more confounding and enticing.

The tables hadn't been righted or cleaned, though some enterprising crew members were taking the opportunity to do just that, but enough of the room had been cleared to allow for a chow line to be set up, complete with plates and utensils at the front of the line, with real protein, carbs, coffee, and something sweet at the end.

There was nowhere to sit, of course, by the time Carrol and her gang got through the line, so it was back out into the corridors, which were packed with bodies. Carrol knew the *Glory* was light on crew for this peculiar inaugural voyage. She'd seen the manifest numbers, which were a fraction of what she could hold, but one wouldn't think it from the hustle, bustle, laughter, and raised voices the filled the passages. For the first time since she'd been on the ship, it felt alive. It was amazing what a hot meal could do. Morale was the secret ingredient, even though hers was in the toilet.

Or was it?

"How in the hell did they manage to put this together?" Carrol wondered aloud as they grabbed a piece of free deck plating and plopped down. Having come from down on the lower decks, they were among the last to go through the line and the last to come outside to find a place to sit, so they were almost alone at the edge of the hubbub. Almost.

"Drake pulled a favor with the dockmaster," a thin voice said through a bite.

Carrol turned to see Fredrickson sitting there. The chief

engineer. He gave her a grimace she assumed was supposed to be a smile. She smiled back at him. "Fredrickson," she said with a nod.

"Well, three cheers for the captain," Zed said between shoveling food into his mouth.

Carrol did the same and her group followed suit, including Efremova, Smith, and a couple of the other pilots. She found the engineer's demeanor off-putting, but at the same time, she was curious to finally meet him, see what he was about, and it wasn't like there was anywhere else to sit. "It's impressive he was able to do it," Carrol said eventually between bites, referring to the captain's hot meal.

Fredrickson shrugged. "Anything can be impressive with the right theatricality."

"You're kind of a sourpuss, aren't you?" Zed asked the engineer, throwing it out there like an insubordinate little shit.

Efremova chortled. "Kind of?" she asked, echoing the sentiment.

Fredrickson stiffened. "I simply have a healthy skepticism for our disgraced captain," he said in a haughty tone.

Carrol frowned and cocked her head to the side. "Disgraced?"

Fredrickson raised his eyebrows at her. "Didn't you pull his Fleet record?" She shook her head. He looked at the rest of the group, satisfied with the size of his audience. "When you came on board? Didn't any of you?"

"We been a little busy," Zed said with an intentionally sloppy smile full of food aimed right at the engineer.

Fredrickson glared at him. "By design, I am sure," he said, and he leaned forward to speak quietly. "Our skipper, good ol' Captain Drake, was run out of the Fleet twenty years ago. Court-martial would have stripped his rank, so he resigned."

"No shit?" Zed asked, over-playing his dramatic interest.

"No shit," Fredrickson spat back at him. Carrol hid a smile. She knew Zed had a talent for getting under someone's skin, and while it was torture for the target, it could be entertaining to see it in action on someone else. Fredrickson struck her as an easy mark. "He was to be brought up on war crimes charges," he continued. "Some mission out in Paragon space gone wrong. But those were dropped when he resigned."

"You're kidding." Zed overplayed a gasp. It infuriated the engineer.

"I am not kidding!"

"So, what happened then?" Carrol asked, heading off a Zed-induced explosion. "On this mission?"

Red-faced, Fredrickson turned his attention to Carrol and took a breath. "Classified and redacted," he said once he'd gathered himself. "So I don't know. But just look around you. All the structural damage we've been patching up, the soot and fire-scoring everywhere, you can get an idea."

"Wait, wait," Efremova piped up to join the conversation. "What are you talking about?"

"Jesus," Fredrickson said to the entire group. "You guys really haven't looked any of this up?" His question was greeted with a snort from Zed and blank faces from the rest. He gestured at the corridor they were sitting in. "This is his old ship. *Glory* was last under the command of Augustus Drake." That seemed to help it sink in. It did for Carrol. Even Zed went quiet. "You don't think that's suspicious as fuck?"

"It's true," she said, thinking back. "There was an, uh, old welcome sign when I first came aboard. Drake's Demons." She wondered why it hadn't sunk in for her then.

"Great name for a doomed crew," Fredrickson said grimly. "Barely half of them came back from whatever that last mission was that got him stripped and run out of the service."

"I wonder what happened out there?" Carrol mused, starting to wish she'd looked this stuff up herself rather than hearing it from Fredrickson. Then again, she was trying to find out why she'd been assigned to *Glory* versus anything else.

"I wonder what's going to happen *here*?" he asked. "To us. Do any of you actually know what we're doing on this 'mission?'"

Carrol shook her head. "Shoving off in sixteen hours for Neptune. That's it."

"Neptune?" one of the pilots asked. A young woman, Wallace. The entire group was now huddled close, listening intently.

"I thought we were part of the peace talk convoy," another crew member stated, this one from Efremova's enlisted.

Wallace nodded. "Isn't that why we shove off in sixteen? That's about when the Paragon delegation is supposed to arrive, right?"

"I'm sure our mission has something to do with the Paragon," Fredrickson said, relishing the attention and gaining steam from it. "But it's not going to be about peace. Please tell me you know what is out there at Neptune."

"It's an Armory," Carrol said.

Fredrickson nodded. Damn. She hadn't thought about that either. "Weapons," he said, then he shook his head gravely. "I don't know what Drake has planned, and I don't know how in the hell he got this ship back and us on it, but none of it's good, whatever it is."

"Oh, come on," Zed said, tossing his now-empty plate on the deck with a clatter, which broke the spell the engineer was casting. "You don't know shit for real, do you?" Fredrickson regarded him with a flex of his jaw muscles, and Zed pushed forward, no longer joking. "You're just spinning bullshit, man. You don't have any more idea of what we're doing out here than the rest of us."

"I know this much," Fredrickson responded, lifting his chin. "I've already put in a request for a transfer." He regarded the plate he was holding. "I highly suggest you all look past the obvious bribery and do the same." He stood, and with a small, contemptuous nod to Zed, turned around to leave...

And smacked into First Officer Oh.

Someone, it wasn't Carrol, she didn't think, audibly inhaled. His face was bright red, his body as rigid as a boulder, and his fists clenched white-knuckled at his sides. The two stood face to face—well, face-to-chest since Oh towered over the engineer—for an excruciating moment during which it felt like anything could happen.

"Pardon me, Commander," Fredrickson finally said, then he slipped around the larger man and was gone around a corner.

There was another interminable silence before Oh said, "Commander." It took Carrol a moment to realize he was addressing her. She stood. Her plate fell to the deck with an awkward clang.

"Sir."

"May I have a word with you?"

Carrol nodded and swallowed, praying it didn't sound

the gulp it was. "Of course," she said, likewise hoping her voice wasn't trembling the way she thought it was.

How much of that conversation had he heard?

Oh turned sharply on his heel and led her down the corridor before stopping abruptly and turning to face her. His face was still beet-red, and his voice was vibrating with fury. He'd heard a lot of it, Carrol decided. "You are an *officer*," he spat, bringing up a giant finger for emphasis. She instinctively flinched. "You are not ever, and I mean *ever,* to engage in such speculative bullshit scuttlebutt, do you fucking understand me?" Carrol opened her mouth to respond but never got the chance to say anything. She decided to keep it closed. "Support your captain. Shut that shit down before it ever even starts. *Goddammit!*"

Oh turned away from her, his fists flexing and his breathing ragged. He paced up and down the passage a couple of times, looking like he wanted to hit the wall—or something else—before turning back to face her. Carrol wisely kept her mouth shut for the duration.

"You are Second Officer on this ship," he said, his anger one step down from a ten, now. "Act like it." He pointed back down the corridor. "Maintain discipline. And decorum. Stick to your fucking protein bars and water. That food is for the crew, not officers. The same goes for goddamn scuttlebutt. Do I make myself clear? Commander?"

Carrol waited for a beat to make sure she was supposed to respond. "Yes, sir," she said, feeling thoroughly upbraided. Her cheeks were now as red as his.

"I fucking better," he said. He looked at the ceiling and let out a giant sigh that was close to being a shout, then stood there, shaking his head.

"Sir," she said after another beat, wondering how long

she was supposed to stand there. "Was there anything else, sir?"

Oh let out another heavy breath and looked at her. "Yes," he said, and he wiped his face. He was sweating profusely. "Yes. Have your pilots prepped for test flights within the hour. DLC—De La Cruz—has the conversions almost completed, and Cap wants you running drills as soon as possible."

"Yes, sir." She nodded and added as crisp a salute as she could manage.

Oh returned it half-heartedly, reminded of decorum but still seething on the inside. "Get to it," he told her. "And don't ever let that shit ever happen again."

He turned away and stalked down the corridor, leaving Carrol at attention.

CHAPTER SIXTEEN

Oh had always been a hothead to a point. It was something Drake had appreciated about his first officer. Drake liked to keep it cool. Say less. Do more. Which wasn't to say Drake didn't have his limits. He did, like choking out an Admiral when the bastard deserved it. But within those limits, when he spoke he liked his words to be listened to, have an impact, deliver what was necessary and let the other person fill in what they needed to. That was not Oh.

At his best and most gregarious, the Commander could enchant a room with his stories and laughter. He could charm the stripes off a tiger or talk circles around a square. All that energy radiated into those around him. He wore his heart on the sleeve of his uniform, and crews generally loved him for it. But the same went for when he was upset or angry.

At his worst, Oh burned hot enough to melt titanium, and he was currently whipping up an inferno.

"He should be in fucking irons is what he should be!" Oh said, spit flying across Drake's quarters from his fury. "It was beyond insubordination, Captain. He called you a war criminal." Drake attempted to speak, but Oh steamed on, fueled anew by the memory. "I could have squashed him right there in that corridor and not had a second thought, the little shit. It was seditious. Sitting there with the others and talking ill of you, sir. You!" The thought that someone could do such a thing was so inconceivable to him that he finally found himself at a loss for words.

Drake seized the chance to slow him down. "I'm glad you brought it to my attention, Commander. I'll certainly have a conversation with him about it."

"I want him off this ship, Cap. We should just get rid of him right now." Drake raised a hand to his XO. Oh pushed through. "Please, Cap. Just let's get rid of him. Toss him to some other nowhere post where he can keep his bullshit to himself."

"He's our chief engineer."

"Promote that other kid! Sudan, I think is her name? She can take over."

Drake shook his head. "Sudan isn't rated on our power core." Oh let out a frustrated growl. "No one is except for Fredrickson. That's why he's here."

"But Cap," Oh pleaded. "He's a fucking shit." Drake almost smiled, and he put his head down to hide it. "He'll become a cancer, sir, if we let him."

"I grant you, Commander, that Fredrickson is a...bit of a shit." Oh snorted as if that were a colossal understatement, which it was. Drake let out a sigh that shared his XO's frustration. "We need him. We do. He's the only one who can get this ship back up and running without blowing everything to stardust."

Oh cursed in Mandarin and waved off Drake's argument, but from the slump in his shoulders, Drake knew the fury was ebbing and reason was starting to take hold. His volcanic outburst had hit its limit, where his emotions found the line they could not cross. As fiery as Oh could get, he'd never gone beyond that line. It made him one of the finest officers Drake had ever served with. He spoke his mind. He pushed the limit, but he never broke it. Almost never, anyway.

"I wish Oliveras was still here," Oh said eventually. He looked at the low ceiling, wistful and sad, speaking of their former engineer.

Oliveras had been a kindly man and a genius. He was equal parts big smile and master technician. He'd had the *Glory* operating well beyond her specs on a regular basis. So much so, he'd written the book on what this class of ships could do. And the man could cook. Could he cook! Whether it was on leave or in the mess during a quiet deployment, his old-world Latin meals had been the stuff of legends. He'd been an indispensable part of the old *Glory* crew until their last mission together had cost him his life. His and so many others.

"Am I interrupting?" Doc had poked his head through the hatch to Drake's quarters.

Drake waved him inside. He entered, letting the hatch clunk shut behind him.

"Just lamenting the boat full of children our dear Admiral Sturgess has seen fit to saddle us with," Oh said, putting his hands on his hips as if he didn't know what to do with himself.

"Any children in particular?" Doc asked, looking know-ingly at the other two men.

Drake smiled a grim smile. "Fredrickson."

Doc nodded. "Is that prickly fellow destined to end up in my Sickbay with a broken face?"

"Not from me," Oh said. "I was as close as I think he

could push me today, and I didn't do it. We'll see if the rest of the crew can show as much restraint." He shrugged.

Doc reached into his uniform jacket and pulled out a flask. Drake went rigid at that and was about to reach for it and give him an earful, but Doc waved him off. "Hush hush," he said, jiggling it. It sloshed lightly enough to indicate it was almost empty. "Last one from my quarters, Cap. Brought it here and figured you two could afford a swig to finish it for me once and for all."

Doc was around Drake's nearby desk before the other two men could say anything, and he dug through overturned drawers, books, and knick-knacks thrown off the small shelves behind it, as well as the hastily half-filled crates that were strewn over the floor. Drake's quarters were a mess from the rapid exodus over twenty years ago. Leaving and not looking back. *Glory* was a monument to a battle and crew lost and a testimony of the crew's resolve in bringing such a battered ship home. It was in such an arrested state as to be unnerving. It assaulted Drake's long-suppressed memories, things he'd rather not remember, and choices he never wanted to make again. Nothing had changed, a moment frozen in time. Nothing had been touched since he'd last stood in the small room—albeit much larger than any other private space on board—nearly twenty years previous.

It snapped him back to that time, the dazed stress of limping home missing more than half his crew, the weight of an impossible choice he'd had to make, and the dread for the coming inquiry, knowing that his ass was exposed like it had never been before.

He'd left these quarters intending to straighten them up when he returned. To recover what was worth keeping and toss the rest. To start over. Next mission. But he'd never had the chance. There had been no next mission, and he'd never returned. So many who'd left the ship had never come back.

Drake found himself thinking of one in particular, and it wasn't the old engineer.

With a flourish, Doc produced three glasses from the chaos, and he set them down on the small wooden desk in the center of the room. With three clinks and sloshes, he emptied the rest of his flask, delivering less than two fingers of the honey-golden spirits into each. Aged rum, almost certainly. The last pour ended with a solitary drop, and Doc tossed the flask into the mess. He handed the glasses out, and the men drifted in to face each other.

"I feel like Elbin would have had something to say here," Drake said, speaking aloud the name that was on his mind. XO's and Doc's faces went particularly solemn at the mention. Drake tried to smile it off but did a poor job of hiding the very personal pain that came with the mention of that name. "He was a poetic bastard, wasn't he?"

The other two officers nodded. Elbin had been their Navigator, a very old, very wise Navid, and Drake had been particularly close to him. Their end together had been particularly painful.

"I may not have the wisdom of an old Navid," Doc said, looking each of them in the eye, "but I do know it was an Englishman who once said 'a man is not dead while his name is still spoken.'" He raised his glass. "To Elbin."

Oh made a solemn line with his mouth and sighed in agreement. "And to Oliveras," he added.

"We might as well add in Admiral Jack," Doc added with a shake of his head. "Poor bastard."

They all clinked.

"To *all* of the old crew," Drake said softly. "How dearly we miss them."

He took a mouthful of the drink and savored the rich liquid, letting the fumes of molasses and smoke drift up his nose and sting his eyes, then he swallowed. It was silent in the room, and Drake realized they'd never done this back then. They hadn't the chance to toast the fallen those two decades before. They'd been fighting for their lives, holding the ship together, and then fighting for their careers after they docked. There hadn't been a quiet moment such as this to sip something fine and strong in the company of their brothers and sisters and think about those who had been lost, to give them the proper quiet respect. Nothing further was said because nothing needed to be.

Drake looked down at his glass and swirled the last of his drink. "And to McCourt." He took another drink, this time to their newly-deceased Command Master Chief, and so did the other two men. It served to underscore their current stakes, which were also life and death, as they had been so many years before.

"How's CAG?" Oh asked Doc.

"Stable." He shrugged, frustrated. "It will be touch and go."

"Going to need you clear-eyed for her," Drake said to him.

Doc responded with a steely stare. "That was the last flask, Cap. Swear."

Drake nodded, accepting him at his word and hoping that wasn't a mistake. He turned to XO. "We know what caused the accident yet?"

"Not specifically, no, sir. We can look further once we're underway, but we're breaking our necks right now just to hit the admiral's underway time."

It would have to be good enough for now, even though it gnawed at and terrified him that they didn't know what had gone wrong, what had taken yet another member of his crew from him. One day in, and already someone else was gone.

"Do we have any idea, sir, why we're on such a tight turnaround?" The same heaviness that Drake was feeling was reflected in Oh's expression. The same frustration.

Drake shook his head. "I've shared with you as much as I know. Jack wants us in flight to Neptune by 0700 Standard."

"Before the Paragon delegation is supposed to arrive," Doc observed.

Drake confirmed.

"You thinking this all has something to do with them?" XO asked.

Drake confirmed again. What, he couldn't say, but it wasn't going to be good, whatever it was.

"All kind of feels like a Hail Mary," Doc mused.

"I think that's probably right," Drake said. Jack had laid out a trail of breadcrumbs. All they could do for now was follow it. And be ready. He straightened. "I know the majority of our problems with the crew—and yes, that is Fredrickson included—stem directly from that. They don't know what they're doing here. Why they're out here. What's coming. In lieu, gentlemen, of being able to tell them exactly that, we can at least make sure they stay busy *doing* something and be ready, as ready as we can, for whatever it will be." He leveled a look at Oh. "Maybe, in the end, they'll come around. And we'll all be the better for it."

He looked down at his glass to see one last swig inside, waiting to be downed. He raised his glass, and the other two followed suit. "To *Glory*," he said.

"To *Glory*," the other two echoed. And they drank.

CHAPTER SEVENTEEN

CARROL WAS LOST. It took her a while to realize it. She was on a *ship*, after all. One could only go so far before you ran into its edges. Yet here she was, wandering corridor after corridor on the lower decks and not sure which way was which. *Glory* was a big boat, bigger than she'd given her credit for. With nobody around and half the lights out, it had become a labyrinth.

She forgot why she'd gone down there. Took her a while to realize that, too. Maybe it had been for a moment of peace after the chaos that had been her squadron's first flight test. Each pilot in that group had flown in an actual cockpit before; it was part of Academy training for moments like this where remote flight was not practical or available. One would never have known it from the way they flew today.

"Fucktards!" she shouted down another litter-strewn corridor.

She'd nearly lost half of them when they'd failed to form up properly and clear the launching area for the second wave. It had descended into chaos from there. Formations were impossible. Another half of them managed to over-choke their birds somehow and went drifting. It had been an inauspicious start that had left everyone frustrated, tired, and ready to throw in the towel.

Someone had asked why the hell they needed the squadron flight-ready if they weren't going to be part of the upcoming festivities, and Carrol didn't have an answer. She didn't know. None of them did. It seemed like an impossible ask and a colossal waste of time.

What in the stars *were* they doing out here on this ancient junkheap? Unspoken for all of them was what Fredrickson had planted in their heads, that they were the subject of the wild experiment of a madman hell-bent on reclaiming some form of his old glory. A man with a violent and secret past with the very Paragon who were about to arrive on Earth to make peace. It had seemed easy to dismiss the recalcitrant engineer at the moment—he was an asshole, after all—but what if he was a tactless, sensationalizing but truthful asshole?

It was around that impasse, while DLC had arranged to deploy cargo loaders to coast out and retrieve the floating fighters—a task that would take a couple of hours, he had assured her—that Carrol had opted to go for a walk. Clear the head. It wasn't working. Lost down in these corridors, she was more confused than ever. Her head hurt, and so did her hands, which she saw were streaked with grime. She rubbed them absently on her uniform. Must have been from the walls down here.

These were the engineering decks. They were more claustrophobic the deeper one went, with pipes and conduits crowding the walls and winding overhead and under the deck plating. It was down here that one could hear and feel the heartbeat of the old ship, the thrum of the power core and the throbbing of the propulsion system, both awakening slowly as the ship came back to life. It groaned, stretching out as if from a great slumber. Gasses and steam hissed from release valves. Energy coils hummed, and plasma knocked in pipes. Heat expanded metal, popping and screeching its dismay at having been roused from its fitful sleep. The air was thick with the sounds, which closed the ship even more tightly around the commander.

Then Carrol turned a corner and found herself at the hatch to a room that was covered in caution tape. Beyond, was everything the crowded corridors behind her were not. The room was spherical, wide-open, and expansive. At its very center was a pedestal covered in a shroud. She'd never seen anything like it. The dimensions looked so much more precise than all the twisting tubes and noise outside.

The caution tape had been disturbed already. It was hanging in several places, ripped aside. The seal to the room had been broken long before. Carrol ducked around the tape and stepped inside.

Everything went quiet. There were no lights, she realized, yet somehow, there was light. Everywhere. She didn't understand how that was possible until she reached the center of the room.

With a gasp, Carrol saw that she was surrounded by stars, up, down, and all around. Well, almost every direction. Jupiter dominated her view in one plane, slowly turning, slowly swirling. The dry dock was around them too, above and below, but beyond that, in every other direction, there were stars. Multitudes of them. She wasn't sure how she was seeing them. The whole sphere was portal windows clustered so tightly as to appear as though there were no seams between them. How those windows could see through the ship to the stars, station, and planet around them, she couldn't fathom. There were solid metal decks above, below, and around them. This chamber was not placed at any one of the ship's outer regions that could offer her this naked view.

"View portals all over the ship," a voice grumbled from the darkness, which made Carrol yelp in surprise and whirl, looking for who it had come from. A pair of glowing eyes greeted her from the edge of the sphere, and the Marine stepped out and into the light. Smith. He pointed at the top and sides of the sphere. "Run 'em through light refraction tunnels to here just so. Makes it look like you can see three-sixty."

"Crazy," Carrol replied, still catching her breath.

He nodded and continued to look around the chamber. "They need it that way."

"Who does?"

Smith blinked as if the answer were obvious. "The Navigator."

It finally dawned on Carrol what she was looking at. Where she was. "Navigator," she repeated. "This is a fulcrum?"

Smith pointed at the shrouded pedestal. "That's the fulcrum."

"But this is where they'd jump the ship from? No gate? Just fold space, right from here?"

Smith nodded. "They need it quiet too, which is one reason why there's extra shielding. Other reason is to protect from attack, of course. It's more shielded here than the command deck."

These were the most words Carrol had heard the giant Marine speak. His voice, once she got used to the low rumble and soft cadence, was quite pleasant. She realized that she felt at ease in the room with him. Not on alert, like the first time she'd met him. Or perhaps it was the room. She wasn't sure.

"I didn't know this ship was that old," she said after a prolonged silence between them in which they each soaked in the quiet. They didn't make ships with spaces like this anymore. Navigators were a thing of the past, ancient relics of a mystical time, like witches or wizards. It was well-known that the Navigators were not based on science, not as reliable as the gateways, and there had been good reason their kind had been purged from the Fleet and rooms like this had stopped being built.

Still, Carrol was struck by the elegance of the room around the fulcrum, imagining a single person standing there, doing something that now took an entire facility of a thousand people and the power core of a planet to accomplish. "It must have been something."

"It was."

That Smith could remember a time when Navigators were still in use struck Carrol as impossible for a split second. After all, the Marine barely looked older than she. Then she remembered that the man she was talking to was two times her age, probably even three, older than any other person on this ship, and she realized he was very much a relic as well. A holdover from that same ancient-seeming time when wizards flew their ships and humanity dabbled in the creation of superhumans like gods. A more majestic time and a more savage one.

"What are you doing down here?" she asked, rousing herself.

He pointed at a pile of rack pads on the deck. Carrol hadn't noticed them blotting out a small portion of the otherwise naked cosmos. There was a bowl beside the pile, with food in it from the mess. "I think this is where he sleeps."

The dog. He was referring to the dog. "You're trying to catch it?"

Smith nodded. "He's injured."

Carrol felt a pang of guilt. The memory of her part in that injury flashed in her mind, pulling the trigger and the yelp. "I hope you find him."

"He'll come back here eventually." Smith sounded confident. "What are you doing down here? Working?" He pointed at her grimy hands and the streaks they'd left when she'd wiped them on her uniform.

Carrol frowned and felt her headache return. "Just looking for a moment of quiet before the big day, I guess."

Smith nodded before retreating into the shadows at the edges of the sphere. "Leave the hatch open on your way out."

Carrol did.

CHAPTER EIGHTEEN

THE COMMAND DECK WAS HUMMING.

It was nearly time, and Drake had a pep in his step. He'd made one last call to Ellen before comms blackout, and with her well-wishes, he'd wrapped up his own loose ends from XO's operations plan and headed for the bridge.

Drake drank in the flurry of activity. Officers and crewmen chattered, sharing printouts and analyzing status screens. Orders were called, chairs turned, buttons and switches pressed and clicked, computer readouts dictated, and statuses chimed. Above it all, a light red chronometer slowly ticked toward 0700.

"Captain on deck!"

XO's barrel chest broadcast the announcement that filled the room with his voice, and everyone stopped and snapped to attention. It was an old tradition, the kind of ceremony that was usually an annoyance. In cases such as these, Drake found that a little ceremony helped. It underscored that something momentous was happening, something they'd been working hard together to achieve. It was a moment to be proud. To be reverent. To show the proper respect for this giant machine they were about to take control of and sail off into the Dark Sky. Standing on a little ceremony here and now filled everyone with the sense that they were part of something bigger than themselves. They were the crew of the *Glory*.

"As you were," Drake said, releasing the crew to return to their activities. The bridge once again filled with the hum of activity.

Oh strode up to him, a kinetic mixture of stress and excitement. Progress had been made; that much was obvious. "Welcome, sir," he said. Close up, Drake could see that he was sweating, and Drake was transported back to every deployment the two of them had taken together. He always sweated. That much of this moment was right. Drake took a breath and wondered how much else was the same.

"Status?"

"Engineering reports the core is operating at thirty-five percent capacity, propulsion system at the same."

It was less than Drake had hoped but enough to cast off. Fredrickson had held up his part of the bargain. They had lights, and they had thrust. "And other systems?"

"That's enough to power gravity on all decks. Repair crews have sealed all compartments. Environmental systems are operating at full capacity, so we have pressure on all decks as well."

"That's excellent." Bare minimum, but still, anything fully operational *was* excellent. *Glory* was old, and a day ago, she had looked like scrap.

"Imaging and sensor systems are online. Comms are still spotty throughout the ship, as is short-range wave—I have crews working on those—but long-range QE is fully operational."

"Defensive?"

That was where Oh sighed. "Hull plating still has the same holes, Cap. Replacing that was down the list. Same for weapons."

Drake nodded. They could fly. That was about it. He'd expected as much, but it was still disappointing to hear. Even within the cozy confines of Earth's system, a warship without the ability to defend herself was no warship at all. Then again, Neptune could fix all that, and perhaps more.

Oh stood to Drake's right, expectant. The captain gave him an appreciative nod, which was what he was looking for. "Thank you, Commander," he said. He'd done the best he could. They all had. "Commander Carrol," he called, his voice raised to cut through the surrounding din.

"Yes, sir," she responded. Drake found her posted at a communications panel. She rose from it, pulling a headset from her ear and snapping to attention.

"Is your squadron ready to launch?"

Someone squawked from the headset now resting on her neck, and Carrol winced. "Uh, yes," she said, attempting to catch what they were saying. An involuntary grimace invaded her attempted poker face. Drake raised his eyebrows. Not a convincing yes. She flicked off the squawking voice, straightened, and put more conviction behind her words, whether it was earned or not. "Ready as they'll ever be, sir."

That sounded like the truth.

Drake drew himself up to full height and inhaled. The noise on the bridge quieted unprompted. For all the activity, all the hustle and bustle, they'd been watching and waiting. It never failed to amaze Drake just how intense the attention that came with command was. It hummed in the air like electricity, flowing toward him. The gaze was constant and equal parts reverent, critical, and dependent. One word from a captain could lift a crew into the heights of ecstasy or drag them to the lows of despair or anywhere in between. They couldn't move forward without him. He couldn't move anywhere without them. They were locked together for better or worse. Drake intended to make it for the better.

"You've done well," he said, sending energy out to them. "I know these have been less-than-ideal circumstances for all of you, and we've asked for somewhat of the impossible." He looked at the command deck's large chronometer, which hung over the forward-most bulkhead. It read 0650. "But the Fleet launches on time. You've honored that with your efforts over the past twenty-four hours. Thank you." There was a quiet murmur and a nodding of heads. Drake even spotted a few smiles in the group. He tipped his chin in appreciation. "To your stations." He turned to Carrol, who'd stood for the short speech. "Escort formation," he commanded. "At your convenience."

Carrol gave a quick ceremonious nod, clocked the last little bit of tongue-in-cheek sarcasm, and smiled slightly. She hid it by pulling the headset back up over her ears and turning to rattle off a series of commands to the flight deck that ended with "Go! Go! Go!" After a few moments, she reported in a strong and proud voice, "Fighter squadron has launched."

Drake nodded his thanks and was about to tell Oh to light up their tactical multipurpose console to track them, but the first officer had already done that.

In three holographic dimensions, *Glory* dominated the center of the table's projection at eye height, outlined and shaded in light green. From her sides, two dozen yellow fire-flies burst forth and swarmed this way and that. The fighter squadron coalesced, slowly and awkwardly maneuvering around the docking facility, and headed to a point ahead of

Glory where the ship would be in the clear once underway. They would surround her in groups of six, top, bottom, starboard, and port—a standard escort formation. Except—except several of the fighters weren't in position. Some moved between groups, unsure of where they were supposed to be, and more alarmingly, several more were listing out of formation, appearing to drift.

"Commander?" Oh called to Carrol, anticipating what his captain wanted to know. She had her headset back on and had turned to face her communications station. Drake watched on the tactical projection as several fighters broke formation to go after their drifting comrades. Beside him, Drake could hear Oh grind his teeth. "Commander?" Oh repeated.

"I'm sorry, sir, I'm..." Carrol barked something into her headset, strained to listen to it, and then ripped it off her ear in disgust. She turned to face her superiors. "We're having trouble with the short-range. I can't talk to them."

Drake looked at Oh, who had grabbed his own headset and was speaking low and urgently into it. He paused to listen, then looked at Drake with a flex of his jaw and a short, punctuated shake of his head.

"Are they unable to communicate with each other as well?" Drake asked Carrol, pointing at the devolving formations and the craft that appeared to be drifting.

"I don't think their short-ranges are the problem, sir," she said, then grimaced. "I think some of the pilots overchoked and flooded their propulsion systems. It was a problem during test flights."

"I see."

"Short-range is down," Oh confirmed with a clatter of his headset as he tossed it on the tactical table. The holographic projection rippled in response.

"We could switch over to the QE system," Carrol suggested.

Drake mulled that. Every ship had three essential communication systems. The first was a network of hard-wired comm panels placed at regular intervals throughout all decks, as well as clustered in the various main areas. Those were supplemented with high-frequency micro-range transmitters for handheld comm devices whenever those might be necessary. The second comm system was a short-range wave system that was used for ship-to-ship or ship-to-surface communications that didn't exceed a few hundred thousand kilometers, where the speed of light would not cause too noticeable a delay. That was the system that was currently down on *Glory*. It was also the system usually used for comms with fighter groups. It was easily coded, separated from other Fleet comms by frequency.

The third system, dubbed QE ("kew-ee"), was based on quantum entanglement. It was faster-than-light. It was also easily coded, but those codes, because they were reserved for crucial long-distance communications, were constantly monitored throughout the Fleet. When one sent a message over the QE system, every receiver that was tuned to that encryption received it simultaneously. It was the way entanglement worked. To use that system in an instance such as this would not only be an incredible breach of protocol, but it would also ring up every comm station in the Fleet.

"No," he said wisely. "No. Commander, you will simply have to go out there and clean them up."

Carrol blinked. "Sir?"

"You said their short-range waves are not the problem?"

"Yes, sir."

"Then get out there and use your fighter's comm to get

your people into the proper formation." Drake's voice allowed for no counterargument. It was an order.

Carrol looked flustered. "I...don't have an assigned fighter, sir."

"CAG has one on the flight deck, does she not?" Drake turned to Oh for confirmation. He nodded, and Drake turned back to Carrol, placing his hands behind his back. "I'm sure she won't mind if you borrow it."

Carrol hesitated, her mouth working for several seconds, but to her credit, she ended the pause with a sharp nod of her head. She matched Drake's stance, upright and with her arms behind her back. "Aye, sir," she said before walking swiftly off the command deck.

"That officer does not want to fly," Oh murmured into Drake's ear once she was gone. "I wonder why?"

Drake shook his head. He didn't know. Her personnel file hadn't indicated why she'd abandoned it. "Let's get our short-range comms back up, Commander," he said to his XO to refocus on the first problem that had led to second- and third-order effects. Drake glanced at the chronometer. It read 0705.

They were going to launch late. Goddammit.

CHAPTER NINETEEN

The flight controller's voice grated through Carrol's helmet, more of a squawk than words, and the advice was more perfunctory than essential. "DW-47, you are locked in for rail launch. Buckle up and standby for the push."

She was already "buckled up." Preflight checklists were insanely detailed, and it would set off every alarm in the cockpit of her delta-wing Fighting Falcon, not to mention in the flight control room, if she were to unbuckle so much as her chin strap. It didn't make it any better that this wasn't her helmet. It was CAG's, and CAG had a meatier head than Carrol. It wobbled with every small movement she made.

Carrol breathed heavily into her oxygen mask and felt her organs press against her chest, pulled down by the gravity of the *Glory*. She was oriented perpendicular to the ship's decks, and thus the gravitic fields they generated, held by three large clamps affixed to the fighter's wings and tail.

A fighter didn't need wings and a tail in space, to be sure, and there were specialized fighters in the Fleet that were built solely for space maneuvers. Space lent itself to the utilitarian, so those craft were boxy, ugly, and unwieldy in any context that concerned gravity, such as standing there and looking at them. But not the Delta Wings.

Delta Wings were the Fleet's workhorses. They did everything, including atmospheric combat, and they needed wings to maneuver through the air. It gave them a look that harkened back to ancient military times, back when the fighting happened on Earth, and anything that was built to *fly* was inherently sleek like a raptor. Its wings were slung low, nose sharp and aggressive, cockpit a streamlined curve, and it widened out in the back with the exhaust nozzles poking out like spikes. Carrol had never had a problem with the way they looked. It was the flying that made her sick. Literally.

In seconds, her Falcon would be "dropped" from the clamps, and two magnetic grips on the underside of the bird would be propelled along magnetic rails that would boost her speed to supersonic, to use an ancient reference appropriate to the fighter's design, in just over a second. Orienting to the relative gravity like this boosted the efficiency of the launch by fifteen percent with no extra effort from the launch rails, and the time to supersonic was *just* long enough to avoid pilot blackout. All of it was carefully calculated to launch the fighters at maximum velocity from beneath a warship so they were harder to pick off in the heat of battle.

Or that was the way it used to be. With droned fighters, none of this was necessary. You could launch a pilotless fighter at any speed you wanted, and the only thing you had to worry about pilot-side was that they didn't fall out of their simulation couches from the visual disorientation. This? This was a headache. An everything-ache.

Carrol hated it, even the feeling of hanging there in

painful anticipation of the sudden reversal of the drop and the magnetic rails kicking in, her organs smashed against her back instead of her chest.

That was the *real* reason Flight Control gave their "buckle up" command: anticipation. Launch was coming. Carrol wished with all her being that they'd just do a goddamn countdown, but they didn't. They never did. Too many variables, Control said, in the careful scans they took of the space outside the ship to make sure they weren't launching their fighters into debris, other craft, or anything else that might kill the craft and the pilot within.

Carrol suspected that was bullshit. Control liked fucking with their pilots so they didn't know when the "push" was coming. She'd seen the tally marks in the control room for each time they'd made a pilot squawk over the radio. Bonus points for any time someone pissed their flight suit, which of course, registered as a little alarm in the multitude of sensors. **Moisture detected**, it read.

Fuck that.

SLAM!

Carrol's head was thrown back into her helmet as the fighter was suddenly and instantaneously accelerated down the launch rail. It was enclosed like a tunnel, which matched Carrol's vision as it narrowed from the pressure in her head. She gritted her teeth to avoid making a sound and strained as she'd been taught to keep the blood from pooling in her limbs while closing her eyes until she felt the magnetic rail give way and the fighter's propulsion systems take over. There wasn't anything she could do until that happened anyway. It lasted less than a full second, but time was relative for Carrol during that interval.

Finally, with her engines engaged and the bird in free flight, she opened her eyes.

Jupiter bathed her in light, and she was about to raise an arm to keep from being blinded when her cockpit glass—it wasn't glass but a transparent metal composite, she'd learned in her science classes at the Academy, but no longer remembered the name of, nor did she care to—darkened automatically, and her holographic navigational and tactical overlays flickered to life on its surface. Carrol sent a silent "Thank you" through the void to De La Cruz. He'd done a bang-up job getting these fossils ready for manual flight.

Space sickness quickly overcame that instant of gratitude as she felt her viscera start to float in her torso. As unpleasant as the feeling of hanging in launch position had been with *Glory's* gravity field pulling her down, weightlessness was a thousand times worse. Fighters were too small a craft to support gravity plating. It was by far Carrol's least favorite aspect of flying. She retched and nearly puked into her oxygen mask. Nearly.

"Carrol," came a new voice over her helmet. "That you?"

She recognized Zed's voice. The fighters' short-range comms were fine. As expected.

"Lieutenant," she said, doing her best to get the quaver out of her voice.

"You all right in there?"

Carrol reddened. The oxygen mask doubled as the pickup for the comm systems. She'd nearly puked with her entire squadron listening.

"Fine," she said.

"So nice of you to join us."

Carrol set her jaw. "Ship-to-ship on *Glory* is down."

"We figured."

"And you are not all in formation. Let's fix this shitshow you're putting on display. This mess looks like ass. You're better than this. Now unfuck yourselves because you know what you're supposed to do. Clear the floods through manual purge and bring your dead engines back online. Then. Get. In. Formation. Right-fucking-now."

THE CHRONOMETER READ 0745 when XO finally reported that Carrol had her flight group in something resembling an escort formation. It would have been easier under normal circumstances to simply recall the fighters, even if it took Carrol to go out there and tell them. But without ship-to-ship comms, doing so would mean each pilot would have to land in the hangar bays manually. Automatic guidance only worked over the short-range comms.

Too many of the pilots were struggling in their fighters, flying manually for the first time in a long time, and with one deadly accident already on the docking bay books, Drake figured it wouldn't be wise to add to that disaster total.

To the commander's credit, she'd wrangled them faster than Drake had thought possible. But they were now undeniably late. That stuck in his craw and irritated his sensibilities. It also nagged at his concern over the cloudy and desperate nature of their mission. Jack had told him to launch on time. Drake knew there was likely a good reason for that, a life and death reason, though he didn't know why except that it was awfully close to when that Paragon delegation was supposed to arrive. That was now fifteen-ish minutes away. It put him on edge.

"Communications reports short-range comms have been restored," Oh reported from one of the side stations on the command deck.

Drake nodded a terse appreciation.

Oh called Carrol. She answered, and he put her on a bridge-audible channel for the captain.

"We're ready, Captain," she reported, her voice sounding over the command deck speakers.

"Appreciated, Commander," he responded. He had no need to extract a pound of flesh from her over her squadron making them late. She had almost zero responsibility or time in training the newbs. They struggled just like *Glory* to meet what was asked of them, but they were out there and mostly functional. Maybe that called for a medal. Definitely not an ass-chewing.

Oh closed the audible channel and returned to the tactical display to join him.

Drake inhaled and regarded his XO. "Take us out, Commander."

Oh rattled off a series of practiced commands. "Ship the gangways, secure from external power, seal the locks. Damage Control to stations. Report green when secure for movement." The commands translated to the various stations on the command deck, and a chorus of voices swelled to forward those commands to appropriate locations throughout the ship. The exterior gangplanks and causeways were removed and hatches closed off from the drydock. Communications relayed departure readiness to Dock Control. Engineering began the final spin-up of their core, readying to be cut from their power umbilical, and propulsion systems were primed and ready to take over once the ship was released and dropped into the void of space. It was an intricate dance, and Oh stood in the middle of it like a conductor. He made this new crew look good.

Drake stood at the center console, observing his ship

running as it was supposed to. Each crew member was doing their job.

"Engineering reports ready to assume full power generation," he reported to Drake after a signal from one of his subordinates. There was an ear-piercing squawk from that station, and the crewman seated there winced. Oh did the same with his headset, hearing the same thing. Drake raised an eyebrow. "Mr. Fredrickson would like to remind the captain that the core is still at less than fifty percent and that the power grid is heavily bypassed. He requests no bumps in the road or 'fancy maneuvering.'"

Drake bit his tongue, then said, "You may inform him that I am reminded. Commence undocking, and let's get out of here. We're late."

"Aye, sir," Oh replied.

The lights on the command deck dimmed, the consoles along with them, and a background hum one wouldn't even have noticed was there before it faded. The image of the *Glory* nearly disappeared from the holographic display, and in the silence that followed, there was a collective inhale from the bridge crew, wondering if they would lose power now that their tether to the dock had been severed. Drake held his breath along with them. A second later, the lights came back on, and the noise of their equipment along with it. There was a thrum, too, that coursed through the deck plating a moment later, slow at first. It rattled the plating at their feet, then rose in pitch and frequency until it slowly leveled off and faded into the rest of the background noise.

"Power and propulsion are...online," Oh reported, consulting the readouts that had appeared alongside the holographic image of the ship and over his headset. He smiled and delivered a tight fist-pump. "*Glory* is under her own power, sir."

A small round of applause broke out awkwardly across the command deck. It wasn't sardonic from what Drake could tell, but an expression of genuine relief. Drake shared it with them, though it wasn't over yet, and he let it continue until it died out.

"Comms," Oh called. "Request permission to depart and contact System Control for a flight path."

"Aye, sir," came the response.

"Helm, station-keeping."

Another "Aye, sir."

"Dockmaster has cleared us for departure," Comms reported a moment later. "And System Flight Control has transmitted our transit lane to the navigation station."

"Flight path locked in," Helm followed up.

Oh nodded in satisfaction. "Ahead on maneuvering thrust."

The deck plating at their feet thrummed, and there was a slight feeling of acceleration. Drake clocked it, and he shared a look with Oh, who noted it with a raised eyebrow and tapped in a note onto the command console. They shouldn't feel anything at such a low thrust, which meant the gravity systems still needed work.

"We are clear of drydock, sir," Oh reported to Drake a few seconds later, referring to the tactical display even though Drake stared at it intensely. "We are five by five in the transit lane and will exit the Jupiter complex in forty seconds."

So far, so good.

"Keep an eye out for traffic," Drake reminded XO. Transit lanes, by their definition, were strictly controlled like airports of old. Incoming and outgoing vessels were rigorously tracked, assigned lanes to stick to, and everything was kept running nice and smooth so long as everyone was where they were supposed to be. This was the *Glory's* first true test. Could they stay in their lane at the speed they were supposed to? Drake thought so, as long there wasn't anything in the way.

Oh zoomed out the tactical display to show a larger representation of the shipyard facilities. In the center of it was *Glory*, now a green blob centered on a shining yellow line that represented their flight path. Other blobs and dots swirled around them in blues, purples, and reds, representing other craft of various sizes in motion on their designated flight paths. One in particular stuck out to Drake. A large blob lit up in red was angling from a drydock to intersect their yellow transit lane.

Drake pointed at it, his hand causing the hologram to waver. It was more than just an interruption of the projected light. The command display was spatially interactive; it responded to gestures and touch in the projected space, not just from the various controls around its edge. A new feature. Drake would have taken a moment to appreciate the upgrade if he hadn't noticed something that red blob was doing that concerned him. "Who is that?"

"Uh," XO began with a frown. He looked down at his controls, then reached out to grab the red dot and pull it closer to him. A holographic readout appeared when he did so, rattling off information such as name, registry, hailing frequencies, tonnage, vector, velocity, etc. It was the last couple bits of information that concerned Drake, and when XO related them, they concerned him as well. "That's *Olympia*, sir." Drake didn't need him to tell him that once her curved hull had been enlarged enough to see. Of course it was *Olympia*. "She's been given clearance to enter the same transit lane. Supposed to do so once we're clear, that is."

"Not at that acceleration," Drake noted.

Oh nodded. He'd seen it. "Comms, hail *Olympia* on channel Alpha-Six-Five-Seven. Advise them that they're coming in too hot."

One of the comms crewmen nodded and turned to his panel, spoke in low tones over his headset, waited what seemed like an interminable amount of time, and then turned back to the commander. "*Olympia* says they're on course for the ceremony, sir, and have adjusted their speed to assure a timely arrival."

"They're fucking late," Oh growled out the side of his mouth.

"So are we," Drake said just as quietly.

"They've requested that we brake in order to allow them to pass."

"That *we* brake?" Oh repeated.

Drake could almost see the hairs on the back of the man's mostly-bald head rise, and he was inclined to agree with the sentiment. *Glory* was where they were supposed to be.

"Tell the commander of *Olympia* that we too have a schedule to keep," Drake said, addressing the crewman directly. "We'd appreciate it if they keep to their prescribed lane and matching velocity."

Another moment passed as the crewman turned back to his comms panel and relayed the message to the giant oncoming ship. As he did, the *Olympia* continued to move as it had, its intersection with their transit lane getting more imminent. Drake's blood pressure rose with every second that ticked by.

"Crewman?" Oh asked, urgency creeping into his voice.

"They're repeating the braking request," the crewman answered.

"Goddammit," Oh said. "Get System Control on the short-range and have *them* tell *Olympia* to slow down, then."

Everyone on the command deck tensed. Activity froze as all eyes zeroed in on the exchange. Several more precious seconds went by with the two ships barreling toward each other before the crewman turned again, a desperate and frustrated look on his face. "System Control is ordering us to brake."

"Sonofa*bitch*," Oh spat under his breath. "Helm."

"Braking, sir."

Drake braced himself for the change in inertia, a conscious move given what was leaking through their gravity field already under more minor thruster maneuvers. He eyed the spatial display of the two ships. There was just enough time, thankfully. But...

No change in inertia came.

Drake hoped for a split second that it was an improvement in the inertial dampening systems, but that was dashed in the heartbeat that followed by a look to the display. The two ships' vectors and velocities had not changed.

"Helm!" Oh barked.

"I've fired braking thrusters, sir," Helm cried in desperation, pounding his console for good measure. He turned, face white. "They're malfunctioning!"

The center display turned all red. A giant warning symbol flashed, accompanied by a blaring klaxon that shook the command deck—a collision warning.

"Hard to port!" Drake shouted over the din. "And keep firing braking thrusters!"

"Brace for impact," Oh bellowed. It was too little, too late.

The ship lurched to the left, sending unrestrained crew into the closest immovable object. Drake ground his teeth, wanting to worry about them but unable to take his eyes off the center display. They were turning, but slowly. Too slowly. Drake pointed at the streaming data, but Oh was already on it.

"Engineering!" he shouted into his headset. "Prepare for one-quarter maneuvering burn." Drake could hear someone, almost certainly Fredrickson, shouting through the tiny earphone, but Oh snapped off the communication before a full retort could make it back. "Helm, down twenty degrees Z-axis at one-quarter, one-second burst. Now!"

What had been a pleasant affirming hum that vibrated up from the heart of Engineering through the metal and plastiform of the rest of the ship now became a scream. The main propulsion drive was not meant for maneuvering. It was meant to *propel*, as in straight lines. At immense speeds and with substantially more power by orders of magnitude than thrusters. Thus, *Glory*, under that burst of acceleration, dove so quickly that everyone on the command deck was thrown as if the inertial dampeners were nonexistent. Drake elevated into mid-air, gripping onto the console handholds with every ounce of strength he had. He was slammed down after the one-second burst of acceleration ceased and the gravity systems caught up with the maneuver and compensated.

Drake was in the process of hauling himself to his feet to see if the maneuver had worked when every light, display, and console on the bridge shut down. They'd lost power.

"Shit." It was Oh's voice in the darkness.

Drake was the first to turn his flashlight on. The rest of the command deck crew followed his lead. "Switch to battery," he called, looking for the manual switch on his center console. It should have happened automatically, the switch to the backup power supplies, but that was obviously another system that was lower on that goddamn checklist. The batteries themselves had better not be.

His console turned on. Others flickered to life across the command deck. "Where in the hell is that fuckhead in his brand-new ship?" Drake requested to focus the crew on the goal and not the tools.

The holographic display showed red for everything that was color-coded, though not with a collision alert with Olympia. That had been avoided. Now they were barreling toward something else, which was what happened when you dove out of your transit lane. It was a part of the junked shipyards, it looked like. A cluster of half-disassembled ship parts dead ahead. With the burst from their main engines, they were going too fast. They were going to crash.

"Main propulsion is offline," Helm reported, panicked.

They couldn't pull the same trick a second time.

"Where are the goddamn braking thrusters?" Oh shouted. At first, Drake thought his XO was talking to no one in particular, but then he saw the light flashing from his headset and realized he was back on with Engineering. "I don't give a shit," he screamed into the microphone. "Now, Fredrickson. Now!"

Drake and everyone on board were thrown forward when the braking system finally kicked in.

The deceleration was accompanied by a burst of electrical sparks at the aft end of the command deck, punctuating the strain on an overloaded system. However, the inertia told Drake it was working. He clamped himself to the center console, keeping his eye on the display and the moving dot that was his ship relative to the debris ahead. Everything stayed red. They were still going to hit.

"Helm to starboard," he called when a potential last-minute window of escape presented itself. "Hard as you can!"

Glory groaned under the twisting thrust of multiple simultaneous course changes, and Drake was afraid that given *Glory's* current state, she might buckle from the strain. It wasn't something he'd have given a second thought in her heyday, but now...

The shipyard loomed closer. Three large derelict hulls devoid of their interiors hung in their path. No ability to move out of the way on their own. They floated there, waiting as *Glory* decelerated toward them. Slowing, turning, but Drake's display told him it would not happen fast enough.

"All hands, brace for impact!" XO called over the ship's broadcast address. Hopefully, his warning was in time.

With a violent lurch, they kissed hulls with the closest scrapped vessel. A glancing blow, and if they'd been at their luckiest, the hull would just have bumped away from them and it would be over. But the deck gave a teeth-rattling shudder that didn't stop. Although the command deck was too far into the interior of the ship to hear it, he could imagine the shriek of metal getting peeled off Glory's outer skin, a cry of pain and anguish but not an ingletu, a ship's death rattle. Glory was made of sterner stuff. Drake bared his teeth, nonetheless.

They'd hooked a part of the junkyard hull and were dragging it with them, still turning, still slowing. Two hulks married in space by a minister called *Olympia*.

With one more heavy lurch, the inertia stopped, and the

scraping shudder died along with it. They'd achieved station-keeping.

Finally.

They hung there for a moment together, Drake, XO, the command deck crew, and *Glory*. Overhead, the low-intensity battery lights slowly flickered, a reminder that they were on borrowed time and dying.

In front of Drake, the center display was still glaring red, with the collision alarm slowly flashing. Drake waved a hand on the console to minimize the alarm. The gesture allowed him to zoom back in on the ship and analyze their predicament. No casualties, but they had indeed tangled with one of the hull shells. It was currently jammed at a grotesque forty-five-degree angle to them, caught at midship, hanging on like a leech. Beyond, in the transit lane, *Olympia* was steaming away.

The sight infuriated him.

Drake activated his short-range comm channel and let his rage grow. "Captain of *Glory* to the captain of *Olympia*." There was no answer. "Answer me you miserable piece of shit!" He felt Oh's presence next to him. He turned.

"Short-range comms are down," the first officer said softly. "Again."

Drake fumed. "Asswipe," he said with a spat. He then gestured, frustrated, to the command display. "Let's get ourselves fixed and to the depot. We have our orders."

He wanted to toss his head back and scream, throw something heavy, or punch something as hard as he could and get it bloody. Maybe the captain of the *Olympia*. Outwardly, he ground his teeth with a flex of his jaw muscles before looking to help the injured, even though they were already starting to pick themselves up off the deck.

Oh didn't say anything else. He waited patiently and silently for his commander to contain his frustration and anger. But that wasn't going to happen just yet.

"Sir," a voice called from the comm station. It was a new one this time, at a different console. "Commander of *Olympia* is hailing."

Drake looked at XO. "I thought you said our short-range system was down?"

Oh opened his mouth to respond, a look of confusion on his face, but the crewman interjected first. "This is over the QE net, sir. And they're asking to speak to you directly."

Drake almost laughed. *Olympia* was hailing *them*? Over the *QE*? He took a deep breath. "Put them through."

"*Glory*," a voice boomed over the command deck loud-speakers. Even disembodied as it was, it dripped with smug-ness, broadcast over the entire Fleet network. Salt in the wound. "This is Captain LeVoit of the *Olympia*. You all right over there?"

"Captain LeVoit," Drake responded, taking care to keep his tone measured. "This is Captain Drake. We had clear-ance for the transit lane. You did not. No one was killed over here, despite your best efforts. So, thank you for your concern, but we don't need it."

There was a long pause on the other end.

"We saw your short-range and main power are down, leading to your crash. I could dispatch a tow squadron for you. They might be able to sort the junk from your hull plating."

Junk. The audacity of this fuck. And Drake had never even heard of the guy. He thought he could hear laughter in the background of the transmission. Hard to be sure, but the scowl on Oh's face suggested he heard it as well because the color in his face reflected a temperature just short of a nuclear detonation. Drake headed off his XO's outburst by tipping his chin in the direction of the loudspeakers and directional microphones that surrounded them.

"Captain, let me be very clear with you." His words were coiled tight, like the springs on a bear trap. "I'm going to assume that because you are running so very late for your very important appointment at the Jupiter Gateway, you didn't hear that we had clearance in the lane, which led you to be in the wrong place at the wrong time; something, mind you, that has fuck-all to do with *Glory's* power systems. I'm also going to assume that you earned your command because you have your head so far up someone's ass that your faculties are negatively affected, because if I *ever* find out that you endangered my ship and crew on purpose, Captain, I will personally make sure there's not a tow squadron in the galaxy that could separate your ass from a goddamn shit stain. So, how about you keep your tow squadron? You'll probably need it next time you forget to take the training wheels off your shiny new ride."

The air sucked out on the command deck, as it did on the other end. Shock.

Drake didn't wait for LeVoit to respond. "*Glory* out," he ended, making a sharp cutting motion to the comms station. Blessedly, the communication terminated, and Drake allowed himself a moment, just a moment, to stew.

Oh guffawed. He couldn't help himself. A few others on the deck did the same, though most just looked at Drake wide-eyed in shock.

What a goddamned disaster. Get a ship marginally operational. Throw in one asshole and stir. And *he'd* been the one to air it all out on the open QE for everyone to hear. Dammit. Drake would probably be the one to get a reprimand for it, too.

He stepped away from his console and regarded the command display in front of him in an attempt to move on. "Tell Mr. Fredrickson," he said and took a breath, trying to calm himself, "to have power and propulsion restored on the double and have our fighter squadron cut that scrap metal off of us."

"Yes, sir." Oh said, swallowing a giant 'fuck-yeah' smile. "How, uh, should we communicate with the fighters, sir, with comms down?"

"Use Morse code if you have to. Just make it happen."

"Yes, sir. And sir?"

"Yes, XO?"

"Fuck that guy."

Drake nodded. Oh was right. It was worth a reprimand. Anything was worth it to protect his ship and his crew. He could see what it meant in their faces. Disrespect demanded response.

Looking like a schoolboy hyped up after a brawl, Oh moved off to coordinate over his headset with the department heads throughout the ship. Drake looked up at the chronometer. It read 0813. They were now more than an hour later than Jack's ordered underway time. Damn.

"Commander," he called across the deck.

Oh finished talking into his headset, then turned to face his captain and listened.

"When does the big hoopla kick off?"

"Paragon delegation is to arrive at 0900, sir."

Drake nodded and let his first officer get back to work. They needed to be underway before then. Jack hadn't said why they needed to be off when he'd ordered them to be, but in his gut, Drake knew it was that.

Whatever was coming, it was going to happen then.

CHAPTER TWENTY

"DW-47, YOU ARE CLEARED TO FIRE."

Carrol acknowledged the command that came over *Glory's* newly-restored short-range comms, triple-checked her positioning to execute a nice, clean shot, and pulled the trigger on the joystick she straddled. Her fighter quivered as the rotary plasma cannon mounted in the ship's nose spat a white-hot ball of plasma at near-light speed. It ripped through the space between her and *Glory* and cleaved a gnarled shard of hull plating in two, the last bit of tangled mess that was intertwined with a protruding plate from the derelict hull. The junk metal floated away under the inertia of the plasma bolt, a line of red-hot metal on its trailing edge cooled in the vacuum, and the job was done. A perfect shot. The hull floated toward the station.

"*Glory*," she called, adjusting herself in her seat. "You are free and clear."

"Roger that," the voice of the comms crewman replied. "Reassemble escort formation."

"Understood," Carrol responded, hoping it didn't sound like a giant sigh.

She was done. Her body ached from being in the tiny cockpit for so long, from tensing and untensing her arms and shoulders as she learned how to fly these things from what felt like scratch. The craft was much more viscerally responsive in person; it bucked and moved with each slight touch on the control stick as if it were alive. Carrol constantly had to rein in its movements to adjust.

And the cockpit was so *small*. She was ready to call it quits, go back inside where there was gravity and room to move her damn legs. They were in Earth's system. What did *Glory* need an escort for? They weren't even heading to the delegation's arrival. What was the need for such pomp and circumstance?

But the order had been given.

"Slagoffs," she called over her short-range when she reached the top of the ship and the rest of her self-assigned escort group. "What the fuck is this formation?"

Her subordinate fighters were huddled close enough to see each other through their cockpits, which was close enough to run into each other with the slightest misplaced bump of the flight controls or to be shot down by a single small-sized area weapon. The latter was not an imminent danger at the moment, but the former was, and it was entirely against procedure.

The huddle dispersed in a flurry of low-powered maneuvering jets, little more than compressed gas that hissed in white puffs against the darkness of the starscape. It looked like a bunch of kids waving off smoke and scattering from behind the bleachers.

"Sorry, Commander," came Zed's voice over the comm. "Playing five-deck poker to pass the time, and we wanted to see each other's cards so no one could cheat, namely fucking Erron."

There was a protest in response, presumably from Erron. Carrol hadn't met him yet, not personally, but he sounded like the type to follow Zed's lead into insubordination.

Carrol suppressed another sigh before flicking her comm back on. "We're about to be underway, so form up properly, and eyes out." There were chuckles on the other end. Carrol flexed her jaw. "You got a problem with that, Lieutenant?"

"Just wondering what we're supposed to keep our eyes out for, sir. We fighting off any more space junk today?"

Carrol coughed. It was the result of simultaneously wanting to laugh and tell Zed on an open channel to shut the fuck up. *Glory* was listening. She hoped not too closely since she opted for the second option once she had her voice back. "Just form the fuck up, smartass," she said as sternly as she could manage. She switched to a broader channel. "All escort groups, return to escort formations. We're heading out."

She switched over to a tactical display on her cockpit window and watched with skeptical optimism as the fighter groups coalesced around the ship into shapes that roughly resembled what the formations should look like. They were still a bit slow, but everyone was flying. The extra time had done them a small favor. It seemed as though the pilots were starting to get the hang of the in-person craft. Training nobody thought they'd ever need, but here they were. Maybe Fleet had some institutional wisdom left in it after all.

Carrol received a coded flash from *Glory* that indicated she was engaging propulsion. The great ship below her started to move slowly at first, then picked up speed and turned in a great, slow arc. Carrol matched her in both speed and heading. She kept an eye on her group and on the rest of the formation around the ship and was moderately pleased when they did the same. The formations were maintained. Granted, this was the *lowest* bar possible, crawling along as they were, but it was progress. Maybe they'd get to come back inside soon.

Time passed slowly. It quickly became tedium at the manual controls to match the ship. Carrol busied herself for a little while by looking the ship over in detail, something she hadn't done since first coming aboard.

Glory was roughly shaped like an I when viewed from above. From the schematics she'd very briefly looked over in her nonexistent free time, she knew the boxy hammerhead front contained most of the ship's sensor clusters and navigation equipment, as well as an impressive array of front-facing weapons. That gave way to the broad main body of the ship, all utilitarian squares and right angles. This was where the teeth of *Glory's* defensive capabilities lay, however. Dozens of plasma cannons and missile and torpedo tubes lined each broadside of the ship, and the lowest sections were lined with hangar bay openings. Deep inside the main body was the command deck and, Carrol now knew, the Navigator's fulcrum. The main body ended in another wider hammerhead shape in the rear of the vessel, which both rose above and dropped down below the main body. The top of the wide rear section mostly housed main propulsion, with giant exhaust ports ten times the size of Carrol and her fighter. The bottom sections housed the fighter runways, one on each side. That made landing a fighter when the ship was at full burn quite tricky—one wrong move and you ran into one of those super-hot plasma trails—but it was possible. If you had the globes.

Carrol didn't spend much time envisioning that. What

struck her the hardest when looking at this ugly, unpolished ship was a giant gash that ran from the top of the rear hammerhead down nearly the full length of the main body's top. It was blackened and warped, but it wasn't like any other damaged section on the ship. There was no splattered and varied evidence that one would recognize as from plasma fire or other explosive damage. When she took the time to get a good view, she could see that there were braces along the gash where something was missing. Something huge and long used to sit atop the *Glory*, running from stern to bow, and it had been removed. She couldn't fathom what it had been, but from the dark line that ran the length of it, terminating in the power plant of the ship, it had been immensely powerful, and it had left a deep scar when it had been used. A weapon, maybe? Surely not this size. What could possibly require a weapon the length of an entire ship?

Carrol's head involuntarily filled with Fredrickson's smug voice. *War criminal.* That was what he'd called Drake. A madman. He'd led his crew into death and destruction once before, and the evidence of that was all over the ship. Looking at this giant charred gash, however, it felt like something beyond that. Something beyond the old tales of battle. Something much more powerful and fearsome. Whatever Drake had done, Carrol instinctively knew that scar on *Glory*, and whatever caused it, had something to do with it.

"So, Commander." Zed's voice chattered into her helmet, which nearly caused her to jump and jerk herself out of formation. "Are we going to get to watch this peace delegation broadcast, or what?"

Carrol's heart was racing, though she didn't know why. She had to take a breath before responding. The small chronometer on her control panel, hardwired there with its own little battery so that it never lost power, read 0900. It was showtime. Outside her cockpit, above and around *Glory,* Jupiter swirled in majestic orange, white, and brown. Cloud formations the size of continents billowed and churned. A white thread rose from the clouds and terminated in a structure that was too distant to be seen with the naked eye, but the fighter's tactical display highlighted it whenever Carrol looked at it. It was the Jupiter Gateway, and what appeared at that extreme distance to be a white thread was a massive power-tap column the width of ten *Glorys* that burrowed into Jupiter's super-dense core and made the jump gateway work.

It was there that the Paragon were about to arrive, and it was there that Carrol realized she wished she could be. With *Olympia,* despite the case of ass they had just shown, and all the other Fleet vessels, shining and proud, waiting to welcome the Paragon, an enemy of mankind for two centuries, to stand down, shake hands, and end hostilities once and for all. To be important. Recognized. A representative of peace.

Not out here in the dark. Not out here in a cramped cockpit, escorting a broken old ship captained by a war criminal. *Accused* war criminal. Not so far on the outside of the Fleet she'd worked so very hard to get to accept her.

"Commander?"

It was Zed. She must have forgotten to answer him. "Checking, Lieutenant," she said more sharply than she'd intended. She switched to the ship-to-ship channel and raised *Glory's* comms officer. "Hoping we can get the live feed from Jupiter Gateway."

She waited patiently for a minute or two, and in the silence, she realized she wasn't sure she wanted to watch.

Half of her wanted to see history in the making, but the other half knew it was a reminder of everything she was missing. Perhaps Drake would eschew the request. Keep his crew focused on their mission, whatever the hell it was, and do his best to make everyone ignore the goings-on that didn't concern them. Carrol half-wished for that response, but a moment later, it came back that the *Glory* would indeed pick up the local broadcast feed and transmit it to them and the rest of the ships.

"Delta Wings," she called to her fighter group once the feed was live. "Tune into channel C on your feed displays if you want to see history being made."

There was a chorus of excited "Thank yous," and she maternally warned them all not to get caught up and lose these damn formations they'd spent too much time getting right, but that was just a distraction from her looming decision of whether to turn the feed on for herself. She surrendered to it eventually. Check the damn feed quality, she told herself. Her heart did sink, as expected, when the view of the Fleet flashed up on her cockpit display in all its projected three-dimensional glory.

The Fleet was truly glorious. Most of the ships there were new, as Carrol recognized from her obsessive porings-over of every vessel that had been commissioned during her past couple of years of command-hunting. They all shared the graceful, sloping lines of *Olympia*, though she was nowhere to be seen yet, and they were in clustered formations around the Jupiter Gateway like jewels in a crown. Hundreds of other ships were there too. Smaller craft, some of them private, along with almost every support craft in the system and a fair number of ships from other militaries. Some were from human colonies in the mid-systems, some from Earth's allies like the Friskans and the Q'ng'oxtu.

And more, Carrol was sure, but she couldn't see them. In the center of them all, roiling with an ever-churning energy field of intense blue that stood in stark contrast to the orange of Jupiter, was the gateway. It looked like an inferno. Though Carrol knew it was safe, she couldn't help but be terrified at the sight in an instinctive way, like looking down from a great height. She'd never been through one. Even on a holographic display, it was captivating.

"An historic day," a reporter said, stepping into view while the holocam pulled back to reveal it had been looking through the large portal window. From the shining white floors he stood on and the distinctive oval shape of the window, Carrol knew the man was standing on the deck of the *Olympia*. No wonder she hadn't been able to see her in the Fleet beyond. "Truly historic." The reporter was shiny with sweat, though from the unabashed grin on his face, it was from excitement more than nerves. Every gesture he made was unnecessarily large, and his voice was an octave higher than normal. He was floored to be there, a good choice.

The cam pushed back in toward the window past the pointing arm of the reporter and re-centered on the swirling gateway. "In just moments now, the first of the Paragon delegation is due to arrive. We're expecting a ceremonial vessel of some kind, what they call a 'Herald' I'm told, as is their custom, to announce their peaceful intentions. The vessel I'm on here, right now, the, uh, the *Olympia*—she's brand new, folks, brand-spanking-new. Nothing but the absolute finest is out here today...um, the *Olympia* will be acknowledging the Paragon Herald ship and welcoming them to the Earth system, and then this group of the Fleet here." The reporter's finger appeared in the display to gesture at the dozens of ships visible around the gateway.

"These ships here will escort the full delegation of ships, once they arrive as well and bring them to the rest of the Fleet, which is waiting around Earth for them to arrive. It should all be very, very exciting, the pomp and circumstance, folks. The first time the Paragon have ever been inside the Earth system..." The reporter's voice trailed off, and when it returned, it was constricted with emotion. "The first time ever inside our Solar System, and it'll be to set aside hostilities between our people that go back two hundred years."

Carrol found, despite the reporter's saccharine emoting and her own feelings of disappointment, that she was caught up in the magnitude of the moment. It was all true; this *was* history being made. Tensions with the Paragon had cooled significantly in the last few decades since there had been a concerted de-escalation of the Human-Paragon war through a mutually beneficial ceasefire, but not peace. The scars of that war were still everywhere to be seen, not the least of which showed on the ship below her. They were echoed in the images on her holoscreen. The Jupiter Gateway, as massive as it was, was twice as large as it needed to be. The rest of the massive structure, some of it stretching out from the gateway in mile-long columns, were weapons platforms that dwarfed any other collection of firepower elsewhere in the Fleet.

War with the Paragon, who were more technologically and militarily advanced than humans in almost every way, had been brutal and bloody. There were always far more losses on the human side than the Paragon, but such sacrifices had been necessary to keep them from gaining a foothold in Earth's Solar System. The Paragon had never reached Earth, not once in two centuries of warfare. That was about to change. In the name of peace, no less. If there was such a thing as generations in the Fleet, a way to describe the chasm between old warriors such as Drake and new soldiers like her, Carrol knew this moment was her generation's legacy. They had pushed for peace after too much bloodshed. They had made this day possible and were ending a war that was, by all accounts, unwinnable.

"Oh, look!" The reporter's voice refocused her attention on the holovid images from Jupiter Gateway. "The first ship is coming through now."

Carrol leaned forward against her seat restraints to get a better look. A dot appeared in the center of the massive gateway. The holocam on the *Olympia* shakily zoomed in on the emerging ship, which appeared as a growing point of light. It was impossible to tell what it looked like from the overexposure of the camera. The image shook again as the holocam operator adjusted the controls, then the image darkened sufficiently to allow a good look at the first gleaming Paragon ship.

The reporter gasped. So did Carrol.

The ship was on fire.

And it wasn't a Paragon ship. It was a Fleet ship.

Cruiser, it looked like, one of the ships that would have been stationed on the other side of the gateway to first greet the Paragon. Explosions burst from its every section, brilliant flares of red-hot gasses quickly snuffed out in the near-vacuum of space. The ship was moving too and fast. Really fast, and not straight out of the gateway, but at a sharp angle that Carrol didn't understand until it was far too late.

A potent explosion rocked the cruiser into a spin end over end, and Carrol couldn't even process what it would mean for the poor soldiers inside the ship as they were tossed and pulverized inside their own hull. Then the ship slammed into one of the towering weapons platforms.

"Oh, my God," came the reporter's voice.

The weapons platform exploded at the point of impact, and the burst of light blinded the holocam. That was the first explosion. A second much larger explosion rocked the holocam image, sounding like a thunderclap even though sound shouldn't have traveled through space. There were screams beyond the edges of the image, which was showing an indecipherable view, presumably because the operator had been thrown to the heaving deck.

Carrol couldn't process what she was seeing, nor could anyone else who was witnessing an event that was diametrically opposed to what they had expected. Somehow, the holocam operator had managed to get back to their feet and point the equipment out through the portal window. The weapons platform was broken in half, on fire, and the cruiser was gone. Completely destroyed. The free-floating hulk of the weapons platform was in grave danger of crashing into a nearby group of smaller non-Fleet ships that was scrambling to get away. Carrol could tell they wouldn't make it in time.

With a mournful wail from those watching on *Olympia,* the weapons tower, propelled by the inertia of the explosion, accelerated into one, then two, and finally three of the smaller vessels, which exploded instantly on contact with the exponentially larger mass. In turn, their explosions caused more of the tower to explode, throwing off more flaming debris.

"I—I..." stammered the reporter, who was shouting to be heard over the screams, alarms, and wails. The reporter's eyes darted left and right as he sought some semblance of normalcy to embrace, but he found nothing but pained looks and horror. "I don't know what's happened, folks. I don't know what'd—there seems to have been some sort of horrible, horrible accident, I think. A ship...a ship has crashed—"

A chorus of screams cut off the reporter's fragmented speech, and the holocam swiveled toward the gateway. Another bright dot had appeared.

Another ship.

On fire.

This one was tumbling end over end in a more advanced stage of destruction, and it was moving even faster than the first. It struck another weapons platform, one much closer to the *Olympia*, but at an angle that made it ricochet off. It spun off on its new vector, straight into a group of Fleet ships, then exploded as its power core went critical. The shine of a mini-nova momentarily blinded everyone, holocam included, and when it had sufficiently subsided a moment later for the camera's light sensors to adjust, three more ships were on fire and spinning out of control.

"My God." The reporter was barely audible. "My God!"

Something started to click for the reporter and for Carrol, pushing its way through the shock and the overwhelming flood of incomprehensible information. One ship was an anomaly, a horrible accident, an inconceivable sick twist of fate.

Two ships were intent.

"Look!" someone on *Olympia* shouted.

The holocam, shaking so much it was almost impossible to see anything, froze for a moment on a view of the gateway. More ships were coming through. These, however, were not on fire. They gleamed with an entirely different light, a golden-white light Carrol recognized even though she'd never seen one of them in person. Everyone had been taught about that golden-white light, a result of how light interacted with the mysterious covering used to clad the ships. Paragon ships. They were pouring through the gateway by the dozens.

"Watch out!" came another screamed warning.

The holocam shifted to show a large piece of flaming orange wreckage seconds away from slamming into the *Olympia*. It was impossible to tell where it came from. It hit with an audible crunch, and the transmission image froze for a second on the deck plating of the *Olympia*, then disintegrated into empty gray static.

Carrol couldn't speak in the silence that followed. She couldn't move. Couldn't breathe. It didn't make sense. She couldn't understand, couldn't possibly *believe*, yet a thought pushed its way through the shock and blared in her mind like a siren.

This was an attack.

They were under attack.

CHAPTER TWENTY-ONE

Glory's command deck descended into chaos.

The battle station's klaxon blared, adding to a screaming cacophony of transmissions across the network. Every level from intraship to interplanetary exploded with traffic as the stunned watchers came alive to vent, look for direction, express their surprise and panic, and share their fear as they looked for stability in a universe suddenly turned upside down. The visual and audible chaos assaulted those crew who had never felt the heat of battle or an ambush. Cognitive dissonance reigned supreme. A third of the crew panicked, suffering a complete loss of control. Another third devolved into a state of instant depression. The last third? They glared and vowed to fight back.

Two panicked souls ran frantically, aimlessly until they ran into each other headfirst and hard, a young man and a woman, crumpling to the deck.

"Shut it off!" Drake yelled to Oh, who was desperately trying to wrangle the comms stations. "Shut it all off!"

Oh dove back to the command console and found the appropriate kill switches for the general quarters klaxon and the overhead speakers. Relative silence returned to the command deck, allowing everyone to hear the whimpers and moans coming from the terrified members of the crew.

Drake didn't let that void last for a second. "To your stations," he said loudly, projecting a fierce calm. "Steady, and focus on your task. Focus on your job. Get us back on course and on mission."

Having a task snapped the crew into the present. They'd survived this moment. The captain had been driving them for nearly two days, sending them in a direction that had saved their lives. He was giving new orders. They hung on those words as the lifeline they were.

Drake stood, feet shoulder-width apart, balanced easily. He schooled his features, wearing the expression he had perfected twenty years earlier. The captain was the bedrock upon which everything else was built.

The sounds died down, and the level of panic lowered with them. Not gone. It was virtually impossible to extinguish panic once it reared its ugly head, but the captain could stay in front of it and teach the newcomers to manage themselves by focusing on their jobs. The little things led to big results, like being ready to fly when they had to be.

The crew's anxiety could be sharpened to a razor's edge, just like the crew that had survived what should have killed them all those years ago. Drake felt that edge trimming the fat from a mind that had been allowed to atrophy, giving him a focus he hadn't had in a very long time.

"Status," Drake said to Oh in a low voice.

Oh matched it and started with the obvious. "Comms are overwhelmed."

"Can we get eyes back on Jupiter Gateway?"

Oh shook his head. "Jamming appears to have been in place from the moment the public feed shut off. Nothing is coming out of there, not even over the entanglement network."

Drake nodded. Typical Paragon tactics. If they stuck to their established methods, in a moment, they'd be broadcasting—

"Incoming short-range transmission from Jupiter Gateway," Comms shouted. Drake casually tamped his hands down to calm the young man. He switched to the overhead speakers with an outsized flourish, and something distinctly alien flooded the airwaves.

The Paragon battle cry had no equal in human history, nor the history of any other species in the galaxy. It was more tones than language, and it was achingly, mournfully, blissfully beautiful. One could lose oneself in the depths of the impossibly complicated harmonies and melodies, and it was postulated that was partly the point of it. Experts had long theorized that the battle cry was akin to the light of an anglerfish, intended either evolutionarily or by design to transfix and paralyze prey with an overwhelming sense of calm. The Paragon broadcast it on all frequencies with a signal power the Fleet had never been able to match. Not only was it a terrifying intimidation tactic, but it was also a devastatingly effective jamming method.

Drake hadn't heard that call for twenty years. It curdled his blood and sent chills running up and down his spine. It played only for a few seconds on the command deck, but Drake could see its trance-inducing effect taking hold. "Shut that off," he called to the comms station, adding a throat-slashing gesture for good measure.

When the crewman didn't respond, XO took three lumbering strides and did it for him.

The call ceased.

Flustered, the crewman and the rest of the command

deck roused. "Uh—uh, translating, sir," Comms mumbled, trying and mostly failing to return his attention to his console.

Drake waved that off too. "No need," he said grimly. "I know what it means. It means 'we come in peace,'" Drake answered, not needing anyone to ask.

"Well, that's good then," a voice said from elsewhere in the room, grasping at the hope that all this wasn't real. "Peace?"

Oh shook his head knowingly. This was real. Very real. "Their idea of peace is the complete domination of other species through genocide or slavery. Stars save us all from their brand of 'peace.'"

Its real translation was "silence," as in, to silence every song in the galaxy that wasn't their own.

A burst of static from the overheads brought Carrol's voice. It was filled with static and distorted echoes because of the Paragon transmission, but they had enough juice at this distance to talk to their fighters. That was good.

"What are we doing, Captain?" the commander asked, her voice tense. A trigger ready to be pulled. "You want us to assume an attack formation?"

"Tell your squadron to remain in escort formation," Drake ordered. "Weapons hot."

"Are we changing course to Jupiter Gateway?"

"*Remain* in escort formation," Drake said, adding more authority to the command to indicate he didn't appreciate repeating himself and wouldn't explain further.

XO returned to join Drake at the command console. He was coiled and ready to spring. His stare wordlessly communicated the question on everyone's mind, and Carrol's open channel, thick with the static echoes of the

Paragon battle cry, underscored the tension. *What are we going to do?*

"Our orders are to proceed without delay to the Neptune Armory," Drake said to everyone listening, his voice even and measured.

"Captain?" Carrol responded, frustration coming through the distortion loud and clear.

"You have your orders, Commander," Drake said with outright force this time, and he found the appropriate command on the console in front of him to mute her on the deck speakers.

The words tasted bitter in his mouth, but goddammit, it was foolhardy and suicidal to rush into a battle they knew nothing about and where they were outnumbered a hundred to one. To say nothing of the state of the *Glory* and her crew.

They weren't ready. They simply weren't. And even if they had been, they were not, absolutely not, jumping into a fight they had zero tactical information on. Drake would never fly his ship into such a blunder, no matter what shape they were in.

"Keep trying the QE," he said to XO, grinding his teeth. "Any kind of picture of what's going on over there. And get us weapons hot with whatever we have."

XO nodded and turned his tension into furious action. Drake wished he could do the same. All he could do was stare at the holographic image of the *Glory* as her long-dormant tactical systems came online. The space around them remained still and silent. It was excruciating.

After was seemed like an hour but was mere minutes, the comms officer had not yet gotten over his excitement. "Incoming short-range!" he shouted.

Drake hurried over and leaned close to the young man's

head. "You better get your fucking self under control. You are the first point of contact for everyone here," Drake waved a hand to take in the command deck crew, "so you need to project calm, even if you don't feel it. Do you get me?"

"Sir." The comm officer bowed his head. The poor kid was slick with sweat, every inch of him trembling. He turned to face Drake, wide-eyed. "It's a distress call," he said, his voice trembling to match. "From *Olympia*."

In another life, at another moment, Drake would have thrown his head back and laughed. He thought of that alternate reality, detached and wishing it could be his own.

"She's under attack, sir," the comms crewman continued, and Drake decided that if they were going to be conversing so much, he needed to get the young man's name. "Requesting immediate assistance."

"Name, Crewman?"

"Hollis, sir."

"Mr. Hollis, request identity verification on that distress call."

"Yes, sir." There was a long, tense beat as Hollis transmitted. Then, with a shake of his head, he turned back to Drake. "No response. It's an automatic signal, sir, but they're on the right channel."

Drake nodded and thanked him before returning to the center console.

Once again, Drake found XO moving closer to him, the same tense question on his face. "We have enough for a few shots, sir. And some countermeasures. Enough to assist, depending."

"Depending" was the keyword that drew a line between life and certain death. *Depending*. "Navigation," he called, "push our sensors to their limit. Let's try to get visual on

Olympia." There was an "Aye, sir," and the holographic tactical display expanded, shrinking the image of the *Glory* along with it.

A red dot appeared at the outer fringes of the display, the extreme range of their sensors. Oh pointed at the dot, which under scrutiny wasn't just one but two, moving in near-perfect synchrony. The forward dot would zig, and the trailing dot would match a split second later. The pursued and the hunter.

"*Olympia*," Oh said of the former, then pointed at the latter. "A single Paragon ship."

Drake nodded. *Olympia.* How ironic.

"Live audio coming in!" Hollis said too loudly. A glare from Drake silenced the outburst, and the comms officer patched it through the main speakers with a look of apology.

"Any vessel in—pia, please assist! Paragon—pursuit. My God, they're—our tail. *Please!* We can't—Any vessel in range, respond!"

There was a horrible cacophony of screams and crashing metal, then the transmission cut off with a screech, leaving the command deck in silence.

Oh looked at his captain.

What are we going to do? Again, he was looking to the bedrock for support.

Drake lamented the situation. Lamented they hadn't been able to launch on time. Lamented that they should already be out to Neptune, picking up whatever the hell Jack had left for them out there. Lamented that the secretive fuckhead had known this was coming, had known they wouldn't be ready, and he hadn't told them—though Drake knew if he were to search his gut, he'd find down there that he had known it would come to this. He hadn't needed Jack to tell him. It was always going to come to this, and here they were, right back in the thick of it. Not ready, even though they had to be.

"Captain?" Oh asked, waiting for orders.

They were all waiting for orders.

"Battle stations," Drake called. "We're going in."

JUPITER GATEWAY

Terran Federation Space

CHAPTER TWENTY-TWO

THE MOOD on the command deck of *Glory* was an unpracticed mixture of excitement and terror. A ship-wide comm was left open. It rang across the bridge, voices at a screeching volume, laced with static and distortion from mouths too close to their microphones. Oh had to snap at the crewman in charge of that console to shut it down. People walked clumsily and too quickly from station to station, tripping as they went. They forgot what they meant to bring or say in their rush, doubling back, standing lost, filled with urgency while losing focus.

Drake stood in the middle of it all, thinking about how many more drills he would have loved to run. That was what they called OBE, overcome by events, and it was not from lack of crew desire that he couldn't run them. No, the new recruits had been eager. At least, until they saw the ferocity of battle and how quickly their fortunes could change. It was no longer a video game or playing soldier.

Oh had wrangled the crew into a satisfactory hum of purpose and gregarious effectiveness, if not efficiency. By and large, people were where they were supposed to be, doing what they were supposed to do. "Weapons complement confirmed," he said, ever so slightly out of breath. "We have enough for one, maybe two salvos."

"Countermeasures?"

"Barely enough for one full spread."

Grim.

Drake dialed the tactical display in on the incoming *Olympia* and her pursuer, watching intently as more information poured in the closer the two vessels came. Options, if there were to be any, depended entirely upon what was out there.

"It's a single cruiser," Oh murmured as the sensor information flashed up a confirmed model on the pursuing ship.

Olympia was burning plasma as fast as she could to stay ahead of the Paragon ship, hardly even putting up a defense. It was easy to see why. She was swamped with fighters and took potshots from the cruiser any time she slowed or turned sharply enough for her to come into their weapons range. The fighters swarmed around her like wasps, far faster and more maneuverable than she could ever be, stinging her until she'd decelerate enough for the trailing cruiser to overtake her for the kill shot. It was better to stand and fight, let those shiny new guns rip. Fight back; it was all they could do. But there was no sign of such a maneuver. No sign of the right proactive tactics from her commander. *Olympia* would die tired, out of plasma and coasting on a ballistic trajectory to her final resting place.

More interesting to Drake than Captain LeVoit's failings was the trailing Paragon cruiser. XO followed his gaze and pointed when he saw it toward the rear of the vessel. "No escorts," he said.

Drake agreed. Hubris. They were confident of their tactical superiority, sure they had the Fleet on the run. It was inconceivable they could be outflanked, and they'd positioned no protection for the rear of their ship. It was also an option. A sliver of one, but... "We'll have one salvo before they turn." That was it. One shot, and their element of surprise would be over. It wouldn't be enough. Not on its own.

Oh circled his finger around the swarm that crowded the *Olympia*. "Might I suggest, Captain, that we, too, have fighters?"

Yes, they did, and they were armed to the teeth. No shortage of firepower there, and while their armament didn't measure up to the punch *Glory* packed when fully taped and laced for a fight, when pointed at the right soft spots, fighters could do critical damage. They were also, when properly hidden, harder to detect until the very last moment.

"Raise the fighter squadron," Drake called over the command deck.

He looked at the tactical display one last time. *Olympia*'s speed was lessening. Dangerously. They weren't yet close enough to see her, but Drake knew that meant the damage was serious. She wasn't going to make it much longer unless that cruiser and its fighters had someone else to fire at. And maybe, just maybe, if the fight turned into a two-on-one, they had a chance.

"Inform Commander Carrol we have maneuvering instructions coming her way."

———

CARROL'S ATTACK strategy called for the fighters to break ahead of the *Glory* and use the background radiation of Jupiter and the plasma trails of the two ships to come in from behind the Paragon cruiser. She was still having an impossible time wrapping her head around it. Paragon. Here. In the Earth system. Attacking. It was inconceivable.

She haltingly relayed the information to her squadron. Fredrickson's words kept ringing in her head. Drake was a madman. A war criminal. He was going to get them all killed. This was all a mistake. It had to be. Drake was wrong. Oh, how she wanted that to be true, but she could feel the fabled era of peace slipping through her fingers, through all their fingers, with every glance at her cockpit's holographic display. *Olympia* was out there, running, and it wasn't from nothing.

"Delta squad." XO's voice crackled over her helmet radio. "Get your asses moving!"

"Yes, sir," Carrol said, abruptly shaken from her reverie.

"And stay in that plasma wake."

"Yes, sir." She switched to the intra-squad channel. "Form up and burn. Cut engines at the terminator. Fingers off your triggers 'til we're a klick out, and *don't* over-throttle when we fire back up. You'll stall out again."

She watched her tactical display intently as the fighters reformed around her group into a wedge formation at the top of *Glory*, with her in the lead. They moved well for the most part. Much better than a couple of hours ago. She took that as a good sign. Technically, there were several tricky parts of their attack plan, including gliding in on their final approach with main propulsion offline, but it was XO's last message that was the most crucial: stay in those plasma trails. If they were going to be able to get within a kilometer before being seen, close enough to fire and hit targets with pinpoint accuracy, it was only going to be through hiding in the ships' sensor-blinding wake. That meant precision maneuvering and ace-level flying. There was a reason to be optimistic when she looked hard enough. Thank the stars.

Looking at them filled her with a surprising sense of pride and purpose. *Olympia* was out there, in trouble. Carrol and her fighters were now an arrow being fired to help the ship she thought she wanted to serve on. She'd never been in combat, not for real, and the adrenaline rush was something else. Her heart was pounding in her ears, but she felt ultra-sharp like time was slowing just for her. She saw everything with exceptional clarity. Felt every movement. Controlled her actions to a microscopic degree.

Gone was the motion sickness, the headache, all of it. She was one with her ship. She was ready to fight. She reveled in the feeling. It was like nothing she'd ever experienced.

With a twitch of her joystick controls, her fighter shot forward into the void. The rest of the squadron followed, and they soared as one through the darkness. A sharp banking turn took them swooping toward Jupiter, and the darkness was replaced with the roiling orange and white clouds of the gas giant. They were in the shadow of the planet for the first half of their looping flight path, Jupiter as luminescent as the stars that surrounded them. But they were quickly approaching the planet's terminator, beyond which they'd be in sunlight for a moment before putting it directly behind them. It would aid in them coming in undetected.

Carrol underestimated how bright it was going to be.

She screamed up and over the glowing, curved horizon line at full speed and caught the sunlight full in the face. She threw her hands over her eyes before the cockpit's smart glass could compensate for the sudden thousand-fold increase in illumination. Her eyes burned and spotted with the light even after the cockpit dimmed, and it was hard for her to see her controls.

That wasn't supposed to happen!

Rookie-fucking-mistake.

"Sunburst!" she sent over the short-range, forgetting the radio-silence orders of their mission for a split second. She quickly cut her fighter's power to float in the rest of the way, but even that was too late.

With her vision still spotty, she watched with a sinking feeling as her perfectly formed arrow-tip fractured as the other pilots, like she, lost their eyesight for several critical seconds and spun out of formation just as they were making a tight turn into the fray and cut their engines. Those she could see winked out one by one.

Carrol scanned her heads-up-display, heart pounding from desperation instead of adrenaline. She searched for the sensor readouts of the plasma wake, frantically hoping that perhaps they were still inside it. That her gaffe hadn't cost them their cover. What she found instead was the battle.

Olympia was on fire and besieged by Paragon fighters, streaks of golden-white light like a swarm of fireflies. She shuddered with every plasma strike. Red-orange belches marked hull breaches, plasma-hot eruptions from fires raging within, extinguished by the vacuum of space. The cruiser was right behind her, firing at will.

Energy and projectile weapons landed like roundhouse punches, and *Olympia* staggered under each blow. She changed course every few seconds, sometimes with frantic, desperate firings of her propulsion drive, other times from the kinetic impact of the shots she was taking. Her hull was cracking. Tiny dots ejected into space with each explosion. Bodies. She was near death. Everyone aboard her was dying.

Carrol wanted to cry from horror. The crisscross of plasma fire and torpedo trails was blinding, nearly as intense as the sun, a latticework of death and destruction that was inescapable.

Every move *Olympia* made was hounded by the cruiser, which fired shot after shot, blow after blow, merciless, deadly. All of that adrenaline Carrol had felt before drained from her and was replaced by dread. What she was watching was the brutality of war. Space was supposed to be enlightened. Beings intelligent enough to develop space travel should have been more peaceful. That was what she wanted to believe. The truth of life arced and exploded before her. A dream ship, newly launched, was dying, and the worst thing was, they'd never had a chance. And Carrol was leading her squadron into the heart of chaos, where darkness and destruction reigned supreme.

For the first time ever, Carrol feared for her life.

A flash from her display made her sick to her stomach. The plasma trail ahead of them was off to the far right, as was the direct sunlight they were supposed to be hiding in. They were bare-ass naked and visible to the Paragon's sensors. Carrol prayed, *prayed* they wouldn't be looking for them. Perhaps the Paragon were so focused on the impending destruction of the *Olympia* that they wouldn't be looking to their rear, and hiding in the light and plasma hadn't been necessary.

An abrupt course change from the streaking Paragon fighters told Carrol something different, unfortunately. They broke from the dying *Olympia* and soared in a great arc across the starscape, then coalesced into a swarm of golden pinpoints heading toward the squadron of Delta Wings.

Fuck.

Sweating, Carrol looked at their distance from the cruiser. Still more than six kilometers out.

Fuuuuuuck!

She switched on her short-range, eschewing the silence orders for real this time. Then she gave her fighter full power, all attempts at subterfuge disappearing. What was the point? They'd been seen. They had to strike as fast as they could and hope they could make up with speed what they had lost in surprise. "Delta squad, engines at full, weapons hot!"

A voice came back. Zed's. "But we're still six—"

"I said, fire it up! We have incoming."

CHAPTER TWENTY-THREE

Since the command deck was located deep in the heart of *Glory*, it didn't have any windows. Views of the outside were provided by sensor readouts, holographic wire displays of objects and bodies, colorful representations of energies and gasses, graphical representations of vectors and power curves, and glowing displays of numbers and statistics. All that organized data was far more helpful, generally speaking, than the limited visual information one could get from their eyes, but not always. In those instances when *seeing* something was the only way to truly understand it, there was a large array of holographic emitters over the center command console that could project a three-dimensional visual image from floor to ceiling.

Olympia dominated that space. The ship was cracking open like a skull, bleeding fire and bodies in real-time. The cruiser behind her was a predator, deadly and relentless, and the holographic projection of the damage it was inflicting upon the *Olympia* was hard to watch. What had been nervous excitement among the inexperienced crew was turning to horror. Drake let them take it in. This was war. This was what they were up against. Not drills. Not games, with trophies or slaps on the back and discussions with the loser about how to do better next time. The winner got to live, and the loser died. There was no "better luck next time."

Drake shuddered and put all of that out of his mind.

He stepped through the holographic image of destruction, the overheads switched back to the tactical display hovering over the table, and the gruesome image faded. He turned his focus from the *Olympia* to the Paragon ship. They were coming out of the terminator sunlight behind the fighter squadron. In seconds, they'd fire their engines and light up like a beacon for every sensor on that ship. He hoped to all the deities in the universe that Carrol had her squadron where they were supposed to be and could execute their run as planned.

Oh leaned over the table, looking over the display, and thought the same. "We have to make her turn," he said, going over the plan one more time.

Drake didn't mind. It was crucial that it worked. There was no margin for error. "Turn and slow. It's the only chance *Olympia* has to get away."

XO pointed at the fighters, which were breaking away from the beleaguered ship. "They'll come right for us."

"Our fighters, most likely. It will be the cruiser we have to worry about."

"Countermeasures are ready."

"We can handle one volley. Maybe two."

Drake shook his head. "One. By then, our fighters should have completed their back-end run. Disabled their engines."

Drake nodded. That was the lynchpin. "And we can get the fuck out of here. Us, and *Olympia*."

It was a desperate plan, but it was the only plan they had come up with in the thirteen seconds they'd had to prepare. *If* Carrol and her squadron could do their job. It was much to ask of a group of pilots who'd never seen real combat. Drake prayed they would do it anyway.

He looked at his first officer and took a deep breath. "Intercom Doc. Tell him to expect casualties."

XO nodded.

Drake was surprised to feel a calm settle in over him in stark contrast to the nervous energy in the room. It had been a long time since he'd felt it, but not so long that he'd forgotten what it was. It was the sharp edge of combat, an edge he'd had a lifetime ago and one he'd feared he'd lost. But there it was, like a razor blade. It took him another moment to realize what he was feeling wasn't surprise but relief. He let go of that too, and all that remained was the sharp focus. He could see clearly, think fast, anticipate, react, thrust, parry, guard, attack. It was all laid out in front of him like a script he'd read before, a game he knew every move for.

That cruiser out there might be deadly, but so was he.

"Tactical, ready weapons," he commanded. "Let's give those bastards hell."

———

"Son of a *bitch*," Carrol shouted as a flurry of plasma bolts ripped past inches from her cockpit glass. The anti-spacecraft fire coming from the Paragon ship was intense. Far more than Carrol had expected coming from the cruiser's six o'clock, and with the larger guns, they were firing with much more precision and accuracy at their distance than she could from her fighter's cannons. It was a cost of their approach blunder, and it was a dear one. The Paragon had superior firepower. For now. "Maintain speed and formation!" she ordered her squadron. They didn't even have the Paragon fighters to contend with yet, and things were hairy. Her joystick bucked and shuddered along with her fighter as the space around her rippled with super-heated plasma fire bolts.

A burst of light followed by streaking trails of plasma burns fanned out ahead of them. "Warheads incoming!" someone called over the channel.

"Break! Break!" Carrol yelled, telling her squadron to split up. It was an unnecessary command. They should know from their training that when area-explosive weapons were deployed, everyone was to get as much distance from the rest as they could. Carrol couldn't take that for granted, however, not even for herself. In the cacophony of light and sound, it took everything she had to remember how to fly her spacecraft.

Her stomach bottomed out as she jerked hard on the joystick, and suddenly she was flying back up toward Jupiter. She lost sight of the incoming missiles, but that was brief. Their synchronized explosions were impossible to miss, and they lit up space in front of her like a supernova. Area-explosive missiles contained compressed gas and liquids, along with deviously sharp small projectiles. The combination was a giant, widespread explosion that ignited the matter into a plasma cloud and sent superheated ballistic shrapnel streaking out from it for whatever the cloud couldn't catch. Effective and deadly. She slammed into the expanding flames, which were white-hot and brighter than the sun. Her joystick knocking against her thigh was the only thing that told her she was still alive when her fighter reached the other side.

An alarm blared in her helmet's headset. She had multiple breaches along her wings and fuselage and one critical breach in a torpedo warhead on the port side. The latter was a ticking time bomb, so she ditched it with the flick of a switch, desperately hoping there was no one directly behind her to run into it. An intense, glaring concussive blow followed a moment later as a plasma bolt streaked past her and presumably hit it dead-on. Probably not friendly fire, thank the stars.

She closed her eyes fast enough this time and saved herself from the worst of the blinding effects. When she opened them and redirected her craft into its diving run on the Paragon ship, she was surrounded by fewer of her compatriots.

"Sound off!" she called. "We lose anyone?!"

In response, she got overlapping shouts, then the Paragon's jamming battle cry cut through. They were close enough that even their squadron radios were interfered with.

A glance at her tactical readout—and it only could be a glance; the anti-spacecraft plasma fire from the cruiser had not abated—told Carrol her squadron was mostly intact but was in serious danger of losing formation. Only the tip was still together. Her, presumably Zed, and five or six others. The rest were scattering at an alarming rate in a desperate attempt to get into clearer space, away from the cruiser's densest firepower. It would make them harder to hit with anti-spacecraft fire, but it was a desperate move that made them vulnerable to enemy fighters—a critical error.

Carrol screamed at them to regroup, but all she got back was the haunting alien battle cry. Losing formation fucked her and their mission on multiple levels. First, since the shortest distance between two points was a straight line, it was going to delay all of them from reaching the cruiser and give the enemy more time to maneuver. Second, it was only delaying the inevitable since to hit a target, you had to aim at it, so they would be in the teeth of those anti-spacecraft plasma cannons again anyway. Finally, those Paragon fighters were coming in fast, and once they arrived, orphaned Delta Wings would be fish in a barrel to pick off one by one.

A fourth downside made itself apparent an instant later —plasma cannon fire intensified by an order of magnitude with fewer targets for the cruiser to shoot at.

"Fuck!" she shouted as she grasped the joystick with both hands. Her cockpit display showed her myriad blinking warning signs and a constantly changing array of flight paths that led her up, down, side to side, and corkscrewing through a latticework of deadly white plasma fire. Something exploded just behind and to the right of her. She knew it was one of her squadron, but she didn't dare take the time to see who. She found herself praying it wasn't Zed. A surprise there.

Another flurry of plasma fire was coming in, and her tactical navigation assist tied itself into knots, trying to avoid the deadly cluster. Three options appeared simultaneously, but Carrol hadn't the time to choose, only to react. She slammed her joystick forward and felt her stomach rise into her throat as her fighter dove, then corkscrewed in the maneuver the assist threw her into to avoid even more plasma fire.

Suddenly, everything around her warped sickeningly, like space was circling a drain. It tore past, tight in a horrible, streaking circle if it was too close and flung out in random direction if it was far enough away to escape. Plasma bolts refracted wildly, chaotically changing course.

Carrol's fighter was yanked sharply toward it as it came past. She was whipped to the side, then snapped back like a rubber band, which flung her fighter out of control. All Carrol could do was hold onto the wildly bucking joystick as the craft spun off in a new direction. It took a long moment of fighting her joystick and the navigation assist to steady the craft. It took her an even longer moment to realize what had just happened.

It had been a gravitic warhead. The enemy had just shot a mini black hole at her. Decent people didn't use such weapons. The evidence that the Paragon weren't decent had just tried to suck her in and crush her to death.

It had fucked with her tactical and navigation controls as well as her perception of space and time. She had no idea how long she'd been out of it, but from where she was and what was dead ahead of her, she figured it had been a couple of seconds.

She was close now. The cruiser loomed like a behemoth. She hadn't expected it to be so large or so bright. It shone in the light reflected from Jupiter, a majestic golden hue. Where *Glory* was boxy and utilitarian, the Paragon ship was sharp, like a set of knives; three of them connected at the rear by a massive propulsion array. That was her target.

But those evasive maneuvers had her coming in too high for a direct run at the engines. Either that or the cruiser had had enough time to start a roll and had pitched upward relative to her attack vector, bow rising and stern falling. From the cruiser's movement, she could see it was a combination of the two.

"FUCK!" No other word properly articulated how she felt.

There was no time to slow and adjust. It would either

make her a sitting duck for the enemy's defensive weapons, or she'd smash into the Paragon ship. She strafed what was directly ahead of her with her plasma cannons to eliminate as much anti-spacecraft fire as possible to help with a second run—if any of them survived for a second pass. She fired her warheads, desperately hoping the AI systems could guide them to their intended targets despite the less-than-ideal angle.

Whoosh-whoosh-whooshwhoosh.

They were away.

Carrol yanked back on her joystick and pulled up at the very last second. She screamed past the cruiser within meters of its gold-plated hull. She dared to flick a look at her tactical display to watch her missiles arc out from behind her, plasma trails lighting their path, seeking their pre-determined targets on the cruiser's main engines. Carrol prayed that they'd hit.

The first one slammed into a harmless part of the hull, exhaust ports protruding on the starboard side of the ship, not even close to the rear. The next two arced too far out, too slow, and were shot down by expert counterbattery fire guided by the rear plasma cannons. Fired by a living being, or were they computer controlled? There were those who believed the Paragon to be a race of AIs, but Carrol didn't anymore. Not after what they did with the last missile.

Rather than destroy it outright, with a burst of guiding cannon fire, they cornered and drove one of Carrol's fellow Delta Wing fighters right into it. There was a brilliant flare, out of which the fighter spun end over end, on fire and out of control. For a brief second, it looked as though the fighter might make it to the rear of the cruiser and impact there, or at least cause some damage in its death, but alas, that was not to be. It flew into one of the large engine's plasma trails and exploded again, vaporizing this time. Nothing was left, not even smoke.

Carrol watched with sinking horror as her fellow fighters' missiles were easily sniped by cannon fire or exploded harmlessly one by one on the cruiser's armored sections as it spun away from harm.

Not a single warhead hit its target.

A plasma bolt clipped the rear of her fighter, which brought her attention back to a fresh new horror: *surviving* the first run to make a second. Streaking away from the cruiser's anti-spacecraft fire made it easier to avoid, but that hope was quickly dashed, as were any thoughts of turning to take another shot at those engines.

The Paragon fighters had arrived. They outnumbered Carrol and the remainder of her squadron ten to one, and they were dead ahead, which meant her people were flanked.

There would be no second run, she realized. No, barring a miracle, they were going to die. All of them.

She was going to die.

The Paragon opened fire and Carrol did the same, fighting for one more second life and then another after that.

CHAPTER TWENTY-FOUR

"WEAPONS AWAY!"

The cruiser was already turning broadside to meet them. It was the advantage of getting off the first shot—a larger target. Missiles were smart weapons. Maneuvers such as turning bow-forward to minimize the dead-ahead surface area facing a foe weren't effective against a missile that could turn to hit wherever it needed to, but missiles were only half of a warship's arsenal. The other half were plasma cannons, which were not guidable, and what part of your ship faced the other was a huge deal.

The Paragon, apparently, were willing to take a hit to target their full firepower against the incoming *Glory*. That was what Drake had counted on them doing.

The *Glory's* plasma fire hit first, sending flames, plumes of superheated gas, and debris exploding off the cruiser's rear starboard side. The missiles struck less than a second later, doing more of the same. The combined firepower whited out their sensors for one glorious moment and made the cumulative damage look much more impressive than it likely was.

A cheer went up across the command deck.

Drake tempered his own response. They'd struck a blow, yes, but only one.

"*Olympia* is away!" Oh called from where he hovered over the tactical and navigation stations.

There was another cheer.

Then the whited-out sensors regained their view of the cruiser, and the cheers petered out. She had finished turning broadside, and although there were craters along her hull and glittering debris floating away from her thanks to *Glory's* opening salvo, she was still very much intact. Her cannons sparkled to life; a hundred of them dotting her golden hull in strips of ten and twenty lit up like jewels. Missiles burst forth first, followed by waves of plasma fire. They streaked through space between the two ships, lighting up the darkness with hellfire.

"Countermeasures!" Oh shouted into the ears of the tactical crewmen.

The deck shuddered as a hundred projectiles hurtled from their port side. Invisible, they streaked several kilometers from the ship, then popped open in near-perfect synchronization and spread millions of gravity-plated plasma-loaded spheres across an area four times the size of *Glory*. It was a net of matter, gravity, and energy. A wall into which the incoming fire from the Paragon cruiser would crash well before it reached the ship.

"Shall I turn head-on?" Oh called to the captain once the countermeasure salvo was away. He thought that if anything got through, that would give the Paragon cruiser less of a chance to get lucky. It was a standard evasive action, even with countermeasures deployed, and a wise one.

After a look at the Paragon cruiser, however, Drake shook him off vehemently. No. He had a plan.

The Paragon volley slammed into their countermeasures with an explosive force in the hundreds of megatons. Plasma hit first, which ignited the network of mass. This, in turn, ignited the missiles that followed a second later, then the following waves of plasma cannon fire. If one thought the radiation and light burst from *Glory's* first salvo hitting home on the Paragon cruiser was toe-curling, this would have blown their socks clean off, and the effect was much longer-lasting this time. Everyone in several hundred cubic kilometers was effectively blinded.

Exactly what Drake had been counting on.

"Tactical, fire second salvo!" he shouted as a few stray shots from the Paragon struck home. He pitched forward and had to hold onto the command console to keep from hitting the deck. Nothing too bad, though. The countermeasures had held up. Now, to counterpunch.

"I can't see anything!" the tactical officer cried out in response.

"Neither can they!"

The deck shuddered again a moment later from their port-side cannons and launchers once again emptying their arsenal. This was why Drake had ordered Oh to keep them from turning into an evasive position. Staying broadside meant they could pour it on for a second shot. Maybe cause critical damage before the Paragon saw the incoming. That, combined with the damage Carrol and her squadron should have inflicted by now with their bombing run on the cruiser's engines, might let them disable the ship and get the hell out with their hides intact. It might actually work.

"Several direct hits!" Oh called triumphantly several excruciating seconds later, scanning the cruiser the instant the sensors came back online. They'd also stayed broadside, and many of their offensive weapons clusters located there were now on fire. Then he saw what the sensors were showing him and snapped a desperate look at Drake.

He'd seen it, too: dozens of energy signatures incoming. The bastards had done the same thing and fired through the sensor whiteout. *Glory* was a sitting duck.

"Y-axis hard to starboard. *Roll roll ROLL!*"

The command was shouted without thought, like the reflexes of a boxer. There was no time to launch more countermeasures. The volley would be upon them in seconds. It was going to hit. There was no stopping that, but *Glory* had more armor on her underside and fewer vital systems.

The deck pitched violently when, as ordered, the ship rolled to the right. The gravity systems couldn't keep up. They likely wouldn't have, even if they'd been working at full efficiency. Anything that wasn't bolted down went sliding, which included Captain Drake. He grabbed a side console's chair leg to save himself from crashing into the bulkhead just in time for the command deck to explode in a shower of sparks.

The Paragon barrage hit home in a bone-shattering fashion. Drake was torn from his handhold and slammed into the bulkhead. Gravity returned to normal a split second later, which indicated they were no longer executing their roll maneuver, and Drake next slammed onto the textured grating, hammering his shoulder against the metal. A spark surged through his body from the injury, letting him know he was alive but hurt. The pain continued unabated, like a plasma fire burned inside his shoulder socket.

It wasn't the only thing burning on the command deck. Several consoles were on fire. In front of Tactical, a crewman was scrambling to get away from a screen that was sending sparks streaking toward him. Another of the crew, a young woman, was being pummeled furiously by a fellow crewman, her uniform sleeve on fire. An officer at Navigation was doing the same to his cluster of controls to put the fire out.

Drake, grunting with the effort, pushed to his feet and staggered back to the command console. Oh was already there. Drake must have been wearing his pain in his expression because the first officer asked him if he needed a medic.

"Not for me," he grumbled, straightening and gesturing with his head toward the more severely injured. He took in the various states of panic and ongoing damage response.

XO nodded and called into his headset for the appropriate fire and medical teams to be dispatched. He then rattled off a report for the rest of the ship.

"We have fires on decks twenty through twenty-five, port sections one through three. Several sections on twenty-five are not responding at all. We can vent the lowest decks to extinguish the fire. Dispatching crews to twenty and twenty-one along midship. Heavy casualties there, sir."

Drake nodded gravely at the verbal confirmation of what he had seen on the holographic display of the *Glory*. It highlighted several areas with oranges and reds to indicate fire and other forms of radiation damage, blue for areas that were not reporting atmosphere. The brighter and more saturated the color, the more severe the damage. He tried and failed not to think of the young men and women caught in those sections.

Tactically, it could have been worse. Their roll had caught most of the Paragon's fire on the largely empty sections in the lower decks, but it hadn't been perfect. They'd been struck in several of their cargo and hangar bays along the lower port side. The roll hadn't quite been completed when the plasma and missiles had hit home. Several of their lower cannon turrets and missile launchers had also taken direct hits, expanding the damage. Their hull was cracking in those areas, lit up in the most dazzling of the oranges. They could not take another hit in that area without risking losing the whole ship.

Drake swiped away the damage report in favor of a larger tactical view of them and the Paragon ship and glared at it.

The cruiser appeared to be mostly undamaged.

Of course, they were. The Paragon had never lost their stomach for battle like the Fleet had, and now they knew the *Glory* had it too. The edge. The fire. There would be no more easy shots such as their first or even their second. Whoever was in command on that alien ship was awake now. Awake was deadly.

The cruiser was head-on with them, steaming toward them and closing the gap between the two ships, going for the kill. It was endgame from this point forward. Drake wondered if he had any chess pieces left.

"Ready starboard weapons and countermeasures," he instructed Oh, wiping sweat from his brow.

Oh shook his head. There were no more countermeasures and pathetically few weapons.

"What about the Delta Wing squadron?" he asked, but before Oh responded, he knew what the answer was going to be from how fast the Paragon cruiser was approaching. She had full propulsion. The fighters and their bombing run had been ineffective. Those engines burned at one hundred percent.

Oh pointed at a clusterfuck of plasma fire and small spacecraft aft of the cruiser. The holographic display lit them up like a swarm of fireflies like it had when they'd surrounded the *Olympia* what felt like hours ago. "They're engaged in dogfighting with the Paragon fighters. Numbers are ten to one. Heavy losses."

Damn. They weren't going to make it either.

It had been close.

At least, it had felt that way. Maybe it hadn't been. Maybe he'd been more bullish on their chances than reality suggested, but at least they'd landed a couple of punches. *Real* punches. The starboard side of the Paragon cruiser was fucked up. It was the only reason *Glory* was still intact. *Olympia*, too, wherever in the hell she'd gotten off to. Maybe she'd be okay. Maybe that would make all this worth it. The end. Because the end was coming fast. They'd made the Paragon turn, made them take *Glory* seriously, or as seriously as you would take a fly that you were about to swat.

"Helm," Drake called, straightening and radiating as much gallows defiance as he could muster. "Put us head-on with the Paragon cruiser, and Tactical, with whatever plasma and guided fire you don't need for defense, pepper their damned bridge. It's right up on top of that tri-hull, and I'm sending the schematics to you, now."

It wouldn't work; Drake knew that. The arrogant bastards put their command deck in the open as a taunt, but it was heavily shielded. In the heat of battle, one you thought you could win, you'd never waste time or munitions on it. But when the battle was effectively over and you wanted to spit in their eye, fire away. Screw 'em. And maybe they'd get lucky.

"Sir!" a charred face at the navigation consoles called. A young man. Drake recognized him from the communications team. He was filling in. "We have another vessel incoming!"

Oh flashed it onto their tactical console, and Drake

switched it to visual since nothing on the readout helped identify the ship. The whole command deck cheered when they recognized who it was.

Olympia.

Drake was inclined to join them and nearly did until he noticed what was streaming from her engines. Plasma, tons of it. It belched from the entire propulsion assembly. The rest of the ship was on fire as well. The cheers turned into horrified cries and mournful groans. She wasn't swooping in to save them at the last second. For LeVoit to redeem himself for being an asshole and a horrible tactician and join the *Glory* in dispatching this Paragon interloper back to whatever hell gods they believed in. No, from her wildly erratic flight path, she'd been out of control for a long time, rudderless and without direction. She'd found her way back into the fray by accident, her dying throes delivering what training could not—a lucky strike.

She fell like a meteor, streaking between the two ships. There was a brilliant flare from her rear by the power core and a collective gasp from the crew.

Everything went white.

Everywhere.

The visual display was sometimes too accurate and too late to react to changes in light intensity. Drake was blinded and stumbled to grab the console. A shockwave of superheated gas slammed into the *Glory*. It brought a fresh round of cries from the crew, the rending of metal and plastiform, and a shower of sparks from consoles and conduits that could not handle the surge of power and movement.

When it was over, the deck was thick with smoke and bathed in red from the remaining controls with power to them. The command console was one of them, and Drake pulled himself off the deck, desperate to see what had happened.

Several sobs told him the crew could see that *Olympia* was gone. An irradiated debris field was all that was left of the once-mighty ship, the crown jewel of the new Fleet, the flagship for an era of peace. Drake mourned with his crew. Even assholes didn't deserve such a death.

Oh was still down on the deck, coughing violently from the smoke that hung in the air. Drake hauled him to his feet, checking the officer for obvious injuries. There was a cut across the bridge of his nose, but Oh pushed him away. "Fine, sir," he said, falling into another coughing fit. "Just getting my wind," he finished when the coughing had subsided.

The tactical display showed them they had been lucky. *Olympia* had been far enough from them that they'd been spared the worst damage from her destruction. Sensors were still having a hard time with much beyond the ship—a weapons volley whiteout was hard to contend with, but it was nothing compared to the radiation and matter debris an exploding warship threw out—but their internal systems were all registering fine for the most part. Even the weak sections of the lower, aft port-side hadn't budged.

They had been lucky after all. Damn lucky, as difficult as that was to believe. But any fight they survived was a good and lucky day.

And even more fortunate, the Paragon hadn't been.

Through patchy sensor readings and patchy visual confirmations thick with static, Drake could see that the Paragon cruiser was no longer under propulsion. It drifted on a ballistic trajectory through the debris field. They'd been too close to the explosion. *Olympia* had provided the knockout blow they'd been hoping for, the blow they'd desperately needed. Drake gave her a silent prayer of thanks.

"What are your orders, Captain?" Oh rasped next to him.

Bloodlust demanded that *Glory* close on that ship and pummel her into oblivion to avenge the sacrifice of their fallen comrades, whether they had the weapons to do it or not.

A warning blinked on the holographic display, a new one that stood out from the mind-numbing march of warnings that had filled his every glance since they'd left the space dock. Drake had to zoom out the three-dimensional image to see what it was.

Two more Paragon cruisers were closing on their position, just minutes away. The explosion had caught their attention.

"Propulsion status?" Drake asked his first officer, surprised to find that his voice too was raspy and hoarse. He blamed the smoke, though it was probably exhaustion.

"Online." He gave a weary, humorless smile. "Fredrickson is refusing to answer me at the moment, but last report was that we've still got our thirty-five percent."

Drake nodded. "Is the Paragon jamming signal still active on the short-range?"

"No, sir, though it's still spotty through the radiation."

"Send the recall signal to our fighters. We'll wait for them as long as we can, then get us the hell out of here. All available speed."

"Aye, sir."

CHAPTER TWENTY-FIVE

CARROL WASN'T sure how long she'd been drifting before she felt safe enough to start making repairs, but it was long enough to get cold. Really cold.

The dogfight with the Paragon squadron hadn't been much of a battle. Not for Carrol, anyway, or her squad. It had been a slaughter. The Paragon were formidable. Where Carrol was clumsy with her craft, still getting used to its controls after so much time since training—and so little training on manual—the Paragon were practiced to the point of precision. That disparity had been dead obvious when the Delta Wings had engaged them one on one. Every slow move, every overcorrection, every missed shot had been punished mercilessly. Carrol had watched as her fellow Delta Wings were carved up like a holiday roast.

In the end, clumsiness had saved Carrol. She'd flooded her engines during a desperate evasive move, done the very thing she'd warned her pilots against, and in the heat of battle. It should have been a fatal mistake, but through pure, miraculous fate, the Paragon fighter that had been hot on her tail had been distracted by another Delta Wing just as

Carrol had choked the life out of her propulsion. She'd lost power, and the enemy fighter had been unable to reacquire her after the rapid deceleration or assumed she'd been destroyed and had gone off after someone else.

Then *Olympia* had appeared and exploded.

Carrol had mourned the ship's loss and the loss of everything it represented, but she made no mistake: the destruction of the Earth Fleet's shining new flagship had been an incredible stroke of fortune. The Paragon cruiser had been almost directly in its path. It had taken the brunt of the massive explosion and the billions of pieces of shrapnel that had spun and streaked off in its aftermath. That had left it disabled and bleeding, vulnerable to attack. Had the *Glory* a full normal complement of weapons, Carrol was sure she would have destroyed the Paragon cruiser. A killing blow. The Paragon fighters didn't know about *Glory's* deficiencies; didn't know that she was nearly useless for practical purposes. So, the Paragon had raced away from the mop-up portion of their slaughter to protect their mothership, leaving Carrol and anyone else alive in her squadron to float into the radioactive debris, effectively hiding from the universe.

Glory issued a recall order. Carrol saw a handful of plasma plumes light up and go streaking after her, fellow Delta Wings who had the propulsion to get back to the barn. She hoped they made it, though the Paragon were still between them and home, and Carrol wouldn't have risked it even if her engines were working. Which they weren't. Turned out it was lucky she'd choked her engines; they were leaking drive fuel something fierce, and her maneuvering assembly was fried. It would have to be repaired, but not with the Paragon still out there.

That *Glory* was alive and intact enough to issue a recall

order was a relief. Carrol knew a tactical withdrawal was the only move left to them whether they were able to gather their fighters or not. She was sure they waited as long as they could. She simply celebrated that they were still standing, against all odds and reason and despite Glory taking on an intact Paragon cruiser, a maneuver she should not have survived but had. Maybe Glory was not captained by a madman or a ruthless killer bent on the demise of his crew. Maybe he was the best in the Fleet, and others couldn't live with that.

Still, it was a cold pain to be left behind. Left to float in the darkness.

More Paragon ships came. Giant, gleaming behemoths.

Carrol couldn't believe how big they were up close, and they got *very* close. So close she thought they'd spotted her. They hadn't. Closer still, and Carrol thought they were going to crush her, a dinghy rolled over by a man 'o war. They didn't. Their hulls were so shiny, so glaring, that they were impossible to look at in direct light, but in the shadows, they were beautiful. Hulls smooth, lines sharp and perfectly angled, and their movements clean and choreographed. Carrol had seen diagrams of Paragon ships, of course. Holoimages. Seen recordings of battles and skirmishes from the last Great War. She knew the Paragon built their ships like temples, monuments to their superiority. Although they were obsessed with effectiveness, form followed function to intimidate anyone who dared stand against them.

Paragon ships made a statement. It was rooted in their very culture, a precept by which they governed themselves and treated the rest of life in the galaxy. It was a religious fervor they had pledged to set aside in their talks with Earth, a higher purpose they were going to relinquish in the name of peace. *We are superior. You are inferior, and we will destroy you for that.* Carrol could see, hear, and feel that message. She could believe it, too. She believed that it had all been a lie.

The ships glided past to their fallen comrade, the damaged cruiser. After a while, they streaked off in the direction *Glory* had gone. After a bit longer, the damaged cruiser lit its engines again and followed them, presumably to hunt *Glory* down. Make her pay for the insolence of what she'd done to them and that she'd dared to challenge their superiority. She wondered if they'd succeed in their task or if Drake would manage to beat the odds again, as he had here.

What followed was the cold. With her main propulsion system down, her fighter had no power. Not to move, not to fight, and not for the heating system. Carrol's flight suit had internal life support systems. Otherwise, she'd have frozen to death quickly. But as robust as flight suit's life support was, it only lasted so long—a couple hours, maybe—so Carrol had modulated that. Turned it down to half-power, which meant it got damn cold damn fast.

It had been quiet for a while. Just Carrol, the floating debris of the battle, and the swirling thoughts of how she'd gotten into all this. To go down that path was to be sucked into a vortex of cause, effect, coincidence, shock, and mind-numbing circumstances that she'd probably never get off, so she turned that part of her brain off and resolved to get working on her fighter. It was now or never.

As handy as her flight suit was for minimal life support and things like heat and waste extraction—to hell with that; she wasn't pissing in no damn flight suit and sitting in it in a firefight, she would *hold* it—it was not a full-blown EV suit. She couldn't seal in an atmosphere and go outside to fix what needed fixing to get power back up and running. That left her with few options.

One was the articulating servo arm. It was battery-powered, thank the stars, designed to allow the fighter to reach out and grab stuff. In the absence of the holocams arrayed around her fighter, she could see quite a bit out of the cockpit bubble and in the network of old-school, fly-by-wire mirrors everyone in the Academy *hated* using because they were never positioned in the way a pilot needed them to be. Technically, they worked in a foolproof way that powered forms of vision never could.

Carrol was not proficient with the servo arm, not by a long shot. She nearly blew herself up on several occasions using the little cutting torch it came with, but one by one, she cannibalized sections of her Delta Wing's outer hull plating, the sections where she knew there weren't any vital systems underneath, and moved those to the leaking parts of the fighter. The cutting torch had to double as a welding flame, which was also tricky, but after a few test runs on non-essential sections, she got the hang of it well enough to give it a try.

Excruciatingly slowly, it worked. Carrol had to contort herself in her cockpit, and she felt like she was going to break her back, legs, and every tiny vertebra in her neck, but it worked. She fastened what, if everything went well, was the last patch and let go of the robotic controls to flex her cramping hands. Her fighter was now a patchwork of holes. If she needed to fly in atmosphere, the ship would come apart. Her wings were Swiss cheese, but she didn't need wings in space. All that could go wrong now was that her patch jobs weren't good enough, that she'd left holes in the fuel supply lines—and was unable to see them because, well, she couldn't really see *anything*—and when she pressed the ignition starter on her control board, the fighter would blow up and her along with it.

No biggie.

The surrounding death and destruction inclined her to be cavalier about it. She should have been dead five thousand times over in the last couple of hours, but she wasn't. Not yet. She realized she didn't want to die; she wanted to survive. Desperately. And out there, she could feel it in her bones that *Glory* was trying to do the same, as were any number of human ships and stations. Hell, even Earth. Fighting against the apocalypse.

She hadn't thought of that word before then.

Apocalypse. The end of everything.

She pushed the thought from her mind. Surely, this wasn't it. Surely, out there somewhere, the Fleet was making a stand. They'd been caught with their pants down, but they'd respond. They'd survive, just like she had, through luck, through tactics; however they could. Which was what she needed to do to: survive.

She pushed the ignition button.

It somehow threw out her back, reaching for it. Of course. After all that twisting and turning and cramping, reaching for a damn button was the move that pushed her over the edge. But feeling that twinge of pain let her know she was still alive.

And so was her fighter. Power thrummed through the fuselage. The joystick tingled between her legs, alive, ready for her gentle touch. The control board lit up, and there was a burst of static in her helmet that made her wince until she turned it down. She'd left it on full-blast from the battle. She was fortunate, however, that she didn't shut it off.

A quiet voice came through, laced with static. "Commander, that you?"

"Zed?" Carrol could hardly believe it.

"I thought I saw you moving out there, but I couldn't be sure."

"I was leaking inert plasma. Had to cannibalize my hull plating to patch it up."

"Servo arm?"

"Yup. That thing fucking sucks."

"Wilson is doing the same, though his torch keeps cutting out on him."

Carrol's heart nearly leapt out of her chest at that. "You mean, there are more of us?" Relief nearly overwhelmed her, and she had to swallow several times to find her voice again. "How many?" she rasped.

"You, me, Wilson, Jiri, Okongwe, and Jackson, though she can't seem to get her radio working." Zed sounded like he was struggling through some emotions of his own, but it was hard to tell over the tinny sound of the distortion-thick radio. "We've been flashing running lights at her—Jackson, that is—and she says she can fly once the rest of us are up and running. Jiri says he had a good view of the course *Glory* set, so we can follow, maybe even find her."

Six of them, plus those fighters who'd already returned to *Glory*. It was much more than Carrol had allowed herself to hope. Not all of them had been lost. Many, but not all. It wasn't over. Humanity had survived to fight another day.

"Excellent news, Lieutenant," she said, throttling her emotions to put on her commander hat once more. It wasn't just a battle for her life. It was time for her to save her people like Captain Drake had done with the crew of *Glory*. "Excellent."

Zed's voice darkened. "There is, uh, something you should see, though, Commander."

"Oh?"

"We've been drifting toward the Gateway this whole time. It was Jiri who figured out about ten minutes ago or so that we were close enough to pick up visual transmissions over the short-range from there, and, well, you should see for yourself, Eunice."

Carrol would have cringed at the use of her first name, particularly over an open channel to the rest of her subordinates, but the tone of Zed's voice pushed that far from her mind. She reached forward through sharp back pain and flicked on the cockpit's holographic display, tuning it to the short-range and searching for the frequency Zed was referring to. It took her breath away when she finally found it.

It was a view of the Gateway from a video drone that recorded with a slight bobbing motion present in the framing. Too small, perhaps, for the Paragon to realize it was out there. Carrol doubted they wanted anyone to see what she was seeing because if there was any doubt about their intentions in the Earth system before, the moment one saw this, those doubts were dashed.

It was larger than a ship. Larger than any structure Carrol had ever seen. It barely fit through the Jupiter Gateway, filling it, which meant it was several orders of magnitude larger than the ring. There couldn't be more than a few dozen meters on any side of it as it squeezed through the swirling energy field and the massive ring structure that surrounded it. Dozens upon dozens of tow ships with thick physical cables and what looked like energy tethers pulled it through slowly, carefully, and their job was nearly done.

It chilled Carrol to her core to look at the thing. It was a half-dome on top, almost perfectly matching the curve of Jupiter Gateway, as though it had been made to fit through it. The half-dome gave way to a spout below, like if a jellyfish had twisted its tentacles into one thick, tapering stock.

That stock ended in a circular opening large enough to engulf *Glory* or one of the Paragon cruisers three or four times over, and it had a round opening that was unmistakable. A massive cannon.

The thing was a weapon, a moon-sized weapon. Even though she'd never seen anything like it in the recorded history of the galaxy, Carrol knew what it was meant to do.

It was a planet-killer.

"My God," she murmured, not sure what else she could say.

"What do we do?" Zed asked, horror in his voice.

"We need to get back to *Glory*."

SATURN

Terran Federation Space

CHAPTER TWENTY-SIX

"CAPTAIN, WE HAVE A NEW PROBLEM."

Oh punched in a new view on the command console. The display had reverted to a two-dimensional image displaying on the surface of the table rather than the three-dimensional holograms that normally floated above it. Those emitters had been cannibalized to restore function to other displays and controls on the command deck. The patchwork repairs had been hasty but critical in getting the ship to minimal operational capability. Crews were hard at work on the rest, but nearly a third of the stations in Navigation, Tactical, and Communications were still charred and silent.

Drake didn't mind the downgrade of the console. The two-dimensional display was what he'd had for the majority of his command back in the day. The holographic system had been new in the later years.

Except in instances like this one. A fully operational console would have shown him what he needed to know instantly, likely before Oh needed to come to him.

"We're leaking drive plasma." Oh pointed at a vibrant

trail behind a crude eight-bit representation of the *Glory*. "A lot of it."

Drake frowned. "How? Are we in danger of losing propulsion?"

"Unknown, and unknown. Engineering is looking into it."

Drake contemplated his first officer's exasperation. Surely that couldn't be the full report. According to the numbers, the entire ship was about to explode without warning.

All Oh could do was shrug. "Fredrickson hasn't been answering my calls since the issue came up, sir."

"Okay." Drake bit off a totally justified string of expletives and tried to think of the next logical question. "The Paragon?" he started, but Oh was already shaking his head in answer. He changed the view to show the three cruisers approaching from behind.

"Closing. They've undoubtedly picked up the plasma trail."

After leaving the battle site, Drake had ordered Helm to get them clear of the Jupiter Complex and the inner planets with all available speed. He'd hoped that if they could get far away from any other major or minor Fleet facilities, maybe, just maybe, they'd be left alone by the Paragon fleet. They could sneak into the outer system, where the Neptune Armory was waiting for them.

Drake clung to their orders. Jack had had a *reason* for sending them out there, and something was waiting that might make a difference. The old man had been right about too much for Drake to discount him. It could have been folly, but Drake's gut told him otherwise.

Except they hadn't made it out yet. The Jupiter Complex was massive, the hub of the fleet. It extended well past the planet, and stretched back toward the asteroid belt with a secondary station out as far as Saturn, which had numerous facilities on the surface and its moons. It took a fully-powered ship, which *Glory* was not, hours to leave it behind. They were just approaching Jupiter's ringed gas-giant sibling, chugging along at their top speed. The Paragon ships had seen them and were closing the distance.

"Time to intercept?" Drake asked, searching through his head for options.

"Nineteen minutes with the lead ship."

Goddamn.

"Navigation," Drake called, urgently and systematically scanning their surrounding area. "What is our current distance to...Titan?"

"Titan is eleven minutes away at current thrust, Captain," a young woman answered. Crewman Foley. He recognized her vibrant red hair. She had been a comms engineer before. Now she was a navigator.

Drake didn't second-guess her. "And the old Selk mining facility? How far are we from that in minutes, Crewman?"

"The what?" She'd turned to look at him. A confused frown creased her forehead.

"It'll be on your charts," he said, and pointed at her screen to impart the urgency of getting an answer.

She turned back to her readouts to check, and after finding the facility to which Drake was referring and doing the math, she had the answer Drake was hoping for. "Seventeen minutes. But that's because it's on the far side of the moon, sir. There's a weapons platform at B-75-Sigma dead ahead that we can reach in half the time."

The mood on the command deck was tense again. Not that there had been a single moment in the past few hours that had been relaxed, but everyone knew what it meant that the Paragon cruisers were closing. They hung on Drake's interaction with Foley like it was a lifeline, desperately waiting to hear what he was going to do.

If they were going to make it.

Drake calmly shook his head. "Selk will do nicely, Ms. Foley. Set a course, Helm. All the speed we have, please."

Helm was manned by a young male enlisted with a crewcut so high and tight he looked fresh out of boot camp. Shannahan was his name—Drake was getting all of them down, he was pleased to realize—gave an "Aye-aye, sir," and *Glory* began to turn toward the largest of Saturn's moons, and its cloudiest.

Oh was by his side, silently questioning Drake's plan. However, he kept it to himself out of superstition. It was bad luck to speak aloud something that would only work on faith and good luck on board a ship held together with spit and baling wire and duct tape.

Visual monitors over the helm stations showed the pea-soup brown of Titan's horizon looming ahead of them. *Glory* rode the gravitational curve to the far side of the planet. Drake could tell Oh was starting to piece it together when they lost direct sensor contact with the trailing Paragon cruisers, which meant the enemy no longer had direct sensor contact on them, either.

Drake only had eyes for what was ahead. "Readings on the Selk mine?" he asked Crewman Foley.

"Quiet from what I can see, sir, but it's not much. We won't get a full reading 'til we're down below the cloud cover."

Excellent. Hopefully.

"Take us down, Mr. Shannahan." He turned to XO. "Clear all personnel from the hangar bays and holds with exterior egress, and prepare all the warheads we have left for remote detonation."

Oh raised an eyebrow but complied with a flick of his headset, taking a few steps away from his captain so as not to be a distraction. It wasn't necessary, the deference, but it was the mark of a true professional. Oh was an officer in the classic sense. Anything and everything he could do to support his captain, to make his command easier, he would do. He'd pull out a damn chair for him to sit if he had the opportunity. Sometimes it was overboard. Archaic. It harkened back to the days when only lords were officers, the enlisted were of the peasant class, and never the two inter-mingled.

Mostly, it was endearing. Oh was the finest officer Drake had ever served with. It killed him, he realized, that the Fleet had, after all these years of loyalty, not given him a ship of his own.

Glory shook as they entered the atmosphere, and Drake refocused on the task at hand. "Tactical, eyes up for poten-tial targets."

The Selk crater on Titan had once been a furious hub of activity, as it had been a massive and well-producing mineral mine in the old days—days that pre-dated even Drake's time in the Fleet. By the time he had the chance or rather, the duty, it was not a treat to visit the grimy, mud-filled pit. The mine was in the advanced stages of winding down its usefulness. But in its heyday, beneath the freezing cold of liquid methane rain, it had produced fifty to seventy-five percent of the Fleet's raw materials, from iron and nickel to the rarer, more specialized engine core compo-nents like platinum, plutonium, and diamonds. It had been a dreary place even back then, let alone what it must be now, forty years after being decommissioned. A silent, empty hole.

At least, that was what Drake was hoping for.

The shaking intensified as the atmosphere thickened. The tense mood on the command deck thickened along with it. The visual readouts over the helm turned from dirty, swirling brown to orange as the lumbering ship produced friction flames toward her front and then dissolved into static. The other sensors shouldn't have been having an issue, and Drake called for an update. Could they see anything yet? The answer was negative. That made even Drake nervous.

The rumbling tapered off as their flight path leveled and slowed. A report came from Navigation at almost the same instant.

"Nearing Selk crater. No sign of any other ships, sir. No nothing."

Comms confirmed. They were getting no signals from the abandoned mine.

Drake breathed a small sigh of relief. It was the first of several he was hoping to let out in the next critical minutes.

"Commander," he said to Oh, "how's that plasma leak?"

"Raging, sir, and dispersing even less in these clouds. Nothing yet from Fredrickson."

"Excellent." That reaction got another raised eyebrow from Oh. Drake pushed on. "Lower all semipermeable energy fields on the hangar bays, and open all cargo bay egresses." He raised his voice over to the internal systems officer, Ensign Hyde. Or was it Ryder? Damn. No time to double-check. "Fire off all topside escape pods, Ensign."

"Sir?" he said, caught off-guard.

"Now, Ensign!" Oh barked. The first officer had put the

rest of the plan together. The look on his face said, "It'll be insane if it works."

There was a whooshing sound as several of the escape pods surrounding the command deck were propelled along magnetic rails up and out the top of the ship. On the command console, Drake saw them explode out and away from their flight path, automatically detecting the gravity and atmosphere around them as they began to arc down toward the surface of Titan and deploy their built-in chutes. On the visual screens showing the sides and below the ship, Drake could see several tons of crates, waste, equipment, and other objects pouring out as well, falling not-so-gracefully to the surface below like the pods. Some of the falling objects were just stuff: food, beds, and equipment they might use or need. When it laid a swath of debris behind them, Drake was hopeful that his plan might work.

"Nearing the mining facility," Foley reported.

"Slowing to approach," Shannahan added.

Drake called up a tactical view of the last leg of their flight path and touched several points along it. Their plasma wake, which stuck together densely within the atmosphere, embracing it tightly to keep it from dispersing, was vibrant. It lit up their flight path in highlighter yellow. "Here, here, here, here, and here," he said to his first officer. "Deploy warheads."

Oh nodded.

"Tactical," Drake called. "Updated time to arrival of the first Paragon cruiser?"

"Five minutes, sir, based on last estimates. They should be entering Titan's atmosphere now."

This was cutting it close, but they should have time. The Paragon being around for the fireworks might help their cause.

"Cut propulsion to station-keeping. Navigation..." Drake's voice trailed off, and he strode over to Foley's station rather than bark across the room. This way, he could show her where they were going. "Call up a map of the facility, please," he said once he reached her. Nervously, she did. Her hands were shaking. Maps of the giant mine came up on the screen. It was set in the middle of a massive crater that had been mined several thousand meters deep. They were near the top of that manmade hole, which descended into darkness. Drake wasn't taking them down there, however. At least, not all the way.

To go down there was certain death since there was no cover for anything dropped from above. But from the one and only time he'd visited this place a lifetime ago, he knew there were myriad lateral tunnels that branched off from the main pit, and if he remembered correctly, there was one main exit the size of a city—a cavern, not manmade. A giant prehistoric tube from a once-massive ice volcano unearthed by whatever meteor had created the Selk crater.

"There!" he exclaimed, pointing at the schematic when it showed him what he was looking for. "What's the clearance on that opening?"

Foley gulped, again doing quick math that would either save or doom them. "Dead center, we'd have a hundred meters on all sides."

Drake shot a look at Shannahan. "Can you make that work, Crewman?"

"Fuck, yes, sir." Shannahan headed for it. If he was nervous, which Drake knew was the case, he wasn't showing it. Good man.

"Back us in," Drake ordered as he rushed to the command console. "Make it easy for us to blast back out of here."

Oh was waiting for him, sweating as if he were standing in a sauna. "Some of the pods are still airborne, sir," he said, pointing at the escape pods in their wake.

Drake shook off the concern. "Doesn't matter. Not when those warheads blow." Oh nodded and wiped his brow. "They in place?"

Oh nodded again.

A scraping sound snapped their attention to the helm, then to the sensor display of them entering the cavern.

"Just an outcropping!" Shannahan shouted, not taking his eyes off his controls. Holographic wireframe outlines of the opening surrounded him in three dimensions. What had been huge in Drake's memory, and what was indeed enormous from the point of view of a person in an EV suit, was now small, barely *Glory*-sized. They were flying a warship into a fucking cave.

But Shannahan was right. All they'd run into was a stalactite just long enough to protrude into their entry space. The helmsman had them dead center.

"Tactical?"

"Minutes, sir. I don't see them on visual."

It was going to be close. Too close.

"In!" Shannahan yelled, dropping his controls with a massive release that left him limp in his chair and drenched with sweat.

"Ignite warheads!" Oh shouted.

"Cut engines," Drake overlapped. "Cut all power! Lights, everything except station-keeping thrusters. Don't crash us into that wall!"

Nobody on the command deck questioned him. There was only action, nearly instantaneous. With a great shudder and a sigh, *Glory* went to sleep, and inside the cavern, there was nothing but darkness.

Outside, however, went nova.

The warheads Drake had dropped off along their flight path exploded with a significant force of their own, a white-bright burst against the brown-green sky. But that was only the appetizer. When the blast dimmed into the orange-red of fading flames, a second explosion ripped across the sky, and it was *much* larger.

The sky was on fire. The roiling drive plasma, unable to disperse and mixed with the explosive methane in Titan's atmosphere, ignited in a spectacular chain reaction with the warheads. It slammed into the mining facility with the force of megatons, and the air around the ship, even tucked away in the cavern, exploded and howled and crashed. Drake braced himself, but he was unable to keep his feet as the deck bucked and rolled.

For a long, terrible moment, Drake thought he'd miscalculated. That the explosion was too much, that he'd doomed them to die in this pit, that the earth over their heads would cave in and bury them. How ironic that would be after everything they'd done to get out of the scrapyard and into space. All this to get her flying again, to stay alive as long as they had.

The rumbling and booming eventually subsided. There were more thunderclaps as the explosion continued its chain reaction in the distance. Then, it was quiet.

Drake hauled himself to his feet for the second time that day. His voice rasped when he spoke, though this time, it was as much from overuse in the past several hours as it was from the smoke that lingered in the air. "Status?"

A palm beacon flashed in his face, unintentionally blinding him, then swept to the side. Oh reached out to haul Drake to his feet. The captain accepted the hand, then grimaced in pain. It was his bad shoulder. He had to reach with the other arm, and Oh helped him up.

Not everything was off. The command console glowed an ominous red. What had once been a multicolored display was now a single color, the lowest-powered light wave. On it was nothing except *Glory*. Stationary. Quiet.

"I think we can risk battery power," Drake said, and he nodded at the visual displays above the helm. He figured everyone deserved to see whatever would come next. There wasn't anything they could do except hold their breath and watch.

Oh got the displays working, and there was an inhale from the crew when the Paragon cruiser dominated their view. Behind it, the sky was still on fire, burning instead of exploding now and slowly fading but still quite the sight. Columns of fire were slowly changing to gray ash and falling to the ground. They reflected in the gold of the Paragon's hull, which hung over the mine. Its weapons gleamed too as they searched for a target.

And searched.

Drake could feel the shift in the crew as they realized, after thinking the idea had been to destroy the cruiser in their mighty blast, that was not the plan. That would have been a nice side effect, but there had never been any chance that they could destroy all three of the pursuing ships. Mixed with that ash was debris from the junk and escape pods they'd jettisoned, now falling into the new deep, smoldering gash in the moon's surface—a gash fit for a warship.

The plan had been to make it look like *Glory* had succumbed to her injuries, tried desperately to flee and hide in the atmosphere of Titan, and exploded on the way down. The bang had been big enough. All that was left was for the Paragon to believe it.

The cruiser hung there menacingly and slowly circled the mine and its pit like a bird of prey. Its fellow joined it several minutes later. By then, Drake knew with relief that at the very least, the Paragon couldn't see them on their sensors. Their hiding place and the radioactive fallout from their megaton blast had taken care of that.

His relief was short-lived, however. Another gasp and a moan from someone in the surrounding crew accompanied a flash of sizzling white light from the closest cruiser. Drake feared for the split second it took the plasma to reach them that the Paragon had found them, but it scorched past the opening of the cavern and impacted farther down in the pit. The resulting explosion rattled the deck.

More plasma cannon fire followed, then more. The rattling of the command deck became a cacophony as the ship and the cavern bucked and tossed as if they were on a gale-blown sea. And still, the Paragon kept firing.

Perhaps *Glory* would be buried in the cave after all, Drake mused. From the blanketing blasts, he could tell they didn't know if *Glory* or anyone else was down there. They were just making sure. Being efficient.

Ruthless.

It was excruciating, humiliating, and intolerable, but all they could do was hold on and hope that when the Paragon were done, they hadn't razed the entire mine and crushed them to death.

At the rate they were firing, that was exactly what was going to happen.

CHAPTER TWENTY-SEVEN

THE BURN TO Saturn's orbit had been an exercise in faith. Faith that their navigation computers were still working after being hammered in the battle and would take them where they needed to go. Faith when it came to the tracking sensors trying to pick up *Glory's* ion or plasma trail, and faith of an even higher order that the matter compression drugs would take hold as prescribed and freeze their squishy innards in place so they could handle the crushing acceleration.

Fighters didn't have gravity plating. They couldn't jump to the speed *Glory* or any other large cruiser could without squashing the poor soul inside like a bug on a windshield.

Enter compression drugs. Where there was space in a human or an alien, so they claimed, compression drugs closed it. The body became rock-solid, immune to the vagaries of acceleration burns or course changes at impossibly high velocities. It also meant your entire body stopped working. No movement, no sight, not even thought. Total blackout. It essentially killed you, then more drugs undid the process once the burn was over and brought you back to life. Carrol had said a prayer for those drugs too and repeated them for her fighter's automated flight systems just to be sure.

She'd never done a high-velocity burn in a small craft before, never taken a compression injection. Since nobody flew *inside* their fighters anymore, it wasn't a part of normal training. When she reached Saturn, she decided that they were a miracle since she'd come to and she never, ever wanted to take them again. Her head was pounding, and her body felt as though it had been run over by a five-ton cargo sled. It hurt to move her eyes. It hurt to breathe. It hurt to think.

But ahead of her was Saturn. If Jupiter was the king of the Solar System, giant and hulking, Saturn was his queen, graceful and lovely. Her rings shone particularly brilliant in Carrol's approach angle, trillions upon trillions of tiny ice and rock particles glistening under the weak rays of a distant sun.

Glory had last been seen flying this way, presumably on her way to Neptune. She worried for a brief moment that her navigation and tracking computers had glitched and stopped her too early, but that fear was unfounded, she discovered as she worked her way through the planet's interference.

Quickly, she registered the three Paragon cruisers that had been pursuing her, hovering over Titan. *Glory* was down there, probably taking a beating. Carrol wondered if she'd arrived just in time to witness her ship's destruction.

As she watched, something in the way the ships moved back and forth in patterns indicative of a search and the way they fired their cannons and dropped explosive charges on the surface told Carrol a different story. They didn't know where *Glory* was, not exactly. They were either trying to flush her out or make sure she was gone.

Zed's voice squawked over the headset radio. "Do we assist?" The rest of the squadron had arrived at the same time as she. That was another feat worthy of prayer, the thankful kind. All six of them.

But no, they weren't going to assist. There *was* no assistance six fighters could provide against three cruisers. All they could do was cut power, return to the void, and make like holes in space. Carrol told Zed and the rest of the squadron as much.

And they waited.

Back and forth, the Paragon tracked. The weapons use decreased after the initial bombardment and became more sporadic, probably looking for movement. Each time one of the three cruisers found something to fire at, the other two came to join them like wolves when a packmate picked up a scent. They scattered again when they were disappointed with what they'd found. The energy surges showing movement and firing were clearer than they should have been. The atmosphere on Titan seemed different, but she couldn't figure out why.

Eventually, the Paragon either tired of their search or were called off to engage in some other part of the battle. Carrol guessed it was the latter because the ships abruptly and without warning rose through the muck of Titan's atmosphere, broke orbit, and burned back toward Jupiter at what looked like top speed. The moon they left behind smoldered beneath the atmospheric cover, residual explosions lighting the nitrogen and methane clouds like lightning.

Carrol waited until the Paragon were off her sensor grid

and she was sure they were gone before radioing to the rest of her squadron to power back up. She headed into the atmosphere.

"*Glory*," she called into her headset, switching to the ship-to-ship. "This is Delta Wing squadron, do you read?"

Silence and static.

She repeated the call.

Still nothing.

"Stay here. I'm going low," she told her fellow fighters. There was a lot of radiation down there, enough to wreak havoc with their radio waves. There was also a ton of debris on the floor of the crater where all the activity had been and a massive charred gash that was worryingly ship-sized.

"*Glory*," she tried again, pushing the fear from her mind. "This is your Delta squad. Do you read?"

More static, louder now. She wasn't sure moving closer to the damage and radiation had helped.

"Are you down there, *Glory*?"

Static was her only answer. Her will deflated as it went on. The adrenaline that had propped her up for hours waned with every silent second, and Carrol feared for what was at the bottom of that well when it ran dry. She couldn't fathom what to do next if *Glory* was gone. Plus, her ship was starting to buck and fight for altitude with the mess that was her torn-up wings.

What an odd thought. That *Glory,* just like that, had become her end all, be all.

She couldn't be gone.

Drake would have found a way.

"*Glory*, please," she begged herself as much as anyone else. "Please be down there."

Static.

Doubt. Drake hadn't found a way. Carrol was ready to collapse.

The static changed. Spiked.

Carrol sat back up so fast she slammed her head into the cockpit screen. "*Glory*! *Glory*, is that you down there?"

Something unintelligible came through the static. She tried to boost the signal, but that made the static louder.

"Zed," she radioed, her thoughts a whirlwind. "Zed, you can fly, right? In the atmosphere, I mean."

"That's affirmative. My wings are fine."

"Get your ass down closer to the surface and find that signal."

"Yes, sir!"

His fighter streaked into the soupy mess, sending out vapor trails as he disappeared below the cloud cover. Carrol tracked him toward a crater on her sensor display, a mining facility Carrol had never heard of. Sure was big, though, and she took a moment to marvel at how well her pilot was handling his craft. Their crash course in hands-on flight had paid dividends now that they'd survived the ordeal. Carrol could feel it in how she handled her own joystick. The tentativeness was gone, confidence in its place. She allowed herself a momentary hope that her home ship was down there, that they'd all survived and would have a chance to take that newfound confidence and smack the Paragon with it.

"Commander!" Zed called, shouting too loud for the sensitive microphone in front of his mouth, but such was the cost of exuberance. "They're down here! *Glory* is intact. I have them on comm."

"Patch them through, Zed, you idiot. Relay them, over!"

There was a beat, then, still filled with static, came

music to Carrol's ears. "Delta squadron leader, this is *Glory* actual." Drake's voice was hoarse but clear.

"*Glory* actual, Delta actual. It's—very good to hear your voice, sir. We've come a long way to find you."

"Are the Paragon gone?"

"Can confirm, sir. We watched them fly off our sensor screens, heading back in-system."

"Thank the stars for that."

"Do you require assistance, Captain?"

There was a gallows chuckle on the other end of the radio. "We're a bit buried in here. Our forward cannons may or may not be up to the task of blasting us a way out. Any assistance you can provide from the outside of the cave-in would be most appreciated."

Carrol nodded. It was a stupid response given there was no visual feed, but it was all she could do at the moment. She sat there for a while, trying and failing to regulate an overwhelming sense of... She felt everything all at once.

"I'm not suited for atmospheric flight myself, but I believe the rest of my squadron is, sir. I can send them right down."

"Thank you, Commander. How many do you have with you?"

Carrol finally had to blink back the pain, and her voice quivered when she answered. "There are six of us, sir."

"Better than none."

"Sir, I saw thruster flares when you issued the recall order back over Jupiter. How many already made it back?"

There was a pregnant pause on the other end, then, "It's just you, Eunice. You did good. So good. All of you."

Carrol again nodded, and again felt like an idiot, but it was all the response she could manage.

"You hang tight up there," Drake said, voice full of

support and sympathy even over the radio. "We'll unstick ourselves and then bring you home. That sound like a plan?"

"Yes, sir," she answered, and her voice finally broke. "That sounds like a plan, sir."

CHAPTER TWENTY-EIGHT

Carrol collapsed on the flight deck as soon as her feet touched the plating. Gravity had never felt so good, nor had the painted, rusted, and repainted deck.

She lay there and listened to the shouts of the crew, felt the vibrations from their rushing footsteps on her cheek as they poured over her fighter and the others, heard equipment whirring, elevators grinding, tools clanging. The deck beneath her hummed with life. She, too, was alive.

So many weren't.

Images of burning fighters flashed in her mind. Explosions. She tried to stop the rush of images by closing her eyes, but that made it worse.

"Commander," a voice called. She didn't feel like moving. The voice called more urgently, accompanied by a strong pair of hands that hoisted her up until she was standing.

She found herself face to face with Zed. "Lieutenant," she said. Her throat felt like it had been sanded. The single word scraped out like a tumbleweed.

"You okay?"

She nodded unconvincingly.

Zed's face was hollow like hers. He was exhausted, too.

Carrol stumbled but forced her legs to hold her up, then gave him a pained smile. "Those compression drugs are a sumbitch."

"Fuckin' A."

Carrol blinked in the light of the flight deck and took in her surroundings for the first time since she'd landed. Her gaze swept past the empty stalls, the ones whose fighters weren't coming back. She looked at the ones that had, which were pilotless and in various states of repair. "Where is everybody?"

"Rest of the squad is recuperating, sir. Got their shots from the doc and are in their racks sleeping it off. Which is where we need to get."

"Why aren't you racked and unconscious?"

Zed reddened. "I was waiting for you."

To her surprise, Carrol reddened too. A moment passed between them, unexpected but familiar. He'd looked at her like that before. She had, too, a long time ago. It became too much for her, and she looked away.

The two of them were standing there, awkward and red-faced, when Flight Deck Officer De La Cruz came up to them. He gave them a look, then blinked and pushed forward with his own agenda.

"Need you to take this to the captain," he deadpanned gruffly. He lifted a charred black box that Carrol recognized as one of the many flight controllers that were found in the Delta Wings' innards. From the size of it, Carrol guessed it was the main one.

She took it. "Sure thing," she said. She nearly dropped it from the sudden weight, but she recovered in time to keep it from hitting the deck.

DLC nodded in appreciation and glanced at Carrol and Zed again, then raised a mirthful eyebrow and nodded again. "Much appreciated."

He turned to leave, and Carrol called after him, "Where is the captain?"

DLC paused, and any gruff playfulness, real or imagined, fell from his voice and expression. "Sickbay."

VISITING the dead and dying was the hardest part of commanding a warship. Every blank and wooden face, every gasp and cry for help was a personal wound inflicted upon Drake.

On the command deck, it was possible to have the perspective that in mortal combat, when life and death were at stake, there was no way to protect them all. That the contract of the soldier was that they were willing to lay down life and limb in the execution of their duty, and in war, some of them would. But not down here. In Sickbay, among those who were paying a steep price, that perspective was lost. Drake knew from past experience that he would second-guess every decision he'd made, and that would plague him for the rest of his life.

But that was the way it was supposed to be. It was his duty as the commanding officer to take responsibility for the consequences of his command. To look at each wounded and dying face and honor those who had passed. He had never shied away from that duty, hard as it was.

Sickbay was a madhouse. Casualties from their tangle with the Paragon could have been much worse, no question, because enemy forces were still numerous, and in the midst of it all, comparisons of "better" or "worse" lost all meaning.

Losing one crew member was too many. Far more than one had died, and many more were seriously wounded and in danger of dying.

Triage dictated that the most serious cases were kept in Sickbay, with the rest led or carried down the corridor to one of several expanded medical areas. "Overflow," they called it. Cargo holds were filled with cots and pads. Chow hall tables were covered with sheets. Drake had already toured those areas and had seen electrical engineers double as nurses, tending crew suffering from shrapnel wounds, burns from plasma fires, and vacuum exposure. He'd toured the morgues, too, the bodies lined up in rows with sheets covering them from head to toe. But it was arguably the worst here in Sickbay with the injured who were able to cry out in pain and agony—the most serious cases as they clung desperately to life.

Doctor Broussard was in the middle of it all, sweating, cursing profusely, but handling the chaos like a maestro conducting an orchestra. He was focused on saving lives. Drake envied him. He couldn't help but feel as though the doctor's focus was the opposite of his. That his own purpose had put all these people here, and even though he knew it wasn't true, all he had done was sow death.

Damn.

A gasp brought his attention to a patient near him. Drake looked down to the barely conscious face of an impossibly young-looking crewman and recognized it. His heart sank. Snyder was the young man's name, he remembered. He'd helped Drake find the flashlights in the cargo hold when he'd first come aboard. His face was covered in dermal patches, the kind that were placed over serious burns, and his black-rimmed glasses were missing. For whatever reason, that bugged Drake, and he began to look for them by going through the young man's pockets and then around the table.

He found the glasses several feet away on the deck, half-smashed and bent. One of the lenses was shattered, and both of the arms that curled behind the ears were askew. Drake cursed and tried to bend them back, but he stopped when he realized he was far more likely to snap them in two. He returned them to the unconscious Snyder, slipping them into one of his uniform pockets and sealing it.

Snyder coughed, his entire body convulsing. A monitor taped to his forehead beeped, and Drake wildly looked around for help.

Broussard was there as if he'd materialized out of thin air.

The doctor produced a syringe and stabbed it into the young man's chest. He depressed the plunger and retracted the long needle, then reset the forehead monitor. Drake didn't see where he'd pulled it from, but a handheld computer pad was in his palm a moment later, scanning the forehead monitor. Broussard regarded the readings, and with a sigh, nodded and looked at Drake. His face was tired. Worn. He'd aged years since Drake had last seen him just hours ago. Or was it that he was finally showing his age? The age they all were...

"How is he?"

"Dying."

Drake had figured as much, given that he was in Sick-bay, but still. Hearing it felt like a physical blow. He thought about how just the day before, he had crawled over the crates in the cargo hold, eager to please his captain. "How?"

"Plasma fire in the hold. No direct exposure to the fire,

but the superheated air got him. Not before he pulled out his fellow crewman along with him, though."

Drake felt a swell of pride. "How is the crewman he pulled out?"

Broussard shook his head. "She didn't make it."

Drake nodded and swallowed the pride, along with the pain that replaced it.

"We have seventeen dead," Broussard continued. "A hundred or so with minor to severe-but-survivable wounds, and another two dozen or so like Mr. Snyder here who, barring a miracle, will likely succumb to their injuries. Eventually." Broussard wiped his forehead to keep sweat from pouring into his eyes, leaving a bloody streak. He sighed heavily. In the midst of the chaos, pausing to talk about a single case made the situation overwhelming. It was somehow easier to consider the total number of casualties as opposed to an individual. Drake felt responsible for that too, for making him pause. "I've given him the most powerful regenerative agents we have to get those lungs functioning again, but they're not working. He's—not going to make it, Cap."

"That's okay," Drake said though it wasn't, feeling that Broussard needed to hear it. "I just know him." He tapped the pocket where he'd stashed the glasses. "See if we can at least fix up his eyewear for him."

Broussard nodded. "I can search the library for a proper repair. You never see those anymore."

"He was proud of them."

The two men found there was nothing left to say, and both stood in the silence left behind.

"Captain?"

Drake turned at the call. Someone new was entering Sickbay with a person in tow. The young man he recognized, though he couldn't place the name. One of the Delta pilots. Behind him was Carrol. Both looked like hell, Carrol particularly. Drake could see their last conversation weighing on her, how many she'd lost out there, how few she'd come back with. But at least *they* were alive. She was alive too.

The young man gave a smart salute. Carrol did as well once they reached Drake and the doc.

"Dammit all," Doc cursed. "You two need your come-down injections yesterday."

He disappeared, presumably to grab the anti-compression drugs that would speed up their recovery. XO had mistakenly reported to him that *all* the pilots had already taken them and were them sleeping off. That left Drake with the pilot and his second officer.

Carrol was holding something. She raised it. "DLC told me to give this to you."

Drake took it with a frown until he recognized what it was. He looked at Carrol, relieved that he could offer those tired, guilt-ridden eyes a small modicum of peace. "Yes, thank you." He gestured at the controller. "You know what this is?"

"It's one of the Delta Wing control modules. The main one, I think, from the size."

"DLC tell you why he asked you to bring it to me?"

"No, sir."

"He noticed something was off on the first of your squadron's Delta Wings he started maintenance on. Computer wasn't responding the way it was supposed to, thrusters and fins in the wrong configurations, cockpit tech with weird lag times. He was having a hard time figuring out what it was, so I authorized him to do a tear-down."

Drake hefted the control module one more time. "Turns out these have been tampered with."

Carrol blinked. "Tampered with?"

"That's right. Flight logs say you lost your formation in a sunburst, is that right? Coming over the top of the Jupiter terminator?"

Her cheeked flushed. "Yes, sir. A lot of us did."

"So far, every one of you who did had their module hijacked by a bug that made it malfunction and not engage the screen tinting in time."

Carrol frowned at the information. Her mind fought with the revelation, but exhaustion and the anti-compression drugs were winning. "But, I—my approach vector was off. I didn't catch it 'til it was too late. Flew us right into the light. Rookie-fucking-mistake."

She was beating herself up. Drake could see it plain as day. "That may be true," he said. "But your fighter module was designed to prevent rookie fucking mistakes, and someone disengaged the safety protocols."

Carrol blinked again. "Someone?"

"On this ship. DLC swears the modules were in perfect working order when they were installed for the in-person flight retrofits, so it happened in a pretty tight window."

The other pilot chimed in, taking a step forward. "Who, sir? Who did it?"

"We don't know. Yet. But you can be damn sure we're going to find out."

It was quite the wrinkle. Sabotage. On their ship. And it made Drake think of something else odd that had happened this far into their deployment. A few odd something elses.

"I'll start reviewing the flight deck logs," Carrol said, hardening resolve replacing the guilt in her eyes. Good. She now had a bone to chew on instead of herself.

"You will do absolutely no such thing," Doc said, rejoining the group with a pair of dripping syringes and a stern look on his face. "You, both of you, will take your injections, and you will go to *sleep*. Those are my orders, which supersede anything from this man here you might call 'captain.' I am your captain now."

"Doc is right," Drake said after protesting for a moment. He had others who could investigate the snake in their midst.

Carrol deflated. She didn't have the fight in her. Neither did her companion.

"I'll have to write that one down," Doc said, winking at Drake. "Cap agreeing with me. Now, right this way." He took them by their arms and led them toward open beds.

Carrol held up. "Captain," she called. Drake almost stopped her, expecting a last-minute protest against the order to rest. Her expression, however, had changed; she had something else on her mind. Something darker. He nodded for her to continue. "I forgot to offload the recording of it. Otherwise, I could show you right now, but make sure DLC gets it." Drake nodded.

Relieved, Carrol continued. "We saw something out there, sir. Something coming through the Jupiter Gateway. Paragon. And big. Bigger than any kind of ship I've ever seen or heard of. And it looked nasty, sir, whatever it is." She shivered at the memory of it.

Drake saw in her expression that it scared her more than anything else. What she was describing sounded familiar.

"I'll pull your flight data," he promised.

"Thank you, sir," she said, then added in a whisper, so full of horror was her voice, "It looked like it was heading toward Earth."

CHAPTER TWENTY-NINE

"You're saying this is flight-recorded footage from a couple hours ago?" XO asked, scratching his close-cropped hair in horrified disbelief. Drake shared the feeling. He could hardly believe it himself.

"Looks an awful lot like the last one we saw, doesn't it? Watch your head."

XO ducked a sloped power conduit as they rounded a corner deep in *Glory's* belly. They were headed to the portside lower plasma manifolds, which were currently under repair; the ones that had leaked during their run from the Paragon. "It's bigger," XO said, hardly taking his eyes off the image on the small datapad.

"And finished this time."

The Paragon craft Carrol had filmed coming slowly through the Jupiter Gateway had a half-dome on top, with tendrils tapering down from the dome into a sharp cannon-like tip with an opening that was probably the length of the *Glory* in diameter. It was the spitting image of a Paragon ship Drake had encountered once before, albeit larger. The other ship had been sitting in an orbital construction dock, un-deployed. Drake had made sure it would never be deployed.

But one had been.

"It's heading for Earth, isn't it?" XO asked, tearing his eyes away from the planet-killer on the datapad. That's what the mammoth ship was, a giant weapon designed to destroy a planet.

"Mars first, it looks like from long-distance tracking."

"Then Earth?"

"Then Earth."

Drake couldn't shake the feeling that Jack had known about this all along. He'd known this was coming, and he'd refused to tell him. Refused to raise the alarm. Refused to do anything except pull Drake out of retirement and deploy one ship. A single ship. Why was the Fleet not prepared for this thing? Why were they not throwing everything they had at it, and well before it had entered Earth space or had ever flown, for that matter? Bastard.

Drake refocused on where he was going. Answers lay ahead, or the beginning of them, at least, for his ship and possibly for the cloak-and-dagger proclivities of his former superior. He suspected the old bastard *had* tried to raise the alarm and been stopped from within. The cancer had grown, and it was right there on *Glory*.

Ahead of them, a group of armed and armored soldiers snapped to. Efremova was in the lead, with the towering e-Marine right behind her, plus two of her security team, all toting heavy-duty plasma rifles that said they meant business. So did the hardened expressions of the soldiers who held them. Good.

XO peered at the mean-looking group. "What are we doing down here, Cap?"

"Hunting rats," Drake answered through clenched

teeth. Efremova saluted as they approached and Drake swept past, indicating with a head tilt that she and her team should fall in behind.

He led them farther into the belly of the *Glory*, to where people seldom went outside of the engineering maintenance teams. Much of the equipment down there was self-sustaining, requiring only occasional checking and adjusting. The plasma manifolds, which were the sections of the main propulsion and power generation drive that bled off excess energy and dispersed it around the ship, were that type of equipment: hot, nasty to work on, and almost never needed attention. It made it even odder that they'd started leaking, especially in the middle of battle when they were trying to sneak away.

Logs showed only a handful of people had been down in these sections. Of them, the most visits had been made by one man. One irritating, recalcitrant asshat of a man.

"Lieutenant Fredrickson!" Drake called as they entered the sweltering corridor the computer had identified as the current location of their quarry. Someone was standing at the end of it, but it wasn't Fredrickson. Drake realized Sudan as they got closer.

Her eyes doubled in size when she saw them, creasing her shining, sweat-covered forehead. "Captain," she said. She was covered in grime and wearing a maintenance uniform. Plasma residue was nasty stuff, and she wore that too from head to toe. It stank with a particular acidity. Everything in the bilge sections smelled of it.

"Where is the lieutenant, crewman?" Drake asked her.

Sudan glanced at an open manifold port. A toolkit lay beside it. From within, there was a sudden banging.

"Ow!" a voice yelped. "Goddammit."

Drake locked eyes with Efremova, and she nudged the

e-Marine over to call the engineer out. He was the master at arms now. His job, not hers.

He leaned inside, and with a rumble, called, "Lieutenant Fredrickson, can you please come out here?"

There was a pause inside the tube, then, "Sudan? Who's asking?"

"I think you'd better come out here," Sudan said, voice quavering as she leaned into the opening. "It's the captain."

"Captain, I'm very busy."

Drake ground his teeth.

XO stepped forward. "Get your ass out here, mister."

There was another pause, then the sounds of scraping tools and fabric. The engineer was coming.

He emerged a few moments later, reeking of residue. Sudan helped him out, took his tools, and handed him a handkerchief. He stood at the opening, wiping his hands and looking warily between those assembled before him. His gaze finally landed on Drake. "What can I do for you, Captain?"

"I'd like a status report," Drake said.

"You need all those guns for a status report?" he asked, pointing at the security detail.

"Answer the question," XO said forcefully.

Fredrickson swallowed. "I've found the leak. One of several, I'm afraid. I'm about to fix it." He gestured at the open tube hatch with a cheeky grin. "You're welcome to come help me if you'd like it done faster."

"What caused the leak?" Drake asked, stepping forward.

Fredrickson flinched. "The coolant switches never turned on, which engaged the overflow vents."

"How?"

"They're burned out. Impossible to tell how."

"How many switches?"

"Seven of the twelve manifolds."

"What would you say, Lieutenant, are the odds of that happening by chance?" Drake knew his ship inside and out. He knew a failure like that was practically impossible, but he was interested to see how Fredrickson would answer.

"I'd say they're very slim, Captain." His face didn't betray anything.

"The logs show you are one of very few people to have accessed these sections in the past forty-eight hours. Can you account for those activities?"

"I'm the chief engineer," he said, nostrils flaring. His body language was starting to resemble that of a cornered animal. "Of *course* I've been down here. So have others." He pointed at Sudan. "She's been down here just as much as I have." He pointed at the e-Marine. "He's been down here too. I've seen him."

Drake looked at him. The man nodded to confirm.

"Cut the bullshit," XO interjected. "You think any of us have your kind of expertise, Fredrickson? To do something like sabotage the plasma manifolds?"

"Am I being accused of that, Captain?"

Drake could feel Efremova and her armed squad tensing behind him. XO looked like he was ready to jump the upstart officer then and there. Drake flexed his jaw. The answer was yes, goddammit. Yes, he wanted to accuse the man. It made sense. At least, it had several minutes ago. He was the most qualified, had the most access, and on the surface, the most motivation with a captain—and a crew—he'd openly stated he hated. But as Drake scratched a little deeper on that motivation front, that began to fall apart. Being an asshole was a far cry from being a traitor with a death wish, and whoever had sabotaged the Delta Wings and caused the plasma leak was trying to get the ship destroyed and them all killed. Drake wasn't sure that made sense. Still, someone had done it, which was inexplicable. He wasn't sure it would make sense for *anyone*, yet it was true.

"Did you sabotage the plasma manifolds, Lieutenant?" the captain asked.

Fury burned in Fredrickson's eyes. "No." Drake was sure that if spitting in his face wouldn't involve being vaporized by a trigger-happy security detail, he would have done it with gusto. If he was telling the truth, Drake could hardly blame him.

XO scoffed at the response, not considering that an option. "Mr. Smith," he commanded the master at arms with a gesture at the shackles that hung off the side of his uniform. "Kindly take Mr. Fredrickson into—"

"Belay that," Drake said, holding up his hand and turning to his first officer. XO looked at him with a fury similar to what he'd received from the engineer the moment before. "The lieutenant says he is not responsible."

XO looked aghast. "But, sir..."

Drake shook his head. They were not going to arrest someone with no proof. He should never have come down here like this. That had been a mistake, and he could see in Fredrickson that it would likely cost him, but it was too late for that. There was a saboteur on board, whether it was Fredrickson or not, and that had to be dealt with. His standing with his chief engineer could be considered later. He turned to Efremova. "You and Mr. Smith kindly see about assigning security details to all critical areas of the ship: Weapons, Engineering, Life Support. Conscript anyone you require to cover the shifts. No work is to be done on any critical system without a security escort, no one left alone." Efremova nodded. Drake turned to Fredrickson. "We have a saboteur aboard. The evidence is irrefutable."

Fredrickson gave a single shake of his head, his expression hard. "I never denied that, sir."

"Good. I'll expect your full cooperation in the investigation to discover the identity of the saboteur. Starting with your department."

A long moment later, he responded. "Yes, sir." He then gestured sarcastically at the plasma tube. "May I get back to work, please?"

"Mr. Fredrickson. Your work to get this ship flying has been nothing less than incredible. The Paragon have invaded the Solar System and destroyed the vast majority of Earth's Fleet. We're running for our lives. The only way we can do that is if this ship works like it's supposed to. That means you will save us all. I am sorry to have interrupted you. If you need any resources from me, please do not hesitate to ask."

Drake walked away. XO fell in behind him and strode next to him for several yards before speaking. "You believe him?"

Drake shook his head. "I don't know," he said. "But he's right, the list of those with access to those systems isn't super long, but it's also not a single person. We have to narrow down the possibilities. And not jump to conclusions."

XO exhaled in frustration. Drake sympathized. "How in the hell do we do that, along with everything we need to do with a crew that's down over a hundred functional hands?"

Drake had been chewing on that question ever since Fredrickson had brought it up. "I have another place to check."

CHAPTER THIRTY

Two days before, the loading bays had been the busiest areas on the ship. Now, with the skeleton crew currently manning *Glory*, the wide corridors and expansive double doorways were empty and quiet save for the thrum of the propulsion system burning them toward Neptune. Drake both missed the hubbub and was grateful for the silence. The work of flushing out a traitor was best done quietly and alone.

The double-wide door of the hangar bay he was searching for was still taped shut. Caution, it read. Black soot streaked the center divide and ringed the outside like wicked fingertips. Drake broke the tape and overrode the security lock. The doors swung open, and he stepped into the room where the transport shuttle had crashed, caught fire, and killed their CMC in the first accident of this ill-fated voyage.

Soot and the stinging scent of refined fuel filled his nostrils. The hangar reeked, and Drake clicked his flashlight on to carefully pick his way across the uneven deck, which had warped in the heat of the conflagration. The gravity plating had deformed along with it, he discovered when an unsteady footstep nearly sent him flying toward the ceiling. He steadied himself on the hull of the cargo shuttle and got a handful of black char for his trouble. He wasn't there for the shuttle, however.

He found the docking arm. The report stated the fire started there, a malfunction in one of the arms deploying improperly, knocking the shuttle sideways, and setting it on fire. In the tight beam of his flashlight, Drake could believe it. The arm was little more than a twisted hulk, barely recognizable as the apparatus that it had once been: a retractable arm with a claw on its end that was the right size to grab the docking latches of a Fleet shuttlecraft and steady them as they entered the tight quarters of the loading hangar. The equipment latched on while the shuttle was still outside the ship and guided it inside. There was almost nothing left of this one, nor was there much left of the rear of the shuttle it lay next to. This was where the fire had started and burned the hottest.

Drake picked his way carefully to the wall to which the docking arm was attached. Despite the operating room that sat a deck up and directly above the loading bay doors, nobody controlled the docking arms. They were operated by a system comprised of a low-level AI and sensors, much like the control modules on the Delta Wings and to a lesser degree, the plasma manifolds. Tiny instances of computer control were all over the ship. Without them, *Glory* might as well be a steamship run by pulleys and levers. There was no central computer system that coordinated everything; others in the galaxy used advanced AI, but not Earth. It had proven to be unwise. There was a multitude of tiny isolated automated systems that made her fly. The controls for the docking arm were such a system, and like the plasma manifolds, their independence made them vulnerable. Perhaps.

The panel covering the arm's controls was so heat-damaged he had to knock it loose with his elbow, which sent spikes of pain running up into his bad shoulder. It dropped to the deck to disintegrate into a puff of black soot. There was more shielding to get past inside, which was in progressively better states. For the last few, he had to use a multi-tool to unscrew the paneling; then he got to the control modules. There, once again, he encountered the black soot of a fire. Not the same fire that had raged inside the hangar bay. No, this one had started inside the wall, and from the radius of the damage, something had exploded in the middle of the modules. Something small. It looked just like the damage DLC had found in the Delta Wings. Drake suspected Fredrickson would find the same in the plasma manifold diverters.

Not a malfunction.

Sabotage.

Drake had expected the confirmation to motivate him and electrify his anger over what he had finally realized was happening on his ship. That feeling didn't come, however. It left him sick to his stomach instead. The thought that there was an enemy on his ship, someone trying to kill them—someone who was responsible for the deaths of the people in this room, and for two dozen Delta Wing pilots, and had nearly been responsible for the loss of the entire ship—was a hard pill to swallow. It felt like too much.

It also meant that his enemy was prepared to die, which made him or her far more dangerous.

Drake pushed the nausea away and picked his way back across the hangar deck, heading for the control room. Access was a ladder on the side of the hangar entrance, which he climbed with no small amount of discomfort in his damn shoulder. The video feeds were in the control room. Whoever had planted the microexplosive in the docking arm control panel was on those recordings.

The room was dark and silent. The conditions that had been a comfort a few minutes before were now claustrophobic. Creepy. Hiding in the darkness somewhere on this ship was a killer. A coward with the courage of his or her convictions, to be sure; someone who hid behind tiny explosives and lies, but a killer nonetheless. Drake couldn't help but imagine them outside that very room. The door to the control room was open to the corridor beyond. Not the extra-wide straight corridors of the deck below, where cargo was hauled in and out and necessitated such room and visibility. This one was a standard narrow passage with kinks and turns that meant Drake could only see a few meters in any direction.

He tried to close the control room door, but the mechanism was damaged, maybe in the fire. It wouldn't budge. Open it was, then. A shiver ran up and down his spine as he focused on the bank of monitors and controls.

The surveillance setup was simple: each display showed a two-dimensional representation of a three-dimensional holographic recording. He could have projected any of them onto one of the small flat multipurpose displays that dotted the control room console, but the monitors were better because each was tied to a camera. Drake found the one trained on the offending docking arm and ran the tape back.

There was a clunk in the corridor outside.

Drake whirled. "Hello?"

No response.

Drake held his breath, suddenly feeling exposed. He

had no weapon, and there was nowhere to hide in the control room. Though, he thought foolishly, there was no reason to think that anyone out in that corridor would be the saboteur or otherwise have a reason to hurt him. Still, he couldn't convince the panic in his gut otherwise.

Drake set his jaw against the fear, paused the reversing footage, and walked slowly over to the open door.

He could see nothing outside, nor could he hear anything. He switched his flashlight on and swept it from side to side, looking down what he could see of the corridor in both directions. Nothing. He switched it off and stood in the dim overhead lights, half of which were out. Probably as power-saving measures.

Silence.

Drake sighed. He was jumpy. Dammit.

He backed to the display monitors, keeping the door in front of him, and resumed rewinding the footage. He reached the fire and watched it unfold in reverse, horrified. Carrol saving CAG. The light burst of the explosion. The careening shuttle tossed by the maniacal docking arm. It was a miracle the shuttle hadn't vaporized and this section of the ship along with it. Drake suspected that had been the saboteur's goal, and it reminded him that he needed to commend the young commander. What she had done was an incredible act of bravery.

The footage continued to rewind. Workers scurried forth and back like little ground cars stuck in reverse, their hard work being done and then undone as time slipped backward. Nobody got close to the docking arm's control panel, nor should they. It was a self-contained system that rarely, if ever, required maintenance on the panel side.

Wait.

A figure blurred toward it and lingered, then walked in

reverse away from it. Drake might have blinked and missed it. He paused the recording, then played it forward at normal speed. A blurred figure approached the control panel, face hidden in shadow. It looked back and forth, waited as another worker walked near, then opened the docking arm control panel and slipped something inside.

"Gotcha," Drake whispered through clenched teeth.

He brought his attention to the other monitors as the figure walked away. They'd have to exit through the hangar bay doors. He could get a clean look at them there. But the figure lingered at the edge of the hangar door camera's range, still obscured in shadow, until a gaggle of workers carrying an antigrav sled filled the view. The shadowy figure followed them down the corridor, where Drake's cameras lost them.

Rewinding the footage showed the same tactic to enter the hangar bay. They obscured themselves in another group of workers. Damn. It was possible to track them. There were cameras all over the damn ship. That would take a long time, however; time they didn't have. But all was not lost. There was still the moment in the shadows by the docking arm when they'd looked around the hangar bay to make sure no one was watching them. Well, the camera *had* been watching them. Bastard. Drake was fairly certain he could do some light processing on that holoimage and get a face.

He found the moment he was looking for and began twiddling the image controls.

There was another clunk in the corridor behind him.

Drake froze, and the hairs rose on the back of his neck. This time, there was no mistaking the sound, and in the reflection of the monitor he was staring at, there was a movement in the shadows. He didn't turn. He figured whoever it was didn't know he could see them. He didn't call out either, hoping they wouldn't know he'd heard them.

On the screen, the image was coming into focus. The blurry figure had a face. It was seconds away from being visible.

In the reflection, he saw the shadow raise an arm. They were holding something that pointed in his direction.

"Shit!"

Drake dove back and to his left, into the far-right corner of the control room.

A plasma bolt ripped through the air and slammed into the monitor Drake had just been standing in front of. The image of the almost-clear face erupted in sparks and flames, and white-hot glass flew at Drake as he dove out of the way. He felt a sharp pinch in his shoulder before he could turn, and the pinch flared into a burning pain as soon as he hit the floor. A shard had sliced into his shoulder. The same damn shoulder.

The shooter was in the corridor to the left. Drake's dive had moved him out of their sight, putting the short wall the sliding door receded into between him and them, but all they had to do was travel the meter or so down the corridor to stand in the open doorway to take him out. He'd have no cover, no weapon, and no chance.

Drake had been lucky. The side of the door he'd dived toward was the side that had a comm panel. He awkwardly slapped it as hard as he could with his non-dominant arm and it turned on, and he shouted with all the volume he could muster. "Security to Hangar Bay Control Room...Forty-Seven! Active shooter! I repeat, active shooter!"

There was a burst of static on the other end, then XO's voice came through. "Cap, is that you?"

"Get them down here now!" he shouted, gritting his teeth in pain. The other comm filled with shouts and over-lapping radio conversations as Security was scrambled.

In the corridor outside the control room, Drake heard heavy breathing. The shooter was still out there, footsteps away from him.

"Keep the channel open, XO!" Drake yelled. "The shooter is still here. I'll identify as soon as they leave cover."

It was as much a bluff as reality. One of two things was true for whoever was out there: they were there to kill him after failing to kill the ship, and there was nothing Drake could do to stop that, and they needed to keep their identity hidden for a while longer. His gambit, he hoped, had made doing both those things impossible. They'd have to show their face to shoot him, or they'd have to leave so as not to be discovered.

A fresh eruption of plasma fire came from the corridor and nearly made Drake jump out of his skin. At first, he worried that the traitor had found an angle from which to snipe him from the shadows, but no. The plasma bolts found their target on the console Drake had just been watching, and his heart sank when he realized what they were doing. They were destroying the evidence. The face that Drake had nearly seen caught fire, along with the monitor that held it, then the console exploded.

Footsteps receded on the deck plating, followed by more footsteps coming toward him. Drake pressed himself as far into the corner of the room as he could to surprise whoever entered the room. Perhaps he'd miscalculated and it was the shooter, having faked a retreat and then returned to catch him off-guard.

"Captain?" a voice called moments before a figure entered the smoky room.

Drake jumped out of his pathetic hiding place and grabbed at the plasma rifle the figure was holding. He tried to wrestle it away but quickly realized that was folly; he was easily tossed to the ground. A light was shined into his face, which he shielded with his hand.

"Smith?" he asked, peering past the blinding light.

"Captain!" another voice called, and a hand reached out to haul him to his feet. Efremova. It *was* Smith who'd first entered the room.

Drake nodded at them in appreciation. He pointed breathlessly down the corridor to his left, right in relation to entering the control room. "They went that way," he said. "If you hurry, you might still catch them."

"Tell me the minute you have eyes on him."

Efremova was pacing like an animal on the only bare patch in Drake's cluttered quarters. She turned to the captain and Doc, who was tending to his shoulder and his hand while the captain sat on his desk. Drake hadn't remembered injuring the latter of those body parts in the moment, but it was throbbing just as much as the shoulder. Doc had clucked his tongue at him when he scanned it. *Broken.* Had been since Admiral Jack.

The Russian CMC filled Drake in as soon as she'd shut off her handheld radio comm. "Fredrickson ducked his escorts about twenty minutes ago. When they found him, he ran, and they lost him." She was kicking herself, as was Smith, who stood in the doorway, rifle still at the ready along with a million repetitions of "Sorry, sir" to join the hundred he'd already spoken.

Drake waved her off. "Not your fault, Crewman. Either

of you. My orders were directed at protecting the ship, not its personnel. Those orders, it would seem, were not sufficient. The fault is mine."

Efremova shook her head, still stewing. "That bastard." She looked at him, and Drake saw the fire in her eyes. "We'll get him. I have every available armed crew member searching the ship. We'll find him."

Drake winced as Broussard dug deep into his shoulder. The doctor looked at him and shrugged, then told him to be still and injected one of his concoctions. Drake guessed it was a nerve inhibitor because the next tool the doc dragged out, he knew all too well: a cauterizer. When he started on that, Drake blessedly couldn't feel it. Less blessedly, he could smell it, so he returned his attention to his security team.

"Do we have holovid from the corridor? Can we confirm Fredrickson was the one who attacked me?"

"Surveillance was cut," Efremova said between clenched teeth. "Power conduits knocked out with the micro explosives he's been using all over the ship. We're going to expand the search to the surrounding areas, see what we can see, but..."

Her voice trailed off, and she resumed her tight pacing. Drake knew why. It was the same reason he'd been hoping to catch the saboteur's face in the hangar bay: the routes in and out of the hangar decks were multitudinous and highly trafficked. It made searching for a single face, even among a skeleton crew, very difficult.

Something about this wasn't adding up, but he could see that Efremova felt differently. That could be dangerous. "First order of business is to find the lieutenant," he said, wincing again as the cauterizer singed a bit of his non-numbed skin. Efremova's pacing was getting to be too much, as was the medical attention. He wanted to be alone and get a chance to steady his nerves. Maybe take a shower if the damn thing was working. Think about the whole thing.

"We will find the *shluha vokzal'naja*," Efremova said, spitting this time. From her embarrassed reaction, Drake must have shown his displeasure at the act, and on his quarters' floor to boot. "Apologies. We will find him."

"See that you do, and I want it done by the book."

"Yes, sir."

"By the book," he repeated, holding her with the command before she turned to leave. He wanted to see in her eyes that she understood. "We don't know that Mr. Fredrickson was the one who attacked me. We don't know *who* it was."

"Then why would he run?"

"I have no idea. We can ask him once you've found him."

Efremova looked visibly pained by what Drake was asking of her. "By the book" meant no shooting. No arresting. Talk. Not her strong suit, Drake guessed, but he meant what he said.

"By the book," she repeated, then she was out of his room, ordering Smith to personally stand guard outside.

Drake looked up at Broussard, who was sweating and smelled like he too could use a shower. "You finished there, old man?"

Broussard gave a humorless grunt. "Me the old man? I had to use twice the regenerative agent on your flesh wound here than I have on my patients in Sickbay." But Doc nodded, and eventually, he finished.

Drake flexed his hand, which already felt better, then hauled his uniform jacket back over the shoulder and stuck his arm down the sleeve, effectively covering it. "You stink."

Broussard wrinkled his nose in response. "So do you."

Doc gathered his field kit off Drake's piled-high desk and sauntered out the door. There he greeted another security officer who informed him that he'd been assigned to escort him back to Sickbay. "Is this your doing?" he asked Drake from the corridor.

"It's for your own good, Doc. If they were brazen enough to shoot at me, whoever 'they' are, they might be inclined to shoot anyone. All senior officers will have an armed escort moving forward. Including you."

Broussard snorted in disgust, then caught himself, exhaustedly shook his head, and gave the security officer a pat on the shoulder. "Not to you, my dear. Not to you. To what the world is coming to."

They left together. Drake got up, feeling every one of his sixty-odd years in his creaking joints, and told Smith that he was closing the door to take a shower. Smith nodded stiffly and gave him another "Sorry, sir." Drake thought of patting him on the shoulder like Broussard had his escort, but thought better of it and closed the door.

He surveyed his mess of a room. There hadn't been much time to clean it during the chaos that had started from the second he'd come back on board, but there had been a few moments here and there. He just hadn't taken them. He couldn't. Everything was the way he'd left it. It didn't seem right to disturb it.

He shut it out and moved carefully, picking his way through the papers, books, souvenirs, and the accumulated detritus of his previous life toward the rear of the cabin where the washroom was. A shower sounded glorious. He had his jacket half-unbuttoned when he opened the privacy door and jumped back in surprise, crashing into a half-fallen bookshelf.

Someone was standing inside the small compartment.

It was Fredrickson.

He had a gun, and he was pointing it at Drake.

CHAPTER THIRTY-ONE

"ARE you all right in there, Captain?" Smith called from the other side of Drake's cabin hatch.

Drake didn't answer. He honestly didn't know. Fredrickson stood before him, gun drawn, a pistol of some kind, his expression desperate and looking very much on edge, but Drake wasn't sure he saw murder in the man's eyes. Drake raised his hands.

"Captain?" Smith repeated, alarm creeping into his tone.

"Call him off," Fredrickson whispered to him with a flick of the gun toward Smith's voice outside. "Do it!"

Drake half-turned his head toward the hatch without taking his eyes off the engineer. "Fine in here," he called.

Fredrickson nodded and licked his lips. He was sweating profusely.

"Is it?" Drake asked him softly. When Fredrickson looked confused by the question, Drake inclined his head toward the gun, got a good up-close look at it, and kept his hands up. "Fine in here?"

The engineer looked at the gun in his hand, then at his

captain, pained. "It was an accident, you know? Not that you or anyone would believe me."

Drake's heart leapt, and when Fredrickson didn't elaborate, he nudged him gently to do so. "What was an accident?"

Fredrickson blinked like it was obvious. "Getting separated from my security detail."

"Of course."

"I was in the plasma tubes, working my way through the repairs, as *you knew* I was going to—you were there when I said that's what I was going to do—and they couldn't very well follow me in there. I came out on the other side of the access tubes, and I was alone. I called for them, but I guess I was too far away. I figured they'd find me and just kept on working. Doing my fucking *job*. And of course, because you marked me as enemy number one from Day One, Captain, they immediately assumed I'd tried to get away. Came in guns drawn and hot."

Drake knew where the story was going by this point. He sighed, suddenly exhausted. "So, you ran."

"Of course I fucking ran!"

"And you came here."

"You did this." Fredrickson's eyes had fury in them again. "You put it in their minds that it was me, that I'm the traitor. Only you can fix that. But you have to believe me, Captain. It's not me."

Drake sighed heavily again and stared pointedly at the weapon shaking in Fredrickson's hand.

"Do you believe me?" The fury faded, and the desperation returned.

Drake had a moment's hesitation, and then he decided to go with his gut, risky as it was. "I believe you, Lieutenant," he said, and he put his hands down.

Fredrickson blinked in surprise. "You do?"

Drake nodded.

"Why?"

Drake pointed at the gun. "First of all, that weapon is a rail-type ballistic handgun." He pointed at his shoulder. "I was shot just now, presumably by our saboteur, by an energy weapon."

"And the other reason?"

"Have you ever fired a rail handgun?"

Fredrickson shook his head. They were rare on Fleet ships, as they tended to poke holes in hulls and equipment where bad things happened when new holes appeared.

"Generally, they require ammunition." Drake pointed out the lack of a magazine in the pistol grip.

"Could still be a round in the chamber," Fredrickson said, looking at it. "I didn't check, honestly."

"Whoever shot at me fired several times." What Drake didn't say was that he'd seen the saboteur in the video, at least a blurred image of them, and even though he couldn't confirm with his eyes, every bit of his innards and intuition told him Fredrickson didn't look the part. That meant he'd royally messed up in his treatment of the man standing before him. "You have my apologies, Lieutenant," Drake said, taking a small step forward, meaning what he said. "You're right. I inadvertently cast suspicion on you with the way I came down to Engineering with the security team."

"Lie."

"What's a lie?"

"It wasn't inadvertent."

Drake had to give him that. "Perhaps. At least at first. You're not an easy man to get along with, Fredrickson."

"Doesn't make me a traitor."

"No. It doesn't." Drake locked eyes with the man. "I'm sorry." He meant it.

Fredrickson nodded, accepting the apology. He tossed the gun into the clutter on a chair, then stared at it. "Don't fuck me over," he told Drake, and stole a nervous glance over to the hatch.

"Mr. Smith," Drake called. "Could you come in here, please?"

The door opened a second later. "Captain?"

Drake gestured for Fredrickson to come out of the washroom and followed him into the main cabin. As soon as the engineer stepped into view, Smith raised his plasma rifle. "Captain! Step away."

Drake put himself in between Smith and the line of sight. "Stand down," he ordered. Confused, the e-Marine hesitated. "Everything is okay. The chief engineer and I were just talking. That's all."

"We've been looking for him," Smith said, not taking his weapon off him.

"And you've found him. A misunderstanding. My fault, in fact." Drake put more authority in his voice. "Lower your weapon."

Smith hesitated again, then complied.

"Mr. Fredrickson is not our saboteur. In fact, I would say he's in just as much danger of being attacked, perhaps even more, than I was. He is to be assigned a guard for his own protection." Drake looked at Fredrickson. "If that's acceptable, Lieutenant."

"Long as they don't go shooting me, sure."

Drake turned back to Smith. "See to it."

Smith nodded reluctantly, then stepped into the corridor and spoke quietly into his mobile radio to call another guard.

Drake regarded Fredrickson, who looked calmer even though he still glistened with sweat. He considered how differently this could have played out; how differently he would have *expected* this to play out. "This is a big ship. You probably could have hidden for quite a while instead of coming here. Coming to me."

Fredrickson nodded knowingly. "It was a risk."

"How did you know I'd listen to you?"

"I didn't."

"But you came anyway."

Fredrickson sighed and shrugged. "You've kept us all alive this far. I figured you couldn't be all bad. Though you still *mostly* are, to be clear. I still think this entire mission is foolhardy. Even if the world is ending."

Drake had to tighten his mouth into a line to keep from smiling. Fredrickson caught it and had to look away from showing his own. A moment passed without the two looking at each other. To Drake, it felt like a tiny step. Toward what, he didn't know, but it led away from contempt, and that was enough. "Well," he said, "I still have your transfer request to send to Fleet when this is all said and done."

"If there *is* a Fleet when this is all said and done."

"Don't bother me with bureaucratic details. I'll probably deny it just to piss in your Wheaties with a pending final denial that I'll extend in perpetuity."

Fredrickson snorted, and the two were interrupted as Smith returned to the cabin with one of the conscripted security detail. The Marine indicated that the crewman was ready to escort Fredrickson back to Engineering.

The engineer gestured for the crewman to lead on and gave Drake a parting half-smile. "I won't hold my breath, then," he said with a wink in his voice.

"Help us find this cockwad, Lieutenant," Drake said,

soberly. "Otherwise, we'll be fixing stuff that shouldn't be broken until we run out of spares. That would be a terminal shortage."

"I understand," Fredrickson replied.

He left.

NEPTUNE ARMORY

Terran Federation Space

CHAPTER THIRTY-TWO

GLORY'S main propulsion cut out just as they entered orbit around Neptune. Fredrickson called up to the command deck—in person—to give the news and wondered if they'd made it. Drake gave him a thank you. Yes, they had.

Barely, but he didn't share that with Fredrickson. He had done what they needed.

The Armory hung in space before them like a spider's web. It was a sprawling facility, large chambers and docking bays connected by a network of tubes and passageways that glittered in the distant light. And it was quiet. Very quiet. Even the local gateways, the portals that ships would normally use to skip around the Solar System, were much smaller than their interstellar counterparts back on Jupiter, just barely large enough for a heavy cruiser like *Glory*—were dead and quiet. They coasted on maneuvering thrusters, using the gravity well to pull them in.

"Tactical," XO called as they came within range for more detailed scans. "What are we looking at?"

"No movement," the crewman called. Li was his name,

Drake remembered. He was starting to remember everyone. "Wait!" Li leaned forward, frowning. "I'm getting debris."

The center console flickered and shifted as Oh brought up what crewman Li was looking at. There were several places for a ship to dock at the Armory. The facility had cargo bays scattered about like pods, and you could dock with any of them individually. There was also a central hub, of sorts; the largest of the bays could handle several large ships at once, and the spidery access tubes that ran to the other sections were all accessible from it. If you didn't know what you were looking for, or you were loading items from several different sections of the Armory, the central hub was for you. Most ships docked there.

Spinning in front of it was a slowly expanding cloud of debris. A ship had been destroyed there and fairly recently, judging by the dispersal pattern: not that large and distinctly ship-shaped. *Paragon*. Without question.

Oh pointed at an interesting reading. "No sign of energy weapons discharge."

Drake thought about it. Very odd. Radiation clung to the cloud, enough to account for the reactor of the Paragon ship having gone nova, but nothing more. Nor did any of the debris show signs of plasma damage. The Paragon ship had simply exploded.

"Keep on your toes," Drake told Li and the rest of the command deck crew, setting his jaw. "It could very well be a trap."

The Paragon didn't usually resort to subterfuge. Their hubris wouldn't allow it. They preferred to proclaim their intentions and superiority loudly and back both up with overwhelming force. But they also weren't stupid. They used deceit when it was the soundest tactic. They had used a damaged ship to lure him into a false sense of security, then come out of hiding, firing like crazy. They'd never blown up one of their own ships to do it, though.

"We have forward cannons on batteries," Oh said to Drake, *sotto voce*. "Two shots. At most."

Glory was on its last legs. It had taken everything they had to get there. If the Paragon were here waiting for them —well, there wasn't a whole lot they were going to be able to do about it.

"Movement!" shouted Li.

Drake saw it on the center holodisplay: a flicker. The tactical computer tracked it, highlighting the vessel.

"Lock forward cannons on that," XO commanded the weapons officer.

The vessel tracking flickered again, shifting to a spot on the opposite side of the wreckage cloud in the blink of an eye. Drake thought their sensors were glitching because it happened so fast.

"Adjust target lock," XO called.

The command deck rocked with an explosion, but from the way the sound concussed, Drake could tell they hadn't been hit. Something had exploded nearby. The tracked vessel flickered again, back by the main hub. Recognition struck Drake like lightning. He knew what he was looking at.

"Adjust target lock and fire," Oh yelled.

"Belay that!" Drake shouted over him. "Stand down."

Another close-proximity explosion rocked them to the side, but again, he could tell *Glory* had taken no damage. That part of what was happening didn't make sense, but the flickering, jumping ship did. He hoped he had it right.

"Comms," he called. "Send out standard Fleet greeting! Identify us to the new vessel." He tweaked the sensor display on his center console and spoke to Li. "Get me visual on the tracked vessel."

A chorus of "Aye, aye, sirs" followed, then a tense silence. The signal they were broadcasting was automatic, computer to computer; it didn't require spoken words. Li quietly trained one of their visual sensors on the small vessel, whatever it was, trying to catch it before it jumped again. Drake had only seen a ship jump like that under one context, with one person on board. Or rather, one *type* of person on board.

"We're being hailed," Comms reported.

"Put them on. Visual, if they can send it."

Static burst through the overhead speakers, and then a voice cut through. "*Glory?*" it asked. It was timid and very young. "Your signal says that this is *Glory?*"

"This is the Earth vessel *Glory,*" Drake responded. "You are in restricted Terran Defense Fleet space, and you have fired on my vessel. Please cease firing. Will you identify yourself, please?"

"I'm sorry. I thought you were one of them."

"Are you referring to the Paragon vessel we're detecting as a debris cloud?"

"I destroyed them, yes. They were after me."

Drake swallowed. "Will you identify yourself, please? We're requesting visual."

"I don't know how to do that—oh, I see."

The visual display above the helm stations flickered to life to show their mysterious new companion, and Drake's heart leapt into this throat when he saw who they were talking to. He didn't recognize the face, but the features: the large eyes, the glittering blue-white skin, the robes...

Drake gasped. "You're Navid."

"I am Idri, the Second Born," she said, her voice

quavering as though she too could hardly believe what she saw. "I've been waiting for you, *Glory*. I believe I am meant to be your new Navigator."

"He found me, your Admiral Sturgess, on Navidia under the guise of a diplomatic mission." Idri sat in Sickbay, perched on the edge of a medical bed, her legs not quite long enough to reach the deck. "We always met in secret. He wanted to see my abilities, what I could do. And he promised me I could be a Navigator. The first of my kind and the first in a hundred years to leave. So I said yes, and he told me to wait. My escort would come get me, and take me to Earth."

Drake, XO, and Doc listened to the young woman's story with rapt attention, hardly able to believe their eyes, let alone what they were hearing. Drake found it inconceivable. A Navigator. On *Glory*. After all this time.

He let his hand slip into his pocket, and he felt for Jack's orders cannister. The second tube had unsealed itself as soon as they came in the vicinity of the Armory. But, rather than hold further instructions, it had only an object. One Drake never wished to see again, and so he'd sealed it right back inside. The Navid made him think of it.

She sat perfectly erect, clutched a giant ancient-looking book to her chest, and spoke softly and concisely. There wasn't a wasted word or inflection. Everything was delivered with precision, and her movements were the same. Broussard, meanwhile, busied himself by examining her with all manner of scanners and probes, interrupting her now and then to get her to look into something or open her mouth.

"Cough for me," he said.

Idri coughed. She looked the worse for wear. Her journey had not been kind to her. Her eyes were sunken into her face, cheeks hollow, and her hands shook most of the time. But she was still there, and despite the physical fragility, Drake could see something steely inside her, a determination he wouldn't have expected from someone so young. Her eyes, sleep-deprived as she was, sparkled fiercely.

Broussard didn't look convinced.

She continued relating her story to the captain with perfect enunciation. "Warren took me in the middle of the night, and we snuck aboard a Freeley transport to get off Navidia. Every ship we boarded was like that; I was hidden. Warren explained that it was for my safety. That if the Paragon knew about me, they would come for me. And they did, finally, at Corvus. A surprise attack, which Warren said was unusual." A memory forced her to pause before she could throw herself back to her story. "Your Lieutenant Warren sacrificed himself to allow me to escape, Captain Drake. The shuttle had this blue planet on the edge of your system as its destination, and so I jumped the ship here and waited. *For you.*"

Drake didn't know Warren. Not personally, but he sounded like the kind of black ops specialist Jack had once employed by the dozens.

Smuggling a Navid off her homeworld; it was astonishing. When Drake had last been in the Fleet, humans weren't allowed to step foot on Navidia. It didn't sound like that had changed.

"So, you've been folding space?" Broussard asked her.

Idri nodded. "To get here and to destroy the Paragon ship."

Broussard clucked his tongue with a shake of his head and showed Drake the scans' readings on a datapad. It was an image of her brain, with several small sections lit up in an ominous red. He pointed them out to Drake, then showed them to Idri. "Those are lesions on your brain. A nasty side effect of folding space too much. Tell me, do you ever lose consciousness?"

"After folding a far enough distance, yes, though I am getting better at that, Doctor. Stronger."

"Well, you almost killed yourself." Broussard shook his head and gave Drake a knowing look before turning back to her. "You're healing now, and I can speed that up, but you can't exert yourself like that again. It will kill you if you do too much."

Idri blinked deliberately and nodded in the same manner. "I did what I had to do," she said simply.

"And how did you destroy the Paragon ship?" Drake asked, unable to keep his curiosity in any longer. "Your shuttle didn't have weapons."

"It had me," she answered with a blink of her startling giant blue eyes. "I folded one of the small craft at this facility into the engine section of their ship."

It was Drake's turn to blink. XO did too. "You did what?" XO asked.

"There are small shuttle-like craft docked at this facility—"

"Yes, I know what you mean," Drake interrupted. "You said you folded one inside the Paragon ship?"

"Yes."

"And that destroyed them?"

"Yes."

"How?"

Idri frowned as though she was having a hard time

understanding why they weren't following. She looked around. She was sitting on the edge of an examination table. Sickbay was quieter now, but there were still wounded and dying around them. Nearby was a package of gauze. Two of them. Idri set aside her giant book and grabbed them.

Before the men could ask her what she was doing, she tossed one of them into the air. It arched above them, reaching its zenith, but before it fell, Idri focused her attention on the second gauze pack she held in her hands. Her face contorted in intense focus, brow knitted, jaw flexing. In a blink, the gauze packed in her hand disappeared.

Pop!

With a thunderclap that rang the ears of everyone in Sickbay and was strong enough to stagger Drake, Oh, and Broussard, there was an explosion of white fibers. Not fibers, Drake realized as they fell, but particles. Dust, even. Still white, and only recognizable as what they once were from that color, but undeniably what was left of the gauze packets. The explosion still rang in Drake's ears as he turned back to look at Idri with unreserved awe. The young Navid looked at them, bemused. How had she done that?

"Matter cannot coexist in the same space and time," she said. "By its nature, it must remain distinct. If I force it to coexist, like I just did with those wound coverings, it annihilates itself."

Drake was awestruck. The explosion had been much larger than he would have thought, but then again, there was more energy in a single atom than humanity had ever been able to harness. She controlled it.

"I've never seen a Navigator do that before," XO said, similarly amazed. "Were you taught that?"

Idri picked up the book and pressed it against her chest like it was a security blanket. "I am a Second Born," she said with no small amount of frustration, shame, and sadness. "I was taught nothing except what I learned myself from the pages of this book."

Drake recognized it. The Tome he believed it was called, and he recalled that what she said was true; the Navid had a strictly stratified culture. Only First Borns were allowed to develop their innate skills to fold space, a skill that had been absent from their society for centuries due to over-breeding and genetic manipulation. It had grown so bad that no new Navigators had been born in nearly a century. With Idri sitting before him, Drake couldn't help but wonder if their folly had been more systemic than genetic science. They could very well have a cultural blind spot as well. "I've had a Navigator in the past," he mused with an arched eyebrow, and looked back to Idri, "and I don't recall that particular maneuver ever being brought up."

Idri reddened. "Before we parted, your Warren encouraged me to improvise." She smiled slightly. "So I did."

"I think you're sensational," XO said, ecstatic. "Sensational. We'll get you a uniform and settled into the fulcrum chamber."

Oh was referring to more than just the swearing-in that any member of the Fleet would undergo. There was a ceremony for Navigators, one that would bond them to their ship and its crew. Thinking about that ceremony made Drake's stomach churn. "Let's hold off on that."

Oh glanced at him, frowning in surprise. "Sir?"

Drake gestured at Broussard. "Let the doc help her recover. And I want you on the Neptune Armory, Commander, looking for the weapon that Jack sent us out here for."

"I—I mean, forgive me, sir, but wouldn't it behoove us to have her get to know the ship as soon as possible?"

"Those are my orders." Drake was shorter with his first officer than he would have liked, but he suddenly needed to get the hell out of Sickbay and away from the Navid. He turned to the doctor with every ounce of self-control he had and took his leave with a curt nod. "See that those lesions are attended to."

Outside, Drake gulped air, blew past his security escort Smith, who'd stayed outside close to the entrance, and swiftly headed down the corridor, not caring where he was going as long as it was away from Sickbay.

"Sir!" a voice called after him. It was Oh, in hot pursuit.

Drake didn't hear him...or didn't care to. It was several long straights and more than a few turns before he finally slowed down. His heart was still pounding, and he was sweating when Oh finally caught up with him.

"What's the matter with you?" XO's tone carried both challenge and concern.

"Nothing," he lied. He knew he looked as anxious as he felt.

Oh got closer to him and spoke quietly and intently. "With all due respect," he started, pointing back down the corridor, "she is a game-changer, Captain. Universe-saving stuff. When she gets a handle on this ship, gets bonded, we can jump without gating. It's a *game-changer*. Just the edge we need against the Paragon."

"How?"

XO's mouth dropped open, and he frowned.

Drake filled the silence. "There's still the *entire* Paragon fleet to contend with, not to mention the question of our ability to take down the planet-killer once we get there.

We're one ship. The only thing we should be thinking about right now is that cannon. The reason Jack sent us out here."

"How do you know *she's* not the reason he sent us out here? 'Use the 'girl' his orders said. It has to be her."

Drake shook his head. "We know that ship, and we know what can take it down. So did Jack. He sent us *here*. That's the edge we need, Commander. It's here. Find it." XO shut his mouth, but Drake could tell there was more he wanted to say. Drake didn't want to hear it. "Let me handle the Navid."

"She made it this far, Captain. The sooner we get her—"

"No." Drake cut him off with finality. "If we push her too far, she could die, and I won't let that happen again."

Oh studied the captain. The look on his face said, *so, there it is.* He wouldn't let it happen *again.*

Drake ignored the look. This was not up for debate. "Get over to the Armory and start looking."

XO seemed like he wanted to push it further, to talk about what was now unspoken.

Drake shut that down, too. "That's an order."

"Yes, sir."

"Smith," Drake called down the corridor to where his escort had posted up to wait out the heated exchange between the two officers. "I have a new assignment for you."

CHAPTER THIRTY-THREE

CARROL WOKE TO STATIC.

Someone was pounding on her cabin door. She rose from her bunk too quickly and nearly smacked her head on the low ceiling. Her entire body ached, and her head hurt like the rest of her. Damn compression drugs were a sonofabitch. Unnatural. Her body continued to fight the effects.

On the opposite wall, her comm station was on for some reason, blaring static, with white, snowy video noise to match. She must have left it on.

"Coming!" she called and made sure she had clothes on before she opened the hatch. She did. Sweat-soaked. Body odor wafted up to her nostrils, now that she was paying attention to it. Yikes.

The person at the door pounded again.

She shut off the comm station, then reached to open the hatch, making sure she stood several feet away from whoever was outside.

It was Smith.

She must have looked surprised because he shuffled his

feet awkwardly. "I've been assigned to escort you, Commander," he rumbled in his subwoofer of a voice.

"Escort me?"

He inclined his head as if just remembering she'd been out for a while. "All crew are to be escorted by a member of security and stay in groups of no less than two. At all times."

She must have missed something. "What happened?"

"An attempt was made on the captain's life."

Carrol's pulse quickened. "By the saboteur? The same piece of shit who fucked over my Delta Wings?"

"The assumption is that they're one and the same."

"But not caught yet?"

"Hence the need for added security."

Carrol looked the giant man up and down. "You're the meanest mother on this ship, Smith. Why aren't you guarding the captain?"

Smith straightened. "I was, but Efremova is with him at this moment. He assigned me to you while he's on the Armory station."

"We made it to Neptune?"

Smith nodded to confirm.

"Stars alive!" Carrol said, heart now racing from the disorientation. "How long did you let me sleep? Is it safe here? Where are the Paragon?"

Smith arched an eyebrow which gave Carrol the impression it had been a while. "I can fill you in, sir," he said, "on the way to the command deck. Your presence there is required."

Carrol nodded, and the motion of her head wafted her days' worth of grime, sweat, and adrenaline into her nose. Dammit all. She looked at Smith. "You think I have time to take a shower?"

Oʜ sᴛᴏᴏᴅ in the enormous central landing hub of the Neptune Armory and frowned at the computer console he was using. Drake approached him from the loading gangway folded out from *Glory* into the space station. As he passed through the giant exterior hatch, he noticed that the bolted makeshift sign declaring that Where Angels Fear to Tread, Drake's Demons Give 'Em Hell was still affixed to the main entrance. It both comforted him and made him feel uneasy. He was at a loss to reconcile the two and tried with great difficulty to shake it from his mind.

"I'm not coming up with any results when I search for the serial number in the inventory index," Oh reported when Drake got within hearing range, which was nearly next to each other because of the cacophony caused by the activity that was underway.

The experimental cannon wasn't the only thing Drake intended *Glory* to get from this massive facility, and Oh had anticipated that. They were loading all the weapons, ordnance, and equipment they could get their hands on. Torpedoes, missiles, plasma cannon batteries and barrels, mines, sensor arrays... Hell, the kitchen was missing food constituters and dispensers for the mess hall. Everything that had been destroyed in *Glory's* conflicts, long ago or recent, or stripped from her in the years she'd been left to rot, the Neptune Armory had it all.

The cannon was the only thing Drake was interested in finding.

"It's been twenty years, and it was top secret even then," Drake pointed out. "I doubt it's going to be sitting there in the common inventory."

XO gave him a look. "Which is why I was searching for

the serial number, sir. I don't expect it to be *described* or just laying out in the open. But an entry with its registered number is standard procedure."

Drake chewed the inside of his cheek, knowing his officer was annoyed and feeling just as annoyed himself.

"It has to be here."

"Did the admiral *say* anything about where it might be?"

"You know Jack. He only said there was a weapon."

The first officer groaned. "More explicit instructions than 'Neptune 0700,' and 'use the girl' would have been helpful."

"Bastard was almost certainly under surveillance the entire time he and I met," Drake said, rubbing his brow. Damn, he had a headache. He didn't think he'd slept more than an hour at a time in two or three days. Ever since the night the secretive admiral had shown up on his doorstep. "I didn't even know he was sending us to Neptune 'til we opened the orders aboard *Glory*. The Paragon would have beat us here."

"What about the second orders cannister?"

Drake stiffened, and Oh noticed. Its contents flashed through his mind, unbidden. A single, gold-plated object. "Nothing in there about the cannon."

Oh pursed his lips and narrowed his eyes, hesitant to push forward, but he did anyway. "What *was* in there?"

"Something else." Drake had no desire to tell his first officer. "It doesn't help us here." That much was the truth.

Oh accepted it begrudgingly, and then threw his hands up. "What if the cannon's not here? What if the Paragon already took care of it?"

"It has to be here," Drake asserted. "*Has to*. Jack said,

outright, there was a weapon. I have that much faith in him, at least."

Oh sighed heavily. "What the ever-loving mess has the world come to if we're putting our faith in goddamn Admiral Jack?"

Drake sympathized, but here they were. Anxiety gnawed at his stomach. He thought of planet-killer. What if the cannon wasn't here? What could *they* do to stop that monstrous thing? He pushed it all down. It had to be here. Had to be. And it would change everything.

An alarm blared.

Over a loudspeaker, Drake heard his name called. "Captain Drake to the command deck! Captain to the command deck."

Oh stiffened, ready to haul ass, but Drake held him back with a strong hand. "You stay here," he said. "Find that damn cannon."

CHAPTER THIRTY-FOUR

THE DECK ROCKED beneath Drake's feet, nearly sending him into the wall. Strong hands grabbed his arm and yanked him steady, which sent shooting pain through his bad shoulder. He grimaced.

"Sorry, sir," Efremova said, her hands still on his arm.

Drake knew he'd been the one to order everyone on the ship to go no less than two by two while their saboteur was still at large, but Efremova had a habit of sticking too close. He missed Smith. The e-Marine was the perfect mix of hang back and close when you needed him. Marine training and experience. Efremova could learn a thing or two from her subordinate. Still, she'd kept him from falling.

He thanked her. They rounded the corner, came to the stairwell that led to the command deck, and started hoofing it.

"You think we're under attack, sir?" she called from behind him.

No, Drake thought. *Not yet, anyway.* That had been the movement of them disengaging from the Armory. That told him that something was coming, but they hadn't yet been fired upon. He shared that with Efremova, and she suggested that they pick up their speed. Drake concurred.

They took the steps two at a time as they raced upward.

They made it to the command deck in record time.

Carrol was at the command console, looking fresher than the last time he'd seen her. Her face was creased with worry.

"Captain," she said formally as they approached, sweaty and heaving. "Apologies."

"Unnecessary. What's the situation, Commander?"

She pointed at the holographic display. "A vessel has just appeared on long-range sensors, approaching fast."

"Paragon?"

"Doesn't appear to be?" Carrol shook her head, frustrated. "They're just now crossing the terminator, sir."

"Roger," Drake confirmed. "What's *Glory's* status?"

"Still on maneuvering thrusters only. Main propulsion offline, and plasma cannons on battery backups." She grimaced. "We haven't had time to repair the weapons systems, sir."

Drake nodded. He'd figured as much. They couldn't run. They couldn't fight. The only thing to do was wait, which was excruciating for Drake and everyone else on the command deck.

"Comms, try to hail them," he called. "And Tactical, get me sensor details as soon as you can pick them up." They could work on that, at least.

A minute later, Communications excitedly barked, "Incoming short-range."

"On speakers."

Static hissed, far more than there should be given the

distance between the two ships. Drake wondered if it was their equipment or whoever was incoming.

"Unidentified vessel," a distinctly human-sounding voice said through the static. Drake relaxed. "This is the TDF cruiser *Vengeance*. You are in restricted space. If you do not leave immediately, you will be fired upon."

Drake smiled at the pageantry of it all. Exactly what he'd have said if he'd rolled up on an unknown situation, whether or not his ship had the stones to back up the posturing. From the readings that were coming in, he doubted *Vengeance* did. She was leaking energy, her course wasn't egregiously erratic but it was enough that Drake noticed, and it was her comms that were underpowered. She'd been through hell, Drake guessed.

"*Vengeance*, this is the TDF cruiser *Glory*. Welcome to Neptune."

There was a pause. "*Glory*? I don't know a *Glory*."

"We're just about forty-eight hours re-commissioned out of the Jupiter Shipyards. Transmitting call signs and registry codes to you now." Drake motioned to Comms that they would allow for visual if *Vengeance* could handle it. They could, and a moment later, a harried, tired face appeared on their overhead monitors.

"Hell of a time to deploy," the man said with a shake of his head. He was probably the captain, but Drake didn't want to make that assumption, given the state of the command deck behind him. The damage was extensive. Hard to say if it was more or less than what *Glory* had suffered, but there was no doubt that *Vengeance* had been in heavy combat with the Paragon. "Boy, am I glad you're not one of them," the man confessed, exhausted. "Inner system is crawling with Paragon. We barely made it out with our lives."

"Same," Drake agreed. "We're here at the Armory station to resupply and effect repairs. You are welcome to join us. Who do I have the pleasure of speaking to?"

"Sellers," said the man. "Captain William Sellers."

Drake didn't recognize the name, and underneath the grime, blood, and sleeplessness, he could see that Sellers was young. In his thirties, most likely. A child when Drake had left the service.

"And I think we *will* join you, Captain...?"

"Drake."

In contrast to Drake's ignorance of the other, recognition flickered over the younger man's face. "Augustus Drake?"

"The same."

There was a moment of silence, then, "I look forward to speaking with you, Captain."

———

SELLERS WAS CAGEY. He came up the main gangway through the Armory hub and flinched at each of the loud noises he heard along the way. Drake directed them to the command deck through out-of-the-way corridors to give the man a respite from the sounds. His interest in his surroundings increased as they went until he was openly marveling at the *Glory*.

"I didn't realize there were any ships of this class still in service," he said as he stopped to observe one of this ship's older intercoms. He traced a finger over the metal panel, which was thick with decades of paint on top of paint.

"There weren't before about two days ago," Drake confessed.

"Indeed," Sellers said, then turned his gaze on Drake.

He looked him up and down, shaking his head the same way he had when looking at the ancient comm panel. "How exactly *is* it, Captain, that you are out here? You and your ship?"

Drake wasn't sure what Sellers meant or what he'd heard about *Glory* and him. He'd had stature at one time in the Fleet and in the history books, but that had been before the fiery end to his career and the smear campaign led by Jack and his fellow admirals. Some of it had been public—too public. But Sellers wasn't looking at him in disgust. It was more neutral than that, almost reverent.

"Special mission for Fleet Intelligence," Drake said, keeping it vague.

Sellers nodded, seeming to accept it. "It's a miracle you survived this long. I could see from our scans that you've taken heavy damage."

"We have. So have you."

"We were stationed on the planned parade route, outside the asteroid belt along with two other ships, the *Nimitz* and the *Erebus*. We ignored the stand-down orders. Figured those were fake, which they most certainly were, and responded to the nearest distress calls, which came in close to Ceres." His eyes clouded. "We were overmatched instantly. Both *Nimitz* and *Erebus* started to have weapons and propulsion malfunctions as soon as they got within range of the Paragon battleships. They didn't make it." He gave a haunted sigh. "It was like that everywhere we went, ships dropping within seconds of engagement. I'd suspect some form of sabotage on a massive scale."

"Yes, well, we've dealt with some of that ourselves," Drake said archly with a glance at Efremova and the security guard she'd assigned to their guest.

Sellers got a faraway look. "For us, it was our chief engineer. I don't know what got into him, but he went mad. Attacked his own second, and in the scuffle, got thrown into an open manifold. It happened early on; I think we were lucky that way. Not sure how many other ships had similar problems. I don't know how prepared any of us really were for an attack in such numbers, Captain—it's been since your heyday that any Paragon ship has attacked a Fleet ship in any real capacity—but it clearly wasn't enough. There wasn't much of anything we could do to help anyone, and so we ran. All the way out here."

"How did you make it?"

"We tried the local gateways at first. That was unwise. The Paragon were waiting for us on the other side, jumping from Ceres to Enceladus." Sellers flexed his jaw in frustration. "It was one ship, but they cut us down the second we emerged before we could even put up a defense. By some miracle, they didn't get our engines and we were able to slip back through and re-dial the gateway for the Uranus pole. By another miracle, there was no one out there and we burned off as hard as we could once we were through. I'm not sure if they followed or not, but I would bet they did."

So would Drake. It was an ominous possibility. Regardless, he had known their time at the Armory would not be undisturbed forever. The Paragon would come. *Glory* needed to be loaded and gone before they did.

"How long do you think before *Vengeance* can be combat-ready?" Drake asked.

Sellers blinked at him, confusion on his face. "Combat-ready?" he repeated. "There is no combat-ready for what they have, Captain Drake. We're bugging the fuck out of here."

"THIS FOOTAGE WAS BROADCAST over the QE network two hours ago." Sellers stood at the head of the conference room table opposite Drake and gestured at a paused holographic recording projected in the center of it.

In addition to Drake, Efremova, his constant shadow, and Carrol were at the table. The room was still crowded with extra equipment and freshly damaged components, but it was clean to the point of usability.

Small victories.

Projected was Mars, and in a high—very high—orbit around it, looking much smaller than it had when framed by the Jupiter Gateway but still terrifyingly massive was the Paragon planet-killer. Other Paragon ships surrounded it in close formation. In the bottom of the screen was a burned-in timecode. Drake's heart sank at the sight of it all. He knew what was coming.

"My senior comm officer has confirmed its authenticity," Sellers explained. He pressed a command on the conference table, and the frozen projection began to play.

The planet-killer pulsed with an intense white light. Each time it did, energy coalesced from the half-dome top of the massive ship and bled to the tip, and the whole ship started to spin. The pulses increased in frequency and intensity with each pass, and the rotation increased. Carefully, Drake watched the timecode in the bottom corner of the recording, noting every stage as the ship went faster and faster, brighter and brighter. The spin turned into a blur of pure white light, and from the tip where the light was the most brilliant, a particle beam erupted. It cut through the super-thin atmosphere that surrounded Mars, sending wisps of gas and dust billowing away from it.

But, the blast was yet to come. Still, the pulsing continued to build around, increasing until the white light turned incandescent and the vessel became a beacon of pure energy

When the blast finally erupted from the ship, it blinded everyone in the briefing room even though it was only a recording. When it subsided, Mars was cracking apart. The energy beam bored into the red planet until it pierced it, sending rocks, magma, and plasma out the other side. Around the circumference of the hole, the planet's tectonic plates were thrown into space, breaking up as they went.

The officers watched in horror. What they were seeing was inconceivable. Finally, the beam shut off, and the Paragon moved away from the dying planet. The violence of their attack and the explosive forces that were now at work made their location the only safe one for millions of kilometers. The Martian matter being ejected into space moved away from the Paragon ships, and Drake understood why they were huddled together so tightly. They didn't want to get hit by the planet's remnants.

Mars didn't exist anymore, except as space dust and fleeting fire.

The Paragon had done it. They had tried decades before when Drake had been there to stop them, but he hadn't been where he needed to be this time. They'd succeeded in building a weapon that could destroy an entire world. The watchers could not grasp what they were seeing, even as the holographic recording continued mercilessly, showing the prolonged death of the red planet. She'd die a million deaths over a million years as her ashes spread across the Solar System. It was a brutal act, and no human had ever witnessed its equal.

Drake re-keyed the recording into his own data rod. He

knew it would be wise to study that footage carefully over the next several hours.

"How many people were on Mars?" The question came from Carrol.

"Unknown," Sellers answered. His twitchiness suddenly made more sense. "Evacuation orders for the entire Solar System were issued about twelve hours ago. The Paragon fleet, it seems, is less here in force to protect their new weapon as it is to pick off any and all of our fleeing ships. On their approach to Mars, they set up a blockade for just such a purpose. It's doubtful many made it through, even if they did get off the planet before it was destroyed."

He finally raised his eyes from the projection and glanced at *Glory's* crew members before landing on Drake. "The battle is over. The Paragon weapon will reach Earth in approximately twenty-four hours. Our orders—everyone's orders—are to be as far away from here as possible before then. This is an extermination. The only victory we may claim is to survive."

Sellers flopped into a chair, and there was a long and heavy silence. Drake felt as though it might crush him.

"What do we do?" Efremova asked.

"Our proposal is to combine crews," Sellers said, spreading his hands over the conference table. "*Vengeance* is certainly not much better off than *Glory*, but we do have main propulsion online."

"We are currently repairing our main drive," Drake said hoarsely.

"Ours is functional now. As I mentioned, Captain, the Paragon are likely to pursue us here. They've already been here by your own account with the destroyed ship. Our plan is to head out-system. The chances of the Paragon following us into deep space are slim."

"And where would you go?"

Sellers shook his head. "We can aim for Alpha Centauri."

"At sub-light?" Carrol asked, wading into the fray with incredulity. "That would take years!"

"Not to mention the Paragon could gate there at any time."

"Along with the evacuation orders for the Solar System," Sellers said, "all Earth colonies were ordered to destroy their gateways." That statement stunned his audience; its magnitude was hard to fathom. Impossible, even. "Heading in-system is suicide. Our directive now is to survive. Leaving is our only chance."

"I can't believe it," Carrol said, and she collapsed into a chair, retreating into shock.

Sellers once again regarded Drake, a pained look on his face. "In just the hour or so that we've been here, Captain, we've already received dozens of transfer requests from your crew. Our intentions to leave have leaked, and many of them want to come with us. All of them, perhaps, once word has gone around in full."

There was another long, awkward silence. Drake didn't know what to say; his world was spinning quickly. Irrational anger boiled inside him, but it was tempered with growing grief and sadness. How could he blame them? Although he knew it was wrong, knew every one of them who left would regret it, how could he blame those who wanted to run?

"What say you?" Sellers asked. His expression softened since he was aware of the gravity of what he was proposing. Sympathetic to it, but asking nonetheless. "To combining our crews, equipment, and supplies onto the *Vengeance*? I think that would give us the best chance for survival in this strategic retreat."

Strategic retreat. It *was* the best chance for survival. Drake couldn't argue that, but he wanted to. He knew he had to. "I will think it through, Captain," he said when he couldn't find the right words.

Drake didn't elaborate, nor did Carrol or Efremova offer their thoughts on the matter. Whether that was because their captain was visibly stewing or because they, like he, couldn't formulate their thoughts, Drake didn't know. He only knew that he wished Oh was in the conference room to be his bulldog and run Sellers off. Sellers, blessedly, wasn't without fluency in non-verbal communication and acknowledged that they wished to be alone with a nod of his head. He stood. "Of course," he said, then he cleared his throat. "I intend to hold a memorial gathering for those of my crew I have lost. Perhaps, as a first step toward integration, we might hold such a service together?"

Drake flexed his jaw muscles but nodded at last. "That would be acceptable, Captain. Commander Carrol can assist in making those arrangements."

Sellers gave Carrol a nod and they exchanged information about how they'd communicate, then he removed his datarod from the port on his seat at the conference table, smoothed his hair, and left.

"Dismissed," Drake said to Carrol and Efremova once the *Vengeance*'s captain was gone.

Efremova gave him an arch look, and Drake indicated that she should wait for him outside. Carrol lingered.

"What do you think?" he asked when it was just the two of them.

She straightened at the question, not used to being asked her opinion. She should get used to it, he thought idly.

She was a senior officer now and one he had begun to trust with his life. He wanted to know what she thought.

"I don't know, sir. Captain Sellers may be right. What can we possibly do? One ship?" She pointed at the table where the projection of the planet-killer had run. "Against that?"

Drake considered her words, her fears. He rose from his seat to reach the internal communications hub in the center of the conference table and keyed an intercom call.

"XO here," was the response to the hail.

"Commander," Drake began. "Have you had any luck locating the particle cannon?"

There was only frustration on the other end. "No. Sorry, sir. Not yet."

Drake told him to keep looking before switching off. Then there was a long, tense silence.

"What are we going to do?" Carrol asked.

He didn't have an answer for her. Not yet. "Whatever we must do," he told her. It was the only bit of truth he could offer her at the moment, even though he didn't know what it meant yet.

"And what about the transfer requests?"

Drake shot her a look. "Hold them."

She raised her eyebrows, but to her credit, she inclined her head in deference with a quiet "Yes, sir."

"For now," Drake added, conscious of his own reaction. He sank, deflated, into his chair. "Just for now."

Still Carrol lingered. He looked up at her.

"There has also been a request, sir, to use the QE and allow the crew to call home. One last time."

Drake felt that one right in his chest. He'd wanted to call Ellen the moment all this started. His response nearly caught in his throat, it was so painful. "I'm sorry,

Commander," he said. "We cannot risk exposing our position."

Carrol's eyes shone as she nodded. She understood. It was the order he had to give.

There would be more of those, Drake knew. He wasn't looking forward to them.

CHAPTER THIRTY-FIVE

OH HAD long since passed the point of futility and was deep in the territory of only continuing to do a task because he'd been so ordered. He'd lost all hope of finding this superweapon they so desperately needed. He was mentally preparing himself to break the news to Drake, wracking his brain for alternatives and staving off the panic and depression that came when he realized there weren't any alternatives. The data scrolled past him in mind-numbing fashion, cache after cache of not-what-they-were-looking-for.

It therefore came as a surprise when, totally at random and lucky that he saw it, he stumbled across one of the Armory caches that was entirely blank. Every serial number was blacked out, dates of equipment loaded in were likewise encrypted, personnel in and out, everything except the item lines, which were numerous. It was one of the larger pods, without a doubt, and its location in the Armory's spider web was unlisted. It had Jack's grubby secret-loving black ops fingerprints all over it.

His heart nearly leapt through his throat and out onto the data screen. He keyed in his security clearance code, and nothing happened. The screen of his access terminal stayed blank.

Oh pursed his lips and tried to think like a spook.

He had never been great at keeping secrets. He'd never fit in with the intelligence crowd, and those people only trusted others of their type. And while Jack had thrown him to the wolves in many ways, given where they were standing, the admiral had never lost faith in one person Oh could think of: Drake.

He searched his brain for his superior officer's SCC. He'd had it memorized a lifetime ago, such was the trust between the two men. Anything Drake was allowed to lay his eyes upon that came from Fleet, Oh was allowed to see as well. XO had never abused that privilege. He wasn't going to abuse it here either. He punched it in as the numbers and letters came back to him.

The terminal processed for what felt like an eternity before finally displaying a green message.

Cargo Bay Open.

His heart leapt again. It had worked! But where was the cargo bay he was looking for? The number and location were still blacked out on his info screen. How was he supposed to find the damned thing? There were hundreds of cargo bays in the sprawling facility, decades' worth of stockpiles and archives.

He brought up a master schematic of the station, overwhelming in its sprawl, but he quickly filtered down by asking the directory to show him only those bays that were currently open. They lit up in green. A dozen of them were clustered around the central hub where he was standing, where the supplies they were loading onto the two docked cruisers were located.

One cargo bay was on the fringe, isolated. It, too, was unlocked.

Oh tapped it on the monitor to bring up its manifest and entry/exit history. Blank.

That was the one.

He noted its location and shouted for his security escort to join him. Her name was Kuminga. Tall young woman. Didn't say much, which he appreciated.

"What's up?" she asked as he led them to the grav sled station at the back of the cavernous central hub.

"Hop on," he said once he'd fired one up.

Grav sleds were simple two-seater transports with long, wide flatbeds on the back. They ran through the Armory on maglev tracks, and one could load them with whatever equipment was needed when they weren't docked with a cargo pod that had the desired gear. The flatbed had adjustable gravity plating that canceled out mass up to several tons, and they could glide back to the ship with the loot in tow. They were also fast as hell and fun to ride in.

Kuminga got on without question or protest.

Oh entered their destination on the sled's onboard computer, and the message **Put on your seat restraints** appeared. Oh gave Kuminga a look. "I'd suggest doing what the computer says. These things are fa—"

He didn't even get to finish the sentence before the sled rocketed into one of the dozen tunnels that lined the hub's back wall. Neither of them was thrown off, thankfully; the sled would have stopped if they had been, detecting they were no longer in their seats. When he and Kuminga got their belts fastened, the sled picked up speed.

Oh would have enjoyed the ride out to the blacked-out

pod if he hadn't been so preoccupied with his sleep-deprived irrational hope for what they'd find there.

There were long stretches of tunnel between cargo pods where the sides and roof were lined in transparent metals that allowed spectacular views of Neptune, which swirled in deep, gorgeous blues, purples, and greens. It was a planet that didn't often get visited, being so far out on the edge of the Solar System, but it was breathtaking for those willing to look up and take it in.

Oh glanced every now and then before he was invariably drawn back to their progress tracker.

The sled finally started to slow, entered one last junction tunnel, and came to a soundless stop in front of a massive door. The pod number and location outside the door to the damn thing were painted over in black so they couldn't read them. They dismounted from their ride and stood in front of the giant entrance. Oh nodded. This carried Jack's signature like he'd scrawled his name as a tagger might.

He could see from the green-lit security panel to the right of the door that the bay was unlocked, as promised. He punched the release button, and with a heavy rumble, the entrance crawled open, rising from the floor and disappearing into the ceiling.

Inside was darkness. Rather than fumble for the light controls, Oh clicked on his flashlight. Bless Drake; he was always right about that. Amateurs and hitchhikers brought their towels into space. Professionals made sure they had a flashlight. The beam cut through the blackness, illuminating all manner of odd devices, most of which were all the more fantastic-looking because they were covered in canvas or tarpaulins, denying the observer a casual look. Even in a locked, unmarked vault on the far reaches of the Solar

System, Jack intended to keep his secrets to the last. What they were looking for, however, would be unmistakable.

"Woah."

Kuminga was peering at something above them, farther back in the recesses of the hold. Oh followed her gaze with his flashlight and lit up something that was stories tall, roughly cylindrical in shape, and stretched for hundreds of meters into the darkness beyond.

Oh cursed and shook his head. It was hard to believe he was looking at the damn thing again after all these years.

Kuminga glanced at him. "What is it?"

"A fighting chance," he said, then he cursed at Jack under his breath for coming through, the sonofabitch. It was here. It had been here all along.

Oh reached for his mobile radio and called *Glory*. All he got was static, and he put it away and motioned for Kuminga to follow him as he exited the hold. They were out of radio range out there. "We have to get back and report to the captain."

THERE WAS a knock on the hatch.

"Yes?"

Drake turned, expecting to see Efremova poking her head inside his quarters to report some horrible thing. But it wasn't her; it was Broussard. "May I come in?" the doctor asked, head and body askew as he angled through the half-open hatch.

"If you wish."

Truth was, there wasn't anything to interrupt. Drake was standing in the middle of his cabin, surrounded by the mess of papers and fallen shelves and not doing anything about them except staring at Admiral Jack's orders cannister —the second one—and ignoring a flashing datapad sitting on his desk.

"The Navid is back on her feet," Broussard reported. "She's a willful one for a Navid; I'll grant her that."

Drake heard him. It was the news he'd been waiting for, but he didn't react. He only continued to roll the orders cannister between his thumb and forefinger.

"That's the good news, my dear Captain. The bad news is that more than half of my medical staff have put in requests to transfer to that other ship over there."

Drake still couldn't muster a reaction.

Broussard carefully picked his way through the mess to situate himself in front of the captain. No small task. He made a show of grunting and teetering as he went, finally reaching the nearby desk. He perched on its corner next to the flashing datapad and looked at it curiously. Nothing he could see, however, with it fingerprint locked. It was all orchestrated to annoy Drake, which it did.

"You ever going to clean this mess?" Doc asked, dropping the pad and spreading his hands to indicate the chaos.

"I've been busy."

"You're not busy now."

Drake looked away.

"And my medical staff?" Doc pressed. "You going to do anything about that?"

"Like what?"

"Like stop them from leaving!"

"I can't force anyone to stay, Doc."

Broussard folded his arms with a smug shake of his head that made Drake want to punch him. "I said, stop them. I never said force." He looked at the ceiling and thought hard for a moment; whether in sincerity or mockery, Drake couldn't tell. "I can't recall Captain Augustus Drake ever *forcing* his crew to do anything, in fact."

"I forced Elbin to jump us back from Paragon space."

The mention of the former Navigator and their last mission together sobered Broussard, and he crossed his arms with a serious frown. "I'm not following."

"I gave the order."

"Giving an order and having it followed is not 'forced,' Cap."

"Semantics."

"Distinction. He would have done what he did whether or not you gave the order."

"But I did give the order! The responsibility was mine."

Broussard blinked in surprise at the sudden heat from his friend. "Okay," he said diplomatically. Drake could see thoughts cycling over his face as he tried to figure out what the hell his friend was wrestling with. "Again, Captain, I'm not following."

Drake decided to make it easy for him. He popped the top of the orders cannister, and into his outstretched palm, he poured the lone object from inside. It was a small pin about the size of his palm, solid gold, and it gleamed even in the low light. Like the captain's insignia that Drake wore on his uniform, this pin, too, was worn and rounded at the edges from many years of use. But the wear hadn't diminished its details. They were ornate, much more so than any other Fleet insignia, Drake's included, with overlapping circles surrounding a starburst in the center. And there was writing. Not Earth Standard, but alien. Navid. In the center of the starburst was the tiny outline of a warship. *Glory*. It was a Navigator's pin. *Glory's* Navigator's pin.

He handed it to Doc.

His color changed when he realized what it was. "This is his?"

Drake nodded. It was Elbin's, yes. Drake thought the old Navid had been buried with it. But there it was. He held up the small cannister. "Admiral Jack sent it with me, to be opened once we got here."

"For the girl?"

"For the girl."

There was a long moment shared between the two men. Finally, Doc understood.

"I, and I alone gave him the order that ended Elbin's life," Drake said when was able to speak again. "I cannot shrink from that. I am responsible. I don't know if that was the right choice then, and I don't know if it's the right choice here to move forward."

Doc was having none of it. "What you were responsible for, Captain, was saving—*pardonne-moi*—our fucking lives. And pardon me again, but that same, *correct*, choice seems to apply directly to the situation we're facing right now. We do what we must. Always."

Drake made his free hand into a frustrated fist and pounded his thigh with it. "This Captain Sellers...they had it worse than us, I think. Saw more. Lost more. He thinks it's all over and we should run. Commander Carrol thinks he might be right, and so, apparently, does much of the crew. What can one ship do against so many?"

"And what do you think?"

"I think one ship can do a hell of a lot."

Broussard smiled. It was a genuine smile, one that could light the darkest room, and it did. "I think so, too." He darted an eye down to the datapad still blinking on Drake's desk. "I also think none of them knows what you know."

Drake glanced over his shoulder at the hatch and the crew beyond. "Are they going to believe me, though?"

"How do you know they don't already?"

Drake shook his head at the question, which had been asked in earnest, and laughed at his friend.

Broussard shrugged, his smile turning sly. "Hey, you were the one who pulled me out of the swamp, Cap. For this moment right here, I think." He leaned back and folded his arms again. "So, what *do* you know?"

Drake picked up the flashing datapad and unlocked it for his friend. It was tingling in his hands as he showed him the message it contained. "XO found the cannon."

Doc nodded. Of course, he had. "And do you plan to use it?"

Finally, it was Drake's turn to smile. "Indeed, I do."

CHAPTER THIRTY-SIX

The caution tape sealing the fulcrum had been disturbed.

Drake considered pausing to put it back up, but with a conscious effort, he buried the impulse. The fulcrum had been sealed out of no one's necessity but his. If he was the ball and chain that bound *Glory's* ghosts, then it was he who needed to cut them loose.

Someone was inside, moving slowly. Idri. She was looking around the vast spherical chamber with wide eyes, a child seeing a cathedral for the first time.

Drake stepped over the coaming to join her. Being inside the room sent a chill down his spine, and he had to regulate his breath to keep his chest from seizing up. It was suddenly freezing.

Idri whipped around when she heard him. Her cheeks reddened, and she looked as though she was about to apologize for being inside when he held up a hand to stop her. "I'm not here to chastise you," he said. He shifted, uncomfortable, and cleared his throat. "Quite the opposite, in fact."

"I wanted to see what it was like," she explained, regardless. "I've never been inside a fulcrum this large."

"*Glory* is a big ship."

"Yes, she is."

Idri was looking at him as intently as she had the fulcrum a moment before. He felt as though she could read him like an open book. It made him more uncomfortable, but he did his best not to shy away from it. That was why he was there, after all.

"This is a hard room for you to be in," she said. Her eyes were so big. It wasn't a question.

"I haven't been in here for over twenty years."

"Because someone died in here."

"Yes."

"*He* died in here. My predecessor. Didn't he?"

Drake nodded and took a long, very tight breath before forcing it out. "His name was Elbin."

Idri drew her robes close, mimicking his feeling of the cold. "Do you wish to tell me how he died?"

It was an odd way for her to phrase the question, but it struck at the very heart of why he was there. That was it, wasn't it? He did wish to, even though he didn't.

He nodded.

She waited for him to speak.

"We were deep inside Paragon space. Elbin jumped us to safety. Several successive jumps. On my orders. Seven of them."

"And that killed him?"

"It caused lesions on his brain, like the ones Doc showed you on yours in Sickbay, except much larger and many of them. He couldn't recover. There was nothing Doc could do. He collapsed in here after the last jump that brought us all to safety. He died right there."

Drake pointed at the pedestal in the center of the fulcrum. He could still see him there, his long, thin frame folded in upon itself like a grasshopper. Idri followed Drake's finger and took in the image with a shiver, then looked back at him.

"And then, he was forgotten when we got home." Bitterness dripped from this portion of the memory. "Everything he'd done was sealed up like this room and stashed away, like what he'd done didn't matter. But it did matter. It mattered to everyone on this ship because he saved us all. He saved everyone."

Idri nodded. "I can see why it would be hard to welcome another Navigator aboard *Glory*, Captain." Drake blinked. "I can feel the ship's pain," she explained. "The pieces that were lost. She still has ghosts, even after all this time."

Drake was amazed by the woman who stood before him, both by her astonishing youth and the incredible presence that came with it. It wasn't a contradiction, which was amazing, too. It was an integration that made his head spin.

He reached into the pocket of his uniform pants and pulled out the Navigator's pin. Elbin's pin. From her expression, Drake could tell Idri knew what it was. It gleamed in the low light of the fulcrum.

"It will be dangerous," Drake told her. "I may very well have to ask you to do the same as Elbin. To lay down your life. Are you willing to accept that?"

"If you are willing to command it."

Drake hesitated. *Forced.* His conversation with Broussard. Ordered wasn't forced. He couldn't let anyone transfer to the *Vengeance*. They had a mission to save humanity, and now they had the means to do it even if it cost all of them their lives. On his orders. That was why Jack, that old bastard, had wanted Drake to deploy with *Glory*. Drake was the only one who could do it because the crew would follow *his* orders.

He gave a half-smile despite the haunting cold he still felt emanating from the room. He liked her. "I am."

"Then I am Second Born," Idri answered and squared her shoulders. "All I have ever wanted is what has been denied to me: to be a Navigator." Drake watched as her eyes clouded with memories and ghosts. He figured she must be thinking about Corvus. "I now know what that entails."

Drake reached out to the lapel of her thick robes—as much as they had a lapel; it was more of a fold—and with both hands, stuck the pin there. She looked down at it, and he stepped back to take it all in. The immensity of space as seen from within the fulcrum. A non-human Navigator. A member of his crew. The pin suited her. It was no longer Elbin's, it was hers.

Idri, of the warship *Glory*.

She ran her fingers over it, and when she looked up, she sported a smile so wide, so relieved, so brilliant that it could have outshone the sun. For a moment, she looked her age. But only for a moment. She squared her shoulders again and gave Drake a crisp, soldier-like nod and a "thank you," even if she couldn't quite get rid of the megawatt smile.

Drake regarded her proudly. "Navigator."

"Captain."

CHAPTER THIRTY-SEVEN

THE CENTRAL HUB of the Armory was large enough to fit both crews and their dead without an issue. It spoke to the size of the hub and also to the undermanned *Glory*. *Vengeance* was a smaller ship, half of *Glory's* size but with the same complement. And the same number of dead.

The latter were arrayed on the floor, perfectly spaced and shrouded. The crews of each ship assembled in crisp lines and neatly split in half, delineating one ship from the other. Drake wondered how long that would remain the case, how many of his own had mentally already joined the other side, if not yet physically.

The arrangement and the acoustics of the wide space made the most logical configuration putting the speakers on the *Glory's* gangplank, with the deceased and surviving crewmembers facing the larger ship.

The young Captain Sellers strode up to face the crowd. The Drake's Demons sign was affixed almost directly over his head. Drake glanced down. Next to his feet, he'd placed a bolt cutter, primed and ready to use.

"We mourn the loss of our brothers and sisters in arms,"

Sellers said simply, raising his voice to project to those in the back. The man was emotional and couldn't keep it out of his voice. Drake swept his eyes over the dozens of shrouded bodies. "They all fought valiantly and laid down their lives so that we could live. I commend their bodies to space and their souls to whatever God or gods they believed in." His voice thickened to the point of breaking. "For us, we shall carry their memories with us and survive."

Those words rang out among the crews, and Sellers turned to Drake. With a nod, he stepped away from the center of the gangplank.

Drake took center stage. He took a deliberate moment to study the faces turned toward him and found a familiar one. He struggled to maintain composure when he realized who it was: Crewman Snyder. The same man Broussard had told him wasn't going to make it not twelve hours before and who Drake had been sure was one of the inert, shrouded dead stretched out at his feet. The young man was gaunt, pale, and teetering on a pair of heavy-duty crutches, but he was alive. He locked eyes with his captain and gave a weak smile accompanied by a wink. He'd pulled through.

Drake was more relieved at the survival of the one man than he would have guessed possible. With the massive losses humanity had suffered that day, one fewer dead was one more to continue humanity's existence. One more to carry on.

"Thank you, Captain Sellers, for those words," he said before clearing his throat. "I could not have spoken more eloquently myself about our comrades who have fallen in the line of duty. It was an honor to serve with each and every one of them. And—" He cleared his throat again and raised his voice as he found the words he wished to say, "it is of honor I wish to speak to you today, and duty. They are a choice, honor and duty. One that each of us makes anew every time we put on our uniform. A commitment to do what we must, no matter the cost. That choice is something we make inside of us. It's not handed down to us by orders or the chain of command. It's a choice we wrestle with individually, personally. I am wrestling with that choice right now, just as you are."

Drake paused. The crews listened with rapt attention.

"The odds are woefully against us," he said. He found his next words in the bodies before him. "So many have died today, here and elsewhere. An incalculable number that we may never fully understand. And many, many more will. In fact, all of us might." He lifted his eyes to the crew. "That is what I find myself wrestling with the most: annihilation. Retreat, here and now, might very well be our best chance to survive and not add to the dead we see in front of us, but it also means annihilation of our home."

He straightened, and his voice boomed off the hub's high rafters and to the back walls. "I know by now, most of you have seen the holorecordings of Mars' destruction and the Paragon ship which destroyed it. That ship is heading to Earth next. It should arrive within the next twenty-four hours. What you might not know is that we have an experimental cannon in this Armory that is meant to take down that ship."

Drake let that land on the two crews and waited for the resulting murmur to die down before turning to look at the Drake's Demons sign. "We've used it once before," he continued, "years ago. It worked then. We believe it will work again. That has, in fact, been our mission from the start; why this Armory has been our destination. You see, not everyone in humanity's senior leadership was taken in by the Paragon. One man, a right bastard, put the pieces in play and set the events in motion that brought us to this point, to give humanity a fighting chance.

"We also have one other advantage." Drake swept his eyes over the crowd until he found Idri standing near the back. He locked eyes with her across the distance. "*Glory* is an old ship, as I'm sure you're aware, and while that has certainly presented us with *many* challenges, she also has an ace up her sleeve. *Glory* is outfitted with a fulcrum, and we now have a Navigator who can operate it."

Murmurs arose again from both crews, most of them confused, Drake was sure. However, even the most ignorant of the youthful crews would have heard the legends of the Navigators and what they could do. He pressed on, however, to get to the point and let it land.

"I have decided to lead *Glory* back to Earth," he said. And land it did. The murmurs stopped cold. "It may very well be her final battle. Chances are slim we will be successful, but a slim chance is enough for me because nothing less than the survival of humanity is at stake, and a soldier never says die. A soldier never accepts defeat. A soldier never leaves behind a fallen comrade. Running now will mean that we'll live to fight another day, yes, but know that we will have to fight eventually. We cannot stand toe-to-toe with Paragon ships, but we can hit those duplicitous bastards, now, when they least expect it. That is *my* duty. That is my choice."

Drake gestured at Sellers, standing off to the side. The other captain's face was unreadable, but he didn't linger to dwell on that. He had to get out what he wanted to say. The rest wasn't up to him. "The *Vengeance* is leaving the Solar System, and all may go with Captain Sellers that choose to. I will not order anyone to follow me into battle. Living for another day is a second course of action that we need to take in case the first fails, but I must stay and fight for Earth."

He paused, his voice rasping with the effort to carry on. "As long as I have breath to speak, I must never say 'die.'"

Silence dominated the massive chamber as his last words left them dumbstruck.

Drake let the proclamation linger and scanned the crowd. He willed for the looks on their faces to change from fear to determination. Strike back. Give an outlet to their pain. *Vengeance*, the name of the ship running for its life. *Glory*, the name of a relic from the past. But glory was her calling, even if no one knew the ship and her crew had given humanity the last twenty years to live unmolested. Maybe she could give them twenty more.

"I will take anyone willing to go with me," he boomed, then he raised his arm in salute. "To the dead."

"To the dead," came a staggered chorus of replies.

Drake picked up the bolt cutters. He carried it back to the *Glory's* gangplank, and with effort, reached up to the mantle above containing the old makeshift sign. He cut the bolts that held it in place, and when the last was severed, the aged sign clanged on the deck.

He dropped the bolt cutter there and picked it up with both hands, then ran his fingers over the old words one last time. Precious as they were, they belonged to another time. Another crew. This crew would have to find their own words.

He turned to see the throng of soldiers behind him, still watching. With a nod to them, he tossed the sign aside and strode back into his ship.

Their ship.

Glory.

CHAPTER THIRTY-EIGHT

For the second time in as many hours, Drake's solitude in his quarters was interrupted by a knock. He turned to see Carrol in the hatchway, which he'd left open.

"Sir," she said, looking awkward as she stood there.

"Come in," he said with a gesture.

She entered and let out a breath in surprise. "You've cleaned."

He had. Most of the clutter on his floor was now in bins meant for the trash chute, which was most of it, and the rest, the few items he'd decided he wanted to keep, had been put back on the still-standing shelves. He'd decided he'd repair the remaining broken shelves and fill those with new memorabilia and memories. If he had the time.

"It looks good," she said and smiled.

"Did you want something?" he asked with a raised eyebrow. He wasn't cold to her, however. Quite the opposite. He was glad to see her. Glad she was there. And very interested in what she wanted to say and why she was building up the courage to say it.

"That was quite the speech."

Drake smiled. "It was impromptu, but from the heart."

"'Never Say Die.' I don't remember that in the Fleet Creed."

"Like I said, impromptu." He gestured to the shelves of books. "Dickens, I think, actually." Carrol nodded and made a show of scanning the embossed spines. Drake pressed her. "You didn't come here to ask me about my speech, though."

"I want to apologize," she started.

"Apologize for what?" he asked when she didn't elaborate. He rolled his finger to encourage her.

"I didn't want to be here. On *Glory*. I hid that from you, but this wasn't the posting I wanted. I wanted *Olympia*."

Drake almost laughed. "I know."

Carrol reddened. "Was I that obvious?"

"You were that obvious. You didn't hide anything. You are a horrible liar, Commander, and that is nothing to be ashamed of."

"I thought this ship was a shit hole," she blurted, finally letting loose. "Pardon the language, and I thought being assigned here was a mistake at first. And then when it became clear it wasn't, that I'd been stashed here, I thought it was all a giant cosmic 'fuck you.' Again, pardon the language, sir."

Drake inclined his head in acknowledgment and rolled his finger once more.

"But it wasn't," Carrol continued intently, taking a step closer to him. "It wasn't a mistake, Captain. I don't know when it happened, to be honest, but this became, has become, the only place where I've ever felt like I actually belonged. It was a miracle. I think you did that, Captain; made me feel wanted. And even if taking down that fucking planet-killer will take a miracle, Captain, I think you're the one person in the entire goddamn galaxy who might be able to do it. Sir. Apologies for the language."

"What exactly are you saying, Commander?"

Carrol squared her shoulders. "I'm staying, sir. That's what I'm saying."

"If our CAG is staying, so the hell are we," a voice called from the hallway. Drake recognized it as belonging to one of Carrol's pilots. Zed, he remembered from when they'd come into Sickbay. There were another half-dozen pilots behind him, the entire remaining Delta Squadron. They all loudly agreed with their commander.

There was more noise from the hallway. Frowning, Drake stepped into the hatchway.

The corridor was packed as far as he could see in both directions, wall to wall, shoulder to shoulder, with his crew. All of them to the man and woman were shouting to their captain that they, too, wished to stay. Even Fredrickson was there, right at the front of the pack. He looked grimy and grumpy as hell, but he had a crack of a smile playing on his lips.

"Can't have you going there to destroy this beautiful ship all on your own," he shouted to be heard over the din. "Now can we, Captain?"

Drake shook his head. Carrol was inside, still looking at him, eyes steeled with purpose. In fact, everyone had the same look. They were all staying.

He set his jaw before scanning the crew.

"It is my honor," he said.

They erupted into a cheer.

From the back of the crowd, someone shouted to be let through. At first, the crew remained packed too tightly, but they managed to create the space. Finally, Captain Sellers pushed his way through.

When he reached Drake, he was breathless. He gestured, exhausted, at the crowd. "You've really done it now," he got out between gulps for air. "Haven't you, Captain?"

Drake nodded. Yes, he had.

"Well," Sellers wheezed, still finding his breath, "we're in."

Drake blinked. "I'm sorry?"

"*Vengeance* formally requests to be included in your plan to return to Earth. If you'll have us."

Drake smiled, and again the crowd roared its approval. A sea of hands reached out to slap Sellers on the back, head, face, shoulders, and any other body part they could reach.

"After all," Sellers continued with a sly, slightly embarrassed smile, "two ships are better than one."

Drake nodded. "Two ships *are* better than one."

Sellers' smile wobbled. "You do have a plan, right?"

Drake nodded.

Yes. He had a plan.

CHAPTER THIRTY-NINE

CARROL SAW the sliver of opportunity, like a window being cracked slightly to let in the breeze. "Break right! Break right!" she shouted over the squad channel.

G-forces slammed her back into her cockpit seat and yanked her viscera up toward her throat as she accelerated into a tight turn. Her vision tunneled, but not so badly that she lost sight of that window the enemy fighters had left open to outflank them. Nor did she miss that her squadron was right alongside her, formation so tight it could squeeze water from a rock. Hell, yeah.

"Closing speed," she ordered over the comm in the gasp of air she mustered before slamming her accelerator again.

Her fighter surged forward, and the rest of the squad stayed with her.

The group of enemy fighters they were hunting grew rapidly on her cockpit display. Her squadron was an arrow-head, about to pierce them.

"Weapons hot!"

The Delta Wings opened fire. Holographic representations of plasma cannons and missile trails streaked toward the outflanked enemy and caused them to scatter and lose formation, thwarting their bombing run on *Glory* for the moment. Carrol intended to make that permanent and ordered her squadron to break up into leads and wingmen, then pick their targets and destroy with extreme prejudice.

A few seconds later, the battle was over. The enemy had been destroyed. *Glory* had been protected. A cheer went up over her comm.

"Oooo-wee, Commander!" Zed shouted over the radio. "That was some ballsy flying."

Carrol grinned in agreement. "Well done, squad," she said to all of them, then switched to the *Vengeance* squadron channel to revel in the groans of disappointment and frustration she heard from the other side.

"Son of a bitch, Delta Actual," came a voice Carrol recognized as the *Vengeance's* fighter group commander. "I didn't think manned fighters could make a tight maneuver like that. Even the computers didn't see that attack vector opening up."

The "enemy" fighters—Delta Wings from *Vengeance*— kill icons were replaced on Carrol's cockpit display as the war game program reset and both squadrons powered down.

Of the losses *Vengeance* had suffered her fighter squadrons had been hardly affected. She still had three dozen fighters, and nearly twice that many pilots. The Armory had holds filled with fighters, so Sellers had agreed to share any and all of his pilots with extensive—or at least recent—hands-on flying experience. Carrol's squadron had been replenished to nearly forty craft.

And they'd won again. It had been tighter this time. *Vengeance's* squadron had come much closer to succeeding in their attack run on *Glory* than any time before, but

Carrol reveled in the fact that not a single missile had made contact in any of the wargame sims they'd run. Her squadron was unbeaten. They were tight now. Disciplined. Deadly.

"I'm telling you," she told the *Vengeance* flight group commander, "there are advantages to hands-on. You should get out of those sim couches and join us. See the stars for yourselves."

That got a half-chuckle, half-groan from the other officer. Boyd was his name, Carrol remembered. Not *Vengeance*'s fighter group commander from even a day earlier, but he was their leader now, and Carrol found him to be competent. The losses *Vengeance* had piled up had less to do with competency and more to do with Carrol knowing the playbook on standard attack methods and strategies and exploiting those. It was an advantage her squadron wouldn't have over the Paragon, but improvisation and strategic flexibility were skills that translated anywhere, as was synchronization among her squadron. They performed well on both. One might consider it a miracle if they were to think about how it had gone the last time.

"We'll stick to our sims for now, *Glory* Actual," Boyd replied. "Though I may personally have to take you up on a butt-in-seat Delta Wing ride once this is all over."

"It's a deal, soldier."

Carrol was pondering whether they had time to go again when her helmet radio squawked that a new call was coming in, this time from *Glory*. Carrol switched over, sharing it with the rest of her squad.

"Bring 'em home, Commander," a hoarse but unmistakable voice drawled into her ears. "That was some mighty fine flying."

"CAG?!" she blurted before recovering. "Lieutenant Kluger, is that you?"

"One and the same," CAG responded with a slight cough. She was alive and awake. Carrol had no idea she'd even been close to recovery, based on the extensive injuries from the hangar bay fire, but here she was. On her feet, or on the radio, at least.

Carrol had a brief pang of...*something* as she realized that with CAG back up, her status as commander of the fighter group was gone. It had only been "interim," after all. She got a lump in her throat, thinking about handing the squadron back over after everything they'd been through, but she swallowed it.

CAG, on the other end, however, seemed to sense what Carrol was struggling with. "Now, Commander, don't you even think about giving up that joystick," she said, still broadcasting over the general squadron channel. "You're staying right where you are, where you belong. Ol' CAG is simply here to give you an extra pair of eyes over on *Glory*." She must have leaned close to her microphone because her voice was hushed and louder at the same time. "And don't tell Cap this because he'd probably just send me back to bed and fuuuuuck that, but you guys are top-notch. I'll do my best to stay out of your way."

Carrol laughed, relieved. The rest of her squadron did the same, and hellos and welcome backs poured over the channel. "It's good to hear your voice," Carrol said, thinking about how dire CAG's injuries had been.

"Yours, too, kiddo. Now, get your donkey asses back to the barn. You're ready!"

Carrol acknowledged the command, relayed it to their *Vengeance* counterparts, and directed her squadron to return to *Glory's* hangar bay.

As they flew over the ship, which was still docked with the Armory, Carrol marveled at the massive structure being put in place along her spine. From bow to stern, the vacant, blackened channel she'd seen empty was, piece by piece, being filled with an impossibly long, impossibly large cannon barrel. Installation was easier than it should have been, as if it had been there before. Workers were putting the finishing touches on it, and Carrol knew Fredrickson was down where it plunged into the power core of the ship, connecting it and getting it ready. Ready for the Paragon. Ready for their mission.

Carrol was ready, too.

So were her fighters.

SMITH MET Carrol on the flight deck.

He was silently waiting when she climbed the ladder down from her Delta Wing. At first, she thought he was being extra-dedicated to his security escort duty, which was a very Marine thing to do, both endearing and annoying. But as she rattled off some feedback to DLC's maintenance crew about tweaks to her fighter before they went out to battle for real, Smith continued to cling more claustrophobically than usual.

"You follow me any closer," she said finally, "you're actually going to be inside my asshole, Smith. And you're not invited."

He blushed, actually blushed, then stood rigidly at attention. "A-apologies," he stammered. "I was, hoping, sir..."

"Well?" Carrol put her hands on her hips. "Out with it, Marine."

"I was hoping you might be able to assist me with a mission, sir."

Carrol cocked an eyebrow. "Mission?"

Smith, as he explained, had taken the chance while his security charge—her—had been running the fighter drills to go looking for the dog again. Carrol had nearly forgotten about the poor thing, the one she'd almost shot—well, *she had* shot it, though only a graze—a lifetime ago when she had pulled clean-up duty with her squadron. The one she'd encountered him feeding and trying to track in the fulcrum chamber no one was supposed to go into. Apparently, the silent tower of a man hadn't been able to stop thinking about him.

"I would have figured he'd have died from the fighting by now," Carrol observed as they took turns sliding down a deck-to-deck ladder and clanking down on the grated deck plating of dark and untrodden sections of corridor. "I hear these lower decks took a beating in our last tangle with the Paragon."

"They did," Smith confirmed. "And they most certainly will again in the next battle." He looked at her, his soft, half-glowing eyes wide. "It is why we must find him now. Before we leave."

"How do you know he's alive?"

Smith gave her a look that was almost offended. Almost. "He's alive."

Carrol shook her head. She almost asked why Efremova wasn't helping him. The two of them were as thick as thieves. Carrol hardly knew him, but then she remembered that Efremova was glued to the captain these days. No one on their own. She also wondered if he held her accountable for scaring the dog into hiding. She *had* shot the poor thing. "You know where he is?" she asked as they set off down the dark corridor. She saw that Smith was holding a rifle tight to his chest.

Smith nodded. "I think so. And this rifle is equipped with a tranquilizer dart, not a plasma pack."

"Where's *my* rifle?"

Smith looked at her. "If the dog sees you with a weapon, Commander, he will not approach you."

Carrol's eyebrows rose. "What exactly is your plan, Smith?"

He pulled a stick of cheese out of his pocket and handed it to her. It was warm and soft. Carrol shuddered at the feel of it. "You will lure him out of his den with that," Smith said. "And I will be in hiding down the corridor."

"I'm the bait?"

Smith shrugged. "If you wish to frame it as such."

"Shit, man. Can I at least have a hand weapon tucked in my back waist? So I can pull that out if it attacks me or you miss?"

"A Marine dog can sense the weapon even if you have it hidden in your pants," Smith said. "He is enhanced in very much the same way I am." He gave her a stern look. "And I will not miss."

They approached a T-junction in the dark corridor. Smith indicated that the dog was in a machine room at the dead-end of the corridor to the left. He would remain at the corner of the T-junction, where he could see down to the end. She was to get the dog out of the machine room by any means she could.

"He's very hungry," Smith said. "And he likes cheese. I believe that alone should draw him out."

Carrol wrinkled her nose at the stick she held. It stank, too. "What is this, anyway?"

"Cheddar. His favorite." Carrol stared at the deck. A

killing machine who knew the likes of his fellow Marine. Smith deserved a partner every bit as much as anyone else. His happened to be an enhanced dog who was terrified.

Smith knelt in a firing position near the opposite wall and sighted on the machine room hatchway, visible in the dim light because it was cracked open.

With a deep, hesitant sigh, Carrol forced herself to go in.

The floor panels in this section of the ship creaked with each step. Instinct told her that was bad, that she should be *hiding* from the beast. Intellectually, she supposed the noise was good. She wanted the dog to know she was coming.

Carrol hadn't grown up with animals, though she knew other people loved them. Too much as far as she was concerned, with their ooohing and aaahing and "Good boy!" over the simplest task like taking a piss, and their dressing them up in people clothes, or letting them eat from the table and lick their faces with the same tongues they licked *everything*, including their own assholes. Mostly, though, they'd always scared her. Dogs were loud. Big. They seemed liable to use those teeth at any time.

They jumped a lot, knocked you down when you were smaller. They were unpredictable and inconsistent. One would growl, and another would run to lick your face. Which, she supposed, meant she couldn't read them. She didn't know them or their body language. Dogs were scary, especially an enhanced freaking Marine dog.

And yet...

She'd found them fascinating, too. She'd always wanted one when she was younger, until she didn't. Maybe this was her chance to learn more, make a friend. She needed more of those.

"Here, doggy, doggy," she hissed into the darkness.

When she was a couple of meters away from the cracked hatch, she held out the cheese and called again.

Inside, there was only silence.

Carrol looked over her shoulder at Smith, who was so cloaked in shadow, she could hardly see him despite his size. He didn't respond, not even a blink. She wanted to ask him how the hell she was supposed to get this thing out, but she knew he wouldn't answer. That would blow his cover.

"Come on, man," she whispered, turning back to the hatch. "We know you're in there. I got this for you."

She held the cheese in the air and waved it, remembering that most dogs' dominant sense was smell. Again, she wrinkled her nose. If *she* could smell the rank stick, the dog sure as hell should.

Something rustled inside. She saw a pair of beady eyes reflecting the dim light of the corridor. They lowered and blinked.

"Hey," she cooed, feeling like an idiot. How did one even talk to a dog? Like a baby? Sure. Why the hell not? "Hey, buddy. This is for you."

The eyes stayed put about a meter inside the open hatch.

"Come on. Give it a shot. I'm not bringing it in. You're going to have to come out here," she tried. "Be a good boy."

Nothing. The beast wasn't budging.

Carrol broke off a small piece of the cheddar stick and tossed it through the hatch. The sudden movement caused the eyes to disappear, and claws skittered on the metal deck plating. A few moments later, the eyes reappeared, then dropped, and Carrol could hear the beast's tongue lapping as it picked up the morsel she'd thrown. The eyes then rose again and looked at her.

"You want some more?" she asked.

The eyes said he did.

She broke off another small piece of the cheese and tossed it, this time aiming for the threshold of the hatch. She hit it right at the lip, and it fell just inside the dark room. Carrol crouched, hoping that if she was smaller, the thing wouldn't be as intimidated.

The eyes floated toward the open hatch, dipped to pick up the cheese just inside, and then became a wet black nose, a dark-brown snout, and a matted and crusted face full of fur. The two eyes glowed even more as they reflected the light, a fierce yellow.

Carrol swallowed. Fur and all, the dog's face was as big as hers. Maybe larger. He was huge. He trained his upright ears toward her and sniffed. It drew his eyes to the cheese.

"You want some more?" she asked.

The dog stared at her.

Carrol tossed another small piece just outside the hatch.

The dog put out one foot and froze indecisively. He looked at the cheese, which was still several inches away, then at Carrol. He growled at her and curled his lips up to show his teeth. Carrol gulped again. They were huge, the two sharp ones in front easily the size of a human finger.

She gave the beast a nod and slowly, carefully, moved back another foot or two from the hatch. The dog flinched as she did so, half-retreating into the darkness of the room, but once Carrol was still again, he poked back out.

With another careful sniff, he took two full steps outside and gobbled up the piece of cheese on the deck.

"Good," Carrol cooed, feeling like an ass. It seemed to be working, though. She tossed the last of the cheese a couple of feet in front of the half-in, half-out dog.

He eyed the piece, the biggest she'd thrown, then eyed her suspiciously. *Come on, dammit.* Carrol realized her heart was racing, and she tried to slow it. Jesus, this thing was big. She suddenly wondered if this was a good idea. She hadn't appreciated his size before. She did now as he loomed over her crouched figure.

"Go ahead," she said and gestured at the last piece of cheese.

The dog sniffed the air again. Carrol wondered if he could smell Smith. Maybe he'd underestimated how smart this thing was. *Come on. Take the cheese!*

The dog stepped the rest of the way out of the room, and Carrol involuntarily inhaled. He froze and looked at her, then sniffed the air again. She would swear the thing knew something was up.

And it was out. All the way out. Why hadn't Smith taken the shot?

The dog was staring at her, head lowered, sniffing with his ears up and forward, listening intently. Carrol felt exposed in her crouched, unarmed position.

Goddammit, Smith, take the shot!

She looked over her shoulder into the shadows behind her.

Mistake.

The dog growled. When Carrol slowly moved her head back, she could see that he too was staring into the darkness behind her. Damn thing had read her body language. He knew someone was back there just because she'd looked.

The dog barked. It sounded like a thunderclap and startled Carrol to her feet. That made the dog bark even louder, and he crouched, looking like he was about to attack.

Which he was.

"Get down!" a voice called from the darkness.

Carrol didn't hesitate. She dove to the floor as the dog launched into the air.

A shot rang out.

She hit the grimy deck plating face-first, and the dog landed on her with a body blow that drove the air from her lungs.

Carrol screamed and fought for her life, clawing, heaving at the attacking dog—until she realized it wasn't attacking her. It wasn't moving or doing anything except lying on her and breathing heavily.

The weight was lifted off her, then a strong hand gripped her by the shoulder and hauled her to her feet.

Smith was breathing heavily too. "Are you all right, Commander?"

Carrol stumbled but nodded once she'd checked her face, neck, arms, and legs. Everything seemed to be in one piece.

The dog lay on the floor, tongue lolling out of his mouth, eyes closed. He would have looked like he was dead if one didn't notice the chest moving slowly up and down. He was unconscious. Smith hadn't missed.

"Too damn close, jarhead."

Smith nodded. "I believe you tipped me off to him."

That was true. Carrol didn't feel like giving him that victory, however. "Still too damn close." She breathed deeply to slow her racing heart. "What next?"

"We get him to Sickbay."

Carrol regarded the beast with a frown. She didn't even want to guess how much the colossal thing weighed. "And how, my dear Smith, do you propose we do that?"

CARRYING a hundred or two limp pounds up a dozen decks' worth of stairs and ladderways was as close to hell as

Carrol had ever experienced. It was the limp part that ratcheted the challenge to an extreme level, at least for her. Turned out there weren't many places to get a good handhold on a dog while climbing a ladder.

Smith didn't seem bothered much, of course, but by the time they'd grunted and shimmied their way into Sickbay, Carrol was pretty sure she'd thrown out her back, her neck, and everything else one could throw out. It didn't help that everywhere they encountered fellow crew members, there were exclamations of "Oh, look at him," and "That's the dog!"

Like, no shit. If you really think he's that wonderful, why don't you help carry him? They never did, and their enthusiasm only served to get in the way.

Doc was no exception. "You found him!" he exclaimed as they entered Sickbay.

He rushed over to them and immediately started his examination as if he were more than a people doc.

"You think—we could—set him down somewhere?" Carrol gasped, still holding onto half of the dog.

"Oh, yes, of course," Doc said, scrambling to a nearby biobed covered with medical consumables. He swept those onto the deck with one motion and gestured for them to put the dog down.

Outside, there was a gaggle of crewmembers crowding around the hatch, watching with rapt attention. It seemed that word of the dog's capture was spreading throughout the ship. Carrol knew she shouldn't have been surprised.

They set the dog down with a great grunt, and Carrol backed away to let the doc do his thing. Everything hurt. Smith, meanwhile, stayed close to the animal and stroked his ratty, matted fur with surprising gentleness.

Doc brought over an examination light, and when it

clicked on, Carrol got a detailed view of the animal. He was skin and bones beneath a thick coat of dark brown and black fur that was missing in patches. And he was still bleeding from his shoulder. Carrol wasn't sure if that was where she'd shot him by accident, but it probably was. She felt another pang of regret. In the harsh light, tongue still flopped out of its mouth, body haggard and helplessly limp, the dog didn't seem fearsome. He seemed vulnerable. Neglected.

Doc mumbled to himself, checking the animal from head to tail.

"We stunned him," Smith explained in his low, almost meek grumble.

"Yes, I can see," Doc answered, opening the dog's mouth, then shining a penlight into his ears. He did the same with his eyes, opening the eyelids with his other hand.

"Is he going to make it?" Carrol asked, reading the grim look on the doctor's face.

"I think that remains to be seen," Doc said, not pausing in his continued examination, now feeling the dog's chest and abdomen. "There's advanced malnourishment going on here, likely several parasites, and I might be feeling some form of abscess in the abdominal cavity, all of which will need immediate treatment." He finally looked at them with a shake of his head. "I'm surprised the dog has lived this long. It must have been here on this ship foraging for years."

"We got to him too late," Smith said with a solemn but matter-of-fact nod. He hadn't stopped softly stroking the poor thing's head.

Doc wagged a finger, and his grim expression slipped into something warmer. "Not so fast, soldier. I didn't say that. Everything I'm seeing could be treatable. I just don't want you to get your hopes up, is all. It depends on how much fight is left in there."

Smith considered this, then with a nod, said, "There is more fight in him. I can promise you that."

Broussard seemed to agree. So did Carrol. "He almost ripped my throat out," she said. "I'd agree with Mr. Smith on that one."

Doc nodded. "That is another thing to consider. Animals such as this, cybernetically and genetically enhanced, were outlawed decades ago. Not only should we take into account that several of the animal's implants might be malfunctioning in very painful ways, but dogs such as these were observed to be erratic and sometimes dangerous. And this one has been away from regular human contact for a very long time. It may no longer be socialized."

Carrol nodded. She'd been thinking about that in the back of her mind ever since encountering him in the lower decks. "You're saying he may be a danger to the crew."

Broussard nodded. "Possibly."

Carrol looked at Smith, who was staring at her. He still stroked the animal. She could hear what he was thinking without him even saying it. He'd said it down in the cargo hold. *They say the same things about me.*

"What do you think, Marine?" she asked.

Smith blinked like he hadn't expected her to ask him. "He might be a danger to the crew now," he said slowly and purposefully. "But he will not be. I will make sure of that."

"Care will be involved. Hourly medications and regular check-ins here."

"I will manage that, sir. I can keep him in my bunk."

Doc nodded. "You've trained a dog like this before?"

Smith nodded. "Yes, sir."

Doc looked at Carrol.

"I'll ask the captain about it, but I think, as long as Smith takes responsibility for him, that it can be allowed." She shook her head ruefully, wondering if this was a big mistake. "I mean, it's not like there's much else we can do with him for now, is there?"

Doc shook his head.

It was settled. "He's all yours," she told Smith. Behind them, in the hatchway, the gaggle of crewmembers cheered, which nearly gave Carrol a heart attack. She'd forgotten they were there. She supposed that meant this news would likewise travel throughout the ship like wildfire. Smith had a dog. She smiled, bemused. "You're going to have to come up with a name for him," she said to him. "'Dog' and 'It' don't really cut it."

Smith blinked again. He held an expression that told Carrol he'd never considered that. "I will name him," he said with a resolved nod.

"On that," Doc said, sporting a fresh smile of his own. "One thing to consider."

Carrol and Smith regarded him, listening intently.

Doc pointed. "He's actually a she."

CHAPTER FORTY

CAPTAIN SELLERS WAS GRIM.

The plan was grim. Their chances for survival were even grimmer, if that was a word. "Grimmer." It sounded like the name of a troll who lived under a bridge and took gold from unsuspecting travelers. Drake allowed himself the gallows humor, if only in his head. The truth was the plan was desperate, but it was their only option. And it *could* work. There was a chance—a chance to save everything. Drake was counting on Sellers to see that.

He'd just laid it all out to his fellow captain. They sat in the briefing room, just the two of them, the hubbub on the command deck just outside barely muffled by the closed hatch. *Glory* was deep in her preparations to depart. Drake imagined the same buzz, the same purpose, coursing through *Vengeance*. It was loud and electrifying.

Sellers leaned back in his chair and shook his head slowly.

"Thoughts, Captain?" Drake finally asked.

"If I had any other option," the man said solemnly, "I'd take it." There was a long pause, then with a final shake of his head, he added, "But there *is* no other option." He looked Drake dead in the eyes, searching. "Your cannon better do what you say it can."

Drake stood. That was good enough for him. "We'll find out shortly, won't we, Captain?"

Sellers stood as well. "That we will."

"When can *Vengeance* be underway?"

"My XO tells me three hours. I know that means he can have us out in an hour and a half."

Drake checked the most recent tracking on the Paragon planet-killer. That should work. Just barely.

Sellers closed the distance between the two of them. He stuck his hand out, and Drake met it. "Our fate is your hands," Sellers said.

"And ours in yours."

They shook.

The two men turned their heads as the hatchway cracked open and let in a burst of noise. XO was standing there, sweaty as always, looking excited. "Am I interrupting anything?" he asked, noting the handshake with raised eyebrows.

Drake released Sellers' hand. "Not at all. What is it, Commander?"

"Fredrickson reports that we're ready to run a test of the cannon. I figured you'd like to oversee."

He'd figured right. Drake addressed Sellers. "Would you like to observe as well?"

Sellers' eyes lit up. "Hell, yes."

XO opened the hatch the rest of the way, and the two captains strode onto the command deck. It was a hive of activity. The deck plates hummed from rushing footsteps, flying orders, and the raw power of the ship. And it was different than before. The calling voices were confident, the rushing strides purposeful, the raw power harnessed. Before, it had been uncontrolled, even nervous. Perhaps the nerves were still there—they always were—but the crew had experienced them before, tested them in battle. The hubbub now had the edge of *experience*.

They'd need every ounce of it.

Drake zeroed in on the engineering officers and crewmen as they rattled off a series of reports to the tactical team.

"Barrel integrity field sensors five-by-five."

"Inducers at a hundred and ten percent capacity. Main core online."

"Plasma exhaust manifolds open and clear."

"Targeting servos read green."

"Transformers are primed and online, capacity showing at maximum."

The lead officer at the engineering station nodded with each report, then turned to face Drake, Sellers, and XO. Anticipation vibrated from him. "Cannon is primed and ready to fire."

"Tactical?" XO called.

"Targeting computer online and ready," Li reported.

"Helm?"

"Coming up on our target now," Shannahan said, pointing at the navigation display.

"Our target?" Drake asked Oh *sotto voce* with a raised eyebrow.

XO pointed at the command console. A slowly spinning rock was dead ahead of them, trailing from an orbital facility that Drake had trouble recognizing. It had a gravity elevator that plunged deep into the atmosphere of Neptune, and several such rocks floated around it. The one they were sighting on was the largest.

"Diamond mine," Oh explained, smug and very proud of himself.

It had the intended reaction, particularly from Sellers. "You're firing on a *diamond*? That size?"

"Nearly the size of *Glory* herself," Drake muttered, checking the mass and dimension readouts from their sensors.

"Holy shit."

Drake smiled. It would do. He stabbed a finger at the screen. *Continue.*

XO surreptitiously flicked a proposed power curve over to Drake, the force he felt would be sufficient to destroy the object of their test. Drake scanned it quickly and nodded. Looked good to him.

"At your discretion, Commander."

XO put his hands behind his back and snapped rigidly upright. "Yes, sir," he said loudly.

The noise on the command deck dimmed as if a switch had been flipped. Only the hum of the ship remained, reverberating softly through the deck plating and the bulkheads. The crew collectively held their breath.

Oh opened a comm channel to Engineering. "Commence cannon power-up, Lieutenant," he commanded.

Fredrickson came back, "Aye, sir."

"Fire when ready," Oh told Tactical.

The hum dimmed, and the lighting dipped. Power was being diverted in incomprehensibly massive amounts to a single chokepoint, and from there, it would build exponentially until it reached the desired charge. Then it would be unleashed into the cosmos as a tightly focused beam of hyper-heated, super-accelerated, massively dense particles. For an instant, a cubic meter of the stuff had the power of the sun.

A great rumble came from the belly of the ship as the process began. It quickly grew into a teeth-chattering wail, and much of the crew, including Sellers, instinctively grabbed something for stability. Only Drake and XO stood their ground. They'd been through this before.

It wasn't a quick endeavor; when building to full power, the process took well over a minute. An eternity in the heat of battle where the ship would be vulnerable. *All* power had to be diverted to the cannon, including all defensive systems, even life support. The wail built to a shriek, and the consoles, deck, bulkheads, and overhead lighting spiked with energy overflow. The deck plating at their feet began to weaken, and Drake felt his stomach float up toward his throat. Every light on the *Glory* became blinding as the ship desperately tried to slough off the excess energy she carried lest the cannon destroy her. Finally, after what felt like ages, Drake felt the ship groan as she expanded with a great inhale that threatened to tear her apart.

"Firing!" screamed Tactical.

The inhale was released in one raging instant as the cannon fired.

Lights blew out, showering the command deck with sparks. A couple of newly-secured makeshift consoles did the same, drawing yelps from the now-scrambling crew manning them. The ship bucked with the force of the shot, and gravity winked out entirely for a moment, but it was what the monitors showed that had everyone's attention.

A perfectly straight, needle-thin white beam erupted from the tip of the giant cannon and struck the ship-sized rock of compressed carbon. For a brief moment, no more than the blink of an eye, the target seemed unaffected. In the next moment, it and everything beyond it exploded.

The flare of white light accompanying the explosion

blinded the sensors. When it faded, the giant diamond was gone. In its place was a fast-expanding cloud of red, orange, and white-hot gas. Beyond it, in a line that stretched as far as one could see, the dust particles, gas clouds, and ice and rock chunks that comprised Neptune's five irregular rings were ablaze.

Glory rocked in the firestorm, buffeted by the gas, dust, and debris it had created.

After it subsided several seconds later, when everything was quiet again with just the hum of the ship at their feet, the command deck erupted into a chorus of cheers mixed with tears of relief.

"Holy. Shit," Sellers exclaimed, speaking for his entire crew. The lights were dim from losing so many when the cannon fired, but his eyes were wide. He now understood the true power of the weapon *Glory* could wield against the Paragon. Almost understood. There was one small detail they'd kept from him.

"Status?" Drake asked Oh.

"Weapon integrity at full, and all numbers project to hold true with a one hundred-capacity shot."

Sellers frowned. "Wait. That wasn't a shot at full power?"

Oh smiled and shook his head.

"What capacity was that?"

Oh consulted his power curve diagram. "Nineteen."

Sellers almost fell over. "Percent?"

Drake pointed at the readout, and Oh tilted his head to look.

"Apologies, Captain," Oh said with an overly serious nod that made Drake hide his grin. "Make it an even twenty percent capacity."

There was more applause and a fair amount of gleeful

laughter from the deck crew. Drake didn't hide the smile that spread across his face.

"A full-capacity shot, Captain," XO explained, "is a one-and-done. It'll burn out our core."

"And take five times as long to prime," Drake added. "We get one shot. We figured we'd save that for the Paragon."

Sellers turned to him. He stood rigid, and there was a fire in his eyes where before there had been grim doubt. "*Vengeance* will be ready to give you the time you need," he said, his voice full of the purpose and determination that had taken root around them. "Permission to disembark, Captain, and see if I can't whittle that prep time down even further."

Sellers didn't need his permission, but Drake granted it to him all the same.

"Let's light those fuckers up," Captain Sellers said. He left with a haste Drake hadn't yet seen from him, his security escort needing to jog to stay with him.

"Nice to see him come around," Oh said quietly.

Drake agreed. Sellers struck him as a competent commander. He hoped he was right about that. They'd need him.

The euphoria of the weapons test started to ebb. Drake felt it in himself and in the crew. Adrenaline could only be sustained for so long before it wore you out. He glanced at the chronometer. They had a couple of hours, and *Glory* was ready to go.

"Tell the crew to get their R&R now," he said to XO. "Eat. Take a nap. And then we bring the fight to the Paragon."

CHAPTER FORTY-ONE

"I've always liked the name 'Rocco.'"

"It's a girl, Zed."

Carrol folded her arms with a frown and leaned back in her mess hall chair.

"So what? Who cares about gendered naming, anyway? I read about this female wombat named Floyd. It's hidden in a book. Entertainment?"

The mess was open and bustling. Steamed rations for the meal, courtesy of the stockpiles in the Neptune Armory, but the crew were attacking the array of "lasagna," "beef stew," and "chicken dumplings" with ravenous haste, despite the quotation marks necessary for those descriptions.

Carrol was starving. They all were. This was the first chance anyone had had to take a breath or a bite for the past two days. Still, the air buzzed with an electrified mix of nervousness and excitement. Battle was coming. It cut through the exhaustion and elevated it to a kind of euphoria.

With Carrol was the rest of her squadron, her ever-present shadow Smith, Fredrickson with his, and their newest crew member Idri, who just seemed to be taking it all in. The pilots were scraping their plates, but for her part, Carrol was just diving in. Eat last. She hadn't forgotten, and she could see that Oh was right; everyone appreciated the deference.

"What do you think?" Carrol asked the Navid through a mouthful of something that resembled Italian sausage.

Idri blinked her giant ice-blue eyes. "About what?"

Zed snorted good-naturedly from beside Carrol. "About a name for Big Man Smith's dog."

It was all the group seemed to want to talk about. Even Fredrickson had thrown in a suggestion, "Violet," which the group had promptly and immediately decried as terrible.

"I..." The Navid flailed. "What is a dog?"

Smith didn't have the beast with him, of course. She was still sedated and sleeping in a crate in the Marine's quarters, which had been cleared of fellow bunkmates. One of the benefits of a skeleton crew was that there was spare space to do that. No one seemed to mind. By all reports, they'd been quite happy to vacate.

Carrol explained what a dog was. Four legs. Man's best friend, etc.

"Ah," Idri responded as though she was having a hard time envisioning such a creature.

"Navid do not have animals?" Smith rumbled the question in response, head tilted.

"We do."

Smith grunted in approval. "So do humans. One such animal is called a dog. They are soft and loyal."

"And murder machines," Zed added. "Almost killed our dear commander here."

Carrol kicked Zed under the table. "They're not murder machines. She was just scared of me, is all."

"They used to be, her kind anyway. Which is why I think we should call her Rocco. Sounds fierce."

"The animal...dog, is yours?" Idri asked Smith.

"She is under my care."

Idri nodded considerately. She was poised, sitting ramrod-straight, back not touching her chair. "For the Navid, the bond with a companion animal is sacred. The bond is reflected in the name chosen." She blinked at Smith. "What bonded you to this dog?"

Smith thought. "Cheese."

The table erupted into laughter.

"You can't name her Cheese," Carrol wheezed. "That's a terrible name."

Smith thought some more and nodded in agreement. "What about Cheddar?" The laughter returned, then subsided as the new name trickled through everyone's mind. "That's the kind of cheese it was, specifically," he added.

Carrol thought about holding that sweaty, stinky stick down in the lower decks and groaned. "Oh, my God, please no." She shuddered.

"I think it's kind of cute," Fredrickson said with a shrug.

"You would," Zed declared. "You wanted to name her Violet!" He shook his head with finality and spread his hands on the table. "It's gotta be Rocco all the way. Or something badass like Laser or Blade."

"What do you think?" Carrol asked, turning to Smith.

Smith was quiet. As much fun as everyone was having tossing suggestions at him, Carrol could see that he was taking the discussion seriously. As he did everything, but this seemed particularly so.

"She's your charge," Carrol added genuinely. "You get to decide."

There was a long beat. Everyone waited intently, which made Smith even quieter. When he came to a decision, he looked at the watching crowd and blinked uncertainly. "I like Cheddar," he said with naked honesty. "It will always remind me of how I found her."

Carrol smiled. So did the rest of the table.

"Cheddar," Carrol repeated with one last mock groan and a shrug. "I can get used to it."

The table erupted into cheers for their newest crew member, Cheddar. Smith smiled slightly, but if asked, he would deny it.

Carrol turned to their other new crew member. "How are you getting along so far?" she asked the young woman, if 'woman' was the right term. Carrol made a note that she'd need to ask her when they were away from the boisterousness.

"Everything is very different," Idri admitted. "Humans are very loud."

That got more laughter from the table, a loud response to underscore her point. "That we are," Carrol agreed. "Sorry."

Idri shook her head vigorously. "Do not be sorry. I find it interesting. Different is good."

"What is it that Navid do for fun?" Fredrickson asked. It was remarkable to Carrol how polite the prickly engineer was being. He was different now, more relaxed, and like everyone else at the table, showed interest in their Navigator.

Idri inclined her head, again seeming lost about the concept.

"You know," Zed jumped in, "downtime. When you're not...Navigating."

"I practice." She gestured at the large, ancient-looking book that was sitting next to her on the mess hall table.

"And that's fun?" Carrol asked her.

Idri frowned. "Fun?"

"What do you practice?" Fredrickson asked.

"I practice folding space."

"Oh, girl," Carrol said with a sigh. That was the job of a Navigator. "We need to get you a hobby, and before you ask me what that is, it's anything you do that's not your *job*."

"I dunno," Zed said with a grin. "I hear that Idri's folding can be pretty fun." Everyone turned to him, including the Navigator. "I heard about the stuff in Sickbay! Exploding gauze packs with your mind."

"Really?" Fredrickson asked, raising his eyebrows. "I've never heard of such a skill."

"Oh, yeah. It's how you defeated the Paragon ship, isn't it? Folded something right inside them, and boom!"

Idri shifted, looking uncomfortable. "I did."

"Do you think you could demonstrate?" Fredrickson asked, fascinated.

"Okay, guys," Carrol interjected. "Leave the newbie alone."

The table groaned, but Idri was quick to respond. "I'd be happy to demonstrate." She seemed genuine. "It is practice, after all, and I do think you would call the feeling that I get from it 'fun.'"

Carrol raised her hands. "Fine by me. Just don't let these fuckers get you to dance whenever they want you to."

Idri frowned, again not following, and Carrol waved her onward. There was much to teach this one and a certain caution she needed to deliver to the pilots. They could not have their fun at Idri's expense like they did with everyone else.

The young Navid took two of the meatballs on her plate, placed them carefully on the bare table in front of her tray, and stared at them intently. The sauce that covered them dripped onto the surface and began to pool. The people at the table, church-quiet, leaned in intently.

"So, you just merge them together or something?" Zed asked with bated breath.

"Similar," Idri answered patiently. "I move one inside the other."

Zed nodded. "Sorry," he whispered. "Proceed."

Idri's brow furrowed in concentration.

She whispered something inaudible.

Carrol couldn't help it. She leaned in too, fascinated.

POP!

It sounded like a gunshot, far louder than Carrol would have expected, and suddenly, something hot and wet was all over her face. On everyone's face. The entire table yelped and scrambled back in surprise.

Idri silently laughed.

Carrol reached up and removed steaming meatball bits and sauce from her face. The two meatballs on the tabletop were gone.

The table roared in approval.

"That was amazing!" Zed exclaimed and slapped Idri on the shoulder.

"Incredible," Fredrick echoed, and he leaned over to the spot in front of her tray where the meatballs had been a moment before. It was shiny-clean. He ran a finger over the spot, then looked at Idri in amazement. "There's not even a drop of sauce left on the table. How did you do that?"

"All matter is unique," she said simply. She gestured at

her book. "The Tome instructs us on how to tell the difference between unique objects."

"And you can move them that precisely, differentiate them with your mind as you fold them?"

Idri nodded, smiling because Fredrickson seemed to understand. "I can. That's how I can move just this ship, for example, and not the space around it."

"That doesn't fatigue you?" Carrol asked, suddenly wondering if they should be doing this.

Idri, however, shook her head. "Objects so small do not fatigue me, no. Only larger sets of mass."

"Like the ship?" Fredrickson asked.

"Like the ship."

"So," Zed said, leaning farther in. "Could you, say, move one meatball inside the other like last time, then pull it out again? Because you can tell the difference between them?"

Idri frowned. She hadn't thought about that.

In her careful, deliberate manner, she took two more meatballs from her untouched meal and placed them on the tabletop. This time, the group leaned away rather than forward. Carrol covered her face and peered through a small gap in her fingers.

Idri concentrated, then spoke softly.

POP!

The explosive sound was just as loud as before, and Carrol felt hot splatter against her hands.

But lying on the tabletop, rolling slightly without having been touched, was one of the two meatballs.

Zed reached to pick it up, yelped, and set it right back down. "It's hot!" he exclaimed.

Idri breathed heavily.

Carrol had to ask. "Are you okay?"

"Fine," she said with a nod. "That took slightly more effort than I'd anticipated."

"You need to see the doc?"

Idri shook her head and smiled. "I am okay. Thank you." She beamed at Zed. "I would never have thought of such a maneuver. Most unorthodox." The way she said the word "unorthodox" made Carrol think it was the highest compliment she could think of.

Zed beamed back. "Now you only have to destroy one meatball at a time!"

Everyone laughed, Idri included. That gave Carrol an immense sense of satisfaction. The crew was starting to come together. To bond. She wasn't sure she'd take the trauma again that had brought them this far, but perhaps they could bond the rest of the way in moments such as these. Moments of laughter and surprise.

Smith rumbled a question for Idri. "You're going to do that to *Glory*?" Everyone turned to him. "Fold it through space?"

The joviality mellowed. Idri nodded. "Yes."

"Is it hard to fold something so big?"

Idri blinked at the large man. "Yes. I've never folded something as big as your magnificent ship."

"I'm sure you'll do fine," Carrol said, fighting the turn of the mood toward the elephant in the room. Danger was just around the corner for all of them.

"That is why I practice," Idri added.

Overhead, an alarm sounded.

"All hands to duty stations," a comms officer called. The order throughout the mess hall. "Repeat, all hands to duty stations. Casting off in five minutes."

The tenor of the room changed instantly. *Vengeance*

must be on her way to the local gateway. It was time. The battle would soon be joined.

Carrol swallowed. "You heard the man," she barked to the rest of the table as she swiped up her tray and stuffed the last bits of rations into her mouth. They never knew when they'd eat again. "Let's move."

So much for laughter.

They'd have to bond over trauma for a little while longer, wouldn't they?

NEAR-EARTH ORBIT

Terran Federation Space

CHAPTER FORTY-TWO

THE LOCAL GATEWAYS spanning the Earth system were nearly as vital to space travel as the interplanetary gate in orbit over Jupiter. They enabled the free, efficient flow of goods, personnel, and equipment to every planet, moon, and outpost in the Solar System in the blink of an eye compared to long burns of space flight. And they were much easier to build once humanity had figured out the basics of the technology. Where the Jupiter Gateway needed, well, *Jupiter* to power the near-star-strength of a gas giant's white-hot planetary core, the local gateways were powered by manmade reactor-powered singularities since they were folding space for distances that were millions or billions of times smaller.

As such, there were hundreds of such gateways spanning the Earth system: shortcuts from the ice mines on Europa to the solar plasma farm on Mercury, an instant trip from Venus to the asteroid belt. Even the military-only gateways meant exclusively for Fleet travel numbered in the hundreds. It was impossible to monitor them all constantly. Fortunately for the Paragon, and unfortunately for humanity, not all of them needed to be monitored.

The majority of the Paragon fleet moved like an animal pack through the Earth system. Their planet-killer had been designed to fit through the interstellar-sized Jupiter Gateway but was far too massive to move through any of the locals, so the fleet of ships stuck close to the vast ship as it crawled its way toward Earth at sub-light speed. They protected it, running raids along their route, fending off the smattering of attacks by the chaotic Fleet, and probed ahead to clear any mounting resistance that might get in their way.

One such tactic was covering the local gateways as they went. *Vengeance* had encountered this during the initial attack on Jupiter. The Paragon had dispersed to the gateways of that complex and laid in wait for ships to either come through in desperate attempts to aid their comrades or to flee in even more desperate attempts to escape the carnage. In all cases, they were easy pickings. Animals caught at the proverbial watering hole. The local gateways had been a slaughterhouse.

As the fringe conflicts decreased and the planet-killer drew closer to its final target, Earth, the Paragon coalesced their forces around the planet-killer and concentrated their formations on protecting their endgame. The local gateways were well-guarded and well-watched.

When one of them activated, therefore, just as the planet-killer was hulking its way into the orbit of the green-blue marble world, which had a gateway that was within shouting distance of the massive ship, it attracted instant attention.

Several Paragon cruisers broke formation around the planet-killer to intercept whatever was coming through.

It was *Vengeance.*

She spat hellfire from the instant her bow cleared the event horizon. The two closest Paragon cruisers didn't stand a chance. They'd made the mistake of posting up at the gateway and not moving. *Vengeance* was firing at their most vulnerable bits before she was fully through and able to use her sensors. She'd counted on them being exactly where she expected them to be, and they were. Arrogant bastards.

Multiple plasma bolts and missiles hit home on their engines and weapons platforms, blossoming briefly in the vacuum before being snuffed out. Larger blossoms came from inside the Paragon ships as critical systems overloaded and exploded. The tri-hull design split on one of the cruisers, and when its power core went critical in the blink of an eye and bathed the scene in a brilliant, blinding white light, it spun one of those knife-like hulls into its fellow cruiser. That, too, erupted in a blaze of energy.

Vengeance burst through the twin explosions and set its sights on the next-nearest target, not relenting in its deadly barrage for even a second. She was a demon, unstoppable, wildly and viciously attacking against anything within her grasp. The Paragon hesitated for a second, caught by surprise and unsure of how to reply, but only for a second. *Vengeance*, for all her sound and fury, was only one ship. The way to defeat one ship was to throw numbers at her, which the Paragon did.

Six, seven, eight more cruisers broke from their formation to intercept the *Vengeance* as she burned wildly toward the planet-killer.

Just as planned.

As the Paragon moved to deal with *Vengeance*, there was another gleam of light against the starry backdrop of the cosmos. This one came not from a gateway or from the light of the firefight but from something else, something the Paragon had counted on being unavailable to humanity.

A ship appeared from behind the light. Another

human ship. From nowhere. No gate. No engine burn. Impossibly, it was where there had been nothing a moment before.

Glory had arrived.

———

"Position!"

Drake barked the order at Navigation. The command crew collectively gasped. Drake and Oh stood firm. It had been a long time since Drake had had a Navigator fold him through space, and he'd almost forgotten how it felt. How he seemed to expand along with the ship to touch every nook and cranny of the universe all at once, every bit of him from the whiskers on his two-day beard growth to the capillaries in his eyes and the soft skin between his toes touched the stars, intermingled with their white-hot energy, and contracted again, funneling into a single point. Drake had been part of the universe, all of it, for a moment. Now, he was alone again, and so was the ship.

"Bearing on the Paragon ship," Foley responded groggily. The newest members of the *Glory* crew felt the effects of the jump most acutely, but to their credit, they were rousing quickly, Foley included. "Oh-seven-seven mark three-four, down two degrees. We're—we're thirty thousand K out, sir."

"Damn," XO muttered from beside Drake at the command console.

They were out of firing range. Close, but not quite there. Much better than it could have been. Idri had done her part, that was for damn sure, but there was work ahead. It was as good as they could have expected.

"Fulcrum," Drake barked next, this time into the direct

intercom he had set up to their Navigator. "How's she doing, Doc?"

Broussard was with the Navigator. He'd insisted on it, and Drake wouldn't have had it any other way. For all the fire and determination that the young Navid had shown, the jump they'd just completed was the first of its kind she'd ever done, and she had been in a weakened state to begin with. Constant medical attention had seemed the wise choice.

"Unconscious," Broussard reported an instant later. Drake was relieved, more than he realized he would be. She was alive. Then, concern. "I have to go, Captain," Doc said. "She needs my attention."

Drake set his jaw, and the intercom went dead. He'd wanted to congratulate her, tell her that she'd done it and they were where they were supposed to be, or as close as one could have expected if not quite hoped for. It was a colossal achievement, the first jump of a Fleet ship in decades. She was now officially a Navigator.

That would have to wait. He silently wished her a speedy recovery and for Doc's hands and medicines to work their magic like they always did and turned his attention to their next immediate problem.

"Full ahead," Drake called, surveying the current state of the Paragon fleet. Their fleet swarmed the planet-killer like a hive of bees protecting its queen, numbering in high dozens, but *Vengeance* had done her part. There was a hole in the formation where a handful of cruisers had broken off to pursue her. Drake highlighted it on his tactical display and swiped it over to Navigation and Helm with a crisp gesture. He was happy to see they were already heading toward it from his first command. It made his chest swell with pride. The feeling on the command deck was one of practiced focus. The foundation of nerves and terror was now simply the fuel for that focus. Everyone knew their part and worked as one—a crew.

Drake gripped the command console, steeling himself for what was to come. They'd been spotted. Several Paragon ships were moving to intercept them, to try to close the hole.

He exchanged looks with XO.

"Launch fighters," Drake told him with a nod. "Tell Carrol to expect incoming."

CHAPTER FORTY-THREE

THE DELTA WINGS rocketed out of their launch tubes. Carrol's fighter launched last. It accelerated down the magnetic rails at a chest-crushing speed that threw her stomach into her throat. She was *fast*. They all were, and they were going to stay that way.

The stars greeted her as she left the launch tube, and the red-orange engines of the rest of her squadron burned blazingly. They assumed a perfect formation, staggered and arranged to come screaming out from *Glory's* underside in a perfect arrowhead. They stuck to that formation as Carrol angled them away from their ship.

"Cruiser coming in dead-ahead," she called as her canopy display highlighted their first target of the day in a vivid yellow. In vivid red, ordnance fire was tracked, ripping through space between *Glory* and her adversary. No, make that two. Two adversaries. Another Paragon cruiser entered *Glory's* firing range, and she was about to take a pounding. Two on one wasn't fair. Carrol gripped her control stick and angled them toward the incoming ship. Time to make it fair.

"Prepare for bombing run," she said louder than she needed to, but such was the effect of adrenaline.

Another bombing run. Just like back at Jupiter, except this time...

This time, they weren't going to miss.

The second her squadron was within range of the anti-spacecraft weapons, Carrol knew it. Her cockpit lit up with blinding stabs of light and rocked with the explosions of near-misses. "Stick together!" she called over the radio, alive with her pilots' chatter. In stark contrast to the last time they'd done this, the talk was loud and urgent but measured. Deadly. No trace of panic or disarray. Her squadron stayed in formation, moving in near-perfect unison to dodge the incoming fire.

It was easier farther out from the cruiser, with more room to maneuver. It got tighter the closer they fell toward the ship.

"Commander," a fresh voice squawked over the radio in an instantly recognizable drawl. It was CAG. "That there Paragon gunboat keeps most of its anti-fighter weapons concentrated on the top-rear central fin."

Carrol frowned, attempting to decipher what the older officer was trying to tell her. Sure enough, most of the fire lighting up their bombing trajectory was coming from the central and largest knife-shaped vertical stabilizer of the Paragon ship, and it constantly rotated to make sure that section of the ship faced the incoming squadron at all times. That was when Carrol saw it, or at least, what she *thought* CAG was trying to tell her.

"Zed and beta group," Carrol called, speaking as quickly and concisely as she could manage. They had almost no time. "Break off to port, now. Adjust your vector to oh-three-five and burn in like hell." She hoped he got it because she was already preparing for the other half of the maneuver. "Sigma group, with me!" she yelled as she yanked hard on her control stick.

It was with no small measure of relief that her squadron split into two groups and veered away from each other, with Zed's half angling toward the left side of the Paragon ship and Carrol and her group to the right.

They were seconds away from weapons range.

Space was a thunder dome. It rattled Carrol's teeth so hard she thought they might fall out, and still she led her squadron in.

"Gravity weapon incoming!" someone screamed over the joint channel.

It was from Zed's group. Carrol didn't dare to look to see if it had broken them up. She had to keep her eyes on the blinking information on her cockpit display. They'd practiced how to avoid them. It was up to them to implement those emergency actions to save themselves.

"Holy shit," Carrol exclaimed as the fire coming from the Paragon cruiser increased exponentially. It was so heavy it was becoming impossible to react, but she still dove.

As did her squadron behind her. It was a numbers game now, which was why the SOP on bombing runs required maximum numbers of fighters.

Some might have considered it good tactics to reduce the enemy's ability to shoot down friendlies. There were a limited number of attacks. But, they employed counterbattery tactics, they didn't hit the main target; if they only went after the main target, they were susceptible to defensive weapons fire. The commander had to calculate the odds to give her the best chance, balance those two conflicting realities, and she had to count on her people to perform. Make the whole greater than the sum of its parts.

"Fire!" she ordered when her cockpit display highlighted the targets in green. Her Delta Wing bucked as two missiles leapt from her wings and screamed toward two of the highlighted targets. One was what looked like a power coupling, the other an exhaust port.

At least two dozen missiles ripped past her as she pulled hard on her control stick to make sure she cleared the Paragon ship's hull and was far away when those missiles struck home.

And strike home they did.

The wake of the explosions her group left behind spread across the right rear of the Paragon ship so thoroughly, it was impossible to tell how many individual hits they'd scored. That would be something for the squadron to dissect, argue, and settle bets on after debrief. Carrol craned her neck to look behind them as they continued to speed away and let out a screaming whoop as the left rear of the Paragon ship lit up with impacts from the second group's missiles. Zed had broken through, too.

"Punch it," Carrol called to the entire squadron and Zed's group in particular since they were a second or two behind them. She recognized the beautiful pattern of secondary explosions rippling across the aft end of the Paragon ship.

Acceleration compressed her into her seat as she led the squadron away. She checked her HUD for the ship count to see who didn't make it.

Behind them, a massive explosion filled space with blinding white, and a shockwave accelerated to a quarter the speed of light roared past. The Delta Wing squadron had gained enough distance to ride the wave before dropping out as it dissipated, not losing formation, and Carrol's helmet filled with cheers.

The cruiser had been destroyed. A reverse sensor view confirmed it. Nothing remained but a cooling cloud of superheated gas and metallic debris.

Glory, for a moment at least, only had one cruiser to contend with.

"Holy heck, young lady!" CAG's voice called over the short-range once the whoops and hollers of the squadron died down. "That was quite the maneuver. I was thinking of breaking you off to try another vector from the underside and avoid that main central fin, but gawdam. That split maneuver works, too."

Carrol couldn't help but grin.

Hell, yes.

"Oh, drat," came a more concerned word from CAG.

Carrol saw it, too: a cluster of new readings, small craft, hightailing it away from them. "Party's over," she called to the squadron. The cruiser they'd just destroyed must have launched its own fighters before it exploded. They were heading at *Glory* for a bombing run of their own, and they had a several-second head start. "Prepare to engage Paragon fighters."

DRAKE GRIPPED the lip of the command console with both hands as the deck pitched beneath him from a direct hit. His shoulder screamed in pain, but he ground his teeth together to ward it away.

"Hard to starboard," he shouted to Helm over the din. "Spin eight degrees x-axis."

The deck leveled, which enabled Drake to watch the tactical wireframe projection of the ship execute the move he'd just ordered. He was grateful to Fredrickson and his team as he watched the ship turn and spin like a dancer. A salvo of fire from the Paragon cruiser flew past them harmlessly.

Glory was moving like she used to; like she hadn't aged a day. Fredrickson had brought her back—all the way back, as far as Drake could tell. And she was now stuffed to the bulkheads with her own hellfire to throw at the Paragon.

"Port weapons, *fire*." One hundred percent of Drake's focus calculated every move and countermove, trying to get one step ahead. In the age-old battle tactic of observe, orient, decide, act, the OODA loop, the one who could loop the quickest won the fight.

The ship rumbled with a different, more satisfying tenor as a hundred rail guns, plasma cannons, and missile tubes unloaded from the left side of the ship as she rolled broadside to the Paragon vessel. With guided weapons, *Glory* was deadly from any direction, but when aimed weapons could be brought to bear in addition? Well, she was downright nasty.

The Paragon ship was nasty too, though. It had dance moves and countermeasures of its own, and Drake watched in frustration as the majority of the salvo they'd just sent across the void landed no more than glancing blows. And the enemy had loosed another salvo in the time it had taken *Glory* to avoid the last and fire hers.

"Countermeasures!" XO shouted, darting between the helm and tactical sections of the command deck.

This Paragon ship was good. Great, in fact, since they didn't count on their technical superiority to carry the battle. They were trading punches, the two of them, and Drake was loath to admit he was on the defensive despite his attempts to deliver a death blow.

Luck wasn't going to come into play. He needed to out-think the Paragon captain.

Glory's countermeasures were a touch late, and the ship was out of position when the salvo broke through. Drake could feel the ship's anguished cry the instant before the first missile impacted the aged hull.

The command deck rocked as several direct hits slammed into Glory's port side. Drake lost his grip and was thrown face-first into the deck grating. Sparks exploded from consoles and power conduits, showering the bridge crew in burning debris. Someone shouted, "Fire!"

Drake smelled the smoke and tasted it on his tongue, but he leapt to his feet even before the shaking of the ship had subsided.

"All batteries, return fire!" he shouted to the weapons coordinators. "Everything!"

The command console was off when he found it again. He smacked it, and it flickered on. A swarm of weapons was trailing away from Glory in every direction. Wild. Blind. Nearly all of them missed the Paragon cruiser.

Damn.

Drake ground his teeth. The snap-fire defense had accomplished little. It should have thrown the Paragon battlewagon off its countermove, clearing the board for a new round, but it had little to shrug off. The fire was too wild, launched before targeting data could upload.

"Fire on decks thirteen and twenty-six," XO reported, silently sliding up next to the captain.

Drake manipulated the holographic display to show a more detailed view of the ship, with the damaged areas highlighted in various shades of orange, yellow and red, depending on how bad it was. Several compartments on the port side were on fire.

"Evac for vacuum venting is already underway," XO added.

None of the areas were particularly vulnerable, thankfully. That was how *Glory* was designed. Personnel inboard, supplies, and extra armor outboard. Some weapons clusters, but *Glory* kept her explosive ordnance stockpiles far from the outer shell, running them to where they were needed through a magnetic rail shunting network or muscle and sweat when routes were compromised. Power had been cut off during emergency actions, and it would stay off until the fires were out. Venting would deprive the fire of oxygen before the crew could get back to work. The main hull was built to weather this kind of storm.

What *did* concern Drake were the other impact points.

"These look like—" he started and leaned in with a concerned frown.

"Intruder alert!" a young crewman from the operations consoles yelled, turning in his chair to face the senior officers. His expression was stricken. "Repair crews report Paragon troops on Deck Fourteen."

Troop pods. The impact points he'd just been looking at were rocket-propelled armor-piercing pods that carried Paragon troops. A dozen each. At least. Damn.

"Master at Arms!" he shouted across the command deck.

"Yes, sir!" two voices chorused in unison.

Drake turned to see Smith and Efremova stepping toward him from the edges of the command deck. They looked at each other.

"My apologies, Captain," Efremova said, taking a half-step back. She wasn't in charge of weapons and security on *Glory* any longer, not since Drake had elevated her to their CMC position. However, if how personally she'd taken shadowing Drake over the past couple days as his security escort was any indication, she'd never vacated the position in her heart.

Here, it didn't matter. Drake wanted both of them.

"Remove those troops from my ship," he said, pointing to each of them. Efremova still looked torn, but Drake knew what her objection was going to be, and he waved her off. "I'm sealing the command deck as soon as you two get your asses out of here." He gestured to urge them to move.

"Yes, sir," Smith said with a perfect salute. He turned his massive head from side to side, set his jaw, and marched out of the room.

Efremova watched him go, then looked at the captain and gave a hesitant nod.

Drake half-smiled. "Follow his lead," he said, pointing after the Marine. "Go now. Kill the Paragon."

CHAPTER FORTY-FOUR

The Paragon fighters were faster than Carrol could have imagined. Faster than her, faster than the whole squadron. They moved like streaks of light in tight formations, then exploded like starbursts to attack targets in several directions simultaneously. They also outnumbered the Delta Wings by nearly two to one.

It was humbling to watch. Terrifying. That made Carrol all the more determined to punch them in the mouth. She started to see patterns and opportunities, and her team had plenty of punch.

It was clear to her that the Paragon had underestimated her and her squadron. Part of that was by design. She'd purposely had them come in with a loose configuration, wobbly and disorganized, but when they reached weapons range, they snapped tight and plowed through the Paragon formation, weapons blazing. It worked. The enemy scattered, and Carrol's squadron got a few easy kills, which had derailed the Paragon bombing run.

But now the Paragon knew. They had tightened up.

Carrol had earned the Paragon's respect, a compliment she didn't want.

The enemy wasn't going to make any more mistakes. They flew at a distance, adopting a tactical spread formation to make baiting strikes, then closing back into formation and playing near-perfect defense.

A force couldn't play both defense and offense, so it kept them from bombing the *Glory*, but only for as long as the Delta Wings could keep the enemy occupied. Carrol was waiting for the Paragon to make mistakes, but it was a game of give and take, much like the Glory was playing with the remaining cruiser.

It would only be a matter of time before the enemy powered through Carrol's squadron, and then her people would be picked off one by one until no one was left to defend the mother ship.

Damn.

Carrol's blood ran cold as she realized what the Paragon were doing: keeping them sidelined from the rest of the fight and using their superior numbers to grind out a slow, deliberate battle of attrition.

It would work. There was no victory in such a battle for Carrol and her squad, not as long as the Paragon had superior numbers. They would be killed with each tiny mistake, one momentary slip at a time, all while *Glory* was left to fight on her own.

She seized on one piece of the realization: superior numbers. The tactic didn't work if the odds were even. All Carrol had to do was find a way to even the numbers. She cocked her head to better visualize the geometry of the battle.

There was only one area that the Paragon were flying

clear of. So were her own fighters, for that matter. And for good reason, a reason she was going to ignore.

"Delta squad," she called over the general channel, her heart racing. "Line abreast!"

Any of her pilots could have had reason to question the order for them to form up in a straight line, wing to wing. It wasn't a configuration too many situations called for. This one would. To their credit, none of them did.

"Purge your ion manifolds," she ordered. That got its fair share of raised eyebrows, especially as their stationary position caught the attention of the Paragon fighters, who tightened up into their own formations and burned straight for them. "Make it fast!"

Behind the line of fighters, a cloud of ionized gas formed, a byproduct of their thruster exhaust. It was visible to the naked eye, glowing and reactive; it was even more visible to sensors. Normally, such particles were separated from the rest of the exhaust by an elaborate system of manifolds so as to not make the fighter light up like a firefly while in combat. The molecules were sticky, too; they'd attach to anything they came in contact with and be an easy mark for sensors. That was exactly what Carrol was counting on.

The last of the fighters confirmed their manifolds had been purged. It was go time. "Tighten up," Carrol barked, "and follow me to bearing eighty-seven degrees down mark twenty-two. Full burn."

There was a split-second pause as her pilots computed the new heading. She braced herself for the reaction. It came in the following moment as a series of astonished cries, the most vocal of which came in from Zed.

"Are you insane?" he said. "That's directly into *Glory's* firing solution!"

Carrol nodded even though she knew no one could see her. Exactly, and at danger-close range, too. Not long enough to react if a pilot found herself in the barrage of friendly fire.

Their flight path would take them across the *Glory's* enemy-facing broadside; hundreds of plasma cannons, missile and torpedo tubes, and ballistic railguns, all firing in a syncopated anti-rhythm to confuse the enemy, making the void between the ships a wasteland of death.

To fly into the midst of the firepower exchange was suicide, and that was exactly what Carrol was counting on to even their odds.

"You heard the order," she barked with every ounce of authority she could muster. "Breaking maneuver on my mark."

The radio chatter faded into stunned silence. Carrol steeled herself and repositioned her grip on her joystick. There was a method to her madness. She knew they had an edge over their Paragon foils: to follow, they would have to fly through that cloud of ionized exhaust. They would shine like the sun. Easy marks, even at point blank range.

"Remember your firing patterns," she advised. There was another advantage. There were several dozen standard Fleet-wide firing patterns that battleships, heavy cruisers, and other attack vessels used with their weapons, and those weapons each had set reload or cooling times. They rotated such patterns and idle times constantly, creating a dead space between outbound fire where a fighter could find solace. They were, of course, intended for firefights conducted at much greater distances, but if a Fleet fighter found itself in the midst of friendly fire, the well-trained pilot could recognize what pattern of fire was being employed and use the gaps therein to fly to safety.

But the advantage at this range and the advanced state of the battle would be razor thin. *Glory* was undoubtedly using several patterns simultaneously or, most likely, none at all because they were in the midst of a life-or-death knife fight with a Paragon ship. Patterns tended to disintegrate at such times.

Still, the advantage remained the same, and coupled with their nasty little ion cloud behind them making them shining, juicy targets, it just might be enough. She had to whittle down the Paragon numbers, or they'd die anyway. Fast or slow. Choose the manner of her death.

"Break!" she commanded, not willing to give the absurd plan another thought lest she lose her nerve.

Her body was slammed back into her flight seat as her fighter leapt forward, and her innards floated when she dove just as hard. She was able to glance at her rear tactical display long enough to see that her squadron dove with her, and so did the Paragon before she crashed into the outer edges of *Glory's* broadside fire.

It was like hitting a wall. Space shuddered and vibrated around her as energy bursts lit her cockpit like a neon dance party. She steeled herself to keep from jerking her joystick to get her fighter the hell out of there. Every instinct in her body was screaming at her to turn and run, but she shoved that down and pressed on.

Focus.

What pattern would save her people's lives?

She recognized the one ahead. A simple two-one-two burst from a rapid-fire five-gun plasma turret. Two seconds on, one second off, two seconds on. What she didn't know was how long the turret had been firing at that interval and when it was due to change. The ship only used the same pattern for a few volleys. She almost hesitated, trying to guess if this volley would be its last in the current pattern, but it didn't matter. There was no guessing what it would be next. The only way was to burst through now, at the next rest. Everything else was out of her hands.

She surged through.

Clear.

She wanted to breathe a sigh of relief, but she couldn't yet. The mess ahead was even worse, a combo of missile tubes, single-shot large-fire plasma cannons, and an automatic railgun that fired several pitch-black slugs per second. Chaos. It was sure to rip Carrol and her fighter apart. Except...

A pattern. They were off by a single second but still on the same rotation. Eight-four-nine, pause, eight-eight-two. The missile tubes were the wildcard. Carrol resolved to dodge those if she had the time.

She didn't.

Shit.

One screamed right for her. A flick of her joystick got her out of the way just in time. Screams over the comm. An explosion behind her. Carrol didn't dare look, though. The next set of weapons fire was already upon her, more complicated than the last. A dense cluster of outbound projectiles filled space in a final-protective fire pattern, which meant there would be no gaps. It was everything *Glory* could throw, and Carrol's trajectory was sending her right into the cloud, giving her less and less reaction time.

More explosions, one on her backside. It hadn't come from *Glory*. The Paragon were pursuing. Good. And bad. It was fire she couldn't avoid, not with her hands full.

She pulled back as the FPF ceased and a new series started. Two-one-two in three second increments so the bank of plasma cannons could cool before *Glory* hit the Paragon with a full broadside.

A rogue p-beam tower was in constant fire, wildly sweeping back and forth. She dove.

The next. Three separate bolts at once. And the next. And the next.

She didn't think; she just reacted.

Flow state.

Pattern.

React.

Chaos.

React.

Up. Down. Her stomach in her toes, then her throat. Fire. Shouts. Explosions from behind, above, below, in front of her. She flew through a plasma trail, missing the shot itself by milliseconds. No time to think about how lucky she was to be alive. No time to do anything but see. React. Repeat.

And then stop.

STOP!

A wild railgun had finished its re-load just as she was about to dive through, and she slammed reverse thrusters just in time. She smacked into her cockpit window *hard*. Stars burst in her vision, and not the ones from outside. These were in her head.

Then something hit her.

Her view of the real stars streaked as her fighter spun. Carrol panicked, thinking this was the end. She'd been hit by a shot she hadn't seen. Her muddled brain raced. It was foolish to have done this. She'd asked the impossible of herself and her squadron, and now she was paying the price. They would *all* pay the price.

But her fighter didn't explode, and when she realized that in the following second, she reacted again without thinking by grabbing her joystick and righting her fighter. One of her Delta Wings had hit her when she braked, so close in formation were they. They had spun out too, but like her, they were steadying themselves.

A shout came over the comm. "Go, Carrol!" Zed.

A fresh barrage was coming toward her and her fellow fighter. They had less than a second to surge forward again, or they'd be engulfed in plasma fire.

She didn't think, just plunged forward on blind instinct. There was no reading and reacting anymore. Not consciously. There was no time.

The space outside her cockpit canopy was a firestorm unlike anything she'd ever seen or heard. Her fighter shook and screamed and plowed on and on, the joystick shaking and vibrating in her hands like it was possessed. When it all cleared, when Carrol finally broke through on the other side, it took her a very long time to realize it was she who had been shaking and screaming.

For an excruciating moment, it was dead-quiet.

So violently did Carrol's hands tremble, she couldn't manipulate any of her controls, including her joystick. She hung in space, surprised she was alive, and wondered if what she'd just done had killed her entire squadron. She was dimly aware that her right wingtip had sheared off and the remainder was spitting sparks into the void. She wondered how the other fighter had fared.

"That was the most harebrained goshdarned thing I think I've ever seen," said a voice over the comm in a slow drawl. CAG. "But I give you credit, Commander. It worked."

CAG's calm roused Carrol from her reverie. She moved her hands in front of her face to confirm they had stopped shaking, then brought up her display to get a visual of her situation. What was the status of her squad? Where were the Paragon?

She could have cried; what she saw was that beautiful.

Delta Squad was in formation right behind her. They were likewise a bit wobbly and in shock but alive, not a fighter down. And trailing quite a ways behind them, with holes in their formation so big a bad pilot could drive a cruiser through them was the Paragon squadron. What was left of them.

It appeared that the "harebrained" maneuver had delivered Carrol and her Delta Wings the best of all worlds. The Paragon had been split on following them through *Glory's* fire, and some had stayed behind. Those fighters were now orphaned and running from *Glory's* anti-spacecraft weapons. The rest had plunged into the fire and paid a heavy price. Less than half, far less, had made it through unscathed. The Delta Wings now outnumbered them two to one.

The odds had flipped.

"Seek and destroy," Carrol called to her pilots. "Let's mop this shit up."

A chorus of "Yes, sirs" came in response, and Carrol swelled with pride as she watched the fighters explode out of formation to pick their targets and then terminate them with extreme prejudice.

Victory.

From the jaws of defeat.

Damn right.

She resolved to enjoy it while she could. In the distance,

she could see more trouble brewing and coming their way. More cruisers closing. And beyond them...

The planet-killer hung over Earth hungrily. Light was starting to glow in its belly.

They were running out of time.

CHAPTER FORTY-FIVE

EFREMOVA HAD NEVER FOUGHT the Paragon before. Not face to face.

The rifle in her hands was slick with sweat, and her uniform was too tight as she ran down the corridor just behind Smith. His hulking steps shuddered the deck plating, and she smelled ozone in the air. The fight ahead was already furious and deadly. She knew it from the shouting.

Combat wasn't new to her. She'd always excelled at it, from basic training to years of field ops in the red zones and various off-world skirmishes. She'd lost comrades, friends, and even been hit herself. Praise the maker of regenerative medicine and the doctors who wielded it, or she wouldn't have a right shoulder. Efremova was as battle-hardened as a member of the modern Fleet could be, but she'd never faced the boogeyman of the galaxy, the self-proclaimed deadliest.

She'd never faced the Paragon.

It made no difference. She was trained to deliver lethality. She was looking forward to sending the bastards off her ship and to whatever hell they believed in.

"Stay low," Smith rumbled to her as they approached

the line of Fleet security forces. He'd fought Paragon before. She'd listen to whatever knowledge he had to impart. "The Paragon don't miss."

They reached the makeshift barricade the security forces were behind, a collection of hastily piled cargo containers. Most of them were empty, as evidenced by how they went spinning and flying when they got hit by plasma fire. Heavier spare equipment placed at random intervals made much better cover. Efremova could see beyond the barricade that Smith's warning had been right. There were several bodies—human bodies—shot through the head or chest.

The fight was not going well.

"Report," Smith asked the nearest soldier.

It was a crewman. A young one. "Their blanket fire has us pinned down," he said, eyes wide and face shining with sweat. "Lots of activity behind their front line," he added with a grimace. "We need reinforcements."

Efremova gave him a wry smile, a wink, and an easy gesture. "We are your reinforcements."

Smith peeked around the corner of their cover just as the blanket fire paused. How he had intuited that Efremova didn't know, but he was able to get a solid look before jerking back to safety. A spatter of white-hot plasma fire peppered the edge of the old steel crate the moment he was back behind it.

Efremova was about to ask him what he saw when he cocked his rifle, leaned around the corner once more, and fired four shots in rapid succession. There were four matching squeals from the Paragon's section of the corridor, then four thuds. As Smith retreated once more behind their crate, Efremova dared to angle past him and take a peek herself by snapping her head out and back in a single movement.

She nearly got a mouthful of plasma for her troubles, but she saw four dead Paragon troopers lying on the floor, still twitching, oozing a shimmering white liquid.

Stars, were they fearsome to look at.

She'd seen images of Paragon troopers, of course, with their perfectly white suits and the beaming blue dots that lined their torsos and appendages. The theory was that those were sensors, that the Paragon didn't see with their eyes but through an implanted sensor grid. Or, at least their suits did. What the Paragon looked like inside was anyone's guess. Even in the course of the war, not one had ever been seen or examined outside of their suit. They self-destructed on the molecular level once deceased. And it was happening now. She watched in half-horror, half-fascination as the entire trooper turned into smoke and charcoal, its suit collapsing from the inside out. Even the white splatter on the deck smoked and turned black. In seconds, there was nothing left but the husk of a uniform, and even that was starting to smolder.

Efremova had only seen four of them lying on the deck, dead. There were many more behind them, alive and moving fast. The crewman hadn't been exaggerating. The group ahead of them was gearing up and dispersing fast. But why?

Smith was a step ahead. "You and you." He pointed at two groups of five or six huddling security troops, then at a cross-junction in the corridor behind them. "Take left and take right. Barricade and hold them off when they come." He pointed at the remaining group of seven or so. "Lay down cover fire for them to break off."

Everyone did as they were told, and Smith shouted, "Stay low!" as the two smaller groups scurried off.

Efremova saw the wisdom in his orders, and the movements behind the Paragon firing line suddenly made chilling sense. "They're trying to outflank us," she said, picturing in her mind the network of corridors around them.

The Paragon had boarded the ship through the outer hull. It was an inherently disadvantageous position, with their backs to space and very few options to maneuver. But they could spread laterally, probe the corridors, and seek ways to penetrate inboard. With sufficient violence and speed of action, they could outflank opposing forces and swarm them to gain the access they needed. In this case, that access was directly behind them in the form of a ladder. Decks Fourteen and Thirteen above it were mostly crew quarters, nothing that vital. But up that ladder two decks and also down one were some of the main pipelines to the starboard weapons platforms.

They had to hold the Paragon. This far and no farther. They could not yield any more of the ship to the enemy.

Efremova found a window in their barricade to poke her rifle through and squeeze off some shots. Beyond, the Paragon were blurs of movement. "*Suka, blyad*," she spat, readjusting the rifle stock on her shoulder and firing another spate of shots. "They're fast."

All those shots missed too.

Only Smith got his shots to hit home, but he was only able to fire in short, concentrated bursts, leaning around their cover and retreating a split second later. The Paragon's cover fire was overwhelming.

"Incoming!" someone shouted—one of the younger crewmen, his voice cracking with fear.

Something black and metallic clattered on the deck in

front of their makeshift barricade. Efremova had no time to react before it exploded, sending her flying and pounding her head like she'd been cuffed on both of her ears—a concussion grenade. Smoke quickly followed, filling the corridor in front of and around them.

"Blanket fire!" she shouted. She didn't have to wait for the fast-moving shadows behind the smoke to start their rush forward to know what was happening. The Paragon were charging.

The corridor erupted anew with plasma fire. Shots flew into and out of the smoke blindly. Efremova set her rifle to rapid fire and raked back and forth, desperately hoping some of the energy bolts would find a target. Some did. Most didn't.

Shadowy figures burst through the barricade. The blue lights were off during the charge through the smoke, making the enemy less visible. Once through, the lights snapped on, blinding the humans. Efremova fired, but the trooper was upon her. It was massive up close, two and a half meters tall and well over a hundred kilos. She didn't stand a chance, but she fought like hell anyway, smashing her rifle into its helmeted forehead. The alien didn't budge.

It grabbed her by the throat with a lightning-quick strike from one hand, pinned her with a vicious vice-grip, and cocked its other fist. The blow was lightning-quick, but Efremova was no pushover, not even outmatched. As soon as she felt the trooper's momentum fall toward her, she twisted her body to follow, using it against him. Or her. Or whatever a Paragon was. The blow slammed into the deck plating. The vice-grip on her neck slipped just enough for her to gasp in a breath.

She pulled the trigger on her rifle.

The twisting move had allowed her to point the weapon

upward. A burst sent a dozen plasma bolts rat-a-tat-tat into the chest of the hulking creature, and it sagged. Efremova kept firing until the damn thing's weight was too much; then she was forced to drop the weapon and scramble out from underneath, lest she get pinned.

She was up in time to see Smith stab another Paragon trooper in both its chest-level blue sensors with two Marine-issue Ka-Bar knives, one in each hand. He was moving again before the trooper fell, rolling just beyond the barricade. Coming out of his roll, he was suddenly holding a fresh plasma rifle that must have been on the deck. He lifted it and fired two shots into the smoke. Two Paragon bodies fell forward, nearly clipping him. He turned and fired one more shot, this one at Efremova.

She flinched and moved out of the way as it ripped the air next to her forehead, then heard a loud thud on the deck right behind her. She turned to see one more trooper lying there, twitching and bleeding white blood, a huge hole torn through its helmet. She wanted to get a peek, but Smith had other ideas.

"Pull!" he bellowed to everyone at the barricade.

He grabbed the largest section of the barricade and hauled it backward. More Paragon troops surged forward.

Efremova realized they were about to be overrun. Smith was attempting to pull back, cover and all, into the corridor behind them. It was narrower back there—more easily defensible and closer to the cross-junction. In other words, closer to the escape routes.

She pitched in and hauled too, taking breaks only to snap shots at the enemy to maintain a pale semblance of suppressive fire.

The others on the line saw what she was trying to

accomplish. Leadership by example. They followed without having to be given the order. The tactic was clear.

Within a few excruciating seconds, they had withdrawn a hard-earned few meters from the Paragon entrenchment back into the narrower section of the corridor. Their cover was still makeshift, still porous, but much more effective.

The security team fired, retrenched. The Paragon advance stopped. Several troopers found themselves new cover farther forward, but the surge was over for now.

Efremova wiped her forehead, and it came back hot and slick. She panicked for a moment, feeling for a gash or other head wound, but upon looking at her hand, she realized it wasn't her blood. It was a shimmering white. Paragon blood.

It started to blacken and smoke as she held it, so she wiped it off to avoid it burning her, too. She looked at Smith, and grinned. *Efremova, Paragon killer.*

Smith wasn't celebrating. He was having none of it because the battle wasn't over, just one small phase of it. He kept looking ahead, then leaning back enough to see down either side of the cross-junction and listening to the fighting in those directions. He shook his head. "This won't do."

"You worried about our flanks?" she asked.

He shook his head, repeating the look ahead and down the corridors. Efremova didn't know if that meant yes, no, or something in between. He looked at her with resolve behind his eyes. "Hold here," he said. He stood, turned, and ran down the corridor behind them, heading toward the ladder.

"Hey!" she shouted after him. "What the fuck?!"

"Just hold!" he shouted and disappeared around a corner.

Efremova felt like screaming. What was he up to?

She felt eyes on her. Several of the security team were

looking at her uncertainly. She mustered her most Smith-like steely stare.

"You heard the chief. Let's hold this fucking position 'til he gets back!"

It worked. The soldiers set their jaws, turned their eyes back to the line of Paragon in the distance, and continued to fire in small bursts, shepherding their ammunition for the fight ahead.

They all knew it was coming, but they had won a skirmish, and that changed their attitude.

Better be good, she thought. Whatever Smith was going after. *And quick.* Sounds came to her. She could hear what had caught Smith's attention down those two corridors. The Paragon were coming to outflank them.

She was getting back into position to hold them off when the entire ship bucked around her and sent everyone, Paragon included, flying.

CHAPTER FORTY-SIX

DRAKE HEARD his name being called. It sounded far away. Much too far away for the face that filled his vision, yet he could see the mouth on that face moving, making the shape of his name.

"Captain Drake! Are you all right?"

It was Oh, standing over him. Drake pushed himself off the deck plating. He must have fallen. His shoulder stabbed with pain. And still he heard the call.

"Captain!"

It was someone on the other side of the command deck. Drake allowed his first officer to haul him to his feet, wincing in pain from his injured shoulder. He allowed himself to cradle his arm to relieve the pressure. "Report!" he called, not sure who was trying to get his attention.

They were still locked in battle with the Paragon cruiser dead ahead of them, both ships now landing more blows than they missed. Neither ship gave an inch. It was a precarious situation. Whoever could take the most punishment would win the day, and Drake worried about old *Glory* and her groaning metal beams.

A young man at the sensor control station yelled to get his voice to carry over the din. "The Paragon planet-killer has established synchronous orbit over Earth and is beginning to charge its main weapon!"

Drake staggered over to the center console and brought up the orbital schematic on the holographic display. Sure enough, the massive ship hovered in orbit over one of Earth's oceans, the Pacific, the readout told him, and there was a guidance beam aimed into the Marianas Trench. That was where it was going to fire—the thinnest part of Earth's crust.

The image of Mars flashed in Drake's mind, and he slapped the display to a tactical view showing the Paragon cruiser.

They were running out of time.

They needed to get their clear shot within range, and that damned cruiser was in their way at every turn, blocking their path.

There were more cries on the bridge as another volley launched from their foe. Drake wordlessly handed the task of coordinating countermoves and mounting their defense to XO. He stared at the tactical display. His head pounded from his fall. He couldn't remember how it had happened, which probably meant concussion.

His arm ached. Everything ached. But the image of Mars and what that damn ship had done to her—splitting her open like nothing he'd ever seen before—wouldn't leave his mind. It was going to happen to Earth if they didn't act fast.

It focused him.

The problem was the cruiser ahead, staying between them and the planet-killer, in lockstep with their every move.

Their every move...

"Navigation!" he shouted. All heads turned toward him. "Bring broadside to bear at twenty-two mark oh-five-seven, down two degrees. Weapons, fire full volley, everything we have, at those coordinates."

There was a moment of confused silence.

"Guided as well, sir?" a lone voice asked from Weapons.

"Yes! Everything!" The force of his command cut through the confusion. He knew the Paragon ship wasn't at those coordinates. It wasn't even close. But it would be...

He waited for the telltale sounds and the shudder of the ship's weapons to fire in near-perfect unison, then he barked his next set of confusing commands. "Helm! Ahead full to oh-seven-three mark fifty-four, down four degrees."

Inertial compensators strained to keep up with the sudden maneuver, which the two crewmen manning that station executed without hesitation. Drake held onto the center console for extra support. He could feel XO's eyes on him, questioning. They were following the wild volley they'd just fired. Diving below it, in fact, and rushing ahead. The space between them and the planet-killer was clear now, if only momentarily. It was nothing like what they needed to fire their cannon. That would take minutes to spin up. But it was a glimpse of what they needed—a moment of vulnerability in the Paragon cruiser's defensive cover.

And the cruiser reacted.

Its engines fired, and it dove to cover the forward feint. They reacted just as Drake expected them to, the way they'd been reacting since this battle began and he'd only just understood: a maneuver to once again block them from the planet-killer.

"Full stop!" Drake shouted.

The ship jerked to a stop so suddenly that everyone and everything not hanging on with hands, bolts, or both went sliding forward, much of it careening to the deck. Drake kept his balance and was able to see the Paragon cruiser glide perfectly into position between them and the planet-killer.

A perfect defensive reaction. Except...

...it was the exact coordinates where Drake had directed their seemingly wild volley moments before. The timing was even more perfect than Drake could have wished.

The flurry of plasma fire hit on her broadside first, and the ballistic slugs and scattershot slammed into her next. The guided missiles and torpedoes came last, arcing on terminal approach, exploiting the cruiser's vulnerabilities, burying themselves in her soft underbelly.

The Paragon ship staggered before all fire ceased. The ship lurched and twisted, too late to protect herself.

A roar went up on the command deck.

"Again!" Drake commanded. His voice reverberated, and there was no doubt he had just ordered the kill shot.

Another volley launched, this time without the threat of incoming. *Glory* loomed large over the enemy.

The second volley slammed into the unprotected ship, unopposed by defensive fire. The weapons impacted with deadly effect. Lights flickered. The ship was losing power. Explosions rippled and blossomed like a tidal wave had passed over the hull.

Drake was about to shout for another volley when the cruiser split in half, belching fires that burned briefly in the escaping atmosphere, to be snuffed out in the vacuum of space. The ship began to fall, arcing slowly toward the planet below.

Earth, a shining blue sphere dotted with the innocuous

white of clouds, but she was not destined to crash there. The damage *Glory* had inflicted was too intense, too explosive. She burst with a supernova-like brilliance, sending debris in an expanding cloud into the upper atmosphere. Humans on Earth would be treated to a meteoric light show. They would be awed, not knowing their fate rested on the next actions of an aging ship, battered and bruised but still flying.

Our lives for you, Mother Earth, Drake thought, though he had no intention of dying.

"We have a clear shot," XO said, blinking in the brilliance of the cruiser's explosion.

Drake regarded the tactical display through heavily watering eyes as he attempted to clear the fluorescent sparkles. XO was right. In three dimensions between them and the giant Paragon ship was nothing. Several cruisers were moving toward them from other positions around the immense planet-killer; they would be there soon, but too late.

Glory had the shot. She didn't need an exit strategy. That wasn't in the cards. There was nowhere to go.

"Fire up the cannon," he told XO. He pointed at the closing Paragon ships. "And make sure we hold those off until we've taken our shot."

CHAPTER FORTY-SEVEN

CARROL COULD SEE them on her scope and with her naked eye. Six, no, seven incoming Paragon warships. Their weapons were hot, fighters launched even though there were still out of range. Below her, *Glory* was beginning to glow down the top of her spine along the impossibly long barrel of the giant cannon.

The powering-up cycle was beginning.

She needed a clear shot, and she needed protection. The cannon took enormous quantities of energy, so *Glory's* responses would be sluggish, and her teeth clenched as all plasma cannons were shut off in favor of feeding the single weapon. She still had her railguns, missiles, and torpedoes. She wasn't defenseless, but against the fury of seven Paragon cruisers, she wouldn't last through the first barrage.

Four of those cruisers would intercept before the weapon had time to charge. At least. Cruisers five and six would be right behind.

The order came through from CAG. "We have to take those bastards down," she said, her jovial tone now weary and hard. "However possible."

"Do we have a visual on *Vengeance*?" she asked, scanning the surrounding space for the other ship in their tiny attack fleet. She hadn't seen *Vengeance* since the first stages of the battle. Carrol feared she'd been destroyed.

"We do not," CAG confirmed. "It's up to you, kid." She knew what she was asking of Carrol and her fellows. Seven ships. Just under thirty fighters left. Those odds were...

Carrol didn't hold onto the last thought, not for a millisecond. "Yes, ma'am," she replied with full confidence. "Consider those ships fucking handled."

She switched to the squadron channel and relayed their orders, then marked off the pilots into flights of three to four ships per cruiser and shared it with them. "Stay tight and fast and bomb the hell out of your targets. We're the last line of defense."

It made her heart swell to hear back nothing but "Hell, yeahs" and "Yes, sirs." Each of them knew what was being asked and where it was most likely to lead, but like her, they were comfortable with the mission. As Drake had thought, so did the pilots. *We offer our lives to give Earth one more chance.*

A voice caught her attention. "Commander, permission to accompany you to your target?"

It was Zed. She'd assigned him to a different flight and as the lead to boot. But he did have a group of five over there, and Carrol had only three, including herself. Tollison was in that flight, a fully capable pilot. She considered telling him no just because, but that thought evaporated quickly.

"Join my flight as Bravo Section leader," she said and made the change in her tactical plan. A section of two ships, mutually supporting a flight of four. It made more sense. It was fitting that Zed should be by her side at the moment.

He knew it, too. She wasn't going to fight anything except the Paragon ship filling her tactical display.

"Good luck," she told her squadron. They broke into flights and sections and assumed their individual attack vectors.

Before, she would have paused to consider that this was likely the last time she was going to see any of them. She was past that. Now she had only the mission and the resolve to get it done. Her flight of four craft assumed a tight diamond formation, Zed on her left, Valdez on her right, and Darius at the rear since he had the most payload remaining.

Their target was the closest of the incoming cruisers. It was a minute away from weapons range of the *Glory*, maybe less.

Acceleration pinned her to her seat. Her vision tunneled. She thought idly back to how much she'd disliked flying before. It came to her as someone else's distant memory. This was where she was meant to be. Right here, right now.

Zed called incoming fighters, but Carrol told him to ignore them. They were going to protect the underside of the ship, where the anti-craft weapons were thinnest. They weren't heading for the underside. She'd decided it was better to take their chances topside against those weapons platforms than dodge fighters.

They would dive as fast as they could, let loose everything they had, and pray it was enough.

The anti-spacecraft fire, able to focus on the four of them, was intense even before they came within range. Carrol wondered if she'd made a grave mistake. A simple dive wasn't going to cut it. The fire was far too much to maneuver through manually, so she called for a computer-aided spiral dive, set to shift its pattern every second so the Paragon couldn't anticipate. It was as good as they could get.

Carrol held onto her stick as though her life depended on it, even though it didn't. It was just odds now. Math. And luck. As she entered the defensive fire envelope, the incoming was so thick it was like looking through one of those kaleidoscopes she used to hold up to the sun as a kid, twisting patterns forming and disappearing. It was beautiful in a deadly sort of way.

Valdez went first.

Their formation was so tight, shrapnel from her explosion—a direct hit from a guided missile—ripped into Carrol's right wing. It caught fire for a second, but not enough to spread. Her remaining missiles were spared. It also nearly caused her to crash into Zed. Carrol gritted her teeth and blinked back thoughts of the last conversation she'd had with Valdez. She couldn't remember what they'd talked about.

Darius was next.

He was even more unlucky. Their flight path, randomized by computer, swung him into a ball of white-hot plasma. It wasn't even guided. He was in the wrong place at the wrong time. There was no shrapnel from his explosion. He vaporized instantly, spreading the debris of his life into their wake.

Carrol didn't have any memory of a full conversation with him. She'd never had the chance.

Just like that, it was only Carrol and Zed.

"Eunice," Zed said over the comm, transmission so thick with interference from the weapons fire as to be almost unintelligible. "If we don't make it out of this, I just want you to know—"

"Shut the fuck up, Zed."

"Okay." He chuckled as he cut off comm.

The cruiser filled their screens. They were almost too close for defensive fire to be effective. The computer was bleating in her ear that it was nearly time to fire what she had. Several targets lit up the HUD on her canopy, virtually lost in all the tracking of incoming fire.

Ahead was a crisscross of plasma fire. She couldn't avoid it and flew right into it. Her fighter bucked violently and spun.

A scream.

It was Zed. Or was it her?

She was still conscious inside her fighter. She hadn't exploded. Beside her, Zed was on fire.

"Zed?" she called. No answer. She didn't repeat the call. He was still falling, but Carrol thought it was momentum and Zed was on a ballistic trajectory toward the hull of the enemy ship.

Finger hovering over the fire button, Carrol lost her right wing. It ripped away from the acceleration force, spun off behind, and exploded brilliantly when a Paragon shot caught it and its payload.

She was down to half of her missiles and torpedoes.

She fired them before she lost the ability to control her ship.

Her auto-navigation computer screamed that she had insufficient thrust to pull out of her dive with her wing gone. She was going to hit the cruiser around the same time her shots did. Carrol shut it off. There wasn't anything she could do about it anyway.

That was when Zed's fighter, still on fire, loosed all of its weaponry, then screamed past her with a final burst of speed Carrol wouldn't have thought possible.

Zed was still in the fight.

The rest of what happened was a blur separated by snapshots of images. Zed impacted ahead of Carrol by several hundred meters. So did his fired weapons, and the ones Carrol had fired as well.

The explosions before her were too close for Carrol to avoid, and her fighter fell into the middle of it.

Carrol's ship violently spun end over end. Her guts heaved and she puked, muscles tight in anticipation of the crash...that never came. She was through the fireballs and out the other side, flying out of control toward the distant stars.

Her vision tunneled much worse as the fighter spun. She was going to lose consciousness. As she locked in controls with a feeble hand to engage the automatic stabilizers in the hope that they would arrest her momentum and bring the death spiral to rest, she caught a glimpse of the Paragon cruiser behind her.

It was buckling from a massive explosion dead in the center of its tri-hulled structure, right where they'd targeted their bombing run.

It ripped apart in a brilliant flash.

Four fighters against the Paragon's superior technology. By force of will alone, humanity was fighting back. Carrol wondered what had happened to the rest of the squadron. Were their targets falling, too? She hoped so.

If the Paragon wanted Earth, it would cost them.

The universe disappeared into a blackness that consumed Carrol's final thoughts of vengeance.

CHAPTER FORTY-EIGHT

Efremova had just about lost control of the situation on Deck Fourteen.

The Paragon had outflanked them. There was no going back. The firefight on either side of their makeshift entrenchment was now a crossfire that had her and her security force pinned down. The only option they had was to retreat, and they were right up against the ladder access that would allow the interlopers to spread into vital areas of the ship.

This was the stand.

They could not give up this ground. This far and no farther.

To her soldiers' credit, they knew it. There was no backing down from this spot except through death. Too many had already succumbed, although they had hurt the Paragon by delivering death into their ranks, too. But the Paragon outnumbered the humans three to one. They could absorb the losses necessary to overrun Efremova's position. They seemed eager to die, even.

Efremova wasn't ready to stop living. Not yet. They would have to kill her to get to that ladder. It was likely going to come to that, but every second she could hold them off was one more second to live.

Whatever plan Smith had, it was too late now.

Several smoke bombs arced through the air, landing in front of their barricade. *Glory's* deck bucked beneath them as the ship was pummeled by Paragon anti-ship weapons. It made the smoke bombs dance and skitter before exploding and bathing everything in a caustic haze that choked human throats and made their eyes water.

Efremova knew it meant the Paragon were making their move. From all sides.

"Hold fire 'til you can see!" Efremova shouted at her small but stalwart group. A half-dozen? She hadn't the time to count, and it didn't matter anyway. It was what they had. Their rifles were running low too, which meant every shot had to count. Wild sprays of plasma into the fog wouldn't do anyone any good. Not anymore.

Dozens of shadows came at them, lit by blue spots of light along their limbs and torsos. Efremova knew only one thing would stop them—a well-aimed shot.

But there were, quite simply, too many of them.

She switched to her rifle's scope, aimed, and fired.

Sprraaattt.

Got one in the chest, clean through. It staggered, then fell to the deck.

As Smith had done, she was looking for her next target before she knew the effect of her first shot. It had to be a perfect shot. If it wasn't, she would die.

Sprraatt-sprraatt.

Another one, but this time she only caught it in the

shoulder and leg. Damn. Shots wasted. She adjusted and aimed again.

There was a roar from behind her.

In her scope, the Paragon's head exploded.

Efremova whirled. Behind her, teeth bared and panting hot, furious breaths, was the massive e-dog from the lower decks. She was ready to kill, to tear apart, but not Efremova. No, the dog's eyes were ahead, past the barricade that was tumbling apart from the Paragon weapons fire and the bucking of the deck.

Above the dog, just as rigid and coiled, ready to destroy, was a hulking figure dressed in a full suit of body armor. Old armor, blackened and charred on its edges. It was an impossible-to-miss color of faded green and blood-red. A Marine's armor.

Smith had returned.

On his shoulders rocked two plasma cannons, and in his hands, he held the most massive rifle Efremova had ever seen. He cocked it and fired a projectile from the lower barrel that launched with a *thunk*. A grenade shot past the barricade, clanked off the ceiling of the corridor, and went spinning into the smoke.

The resulting explosion threatened to melt Efremova's face off, but from the Paragon screams that followed, the weapon had delivered a deadly blow to the enemy. That was well-worth a sunburn.

Smith tilted his head toward her, face invisible behind his reflective faceplate. The dog wore an expression for the both of them.

"Attack," Smith commanded the animal. It was a command for him as well, and the two of them launched over the barricade and disappeared into the Paragon smoke beyond.

Efremova didn't dare follow. Instead, she put her eye back to her scope and watched as shadows flew and screamed. A body was ripped in half. Plasma fire lit up the haze like lightning in a thunderstorm. Efremova squeezed her trigger in the rare instance a Paragon target appeared. She yelled at her fellow stunned soldiers to do the same. "One shot, one kill! Aim at the blue lights, my pretties."

Their help was limited, secondary to the carnage the Marine and his dog were delivering. They disappeared down a T-junction in the distance in opposite directions, and there was more firing of weapons and more screams ending in wet gurgles.

The Paragon began to run toward them, this time away from something as opposed to an organized charge.

Efremova and her team picked them off as they approached from the front and down both side tunnels. They ran in panic, abandoning their cover and not bothering to fire ahead of them until it was too late.

Smith appeared at the end of one corridor. The dog did the same at the other, jaws dripping smoking black blood. The ship's air handlers fought their own battle against the smoke, and the scene slowly began to clear. The Paragon troops laid unmoving.

Efremova called to her people, "Clean up this mess. Airlock the bodies."

The defenders stepped out from behind the barricades and moved forward.

An arm moved, then another.

"They're still alive!" Efremova shouted and dodged sideways, firing erratically. The security force charged and shoved the barrels of their rifles into the mouths of the enemy to kill them once and for all.

Smith jumped into the fray, using the wicked bayonet

attached to the massive firearm. The combat dog ripped into the nearest suit, shredding the body within.

The Paragon tried to gather themselves and regroup, but the defenders were on them. The best defense is a good offense. Before they could fire back, the Paragon were wiped out. The defenders charged through, finishing the attackers as they passed.

The remaining Paragon had no chance, not even with their superior size and weaponry.

The one closest to Efremova roused since she hadn't blasted its helmet. She fired in surprise, and it dodged the shot and slapped the rifle away from her. Efremova reached for her pistol in a smooth, well-practiced motion and shot it in the chest with a quick draw and rapid fire. It wasn't enough.

The giant alien swept a gloved fist past and knocked that away, too, along with Efremova herself. The woman flew into the bulkhead and fell. Hard. She tried to roll away, but a fallen Paragon on the floor next to her blocked her way. The Paragon screamed inside its impenetrable helmet and raised its weapon over its head, ready to bring it down for a final crushing blow.

Smith appeared in a blur and drove his bayonet through the suit and the creature and out the front. He lifted the Paragon into the air and turned it away from Efremova, then thrust the weapon forward and drew it back quickly to free his blade.

The body dropped to the deck, but it tried to get up. The Paragon still lived!

Smith fell on top of it and smashed both gloved and armored hands into the Paragon's face shield. The enemy writhed in pain, and Smith did it again. And again, and again until the alien went limp and its legs stopped flopping. And still, Smith pounded the ruined helmet and destroyed skull against the deck.

The Paragon's head was a blackening pulp when Efremova finally staggered to her feet.

"Smith," she called.

He continued to pound away at the alien's head. He was denting the deck.

"Smith!" she shouted, and she reached to grab his arm.

With lightning reflexes, he tossed her aside, and Efremova slammed into the bulkhead again. This time, she hit the back of her head hard enough to see stars.

He was on his feet, towering over her, arms raised and ready to strike.

"Smith!" she screamed. It was all she could do to cover her face.

The dog was suddenly beside him, growling with its teeth bared. The two of them had bloodlust in their stance.

Smith halted, arms still raised, shoulders heaving.

Efremova fought the urge to cower, just dug her fingers into the rough holes of the deck grating and set her jaw. "Stand down," she ordered the berserker Marine. She looked at the dog, mustering as much authority as she could fake. "You, too!"

The two stood there for a long heartbeat. The rest of the corridor was quiet, the uncanny silence that happened after a battle when one's hearing returned while time continued to pass slowly. Sights and sounds assumed a surreal state.

The survivors watched, guns drawn. Efremova felt as though her heart was about to burst from her chest, but she knew it was over. She knew it before Smith did. He wasn't going to hurt her, and neither was the dog. They just had to be reminded of that. Efremova didn't take her eyes off Smith, not even to blink, willing him to hear her and remember.

She watched as he slumped. His arms fell, and his body sagged. He staggered and nearly fell but caught himself and took a knee. The dog rushed to him, sniffing and whining.

Smith cracked his helmet open. The escaping air hissed free. He removed the helmet and set it on the deck almost reverently. His face was bright red and drenched with sweat, but his eyes weren't wild. Not anymore.

"Good girl," he said to the dog, who was beside herself, ears back, pawing at him furiously and whining. He patted her. "Good girl."

He offered a hand to help Efremova to her feet. She took it gratefully, and they stood together. Efremova could tell that Smith wanted to remark on his bloodlust, to apologize for turning on her, but Efremova ignored it. It wasn't necessary. He'd remembered in time. That was all that mattered. He had saved them and they him. Everyone had fought together greater than they could have fought alone.

Except for Smith. He was the greatest warrior she had ever seen.

She was grateful. More grateful than she thought she could ever tell him, so why even bother?

Together, they surveyed the battleground, still smoky but clearing. The deck rumbled beneath their feet, a sign of the continued firefight that *Glory* was in.

"Did we get them?" Smith asked, his voice quiet.

"I think so," Efremova said, fighting her body's desire to rest. All she wanted to do was collapse, maybe sleep for the next few millennia.

"We should make sure," he said and looked at her.

She nodded.

Smith put his helmet back on, and Efremova picked up her rifle.

"No one gets past you," Efremova ordered the survivors of the security detail. "And find some more goddamned ammunition while cooling your heels."

CHAPTER FORTY-NINE

GLORY COULD TAKE a hit like no other ship Drake had ever served on; such was the quality of her beams and the care with which they'd been fitted; such was the craftsmanship and pride with which she'd been designed and built. But even *Glory* could only take so much.

They were in weapons range of a pair of incoming cruisers and taking a pummeling. Two more cruisers would be in range shortly, and *Glory* would be hopelessly outnumbered, outgunned, and outmaneuvered. Drake'd had a brief surge of optimism when Carrol had managed to take out the first cruiser, but the other bombing runs had failed. Carrol's had been the only one to succeed. None of the fighters showed up on the tactical board now, and the attack window was closing.

"How much time?" Drake asked XO as if something had changed in the last four seconds.

XO shook his head. The cannon was still charging, and it wasn't going to be charged soon enough for their shot to remain free and clear.

"What are we going to do?" the first officer asked.

Drake didn't say anything. He didn't know. He was out of tactics. Out of miracles to pull from his bag. Out of optimism. They weren't going to get their shot. The Paragon had seen to it. They'd moved fast enough and been lucky enough. It wasn't going to work.

"We could fire anyway," XO offered plaintively, but he knew that was folly.

The cannon needed a clear shot. It was the only way to aim properly, the only way to make sure it hit where it needed to: at the very base of the planet-killer where the energy generation was the most intense and the shielding was weakest. Anything in the way would deflect or dissipate the intense particle energy...

And the planet-killer would survive. The clock was ticking on that damned thing as well. It was minutes from firing.

Before the weapon could charge, two cruisers swept between *Glory* and the planet-killer. They turned broadside at the extreme of their weapons range. Drake knew they readied a massive bombardment that *Glory* would not survive.

"Goddammit!" Drake yelled, and he smashed a fist on the center console. They'd been so close.

"Captain!" a voice called from one of the peripheral control stations.

Drake didn't look to see who it was. He knew what they were going to say from the readouts winking at him in a gleaming green. The cannon was charged. "Two seconds, Crewman," he called to share in the general misery. "We missed it by that fucking much."

"No, sir!" came the response. Drake jerked his head toward the speaker. It was Gerry at Tactical. He flashed something over to Drake's console.

XO rushed over to see a ship coming up behind the growing group of Paragon cruisers and burning like hell's fury to reach them. It was surrounded by a growing cloud of small objects ejecting from all sides of it. At first Drake thought they were fighters, though he'd never seen the Paragon launch from all angles like that.

Then he realized they weren't fighters, they were escape pods. And that ship wasn't Paragon.

It was *Vengeance*.

"Hailing!" Trudy called from the comms station.

"Put them on," Drake ordered.

"You got that cannon ready to fire?" came the voice, followed by a shaky visual connection a second later. It was Sellers, face covered in sooty sweat and a gash across the bridge of his nose. Behind him, his command deck was in flames. Despite all that, his eyes were clear. Hard. Determined.

Drake glanced at his XO. It could only stay primed for a split second, which he knew they'd reached, but it wouldn't take as long to get back to the red line as it had the first time. Seconds? XO gave a nod to confirm. *Seconds.*

"We're blocked by the cruisers ahead of you," Drake confirmed. "Anything you can do about that?"

"I can see."

At that moment, Drake put it together. The escape pods accelerating away from the ship. The approach vector Sellers was taking. The hard look in his eyes. "Now, wait just a goddamn minute, Captain!"

Sellers waved him off. "Save your breath, Drake. It's already decided, and my core's close to critical anyway. I have a couple torpedoes down there, armed on my signal to help get the fireworks started."

Drake blinked, at a loss for words, then, "Eject for God's sake, man!"

Sellers shut that down too with a shake of his head and a glance down. Drake figured he must be at the helm. "No," he replied gravely. "Need to make sure the timing is just right." He looked up, and Drake could see emotion creeping into the hard, determined eyes. He looked decades older than his young face should. "I've always known I would go down with my ship," he said with a nod impossibly full of purpose and peace. "Take care of my crew."

All Drake could do was nod in return. The escape pods, which were falling into the nearest gravity well, would be on Earth soon. Their fate would be the same as hers.

"It's been an honor, Captain," Sellers said.

Drake nodded tightly, lips white as he clenched his teeth.

Sellers nodded back. "Take that big fucking thing down."

The transmission ended abruptly.

There was a moment of stunned silence. A tactical officer called, "Cruisers three and four now also between us and the planet-killer."

The tactical display showed four of the Paragon stood in their way. As *Vengeance* rose behind them, however, and turned to aim at the middle of them all, Drake knew what Sellers was going to do. In their effort to block *Glory's* line of sight and remain at the edge of weapons range, they were clustered together. Too close.

Vengeance was in their midst before they knew what was happening. Bristling with unleashed firepower, Vengeance continued on her final trajectory, the middle of a barrage to clear *Glory's* line of fire. The cruisers staggered, but if it had solely been up to the Fleet cruiser's plasma cannons and missile tubes, she would have been hopelessly outmatched. The Paragon treated the situation like she was. They rearranged themselves to fire back. It brought them even closer.

A fatal mistake. *Vengeance's* greatest weapon wasn't her cannons or missiles. It was the ship herself and her captain's resolve.

Vengeance lit up the entire cosmos when she went, brighter than any star. So brilliant was the release of her power core detonation, those who were left alive to witness it had to shield their eyes lest the light of her death blind them. All except Drake, who didn't blink or lift a finger. It was the least he could do, he felt, to watch her go. She and her damned fool captain; in the end, one of the bravest men Drake had ever met. A soldier.

Bravery was coming in waves. Glory's Delta Wings. The security details fighting Paragon soldiers hand-to-hand. And captains who sacrificed their ships.

The battle for humanity was joined.

Four secondary explosions followed as the Paragon cruisers were caught in the inferno of *Vengeance's* death. They, too, lit up the starscape, but not as brightly as their executioner.

After the light and fire had dissipated, as darkness once again took hold in the void of space, *Glory* had her shot. Free and clear.

"Mister Oh," Drake said, breaking the stunned silence on the command deck.

Oh roused, wiping something from the corner of his eye. "Yes, sir?"

"Spin the cannon to redline and fire."

"Yes, sir."

CHAPTER FIFTY

Carrol came to alone in the black of deep space.

It was quiet outside. Deathly quiet. No buffeting; her ship sat motionless. Carnage surrounded her in the form of a steadily expanding cloud of irradiated shrapnel.

She figured it was from the cruiser she and Zed had taken down, but as she became more cognizant, she realized it was far too large and spread out to be just one ship. It had to be several. Her heart sank, figuring one of them must be *Glory* and their mission had been a failure.

She called over her comm, desperately seeking the ship or any of her fellow fighters, but the radiation caused too much interference. It didn't mean they were dead. She just couldn't reach them. She thought especially of Zed on fire. She wondered if he'd perished back there, or if he'd ejected in time before his fighter impacted. Damned bravest thing she'd ever seen. She hoped, prayed he was out there. An ejected cockpit capsule could keep someone alive for a long time.

Her fighter was intact enough to fly even with a missing wing, she discovered. Always the wings she seemed to lose in battle, though this time, there was no servo arm that could repair it. No matter.

She pulled herself out of the densest part of the debris field and into open space. Her calls from there still went unanswered, but she was able to see again. Her scopes gave her a view of the battlefield.

And what a view it was.

Glory was alive, but in the radiation, she was out of comm range. Carrol was ahead of the ship, but she was alive. And from the glow down the length of the massive cannon on her spine, she was about to fire.

"Yes!" Carrol cheered, pumping her fist at the old ship. *Her* ship. The sacrifice had bought them the shot they wanted.

The only shot remaining for humanity.

"Here's to Zed and every hardcore motherfucker who believed in you, Captain. Give 'em hell!"

In the distance, the planet-killer was spinning up too, glowing from its firing tip. It was also getting ready to fire.

She watched the battle of giants playing out before her. A battered megalith from a time when humanity was better at making war, and an alien ship the size of a small moon serving one purpose. Mars was already gone, a testament to its power.

Earth was next unless *Glory's* shot delivered the endgame.

Who would fire first?

Glory. She was ready.

Carrol wanted to shout and scream to her ship. To cheer them on and tell them she could see, she knew what they were about to do and that they'd done it. They'd all done it together. She supposed she did just that in her cockpit, imagining they could hear her in the moment of their triumph. Goddammit, they'd done it.

They'd done it.

The tip of the cannon at the leading edge of *Glory* glowed white-hot. The ship visibly shuddered, and a wave of energy passed from the rear where the power core was located to the tip. The whole ship undulated with the energy building at the cannon's business end. And again and again, until it was too dazzling to look at and the ship was bathed in the imminent release of more energy than should have been possible.

The cannon fired.

It was a scream in the darkness. It ripped past with such force that Carrol's fighter was blown back by the beam. She turned to see it hit the planet-killer on its glowing tip of building energy. Straight and true. Right on target.

As the energies collided, there was a massive blaze of light, the explosion of competing energies. Kaiju fighting for primacy. Leviathans battling in the heavens.

Carrol turned her head away and still the light was everywhere, too intense to cast shadows. She closed her eyes and the light was still there, burning her retinas. As soon as that faded enough, she dared to open them again. The stars were gone in the residual glow and nothing could be seen, but slowly, timidly, the starfield peeked out from behind the fallout, the dark of space returning to normal.

Carrol looked at the explosion's origination point, hoping against hope to see the planet-killer gone, broken up or perhaps with a massive, ragged hole bored through it. To see it destroyed.

Surely, it must have been destroyed.

What she saw instead, unfazed and exactly where it had been before the cannon shot, was a fully intact, fully operational, and undamaged enemy, readying itself to fire on the planet below.

They'd failed.

The planet-killer had survived the best shot humanity could take.

Carrol blinked and rubbed her eyes, sure they were deceiving her, but when she looked again, the Paragon doomsday weapon was still there and getting brighter.

Impossible.

The truth was so crushing Carrol couldn't bring herself to acknowledge it. It was all wrong. It wasn't supposed to happen this way.

No.

NO!

Her communications console was beeping. She was dimly aware of the intrusion, but she couldn't move. She didn't want to move. What was the point? The planet-killer was still there.

"Eunice," a voice said, also dim and distant. It was familiar, and it brought her back to the present, back to her cockpit.

A familiar paternal face was smiling at her from the center of her canopy display.

"Admiral?" It was Lyle, her former benefactor and mentor. The man who'd gotten her a posting on a starship. Except...

Except it wasn't Lyle. She'd known that, hadn't she?

"It's good to see you," the not-admiral said. She'd had this conversation before. His image glitched. There was static. "How is the posting going?"

Carrol felt nauseous. Disembodied. How many times had she had this conversation? Her head hurt, suddenly, violently. It bent her over in pain.

"No," she gasped.

"I do hope you're settling in nicely," the admiral continued, oblivious.

The glitching became more pronounced. There was static now. Carrol felt something rising inside of her, something dark, something distinctly not her. With it came intense pain.

She moaned. Her vision swam. She tried to fight, tried to stay conscious, to stay herself. She was hanging off a cliff with darkness below, only her fingertips on the edge.

"Big step!" the not-admiral effused. He was standing over her on the cliff, his face writhing like he was possessed and his foot raised. She begged him, but there was no stopping what was coming.

On the cockpit display, the admiral's face glitched one last time with a crush of static.

The foot came crashing down, the cliff crumbled under her desperate fingers, and she fell into the darkness.

CHAPTER FIFTY-ONE

FAILURE.

It rocked Drake into silence, along with everyone else on the command deck. Someone moaned their grief, beyond words, an involuntary sound. Drake would have made the same sound if he'd had breath, but he didn't. He'd breathed everything he could into that cannon shot. His entire crew had. Against all odds, they'd gotten it off, too. And now...

What now?

The planet-killer was still there. Still readying to fire, and there was nothing that could stop her. The Paragon had anticipated the cannon just like they'd anticipated everything else.

Drake's failure was complete, so colossal in scale that it staggered him mentally and physically. He sagged against his command console and would have fallen to the deck if XO had not been there to catch him.

"Captain—" his first officer started, his eyes lost and desperately searching his superior's face for some option, some explanation, *something*.

Drake didn't have anything for him.

He didn't have anything left for anyone, not even anger. No anger for the Paragon and their brutal intolerance, no anger for the degradation of the Fleet that had led to such a poor response, not even anger for Jack, who he should have been the angriest with for giving them hope. Hope for a half-assed plan.

Everything had been for naught. Futility at its finest.

He found he did have some anger for the admiral. If only the old man had shared a little of what he knew with Drake. Given him a chance to help instead of making him a lackey. Everyone was a lackey to Jack.

What had been the point? To come all this way, only to fail? What did Jack know that had given him a reason to believe this would work?

I need you, he'd said that night at the Veterans' Building.

The failure burned into fury. Drake wanted to scream at the man who wasn't there.

A fighting chance, he'd said that night.

Those were the final words Jack had said to him, damn him. Except...

Except, they hadn't been. Not quite.

He'd said something else at the end, something Drake hadn't understood at the time, which was perhaps why he hadn't remembered until just then.

Use the girl.

The girl.

Drake snapped ramrod-straight. The move was so abrupt it sent XO stumbling back. Drake looked at him, eyes wide with purpose.

"Captain?" his first officer asked, reading the change in expression.

All eyes were on Drake. He reached for the intercom,

one of the few systems that Drake knew would be working, and keyed the link to the fulcrum.

"Cap?" Broussard called over the tinny speakers. "What's going on up there? We get the shot off?"

"Never mind that, Doc," Drake overlapped him. "Is she okay? Is Idri awake?"

"She's...she's—"

There was the sound of movement over the intercom, then a new voice broke in.

"I'm awake, Captain," Idri said. Her voice sounded strong. Clear. "What do you need?"

Drake could have cried. He didn't, but he could have. "I need you to prepare for another jump," he said instead. An action. Concise. Simple. It belied just how desperate a move he was finally considering, something he realized he should have considered a long time ago, but that didn't matter now. He had a final piece he would put into play.

"Now, wait just a bloody minute—" Doc began.

Drake cut him off again. "I'll explain when I get down there." He switched off the channel. All eyes were still on Drake, most of all XO's. "Commander," he said with a large swallow. "Make the call to abandon ship."

XO, bless him, didn't even blink. "What's the plan, sir?"

Drake simply embraced the man, hard and tight. A moment was all Drake had to spare, but he took it anyway, then held the man at arm's length. "It has been an honor serving with you," he said. "Now do your damned job, mister, and get everyone off this ship."

XO knew what the hug meant.

Finality.

The large man gripped Drake's forearms and nodded crisply. It was only his voice that betrayed his emotions. "The honor has been all mine, sir."

Drake released him. XO took a step back and gave the most perfectly crisp salute that Drake had ever seen in his life. Then Oh turned and started barking orders to the stunned command deck crew.

An alarm rang out, one Drake had thought he'd never hear.

"Abandon ship," a voice called.

Magnetic locks released around the command deck as it was unsealed so its crew could make it to their escape rafts. Drake rushed toward the hatch leading into the ship.

"Where will you be, Captain?" Oh called after him.

Drake paused at the exit. "Fulcrum."

Oh nodded. "Good luck."

Drake gave a grim smile in thanks. He would need it. They all would.

CHAPTER FIFTY-TWO

IDRI WAS unfazed by Drake's plan.

Doc, on the other hand, was beside himself.

"Absolutely not. No! It will kill her."

"It might." Drake looked the young woman in the eyes to make sure she understood.

She stared back at him with two big, dark pupils. "I understand."

Drake was asking of her what he'd never wanted to ask, ever again. It was the reason he'd resisted her being on board, it was the reason Jack had said what he'd said a million years ago at the Veterans' Building, and Drake knew it was the ask that was always going to be required of him whenever he put on the badge of office that hung from his uniform breast. Fate held him once more in its ugly grasp, and his was the order that would carry it forward, deliver into the hands of the merciless mistress. He had to use a Navigator, sacrifice her to succeed. But she was a survivor.

Maybe...

As she'd done to defend herself at Neptune and she'd demonstrated to the officers in Sickbay, Idri was to jump into the heart of the Paragon planet-killer, taking *Glory* with her. The ship was the only thing big enough that Idri could move. The combination of the two masses would annihilate both vessels, particularly if the ship jumped into the other's power generation core. The chain reaction would be unstoppable—a trump card to win the final hand of life.

Drake was certain the Paragon knew about it. After all, they'd expended an awful lot of energy trying to intercept her before she reached *Glory*. But it didn't matter. The move was indefensible. Once the jump was made, it would be over for the planet-killer.

It would also be over for *Glory*.

"If you can jump yourself free, or send the ship ahead, or whatever other tricks you might have up that sleeve, I'm all for it."

Idri shook her head. Drake could see her mind working behind those two large eyes. She laid a hand on the fulcrum. "A jump of such size requires me to be here. With the ship."

Drake had figured as much. There was much about what the Navigators did that he didn't know, but one thing he did was that their ability was limited to a certain degree by mass. Ships could only grow so big before a Navigator wasn't able to move them with their mind. The fulcrum helped that. Exactly how much and what those limits were, he didn't know. But he took Idri at face value. She would have to be with the ship. With him.

"And you'll do this? Even though it will cost your life?"

"I am Navigator of *Glory*. I will take her wherever you command, Captain."

Drake gave a small smile that said, 'Thank you,' and the young alien returned it. If Drake were to think about it for too long, it would occur to him that it was a shame they'd not gotten to know each other. He was sorry, too, that he'd ever doubted her or resisted her presence even for a second, no matter what his personal reasons were. She was quite the soldier. Better than he'd given her credit for.

"Get to the closest escape raft," Drake said to Broussard, not allowing himself to linger in sentimentality. He pointed out of the chamber's one and only hatch.

"Absolutely not." The doctor shook his head. Drake opened his mouth to make it an order, but Doc held a hand up to stop him. "If you're making a jump this big, this important, you'll want your Navigator in tip-top shape, won't you?" He reached into the medical bag lying on the floor, which was chock-full of vials, syringes, and pills from when he was attending Idri previously. He regarded the Navigator and passed a scanner over her face. "Your f-particles are still low. Let's see what we can do in the next minute or two to get them higher."

OH SLAMMED the hatch shut on the tightly-quartered escape raft, waited for the indicator panel to turn green and indicate that they had an atmospheric seal, then stabbed the launch button with a meaty thumb.

A five-second countdown started and Oh struggled with his seat straps, floundering for a stressful moment before hitching the clasp across his barrel chest. It wasn't a second too soon. The raft launched like the bullet out of a gun. Oh fought to keep his stomach out of his throat as the acceleration ramped up and up, then they were away, outside the hull of the ship and shooting through space. The acceleration slowed, and the raft began to tumble slowly.

"Look!" one of the command deck crewmen said,

pointing through one of the many portals that surrounded the roughly cube-shaped container.

It was *Glory*. She hung in space, her nose offset from her ballistic trajectory, listing from the overall loss of power she'd suffered from using her cannon. She looked like a husk or a deflated balloon. Tired, old, and defeated.

XO knew she wasn't, that she still had fight left in her, but it hurt him to see her like that. He wanted to look away, close his eyes, and picture her the way she had been on the day he'd first laid eyes on her: shining, beautiful, and strong. But he couldn't. She deserved for her people to watch her final act of defiance.

Her final victory.

She *was* still beautiful and strong. Underneath several decades of rust and carbon scoring, her vibrancy lived on. Just like Drake was in there, still fighting with every breath he took. Oh ached to be with his captain, to be down there helping with whatever it was they were planning.

As much as it hurt him not to be there, his captain had asked one last thing of him, and he hadn't made it an order. *Take care of our people.* That was XO's job.

Oh grabbed the status pad that he'd brought with him from the command deck once it was empty except for the handful of people he'd picked as those who would go with him on the last raft out. It was the escape manifest. He scrolled through it, checking to see that every raft had launched and cleared the ship and every crew member was accounted for. They were, but they weren't.

Captain Drake. The Navigator. Broussard. Everyone else was on a raft, right where they were supposed to be. Except...

Oh frowned.

Except that his link to *Glory's* tactical scopes showed a

ship was about to land in her fighter bay. A Delta Wing. One of *Glory's*. Oh tried desperately to hail them before they landed, but it was too late. They disappeared inside the ship.

Oh keyed open a comm channel.

"Is the evacuation of the ship complete, Commander?" Drake asked.

"Yes, sir. Except for one fighter, sir. She just docked. They either didn't hear the abandon ship order, or they confused that for a recall signal. I don't know."

"Did you warn them off?"

"I tried, sir. They landed anyway."

A pause, then, "Thank you, XO. You've done well. You always have."

"Of course, sir."

"I haven't said that enough, but you have. Thank you... for bringing me back." Another long pause, which Oh wanted to fill but suddenly couldn't find the words. "I have to go," Drake finally said without wallowing further in the emotion of the moment.

"I know, sir. Me, too."

The channel switched off. Oh had nowhere to go. He could only watch as the events before him unfolded.

XO looked out at *Glory*, hanging in front of the stars. He decided that this was always how he would remember her. And her captain. In their prime. Worn with experience and weathered with grit. Stronger for it all. The strongest they'd ever been.

He drank it in, putting his hand on the glass as if that would help him feel her. Someone behind him started sobbing. A tear trailed down Oh's cheek, but he refused to wipe it away. He could only stare at *Glory*.

DESPITE THE STODGY old doctor's protests, Drake sent Broussard to find the poor, misguided fighter pilot who'd come to an empty home. He'd been ordered to take them to the nearest raft and throw himself in alongside. And be quick about it. He wondered if he was going to listen. There wasn't time for debate or delay.

The planet-killer was glowing white-hot, but Drake knew from careful study of the Mars footage that it was not yet quite ready. It was down to minutes now.

Idri was quiet and still, meditating and softly reciting to herself. Drake gave her space while he kept his eye on the planet-killer.

He had no desire to die alone, but he didn't want anyone to go on this one-way ride who didn't absolutely have to. With a syringe in hand, instructions to deliver its contents, a stimulant, right before making *Glory's* final jump, and the knowledge of exactly where in the planet-killer Idri should jump them, the only two people who were required for this maneuver were him and Idri. He wished his old friend luck. It would have been nice to spend more time with him too.

A clatter at the hatchway broke the silence, and Drake groaned. "Goddammit, Doc," he said, turning. "I told—"

The sight in the doorway made him stop. Next to him, Idri roused.

The doctor stood there but not alone. Drake's second officer stood beside him and held a gun to his head.

"Carrol," Drake said more matter-of-factly than he expected.

But it wasn't Carrol. It was something else. Her face writhed underneath the skin. Whatever it was oozed out of her skin wherever it went, little tentacles wriggling out of her pores and then slinking back inside her body. Her eyes were vibrating. Her body shook, drenched in sweat. She opened her mouth to speak, but a shriek came out.

The Carrol-not-Carrol flung the doctor aside with inhuman strength. He flew into the nearest bulkhead with a sickening crunch and collapsed in a heap. A gash in his forehead gushed blood. In the same motion, Carrol brought her blaster pistol to bear and fired.

CHAPTER FIFTY-THREE

DRAKE FLUNG HIMSELF INTO IDRI.

The blaster shot ripped through the air where she had been and scorched the far wall of the fulcrum. The air sizzled where the shot had passed.

Drake used his momentum to fling Idri ahead of him, sending her crashing into the fulcrum wall like Broussard had, albeit with much less force. She hit, grabbed its rough surface to steady herself, and collapsed into her robes, making herself as small a target as possible.

Carrol had followed her and fired a shot just before she collapsed that torched the wall above Idri's head.

Drake lunged toward Carrol once he'd sent Idri sprawling.

He slammed into her with the force of his athletic glory days at the Academy. Defensive end. He knew how to tackle. He plowed her into the deck, driving until both of them made contact.

He wasn't as young as he used to be, but the pain in his shoulder didn't hold him back. He grunted as he jumped up to stand over Carrol. She'd lost her pistol on impact.

Drake straddled her and desperately sought to remember other moves from his past, those from his days on the wrestling mat. He wrapped her up, trying to pin her arms and legs with his body. He succeeded, if only for a second or two. The move brought him millimeters from her writhing face.

Slick gray-white tentacles wiggled from her skin, stretching and ripping at her pores. Her eyes vibrated so rapidly her pupils became jagged lines. Drake had to look away because it induced vertigo. Carrol screamed again, and the glimpse inside her mouth was even more horrifying. Something pulsed in there with the same slick gray-white slime, and it was growing.

Her body movements matched the writhing creature, and with a strength that shouldn't have been possible with any sort of pain-intolerant nervous system, Carrol kicked and bucked at Drake with every shred of muscle she had. Drake could feel her joints ripping apart as she heaved to get him off her.

He was powerless to stop her.

Drake still held the syringe Broussard had prepared for Idri. A stimulant seemed like the last thing Carrol and this creature needed, but it was all he had.

Carrol, after another ear-piercing shriek, tossed Drake off with a great kick from her legs. She jumped to her feet and raked her insane eyes over the room, looking for Idri. She found the Navigator huddled against the far wall of the fulcrum, almost directly opposite. Drake had hoped she'd run out, but he and the possessed Carrol had been fighting at the entrance. She'd gotten as far away as she could. Good girl.

Carrol took off in a dead sprint across the room despite the damage Drake had done to the host's body. A disjointed knee. Broken ribs. The creature, whatever the Paragon bio-infestation was, was in complete control, and it didn't care what it had to destroy to get what it wanted.

Idri.

Carrol's path took her past Drake. He dove again, his shoulder screaming in pain as he managed to trip her.

This time, Carrol landed on top of Drake.

All part of the plan.

He yanked the syringe out of his uniform, placed his thumb on the plunger, and stabbed toward Carrol's face, where a large tentacle had appeared, writhing from the corner of her eye.

She saw the move and blocked it.

With vice-grip strength, she squeezed Drake's hand. He cried out in pain as she squeezed. It was his broken hand. He turned that pain and that yell into a howl and pushed back with the syringe.

The creature started to pull out of Carrol's face, dripping onto Drake's. Even the fluid from the thing writhed on its own, sending convulsions of disgust up and down his body. *What was it?* With horror, he realized what it was trying to do: separate from Carrol to possess him.

It tore and ripped at the woman's face, splitting her cheeks, widening the rims of her eyes, and crawling out of her mouth. She screamed, and it screamed too. Drake roared, trying to break her hold and stab the creature, but she held him tightly. He couldn't budge.

A shot rang out.

Carrol lurched. Turned her head.

Drake turned his head, too.

Broussard was standing, woozy from his forehead gash but with a blaster in hand. He'd shot the possessed commander in the back. She screamed at him.

He shot her again, this time in the shoulder she was using to hold Drake's arm.

Her grip weakened slightly.

Drake heaved the syringe forward. It caught her in the cheek and squished through. The creature wriggled inside, shuddering as the needle pierced it.

He injected the stimulant into it.

Carrol went as rigid as a board, and Drake used the opportunity to break free, rolling desperately while scrubbing the alien liquid off his face.

Carrol and the creature didn't follow. He jumped to his feet, hoping he could fight again, but she was convulsing on the floor. The second officer rose onto her hands and knees and dry-heaved several times, then let out the most blood-curdling scream Drake had ever heard.

A mass of white-gray poured from her eyes and her mouth and coalesced on the deck of the fulcrum. It was the size of an adult head, and it was quivering with tentacles large and small that stabbed and jerked in an apoplectic frenzy. It was wired, pumped with the stimulant and going crazy.

Carrol slumped next to it, her face a bloody mess, and fell unconscious. But the creature had no interest in her. Not anymore. The tentacles waved like seaweed in an ocean tide, searching, and it began to move, hesitant at first and jittery. Drake knew who it was searching for.

"Doc!" he shouted, and the creature responded instantly to the sound. "The gun!"

Broussard didn't hesitate. With a toss, he sent the gun flying toward Drake in the same moment that the creature jumped at Drake. He didn't know what was going to arrive first, the gun in his outstretched hand or the creature on his face.

In a fury of adrenaline-fueled action, Drake caught the pistol with his good hand and brought it into the alien's path. The millisecond before it impacted the barrel, Drake blasted the creature backward with a massive hole through its body.

It squealed.

Drake shot it until there was nothing left to writhe, squeal, or do *anything* except smolder.

Suddenly, it was quiet again, save for Drake's ragged breaths.

He whirled as a hand was placed on his shoulder, but it was Idri. Safe.

Doc joined the two of them, also breathing heavily and dabbing gingerly at his wound. "I guess," he gasped, "we know who the damned saboteur was."

That hadn't sunk in yet. Carrol. It had been her the whole time. Or rather, whatever was now smoking on the deck.

But the planet-killer was still out there. It had not yet fired. There was still time. "Stimulant!" Drake barked.

The Paragon ship was close to firing. Less than a minute now.

Drake guided Idri to the stand in the center of the fulcrum.

"Take her and get out of here," Drake told the doctor, gesturing at the unconscious Carrol. She didn't need to be on the ship, and neither did the doc. "You might have just enough time to make the nearest escape raft."

It was only a few meters down the passage outside the chamber's hatch.

Doc didn't argue. He hobbled to Carrol and tried to hoist her onto his shoulder for a fireman's carry, but he slipped in the blood and collapsed.

The Paragon ship began its death spin, twirling like a top. It moved slowly at first, then faster and faster as it began to glow with pulsating energy.

Drake glared at his old friend, but the doc silenced him with a wave. He cradled Carrol's body to him and rocked her while Drake returned his attention to the Navigator.

Drake went to Idri. It was close. Moments. The Paragon ship was spinning exactly as it had over Mars. He knew from watching the recording over and over that first would come a particle beam, then a flash from the tip right before the blast...

"Almost," he whispered, standing so close they were shoulder to shoulder, both pairs of eyes locked on the ship.

The particle beam burst from the ship's tip. Not yet.

Idri grabbed his hand and squeezed. "Thank you," she said.

"For what?"

"For giving me a ship, even for a little while."

He squeezed back.

The particle beam tore through Earth's atmosphere, blowing away clouds and billowing steam where it met the sea, and still the Paragon ship spun faster, and shined brighter. Its tip, small from this far away but larger up close than the length and width of *Glory,* flashed with a blinding light.

"Now, Idri!" Drake yelled.

The Navigator jumped.

OH WAS WATCHING when it happened.

The Paragon ship spun till it became a blur, and then its

weapon's tip flared with a white-hot light. A beam of energy erupted and slammed into the Earth.

In the same instant, the *Glory* flared with a light all its own and disappeared.

The energy beam from the Paragon ship blasted the atmosphere away from it, vaporizing clouds, billowing water the moment it touched the sea, and melted rock miles below...

Then it faltered.

There was an explosion of a different kind very near the tip. Red-orange. Fire! A crack appeared on the side of the half-dome. The ship tilted and cracked some more, then steadied.

The beam ceased to operate. The ocean recovered quickly. Clouds swirled.

And with the force of a thousand ships' power cores, with light equal to a supernova and a sound that would wake the gods of old...

The planet-killer exploded.

Vaporized.

Everything was light and sound and fury, and it sent the escape raft and everything else lucky enough to be outside the blast radius tumbling violently away. Wave after wave of energy pummeled the poor cube for longer than anyone thought possible.

Oh tumbled with it but stayed in his seat. He reached for the thruster controls of the raft as soon as the g-forces would allow, and he stabilized their spin.

Oh was certain he was the first to lay eyes upon the destroyed beast after the fallout dimmed, when heads or tails could be made of what was left of the pinnacle of the Paragon war machine.

Nothing.

Nothing but dust, fast-cooling gas, and one final fireworks show for the people of Earth.

The enemy ship was gone.

The crew around XO cheered, whooped, and hollered, and he did too. More tears came to him, and when he could yell and scream no longer, he shook his head and pounded his fists on the portal window.

"You did it," he whispered when that was all the voice he had left. "Captain, you did it."

He would have been content to look at that void forever, but after a certain amount of time, one of the crew tried to get his attention.

"Sir?" the crewman asked when he finally turned to acknowledge him.

He knew he didn't look like an XO should. Emotions spilled over his face, while his body spasmed from exhaustion and emotional trauma.

The young man held up a control pad, which was blinking a signal.

"I think you're going to want to see this."

CHAPTER FIFTY-FOUR

DRAKE REVELED IN THE JUMP.

He'd never been inside the fulcrum when it happened. It was much more focused, much quieter, and personal.

Everything around him expanded. He grew along with it. And in the center of it all was Idri, and he was right next to her. He was aware of all of it at once. Time had no concept, nor did space. He was everywhere and everything, and it was all right there in front of him, around him, inside him. He could drag a finger across the cosmos and make the stars dance because he was the stars and the matter and energies that held them together.

After everything contracted, after all that enormity sucked back down into a single point, pulled in by Idri, it was loud, more intense. They crashed back into the realm of space and time like a wrecking ball, for there was matter already there. They infected it, invaded it, pushed it out. Drake could feel it, he thought, just for a moment, the heat of the planet-killer in the threshold between eternity and the finite as time ramped up to its unrelenting, unstoppable speed. He existed simultaneously everywhere and in a single already occupied point inside the Paragon ship. He felt its massiveness as he scaled down, its power, and the havoc it was about to unleash on the planet below. He felt Earth shuddering, and then they crossed the threshold.

Annihilation.

He felt his body and everything around him rip to shreds as matter met and the laws governing the universe broke down. Matter appeared inside matter, and Drake was the Paragon ship in addition to himself. Their air his air, their metal his flesh, his energy their energy.

The tear was release. It was order being restored.

Drake felt himself expand again, and in whatever fraction of a second he had to entertain the thought before he was scattered across the stars, he considered that he'd always expected death to be painful.

It wasn't.

It was like jumping.

He expanded and contracted again, then it was quiet. And peaceful. Idri was gone from his side. It was just him.

Expand.

Contract.

He found he could do that if he concentrated, if that's what he was doing. Concentrating.

Expand.

Contract.

Like a breath.

An interesting thought skittered across his mind in that peaceful, quiet place of expansion and contraction. Was this the afterlife? If he was dead and could still ask a question as inane as "Am I in heaven?" Well, then surely it was. And he was.

Imagine that.

The afterlife was real after all.

He laughed.

What a thing to learn.

"CAPTAIN?"

Drake was still laughing when he came to.

A voice called from somewhere far away. "He's waking." Then the voice was close. "Captain, can you hear me?"

Drake opened his eyes to a blinding light. The beam was a dagger through his eyeballs to the back of his head. He had an intense, non-heavenly headache, and his eyes were on fire. He tried to speak, but his throat was bone-dry. There was rustling beside him, and something was pressed into his left hand.

"Drink," said the voice.

It was a cup. Cool liquid sloshed onto him from inside it. Water. He found he couldn't hold it steady.

"Let me help you."

A strong hand helped him lean forward and steadied his arm to raise the cup to his lips. He drank. It acted like rain on cracked soil, disappearing instantly, absorbed into parched tissues. There were more cups of water to follow.

Drake drank them. He blinked his eyes and tried to focus.

He was in a room. Pure white. Quiet.

The light wasn't blinding. It was mellow as his eyes adjusted, coming from two shaded lamps and a window behind him. He turned to see who was helping him and smiled when he saw Doc sitting on a chair covered in blankets, a pillow, and the evidence of several meals. The gash showed purple on his forehead, but it was stitched and healing.

"What happened?"

"'Only a man who knows what it is like to be defeated can reach down to the bottom of his soul and come up with the extra ounce of power it takes to win when the match is even.'"

Drake frowned.

Doc shook his head and smiled. "You saved the day, Cap. That's what."

Doc pressed a button and Drake's bed turned toward the window. Below, in the soft light on the other side of the terminator, Earth lit up as night fell. They were over the old US, it looked like. Home. Intact.

"How?" He could hardly speak, he was so overwhelmed.

"The girl is a miracle worker," a new voice called into the room.

Broussard turned the bed back to its normal position to reveal Admiral Sturgess standing in the doorway. He looked much the worse for wear since the last time Drake had seen him, or maybe he looked the same. Drake still didn't like him. The admiral's arm was in a sling, and his face was drawn to the point of looking skeletal. He was thin.

But he was alive.

"She did something that, frankly, no one has ever heard of, let alone attempted. She jumped *Glory* into the Paragon ship and then jumped her out again." He snapped his fingers. "Just like that. Merged the matter and set off a chain reaction that destroyed the weapon, then somehow untangled you, her, and the ship again and put you right back where you'd started from. Nearly killed her, of course, but she did it."

"I want to see her," Drake said, strength returning to his numb, tingling limbs.

Broussard gently held him back. "She's not up for it yet, Cap," he said, and when Drake looked at him, panicked and worried, he reassured him with a soft squeeze of his shoulders and a smile. "But she will be soon. She's going to be okay. I promise."

Drake looked at the admiral, and the man confirmed Doc's words with a warm smile of his own. It wasn't a look Drake was accustomed to seeing from the dour spy chief. He wasn't sure how to feel about it. "The explosion took out most of the Paragon fleet, and those that survived turned tail and ran. You saved Earth."

Drake swallowed and tried to internalize the immensity of it all. He had been ready to die. He shouldn't be here. His throat felt rougher than sandpaper. "And Carrol?" he asked, mind still running through the loose ends, trying to figure out what happened.

"Recovered," Doc answered.

"Already on assignment," Jack added. "I actually had an encounter with one of those Paragon cerebral parasites myself here on Earth. Nasty things, aren't they? And wholly undetectable, which is quite the problem, but we're working on it." He shuddered, presumably because of a memory. "Thankfully, in the case of Commander Carrol, the encounter wasn't fatal."

"She wanted to be here when you woke," Broussard said. "I think she felt rather ashamed."

"Nonsense," Jack interjected with a firm shake of his head. "She was absolutely not in her own mind when that thing made her do what she did. She shoulders none of the blame. She saved your lives more than once. She made the shot possible."

"Where is she?" Drake asked.

Broussard and Jack glanced at each other. Doc deferred to the admiral.

"You just get some rest, Augustus," he said. "Build your strength. We're going to need you out there."

Doc stood, and so did the admiral.

"I want to see Ellen," Drake said, emotion suddenly welling in his chest.

"She's on her way here," Jack said. "Things are a mess planet-side, but we finally got a hold of her."

Drake nodded, immensely grateful. "Thank you."

Doc slapped his thighs. "I'm going to get you some food," he said, and he left.

Drake was grateful for that, too. He hadn't realized he was starving until the doc mentioned food. Drake was alone with the admiral. "I thought you were dead," he said to him.

"Those reports were greatly exaggerated."

Drake noted his arm in the sling. There was a bandage on his shoulder. "Exaggerated by you?"

Jack shrugged. "Who can say?" His eyes twinkled.

"And the Paragon bugs?"

"Turns out there was a cure, after all. A certain Senator hand-delivered it to me. All a story I'll tell you someday. Maybe."

"You're crazy."

Jack shook his head. "*You're* crazy," he said with about as much warmth and mirth as Drake had ever heard from the lying sumbitch. "Jumping the ship inside the Paragon superweapon. How'd you ever come up with such a wildly madcapped idea?"

Drake blanched. "It was you," he stuttered. "You, Jack. You're the one who told me not to be afraid to use her."

Jack chuckled. "I meant to jump to Earth and use the

cannon, my dear captain. I had no idea she could do such a thing."

"They expected the cannon."

"Yes, they did."

"Did you know that?"

Jack shook his head.

Drake sat back in his bed. It had been *that* close. Losing everything. Plans thwarted. Outmaneuvered. They had been a desperate, improvised Hail Mary away from losing everything.

"It was the girl's idea," Drake said quietly. "She came up with it all on her own. Wasn't even in her book, she said."

Jack nodded reverently. "She's special. Unorthodox." Jack tapped him on the chest. "Just like you, which was why I needed you. All of humanity needed you." He rubbed his face with his free hand, and Drake saw the exhaustion creeping back into his expression as his thoughts turned to what lay outside the quiet recovery room. "We *still* need you," he said, looking down at him. "The Paragon fleet here may have mostly been destroyed, but you and I both know they're still out there and pissed. We don't have a scanner that can yet detect one of those creatures that infected poor Carrol, and I can tell you I fear there are more of them out there. To say nothing of the UE Council, ready to undo all the work we've just done." He sighed, heavily. "I'm up to my ass in gators, I think you or your crew might say."

"What else is new?"

Jack smiled. "I meant it when I said to rest up."

"Yes, sir," Drake replied, and he managed a respectable salute. He eased the movement so as not to aggravate his shoulder, which had not yet healed.

He must have winced in pain because Jack clucked his

tongue and shook his head. "Disobeying orders already." He stretched. "I should be going. I do believe Ellen promised me another crack in the jaw if I was here when she arrived."

Drake laughed.

The admiral turned to leave.

Drake stopped him with a word. "Admiral?" Jack looked over his shoulder, eyebrows raised. "You said that you wondered about the fighting spirit of the Fleet. Whether we still had it in us to stop the Paragon."

Jack nodded, then let his breath out slowly. "I did. Yes."

"And I said that if anyone in the Fleet was giving up, it was you who was giving up on them."

"I remember."

"What do you think now?"

Jack smiled again. "I think, Captain, that I was right." He tapped the doorframe with his fingers, rat-a-tat-tat. "You didn't give up on them."

"No. I didn't."

"And they didn't give up in return, did they?"

"No, sir, they didn't."

The admiral nodded appreciatively.

He left, and Drake sank back into his bed.

CHAPTER FIFTY-FIVE

"Would you stop fussing?"

Drake had to shove Doc away as he adjusted his uniform collar and the rank, insignia, and decorations that hung from his breast pocket. It was hard to do with his limp hand, balky shoulder and the cane that he had in hand. The latter was an embarrassing necessity but nevertheless a necessity. Ellen thought it looked distinguished. He shot her a pleading look, but she only raised her hands in response. Getting gussied up, as she would describe it, was the Doc's purview, not hers.

The shuttle they were in was about to dock, though Drake only knew that from the steady indicator chimes. The windows had been blacked out, admiral's request. And Drake had not been told where they were going, only that it was a surprise and dress uniforms were required.

It had been two weeks since he'd last seen the admiral in the orbiting medical ward; two weeks since he'd been reunited with Ellen safe and sound. Drake had improved considerably, except for the shoulder and a hitch in his leg, hence the cane. He'd been itching to move around, get to work, do *something*, so even a formal event sounded like fun. At least, that was what he assumed it would be. Probably a medal ceremony, which only meant he'd have to fuss more with his uniform than he already had.

"There," Doc said, taking a step back to appreciate his handiwork, which he'd slipped in despite the captain's protests. He squinted one eye and Drake knocked him away, half-playfully, half-seriously. "You look like a right gentleman. Doesn't he, Captain?" The question was for Ellen.

"Yes, he does."

Drake grunted at both and turned to look at the controls.

This time it was Doc's turn to swat him away. "No touching! Everything's programmed in, and we're almost—"

The shuttle slowed, and with a clunk of docking clamps, came to a halt.

"There." Doc finished with a broad smile. He was in a good mood. It made Drake suspicious.

Behind them, the shuttle door opened.

Doc practically skipped to it and gestured his hand toward the opening, inviting Drake to exit. "After you."

Drake kept from rolling his eyes, took Ellen's elbow as she offered it to him, and ambled over and through the shuttlecraft's hatch. He braced himself for some kind of "surprise!" shout or a cake with candles to be shoved in his face or some other cringeworthy pageantry, but none of that came.

The shuttle had docked in a larger cargo bay, and a rather ordinary one at that, the kind you found everywhere at Fleet facilities across the Solar System.

Doc skipped past him. "This way!"

Drake looked at Ellen, and she only shook her head.

Like him, she had no idea where they were headed. They followed the doctor to the back of the bay and through a large set of double doors. Again, Drake braced himself for something, and again, nothing came. He was greeted with silence.

It was unnerving. Protests aside, he had expected more than an excited old friend leading him to the nether regions of a station where spacers were probably brewing the finest rotgut.

Through a curving corridor lined with windows like those in a dry dock. Broussard rushed over to the nearest window, which was double his height and nine or ten times that in length.

Drake and Ellen followed.

"Look at her," Doc said reverently.

All three peered out the window, and Drake felt his breath leave him.

A massive dry dock. And sitting in the middle of the facility, with suited workers and repair shuttles scurrying over her like so many bees in a busy hive was...

Glory.

Damaged, for sure; the repairs she was undergoing were extensive, but she was in one piece. Drake could even see that she had power to her aft section. The core was intact.

"She'll fly again and soon," Doc said, all smiles.

Drake nodded, overwhelmed.

Doc knocked into him, shoulder to shoulder. The good shoulder. "There's more," he said, and he left Drake's side to head farther down the docking ring corridor. "Come on!"

Drake followed as fast as he was able, Ellen in tow, trying to retain some dignity with his cane and a limp.

Doc led him down a gangplank toward the ship. Frequently, Drake kept stopping to point out something on the hull or to point at the work that was being done and ask a question or make a note, but Doc eventually got him to the end of the long docking arm.

At the bottom, Drake, totally unprepared and unguarded, got his surprise in the form of a chorus of applause from dozens, no, hundreds of Fleet personnel packed into the small loading bay just outside the main gangway leading into *Glory*.

He staggered and leaned far too heavily on his cane, but the sight of the crew, assembled, healthy, whole, and cheering together with broad, happy smiles, straightened him. It filled him up, and he couldn't help but stand tall and smile back at them. Ellen gestured, and he handed his cane to her so he could clap for them in return.

This moment was for all of them, even and especially those who weren't able to be there. They had all done it, and the ship behind them was solid proof that their will alone had carried them through.

XO stepped forward; so did Carrol and Idri.

Drake embraced the second officer through a tearful apology that he squeezed right out of her. Jack had been right; she felt guilty. He told her it was for no reason, and she nodded.

He did the same with Idri, telling her how proud he was of her; how she'd saved them all.

XO nearly crushed the air of out him, and Doc jokingly told the burly man to take it down a notch lest their good captain be put right back in Sickbay.

Others came forward. Fredrickson. The Marine. Efremova. Faces he recognized, like those of Snyder and Foley from the command deck, Zed the fighter pilot, who Drake saw was bandaged on half his face but smiling and holding Commander

Carrol's hand, and so many others he didn't but that he intended to know soon. They needed more time together, that was all. Time they were going to get, miracle that it was. Even the dog was there, and Smith introduced her as Cheddar. She wore a sharply tailored canine tactical vest that had been outfitted in the dress whites with various medals and insignia. Drake tried to remember if there was an official canine uniform, doubting there was. On his ship, there would be.

Drake embraced them all. Thanked them all. He thanked Doc, too, for bringing him there, even though the doctor deferred to Admiral Sturgess, who he said had arranged it all. The admiral wasn't there, but Drake looked at the ceiling to send him a thank you as well.

The celebration and the greetings died down, and once again, Doc was at Drake's elbow.

"Cap," he said, getting his attention. "We have, uh, one more thing."

Drake looked at the man with exhausted shock and laughed. Everyone around him laughed too. "What more could there possibly be?" he asked, eliciting laughter from the assembled.

Fredrickson stepped forward. "Sir," he began, and Drake was curious to hear a quiver in the usually unflappable man's voice. He cleared it and continued. "We thought it might be appropriate to put this back up."

Two crewmen, some of the engineer's team Drake recognized, stepped forward. Off a nearby cargo crate, they lifted something long, rectangular, and heavy. It was thin, like a single piece of plated metal. It had a canvas shroud over it, which the three of them were careful not to let slip as they brought it over to the captain.

Once they were in front of Drake, Fredrickson looked at

him, cleared his throat once more, and asked, "Permission, sir, to affix this to the hull of the *Glory?*"

With a flourish, the canvas shroud was dropped.

Drake's jaw fell with it.

It was a piece of plated metal, buffed to a mirror shine. Scrawled in hand-written letters, Drake read the following phrase:

As Long as There is Breath to Speak, Drake's Dogs Will Never Say Die.

Drake closed his mouth and stared at it.

The crowd around him cheered while Drake tried to take in what he was seeing.

"We stashed the old one in your quarters, Cap," XO said in reference to the old placard that Drake had taken down what felt like ages ago. The First Officer's expression was expectant. "So, what do you think?"

"We even have the mascot ready to go," Doc added in, pointing at the grinning Cheddar sitting obediently next to her Marine.

"I think—..." Drake began, and the crowd quieted, leaned in, and hung on the silence that followed. He looked over at Ellen. There were tears welling in her eyes. He smiled at her, and then looked back to the crowd before his own eyes forced him to suffer a similar betrayal. "...—that we're going to have to *work* like dogs to get this ship flying again. And by we—," he pointed to his bum leg, "—I mean you guys."

They laughed genuinely, from the belly. Drake laughed too.

"And!" he continued once the noise subsided. "That sign goes up. Permission granted, Mr. Fredrickson."

It filled Drake to the brim to watch his crew celebrate, see them happy. It was perfect. When they roared again as

Fredrickson directed his fellow engineers up on ladders to bolt the metal sign to the hull of the *Glory* where the old one had been, Drake realized the ghosts of the old ship were gone. Not just for him, but for everyone there.

He was home.

They were all home.

CHAPTER FIFTY-SIX

WARREN GASPED FOR AIR.

What filled his nostrils wasn't particularly good-smelling. Nothing in these damned Paragon tin cans smelled good. It was enough to make him wonder if the beasts had a sense of smell, so rank was the stench, but it was better than the oxygen-depleted muck he'd been sucking for the past hour inside his suit.

He was alive.

That was all that mattered.

And he had a ship now. A Paragon fighter he didn't know how to fly, but it was his ticket off the still-descending *Ulysses*, which was slowly, steadily being crushed in the depths of the Corvus gas giant.

He was days away from his last meal. The only water he'd managed to drink for a week was reclaimed, read piss, and he had a few nasty impact wounds from battling with the Paragon troopers, but if he could get the fighter up and running, he might be in business.

He punched the controls mindlessly at first, euphoric from the ample oxygen in the Paragon cockpit. There was no joystick, no levers to pull or switches to click. The surface was flat and polished, and it responded to no touch of his.

Warren grunted, a new idea occurring to him, and he reached behind his pilot's seat. One of two, with the other in the back. There was a wet crunching sound, and when he pulled his arm back to re-address the control console, he held a severed Paragon arm, smoking and rancid. The armor shell was still mostly intact, however. Black sludge poured out from it if he tipped it too far.

He slapped the hand on the blank surface, and it flickered to life.

"Now we're getting some-damned-where," he muttered and tossed the arm behind him.

It took him a few minutes of trial and error to get the craft powered up. After a few more minutes of slightly more harrowing trial and error, he had lifted the fighter off the exterior hull of the *Ulysses*—he hadn't been down in the hangar bay for quite some time at this point, but that was a much longer story to tell—and he was flying forward, backward, and from side to side.

"Cake," he said to himself, instantly regretting the analogy. It made him hungry, which made him lightheaded.

One thing at a time.

He gritted his teeth and angled the fighter up through the clouds and the sub-zero freezing rain. The pressure decreased as he ascended through Corvus. Light from the distant star began to be visible, and for the first time in as long as Warren could remember, he felt warmth. It filled him with hope. Maybe, just maybe, he was going to get out of this mess alive.

The Paragon fighter burst through the top layer of the clouds, leaving a nice and pretty gas and vapor trail behind him. The fighter was swift, that was certain. He almost liked flying it. Almost. It fought him with every command, or rather, he fought it. Either way, it felt powerful, fast, sure, but alien. Inhuman. Dangerous.

It matched the ships he found himself staring at, dead ahead.

The warmth inside Warren faded.

A fleet of Paragon ships was close. So close, it was impossible that none of them had seen him.

The fleet was stationary. Repair vessels nearly outnumbered the warships, and there were prisoner ships too, a multitude of them, along with countless troop carriers and other support craft.

This was a fleet regrouping, hiding here on an edge system to lick its wounds while preparing for its next battle.

If they'd been to Earth, it meant that, perhaps, the day had been saved. The Paragon fleet had been forced to withdraw. There was relief in that, to be sure. It meant his home was still there. Losing Earth was unfathomable.

From the sheer number of vessels in front of him and the flurry of activity, Warren knew that safety would only last as long as it took this fleet to re-deploy. And that time was not far away.

Warren had to get away, warn the Fleet. But even as he stalled out his fighter to allow him to fall back into the dark, cold muck of Corvus, one of the faster attack ships in the Paragon fleet moved toward him on an intercept course.

"Damn," Warren said aloud, looking at the Paragon trooper carcass behind him, which was missing its head as well as its newly severed arm. "You fuckers just don't know when to quit, do you?"

Earth, or wherever this fleet was about to strike, had to be warned.

Warren decided then and there that he was just the man for the job.

Humanity has survived...
Glory, Drake, and his crew will return in *Glory:*
Humanity Fights Back
AVAILABLE NOW ON AMAZON!

IF YOU LIKED THIS BOOK, please leave a review. We love reviews since they tell other readers this book is worth their time and money. I hope you feel that way now that you've finished this first volume in what could be a six-book series. Please drop us a line and let us know you like *Glory*'s adventures and want them to continue. This is my new favorite series. I hope you agree.

Keep reading since we have a few extra tidbits just for you.

MORE FROM THE AUTHORS

If you liked this story, you might like a couple other military science fiction series that we recommend...

Battleship: Leviathan – One ship against many in a war that has lasted a thousand years...

https://geni.us/BLo1

Metal Legion - **Victory or death!** *Fight to survive* **by CH Gideon (Craig Martelle's pen name)**

The complete set in one package – as much military science fiction adventure as your heart can handle. Aliens. Galactic conquest. Grunts. And firepower. Humanity learns that it's not the biggest or the baddest in the universe, but that doesn't stop them.

https://geni.us/MLComplete

Starstuff – by Ira Heinichen

The galaxy is dying...
   Starstuff is an epic space opera perfect for readers of any age.

AUTHORS' NOTES

Ira Heinichen
Written October 31, 2021

I must start with my most sincere and everlasting THANK YOU to you for reading this book. I cannot begin to tell you how much that means to me. *Thank you.*

My other thank yous must also extend first and foremost to my co-writer, co-conspirator, and military sci-fi legend Craig Martelle. I'm so fortunate to have you by my side as we worked on this together. Thank you for saying YES!

Thank you to my wife for your love, support, and feedback. I'd never have done this without you.

Thank you to Cooper and Coco for helping me write, getting me outside for walk-os, and for inspiring the creation of Cheddar.

This is my second book. It's been a while since my first. Too long. It's good, so very good, to be back. I sincerely hope you enjoy this crew, the adventure they find thrust upon them, and I hope you're looking forward to what comes next.

Writing Drake in particular was a challenge and a joy. There's a lot of Craig Martelle in him, truth be told; we drew on his wealth of leadership experience both in the military and in the private sector. Craig has written a lot on the subject leadership, what makes a good leader, and a bad one. His book *Leader Within*, in particular, was a major source of inspiration for the kind of Captain Drake always intends to be. We also drew inspiration from the accounts of retired Navy Captain L. David Marquet's *Turn the Ship Around!*, which was based on his real-life experiences in taking a demoralized and under-performing crew from 'worst to first.' They're both incredible reads if you haven't already, and they're both available on Amazon. Hopefully some of those inspirations shone through in the Drake that appears on these pages.

There's much more to come, both for Drake, and for everyone else on the old girl *Glory*. I suppose I will end this brief note here and get back to writing the next book. But, before I go, just one last word of appreciation for your time:

It means the world to me you read this story.

Thank you.

PS – as of this note, I only have one other book available out there. It's called *Starstuff*, and if you loved this book, there's a good chance you might love that one, too. It's decidedly not military-scifi—it's much more of a Space Opera-style adventure story—but there's still plenty of action, intrigue and colorful characters. I'd be honored if you checked it out.

One IMPORTANT DISCLAIMER: It is the first book of a trilogy, and it ends on a legit cliffhanger. The next book is not yet written (and likely won't be until later next year when the *Glory* series has several more books in it), so hold off if that's going to make you crazy. But, if you're jonesing for more work from me, that's where you can find it

You can get *Starstuff* here.

Please join my Newsletter (iraheinichen.com), or you can follow me on Facebook, Twitter and Instagram.

You can also email me any time authorira@gmail.com – I would LOVE to hear from you. I try to answer every email I receive.

If you enjoyed this story, please consider leaving a review! I cannot tell you how much seeing encouraging review helps motivate me towards writing the next book.

Amazon—www.amazon.com/author/iraheinichen
Facebook—facebook.com/iraheinichen
Website—www.iraheinichen.com
Twitter—twitter.com/iraheinichen
Instagram—instagram.com/iraheinichen

Craig Martelle
Written November, 2021

Thank you all for joining us on this great ride initially conceived by Ira. We worked back and forth on some of the plot points, but the flowing and almost lyrical prose is all Ira. He is an all-star author, and I was quite pleased to join him on this project.

We've been working on this for about nine months because the story took on a life of it own. A 100,000 word book became 130,000 words because we needed more. The outline for the next book is a spectacular follow-up to hit you right where you feel it the most.

Ira is a Hollywood insider and I'm just an old broken dude from Alaska. Ira brought his cinematography and storytelling, and I added the hard-hitting realism of military life under extreme stress. Together, I think we make a great team. Go team!

If you need something done, find the busiest person and give it to them. That highlights how Ira and I worked on *Glory*. We were both quagmired in life and our other work, but Ira powered through the hardest of it. My hat is off to him.

As I write this, I'm in Las Vegas doing the final preparations for our 20Books Vegas 2021 conference. Some 1700 authors will be here in a couple days. Ira will be here, too. He's in charge of the session filming – we have 150 separate sessions over three days. A monumental effort, but well worth it. This is the biggest and best show of its kind in the world. And we get attendees from around the globe. It is an international affair of the best sort.

And the busy never stops. I have a book on the other screen that I need to get back to, so that's it for now. We keep writing.

While you're waiting for Glory: Humanity Fights Back, we have a few other titles you can check out...

Peace, fellow humans.

Please join my Newsletter (craigmartelle.com—please, please, please sign up!), or you can follow me on Facebook.

If you liked this story, you might like some of my other books. You can join my mailing list by dropping by my website craigmartelle.com, or if you have any comments, shoot me a note at craig@craigmartelle.com. I am always happy to hear from people who've read my work. I try to answer every email I receive.

If you liked the story, please write a short review for me

on Amazon. I greatly appreciate any kind words; even one or two sentences go a long way. The number of reviews an eBook receives greatly improves how well an eBook does on Amazon.

Amazon—www.amazon.com/author/craigmartelle

BookBub—https://www.bookbub.com/authors/craig-martelle

Facebook—www.facebook.com/authorcraigmartelle

In case you missed it before, my web page—https://craigmartelle.com

ALSO BY CRAIG MARTELLE

 # - available in audio, too

Terry Henry Walton Chronicles (#) (co-written with Michael Anderle)—a post-apocalyptic paranormal adventure

Gateway to the Universe (#) (co-written with Justin Sloan & Michael Anderle)—this book transitions the characters from the Terry Henry Walton Chronicles to The Bad Company

The Bad Company (#) (co-written with Michael Anderle)—a military science fiction space opera

Judge, Jury, & Executioner (#)—a space opera adventure legal thriller

Shadow Vanguard—a Tom Dublin space adventure series

Superdreadnought (#)—an AI military space opera

Metal Legion (#)—a military space opera

The Free Trader (#)—a young adult science fiction action-adventure

Cygnus Space Opera (#)—a young adult space opera (set in the Free Trader universe)

Darklanding (#) (co-written with Scott Moon)—a space western

Mystically Engineered (co-written with Valerie Emerson)—mystics, dragons, & spaceships

Metamorphosis Alpha—stories from the world's first science fiction RPG

The Expanding Universe—science fiction anthologies

Krimson Empire (co-written with Julia Huni)—a galactic race for justice

Zenophobia (#) (co-written with Brad R. Torgersen)—a space archaeological adventure

Battleship Leviathan (#)– a military sci-fi spectacle published by Aethon Books

Glory (co-written with Ira Heinichen) – hard-hitting military sci-fi

Black Heart of the Dragon God (co-written with Jean Rabe) – a sword & sorcery novel

End Times Alaska (#)—a post-apocalyptic survivalist adventure published by Permuted Press

Nightwalker (a Frank Roderus series)—A post-apocalyptic western adventure

End Days (#) (co-written with E.E. Isherwood)—a post-apocalyptic adventure

Successful Indie Author (#)—a non-fiction series to help self-published authors

Monster Case Files (co-written with Kathryn Hearst)—A Warner twins mystery adventure

Rick Banik (#)—Spy & terrorism action adventure

Ian Bragg Thrillers (#)—a hitman with a conscience

Not Enough (co-written with Eden Wolfe) – A coming of age contemporary fantasy

Published exclusively by Craig Martelle, Inc

The Dragon's Call by Angelique Anderson & Craig A. Price, Jr.—an epic fantasy quest

A Couples Travels—a non-fiction travel series

Love-Haight Case Files by Jean Rabe & Donald J. Bingle – the dead/undead have rights, too, a supernatural legal thriller

Mischief Maker by Bruce Nesmith – the creator of Elder Scrolls V: Skyrim brings you Loki in the modern day, staying true to Norse Mythology (not a superhero version)

Mark of the Assassins by Landri Johnson – a coming of age fantasy.

For a complete list of Craig's books, stop by his website—https://craigmartelle.com